DANGER IN THE ~~~~

An enormous neck swung out of the woods and a moment later it was followed by a vast bulk, at least ten, perhaps twenty times Bazil's size. With a cracking sound, the whiplike tail erupted from the nearest brush and lashed at Bazil's head.

He dodged back as the tip cracked only a few inches short of his nose. The beast towered over him. Bazil retreated. Even with Ecator in hand he wasn't certain of killing something this large in a single blow. That tail was coming again. Bazil flung himself low and felt a wind pass over him as eight feet of bony tail swept through the air with a huge droning sound.

A moment later, there was a tremendous crashing of vegetation and a second enormous beast emerged behind the first. . . .

A DRAGON
AT WORLDS' END

A DRAGON AT WORLDS' END

Christopher Rowley

A ROC BOOK

ROC
Published by the Penguin Group
Penguin Books USA Inc., 375 Hudson Street,
New York, New York 10014, U.S.A.
Penguin Books Ltd, 27 Wrights Lane,
London W8 5TZ, England
Penguin Books Australia Ltd, Ringwood,
Victoria, Australia
Penguin Books Canada Ltd, 10 Alcorn Avenue,
Toronto, Ontario, Canada M4V 3B2
Penguin Books (N.Z.) Ltd, 182–190 Wairau Road,
Auckland 10, New Zealand

Penguin Books Ltd, Registered Offices:
Harmondsworth, Middlesex, England

First published by Roc, an imprint of Dutton Signet,
a division of Penguin Books USA Inc.

First Printing, February, 1997
10 9 8 7 6 5 4 3 2

Cover art by Daniel Horne

 REGISTERED TRADEMARK-MARCA REGISTRADA

Printed in the United States of America

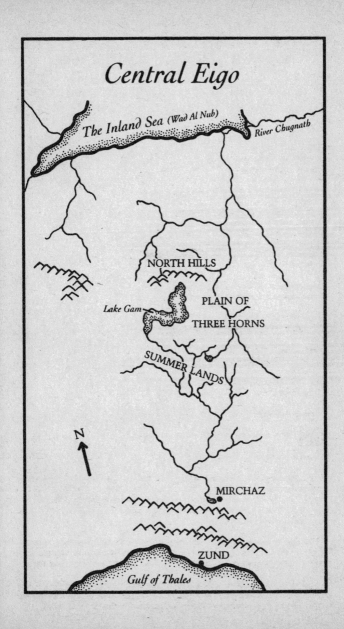

Central Eigo

The Inland Sea (Wad Al Nub)

River Chugnath

NORTH HILLS

Lake Gam

PLAIN OF THREE HORNS

SUMMER LANDS

N

MIRCHAZ

ZUND

Gulf of Thales

Prologue

It was a wet day, and cold due to an incessant wind off the sound. The crowd was heavy, all the way up Tower Street, despite the rain. Folk from all the provinces had come to stand there. Aubinan grain farmers, fishermen from Seant, and sheepmen from Blue Stone, they were all cheek by jowl with the natives of the white city under a mass of dark gray umbrellas, come to welcome the army home.

In fact, the Legion had landed two weeks before, but this was the official welcome and march of remembrance, to consecrate the memorial to the dead that was to be built on Tower Hill. It was an opportunity for the common people of Marneri to show their support for the men and dragons that had been sent so far—halfway around the world, in fact—and asked to risk their lives for the greater good of all mankind.

Up the hill, to the tap of the drum, came the dark columns. Serried spear points packed the wide street and the ranks that went by were filled with the trained, professional soldiery of the Empire of the Rose. The hearts of the people could not fail to be uplifted at the sight. No better troops existed in all the world. But of the units that had gone to Eigo, the ranks were thin and the uniforms under the blue capes and freecoats were tattered. With this sight came the rendings of heartbreak, for there was scarcely a village without loss from this mission.

The regiments came on steadily through the expectant hush, long files of men followed by squadrons of dragons, each with his dragonboy marching alongside. The dragons loomed in the rain like terrifying apparitions, true monsters of war, with their enormous swords riding on their shoulders, their helmets glistening in the rain. In their lumbering, steady progression they seemed to embody the Argonath's determination and strength. With heavy-footed, swaying tread they passed, and men from villages far and wide were left grieving at the losses among the dragons, too.

Folk from the village of Quosh, in Bluestone, a dragon village with a long record of service, had come up to pay their respects. Farmer Pigget and his family were there, as were most of the other leading men, like Avil Benarbo and Tomas Birch. When the 109th Dragon Squadron hoved up, following at the rear of the 8th Regiment, Second Legion, their eyes fixed sadly on the empty space left for the Broketail dragon. There were sobs from a few. The dragon, originally known as Bazil of Quosh, had been the proudest issue of their line of Legion wyverns. He would never be equaled.

Also noted was the absence of dragonboy Relkin, the village's most honored son, even though he was a bastard with no known father or mother. Raised for dragon service since birth, he had gone on to win the Legion Star and become the youngest recipient ever of the highest award in the Legions. Farmer Pigget and the others grieved for Relkin as well as the dragon. Quosh had lost part of its identity with the deaths of the Broketail dragon and his boy. Their hearts were heavy as they joined the crowd walking up the hill behind the regiments.

"A sad day for us, Tomas," said Pigget to Birch.

"Aye, Shon Pigget, that it is. Broketail dragon won the village tax exemption three years straight."

"He was the best we've ever hatched."

"The boy was a rascal, but never malevolent, as I recall."

"Yes, Tomas, as usual you fit the cap on it very tight."

At the top of the hill they found places in the crowd that filled up the rear of the parade ground laid out in front of the Tower of Guard.

At a balcony on the fifth floor of the tower, old General Kesepton, now retired, stood watching the regiments come on up the hill. With him was General Hanth, newly appointed to the Legion Supply Office in Marneri. Kesepton noted with pride that there were no visible puddles on the wide expanse of the parade ground. Not on his watch, he thought. Then he remembered that his watch was over. It was someone else's problem now.

"A damned fine sight," he said.

Hanth sighed. "Dearly bought, General, very dearly bought."

"Indeed, but the witches say they won a victory."

"So they do. It is hard to know anything for certain, so little information was made available, but we are assured that one of the Five was destroyed."

"Yes, they have made a big fuss about that. Everything else, though . . ."

"Is secret, I know. So much secrecy, damned witches are everywhere, no one will talk."

"They also serve, General Hanth."

Hanth shrugged. "Oh, I suppose you're right. It all just seems like hocus-pocus to me sometimes. We needed such myths as witches and magical power once, but surely we're beyond that now."

"Ah!" Kesepton bit his tongue. "Well, if you say so, General, if you say so." Kesepton looked down with a trace of a smile on his lips, but the smile was tinged with sorrow.

The casualties from the Eigo disaster were still being digested around the Argonath. They were terrible, thousands of men dead, lost, swallowed up in the heart of the dark continent. The stories told by the survivors were met with disbelief. Monsters, plagues, savage warriors who thought nothing of death, great empires of black peoples, and ultimately a battle in which stone eggs were hurled from the sky by terrible birds. So many fantastic tales, in fact, that folk hardly knew what to believe, but the casualties were very real, whatever else was true.

Thanks to the Goddess, thought Kesepton, his grandson Hollein had been spared. The young Kesepton had been sent to Eigo, but had been detached and sent on a diplomatic mission before the Legions marched west into the unknown interior. He had returned from Eigo a month or so before the rest, coming on a frigate with a message from the kings of Og Bogon and Puji. Real peace could take hold in the whole region. General Kesepton recalled the immense relief he'd felt when he saw Hollein once more, alive and unharmed, standing in the door of his apartment in the tower. Old Kesepton had known from the outset that a mission such as that sent to Eigo would suffer stupendous casualties.

Kesepton also recalled how Marian Baxander had broken and wept at the news of her husband's death. Such a battle the Legions had fought that it had killed both generals in command, along with forty percent of the officers. If this was victory, it was victory with the bloody costs of defeat, and it brought anger in its wake because the mission had been cloaked in such secrecy. Most people couldn't really comprehend the distances involved, nor imagine what threat the witches had found so far away that required such a sacrifice in blood. But, so the witches insisted, it had to be this way.

Out on the wide plaza below the Tower of Guard the regiments measured themselves out in crisp parade-ground array. At the command they dressed to the right, regiment by regiment, each with dragon squads at the rear. In their place behind the Eighth Regiment stood the 109th Marneri. There were wide gaps in the formation, but still they stood there with pride in every ounce of their massive selves.

Out in front was Dragon Leader Wiliger, still, but he was greatly changed. Something had gone out of his eyes since the last battle with Heruta, on the volcano isle. Nowadays he hardly spoke and was often found staring vacantly into space. It was rumored that he had applied for a compassionate discharge from service.

Behind him stood the dragons and dragonboys. At the right front there was the leatherback Vlok, with Swane beside him, then came pale green Alsebra and little Jak. The rest of the front row was empty. In the second rank stood Roquil, with dragonboy Endi, then old Chektor with Mono, and the enormous bulk of the Purple Green of Hook Mountain and dragonboy Manuel. The rest were gone, from Aulay to the big brasshides Finwey and Oxard. Dragonboys were missing, too: little Roos, decapitated at Tog Urbek, and Schutz, whose body was broken to pieces there. And, of course, there was the empty space for Bazil Broketail of Quosh, lost with his dragonboy in the volcanic doom of Heruta.

The Legion was all present and ready. General Wegan nodded and the cornets sounded to bring the Legion with a crash to attention.

There was a long moment of silence. The queen was helped up the steps to the top of the reviewing stand overlooking the wide parade ground. On the stand were several generals: Admiral Cranx, and representatives of the great institutions of the citystate, Fi-ice the Witch of Standing, and Ewilra of the temple.

Their faces were set in rigid masks of disapproval. The queen was drunk. She had been drinking heavily for a year now and any stressful occasion was likely to send her to the brandy bottle. Standing there on the reviewing stand, General Wegan of the Second Legion could barely restrain his anger. Wegan had been on the frontier in Kenor for most of his career.

"You don't know how things are in the city," whispered his friend Major Looth, who headed the Legion Staff Office in Marneri.

"You're right, I don't, and from what I can see, I don't want to find out."

The queen lurched to her place and did her best to stand tall. Behind her stood her current "companion," a handsome cavalry officer from the Talion Light Horse assigned to Marneri. Whenever she wobbled too obviously, he steadied her.

In a shaky voice Queen Besita read out the proclamation of the establishment of the memorial to the fallen. When she'd finished, someone shouted, "The queen is a slut!" And another voice called out, "No more blood for the witches!"

Tension hung in the air for a long shocked second. The wind snapped at the pennons and guidons, but no more insults came. Many men stared around themselves, hot-eyed, gripped by vague, unfocused rage. As much as they hated what the queen had become, they could not accept any insults thrown at the crown of Marneri. The crowd murmured. Besita was oblivious. She never heard the insulting words. She was thinking of nothing except escape from this place and this gloomy business. When she'd finished reading the proclamation, she stood back and would have retreated to her carriage prematurely if her cavalry officer had not held her firmly in place.

Watching this with a degree of horror in her heart was Lagdalen of the Tarcho, former assistant to the Great Witch Lessis and former adviser to the queen. With Lessis's restraining influence on the queen removed, so was any moral suasion possessed by young Lagdalen. The queen had new advisers, smooth young men from Aubinas and Arneis, men who talked of money and fresh markets for Marneri grain.

Thus, Lagdalen did not watch from the reviewing stand, but from the stand occupied by the noble families of the guard, which included the Tarcho clan. Lagdalen's role in the addictive drama of power had been reduced. She was now just a crown attorney, in charge of the endless case against Porteous Glaves, the grain magnate. She was also a mother and hoping for a second child. Her husband, Captain Hollein Kesepton, was also present, and was currently stationed in the city, attached to the Diplomatic Corps. He'd been to Eigo with the Legion and survived, and for this Lagdalen was supremely thankful, although Hollein was torn by odd feelings of guilt. He had been detached on a diplomatic mission and missed Tog Utbek.

Lagdalen, of course, had seen the battle at the field of Broken Stone firsthand and would never forget it. Much had been lost there, including the sure knowledge that an Argonath army was unbeatable in the field. So many had died that day. She was simply glad in her heart that Hollein had lived. She consoled herself with his presence when the dreams were bad and she woke up terrified and sweating.

Hard as those moments were, what Lagdalen could see happening to the queen was worse, because the effects were so vastly more widespread than her own troubles. Besita was floundering, losing her moorings. She refused to work; she refused to accept the duties of being a queen. As a result of her intransigence, the line of the Bestigari clan was coming under perilous scrutiny. The kings and queens of the Argonath city-states were subtly monitored by the witches. Royal arrogance, mania, bloody perversions, and destructive impulses were not allowed to run on for long before poison or an "accident" intervened. If Besita were to die, the throne of Marneri would move to a new family. Such an event would involve the danger of civil war among the clans and provinces.

Lagdalen was left to wish that Lessis was still among them.

The Witch of Standing, Fi-ice went up and gave the blessing for the memorial. Her voice was high, brittle with tension, but still it carried and the words took effect. Men came down off the balls of their feet. They composed themselves for prayer. She read a short, familiar passage from the Birrak and then led them in a short series of prayers. When finished, she stepped back amid complete and utter quiet broken only by the wind whipping across the parade ground in gusts, snapping at the flags.

General Wegan stepped forward and in a crisp voice, clearly audible across the parade, he called for a minute of silence. Nothing was heard thereafter but the patter of the rain and the flap of flags. The minute lasted well into ten minutes and then to twenty before by general consent it came to an end and the units were dismissed and broke up and drifted away, mingling with the crowds. The hush persisted and the crowd started back down Tower Street in relative silence.

Dragons lumbered to the dragonhouse, followed by the dragonboys. Small groups of soldiers were gathered here and there, most in motion as the parade broke up and dispersed.

Dragonboys Swane and Jak were leaving together when they crossed paths with Captain Kesepton and Lagdalen. The boys immediately came to attention and snapped a salute.

Kesepton returned it. "Well met, my friends from the fighting 109th."

Lagdalen greeted each of them with a hug, but their pleasure at meeting again was dampened by the somber echoes of the service.

"It's a hard day, Lady Lagdalen," said Jak after a moment.

"I know, Jak. It is for me, too. For all of us."

"Hard sometimes to believe they're gone, all of them," said Swane.

"Damned hard," said Hollein Kesepton, who'd served many times with Bazil and Relkin. "They were a great pair and their song will be long sung in the Legions of Argonath."

"Tell me, Lady," said Jak. "How is the Lady Lessis? Do you see her?"

"No, Jak, I don't see her anymore. The lady has gone to her home in the isles and she says she will never leave them again. She took the losses in Eigo to heart, you see. She told me one time afterward that she didn't think she could ever order men to go to their deaths in battle again."

The dragonboys were saddened further by this news. Their lives had been made pretty turbulent by the demands of the Gray Witch, but they wouldn't have traded them for quieter times in camp at Dalhousie. They had been halfway around the world in service with Lessis and had seen things that no one would believe. They had gone to the very edge and confronted the great enemy in his abyss, and still they would have had no other life. They had survived and been hardened in the process.

Lagdalen could see the changes in little Jak. Although still diminutive, his face was creased with lines and he radiated a new sense of strength. The boyishness had gone out of his eyes, he was a soldier now. Lagdalen had seen the same thing happen to Relkin. It changed you, to be tested like that, on the anvil of war.

"How are the dragons, Jak?"

"They are well, Captain. A bit down, as you'd expect. Especially the Purple Green—he's taken it hard. He and the Broketail were close from the beginning. From before I joined."

"Bazil Broketail was the reason the Purple Green joined the Legions," said Swane.

"So it's a little difficult. They get sulky pretty easily."

At this point a tall shape loomed out of the crowd and called to Lagdalen.

"Uncle Iapetor!" she cried.

Old Iapetor, a sea captain for many years, greeted the others warmly.

"A day for grief, a poor day to meet, perhaps, but I am honored. Any friend of Relkin of Quosh is a friend of Iapetor of Marneri."

"Very pleased to meet you, sir."

Swane was about to make their excuses when two more figures, these wearing the long military cloak, appeared, and he glimpsed gold stars on their collars. With a nudge to the ribs he hissed "Generals!" in Jak's ears.

Both dragonboys cut a salute as tight as any they had ever made before. General Kesepton returned the salutes, but not casually.

"At ease." Old Kesepton extended a hand toward his colleague.

"This is General Hanth. He's taking over supply operations here in Marneri. General, this is my grandson, Captain Kesepton, with his wife, Lagdalen."

"Delighted, Captain, Lady."

But General Kesepton had examined the two dragonboys now and noted the number in shining brass on the peaks of their caps.

"And, General, we have the honor of saluting two members of the fighting 109th Marneri."

Hanth looked up. "We do?"

"Yes, General Hanth, this is Dragoneer Swane and Dragoneer Jak. Jak tends Alsebra, the sword-skilled freemartin."

"Ah, yes, who hasn't heard of her? I am honored, boys, honored. The Broketail dragon was your friend. Be assured that all Marneri is suffering with you this day."

"Yessir!" said Swane and Jak, reacting to the presence of general officers with parade ground manners.

Kesepton smiled broadly, at a memory from thirty-five years before, and asked Hollein to dismiss them and send them on their way. He moved on to the old friend he'd seen standing beside Lagdalen.

"Ah, Iapetor, you old fox, how are you?"

Iapetor and Kesepton clasped hands firmly.

"The quacks are after me, General, but I keep 'em at arm's length."

"A sad day."

"And a bad one, old friend. The Aubinans will use this, you know they will."

Kesepton nodded heavily. The grain magnates of Aubinas sought independence from Marneri for their rich province. The struggle to sway public opinion was ongoing, but the forces of Aubinan independence were gaining the upper hand.

Both the older men also knew that Lagdalen was now in the front lines of this struggle, and she was but a girl in her twenties. Still, by virtue of her personality and the power of her position as the assistant to Lady Lessis, she had become the crown attorney for the prosecution of the case against Porteous Glaves. This case had become a cause célèbre for the Aubinans, who claimed that Glaves was being persecuted by a vengeful Marneri government.

Kesepton saw the tightening in her face when Iapetor mentioned Aubinas. He thought to spare her on such a mournful occasion. She carried too much of a burden already.

"The Broketail dragon was a legend in his own times. We don't see that sort of thing very often."

But Iapetor could not be deflected. "The Aubinans will try to blame the queen, and the witches."

"Ah, well."

They both turned to Lagdalen, who kept her face purposely as blank as possible. The case could not be discussed casually and she was annoyed at Iapetor for bringing it up. She would not be drawn.

"We face difficult times, good sirs," she said. "And these losses make them harder to bear. But we will not give up. We will never give up."

On that note they parted, hunched against the rain and the wind, which was colder than before. Workmen began to dismantle the parade stand while a couple of stonemasons took measurements where the monument to the fallen was to be erected.

Chapter One

Two predators slipped silently through the ancient jungle, eyes and ears alert for the slightest signal of either prey or danger. Hunger gleamed in their eyes, while starvation showed in their shrunken bellies and haggard faces.

As usual at this time of the day, the jungle seemed to be holding its breath. A deep silence extended with the heat of the midday. All life except the vegetative was in suspension, and nothing moved except the mists rising over ponds and rivers. The jungle seemed to be waiting for something to make a move, perhaps a mistake. This was a forest made wary to its soul, as they had already discovered. Mistakes were usually fatal.

The hunters made a mismatched pair, the first a little less than six feet tall, his well-muscled body bent over in a stalking crouch, white teeth visible in the dusky shadows. The second, a much larger beast, was twenty feet in length from nose to tail tip, striding close behind, jaws held slightly apart.

Skeerunch, crackle.

There it was again!

They were united by sudden soaring hope.

Directly in front of them, something was making noise. Such indiscretion was rare indeed in this ancient forest, which was ruled by packs of two-legged, running killers. The animals that survived were exceptionally fleet and nervous. The hunting pair had sensed game around them on a number of occasions and had even glimpsed animals as big as elephants, but the potential prey had fled swiftly and almost silently into the forest as soon as they were spotted. In the dense jungle of endless conifers, cycads, and fern trees, these animals were capable of much faster movement than would have seemed possible. They were strong and tough-skinned and paid no heed to the spines on cycads and the sharp leaves of palms, and consequently were in no danger of ever being caught.

The smaller hunter suddenly slowed and pressed himself to the bark of an enormous conifer. His attention was directed ahead through a screen of trees into a clearing lit by the sun and filled with lush vegetation. The large predator crouched, eyes working on the dark ahead.

At last! Could it be? Food?

Through the tree trunks they glimpsed an immense beast with a very long neck that stood on four legs like tree trunks in the midst of the young, lush fern trees that were competing to fill the clearing's slot of blue sky. This beast was engaged in the happy business of stuffing fern fronds down its throat to the system of stomachs in its relatively enormous body. The tiny brain in the diminutive head had little room for any thoughts beyond those concerned with the simple pleasures of ripping off more fern, compacting the vegetation into a ball, and then swallowing it, which took a long time with a neck like that.

It was a young member of its tribe, and as yet unaccustomed to the harsh ways of the world. In time, if it survived, it would become very much larger, a giant with a tail nearly thirty feet long. Now, it was not very much larger than the bigger of the two predators studying it from the green murk beneath the trees. It remained blithely unaware of any threat. When it finished consuming a fern tree, removing all the fresh young growth, it took a step forward and brought its mouth down on the next hapless tree.

"Food for a week," whispered the smaller of the hunters, his hand unconsciously reaching up to tug lightly on his new-grown beard.

"Boy may be right," said the larger of the pair with a faint sibilance to the voice. "We haven't eaten anything since that snake the day before yesterday. This dragon could eat a lot right now."

"So could this boy."

The young man who said this was fairly salivating as he gazed at the young beast, visualizing it as no more than a

collection of chops, ribs, joints, and the like, which might
be roasted, baked on hot stones, or dried in the sun for
jerky.

The dragon, a brown and green monster of about two
tons, wore a massive leather scabbard behind its shoulders and within that it carried a dragonsword.

"You stay here," said the young man with the unfamiliar, dark beard. "I'll go around to the right and get behind
it. When I come whooping up at it, you creep in close."

Both of them knew that if Bazil Broketail could get
close enough to wield that dragonsword, then the beast
would lose its head in a fraction of a second and they
would have a feast on their hands.

"Boy go!"

Relkin moved to his right, making almost no sound at
all. This past week in the ancient forest had sharpened his
stalking skills considerably. But as he went, he bemoaned
once again the loss of his precious Cunfshon bow. With
that bow he could have put a shaft into the eye of this
beast at a hundred feet and ended their quest for dinner in
a trice. Without that bow, they were reduced to skulking
along to get to close quarters with the sword.

A dense stand of cycads slowed him up. Their bark
sprouted long spines that were sharp and fragile, and
could leave agonizing little splinters in one's skin. Being
cautious around cycads was absolutely necessary.

That bow would have made all the difference, but it
was gone forever. It had been taken from him when he
was captured on the battlefield of Tog Utbek. He imagined that it had probably been destroyed when the volcano
erupted and great Heruta was slain.

A sting on his hip told him he hadn't been quite careful
enough. Between the cycad spines that littered the ground
and the spines on the trunks there was a lot to look out
for. Relkin was barefoot, too, having lost his boots in the
Inland Sea. He slowed, moving cautiously to keep those
spines out of his skin.

At last he was in the right position. The young giant
munched on. It held its long, flexible tail off the ground
whenever it moved and occasionally curled and uncurled

it with a vigorous snap. Relkin wondered again how it was that this beast had survived to munch ferns and get fat in these forests, which as he knew were haunted by a great many predators, some of them much larger than even a full-grown battledragon and utterly ferocious.

For the third time he asked himself if it could truly be all alone. But careful scrutiny of the trees showed no signs of any other beasts. Nor were there any sounds to indicate more like this one. There was just this one beast, happily stuffing itself on bright green fern trees. Relkin was too hungry to worry about it. The beast took no notice of him and he approached it within fifty feet. This time they were going to make a kill.

By now Bazil's patience was sure to be stretched to its limit. Relkin took a deep breath and said a little prayer to old Caymo, the God of Luck. Then with a loud shout he jumped and advanced on the beast, waving his arms. He would have laughed at the sight if he'd been able to see it from an observer's viewpoint. A two-legged critter less than six feet tall charging an animal that stretched thirty feet from head to tail tip.

The munching ceased, the head came up surprisingly swiftly, and one eye focused on Relkin.

He came on, screaming like a maniac.

The beast uttered a strangely soft snort, pushed back with its front legs, and reared up onto its hefty hind legs. The muscular tail was now pressed to the ground. It challenged him by bashing its stubby foreclaws together. Come closer and get hugged, it said.

Relkin slowed his step. It weighed three tons at the least. There wasn't a hell of a lot he could do to it with just a short sword. He kept his arms waving to hold its attention as long as possible. It was up to the dragon now.

Bazil was on the move, working through the trees without a sound. He had the sword swinging loosely in one hand. All it would take was one good overhand. And then they would eat. He doubted that he'd want to wait for cooked meat, either.

He took another long step and moved into the direct sunlight of the clearing. Instantly there was a reaction from the other side, among the taller trees. An enormous neck swung out of the woods and a moment later it was followed by a vast bulk, at least ten, perhaps twenty times Bazil's size. Anxious parental eyes glittered at the sight of the dragon, and the huge bulk was thrown sideways. With a great cracking sound, the whiplike tail erupted from the nearest brush and lashed at Bazil's head.

He dodged back as the tip cracked only a few inches short of his nose. The beast towered over him. Bazil retreated. Even with Ecator in hand he wasn't certain of killing something this large with a single blow. There wouldn't be time for a second blow before he was trampled. That tail was coming again; Bazil flung himself low and felt a wind pass over him as eight feet of bony tail tip swept through the air with a huge droning sound.

A moment later, there was a tremendous cracking and crashing of vegetation and a second enormous beast emerged behind the first. There was a small herd of the things over there, silently resting up during the heat of the day.

Scrambling back onto his feet, Bazil staggered away as quickly as he could. Relkin came barreling out of the undergrowth a few seconds later while huge tails zoomed above his head, beating hell out of the cycads and the fern trees. Bazil picked up speed, Relkin moved up beside him running full tilt. They pushed their weary bodies as fast as they could through the thickest area of trees, while the giants followed, crushing the forest wholesale beneath them.

Fortunately, it soon became apparent that the giants were not prepared to expend that much energy on them. After two hundred yards the huge beasts had ceased to pursue. They knocked over a few large trees and trampled them and then they ambled back to the clearing and the youngster, which had gone back to gorging itself. The rest of the herd resumed its midday snooze.

Bazil and Relkin slowed, breathing hard, taking time to lean back against a thick-trunked pine.

"How did those things manage to hide so well?" muttered the dragon at last. There was no hiding the shock in his voice.

"We're getting stupid, Baz, something to do with being

so hungry. We should have known that little one would
have protection around. We've got to work harder."

"Got to eat."

"I know."

Glumly they stumbled on through the jungle, steering
south and east as much as possible. This was the seventh
day since they had beached on the forest strand and
headed into the jungle in search of food. At first Relkin
had been sure they were somewhere on the eastern shore
of the Inland Sea. He recognized the strange forest, which
was the same one they had traversed during the epic
march of the Legions from Og Bogon to the shores of the
Inland Sea. Relkin had thought they should be able to
catch some of the more unwieldy animals they had seen
during that voyage down the great river.

On both scores he had been wrong.

During that hungry week Relkin had come to realize
that instead of being on the eastern shore of the ocean,
they were in fact on its southern margin. Seven days of
heading in an easterly direction had brought them that
morning down to an inlet laid out north to south. Down
the inlet lay the ocean. Clearly they were moving eastward along an east-west shore, which meant that they
were a very long way from the rest of the Argonath army.
They were truly alone, and would have to rely on themselves on the long journey ahead. It was even possible,
as Relkin was reluctantly coming to accept, that they
might never rejoin the army, not until they got all the way
back to Bogon on the east coast. One thing he had refused
to even consider was that they might never make it back
at all.

All in all it was a dire situation, and each of them had
been working hard to keep the other's spirits up. The sight
of the young monster in the clearing had been intoxi-
cating. Unfortunately, it had led to nothing and they were
hungrier than ever.

They entered a marshy area and on a mudbank Relkin
surprised a scarlet, amphibious beast the size of a cat. His
sword pinned it before it could reach the water. In a few
moments it was gutted and cleaned and broken into
pieces, while Relkin looked around for firewood. There

was something wrong, though, a strange smell that made the hair on his neck stand up.

The dragon looked askance at the chopped-up, red-skinned creature.

"I don't think this is a good idea," he said carefully, knowing full well how hungry Relkin was, but distrusting that awful smell.

Relkin cut off some hunks and threw them into a nearby pond where some small fish were circling. The fish attacked the chunks briefly. Two or three were almost instantly stricken with paralysis and floated to the surface, bellies up.

With a sigh of frustration Relkin told his stomach to forget it. He wiped his sword carefully in the sand and washed his hands very thoroughly before they went on.

The mires thinned out and they moved through tropical heathland, with a thin forest cover of dwarf pines. The going became considerably easier and they moved along at a steady pace, eyes peeled for some sign of prey. Ahead were white limestone cliffs.

Relkin heard it first.

"Uh-oh," he groaned.

On a breeze from the south came a distant medley of wailing cries.

"Those things again," grumbled the dragon. "They are too damn common in these parts."

Hurriedly, they moved due east, trying to put a lot of space between themselves and the source of the noise. They had seen a pack of creatures that made those cries, and they had faced their ilk on the ramparts of the Legion camp. They had no desire whatsoever to come to grips with them—a horde of yellow-skinned killers, each with deadly sickle claws on its hind feet that were used to disembowel prey.

They pushed on, working eastward along a ridge of drier ground, where the forest cover stayed thin and it was relatively easy to make good time. The wailing cries died away for a while, and the two travelers were starting to think they'd left them behind, when they were renewed, this time nearby.

They were being tracked. They increased their speed,

and now came to an area cut up by the karst canyons of a limestone landscape. Ledges and pinnacles were abundant.

The cries were directly behind them now. Cursing, they shuffled along, pushing tired bodies into a redoubled effort. A fault had thrust limestone up in a sharp cliff that barred their way. There was no time to waste here; the killers would be on them very shortly.

Panting with exhaustion and fear, Relkin noticed a crack in the cliff face they could ascend, legs on one wall, shoulders on the other. Bazil had learned to climb this way when he was a sprat back in Blue Stone County, although it had been a long time since he had tried it.

They climbed. For Bazil it was an exhausting ordeal, and his energy reserves were already low. Still the chimney was almost ideal for this purpose, being big enough for a wyvern dragon to wedge his feet up on one wall and his shoulders on the other.

Relkin was too small to get the benefit of the chimney effect, but he was able to scale the wall anyway. He, too, felt the weakness that came from lack of food and found himself drained by the time he hauled himself out on top of the cliff.

The pack of sickle-claw killers had emerged from the forest and formed a stolid, goggle-eyed audience down below them. The killers made no sound, except an occasional keening cry of disappointment.

When Relkin reached the top, he looked down at the stiff-legged pack. He counted more than ten of them, waiting patiently, with their long arms drooping to the ground, their tails held out straight behind them, and their big eyes fixed intently on himself and the dragon. Slowly Bazil inched his way up to the top of the chimney. He was sobbing for breath with each heave of his big body up the rock. At last he got a shoulder over the top. The maneuver at the end was the worst for him, since he was already drained of strength and this required the maximum effort from his upper body.

Bazil took a deep breath, twisted, and let his feet leave the opposite wall. His arms and shoulders took the entire strain for a moment, while his claws gouged out dust from the rock face beneath him, and then he managed to boost one leg up and get a talon grip on the edge. For a moment he teetered there and might have fallen back, but for a final convulsive heave, plus Relkin's frantic hauling on his joboquin that brought him over the edge and left him panting flat out on the upper surface.

The mob of killers below were still staring up at Relkin with solemn eyes. He was tempted to find some rocks to heave at them.

Bazil got back to his feet with a groan or two.

"Time we was moving on," whispered Relkin.

Carefully the boy and the dragon inched backward from the cliff until well out of sight from below. Then they rose to their feet and retreated across the plateau to the far side. The limestone region formed a scarp with the steep side facing east. They came to the top of this steep slope and found the country spread out below them. Dimly, far off to their left, Relkin glimpsed an expanse of blue that he knew at once was the Inland Sea. Directly ahead lay a river plain, with the river's serpentine coils spread across it.

His fears were confirmed then. They were way to the south of the Legions and essentially on their own.

"What now?" said Bazil, whose own grasp of geographic details was considerably vaguer than Relkin's.

"Got to get down this slope, get across the river, and continue east. Somewhere over there we ought to find the big river we came down from the mountains on. Maybe we can hook up with the Legions. Find where we left the rafts."

"Not going to be so easy to take a raft up the river as it was to float down."

"I know. But it'll still be easier than walking the whole way."

The dragon fell silent, struck by the hard, obvious truth of this statement.

"Come on. Let's take this carefully; don't want a fall."

"By the fiery breath," grumbled the leatherback, but he fell in behind Relkin as they started down.

Cautiously they descended the steep slope, scrambling down through thickets and dense patches of vines. By late afternoon they were far down the slope, deep in a murky forest fed by springs rising at the bottom of the scarp slope. At one spring they paused to take a drink. Behind the spring Relkin discovered a cave that went back into the hill a considerable distance. The air coming up from the cave was cool. Relkin detected nothing more than the smell of moist stone. Bazil noted the presence of some bats in a side cave, but nothing else. They huddled there for a moment, to get their breath back and plot their next move.

"I think we should stay here, sleep, and move on in the morning."

"You not as hungry as this dragon."

"I'm not so sure about that, but the river's too far for us to reach it before dark. I bet there'll be a lot of mosquitoes down there. You know what the witches said about mosquitoes and the plague."

Bazil remembered the plague too well. He shuddered. "We stay here tonight," he said.

They cut down some boughs and made nests for themselves just inside the entrance. Relkin went off to scout for small game.

He passed down by the spring, which had formed a wide circular pool at the base of a cliff of white limestone. Palms grew around it in a grove that trailed off into the deeper woods where the conifers grew thick.

He wended his way down this path, eyes seeking something small that he could hit with a stone, of which he had a half dozen nice smooth ones, picked up earlier. There were lizards, but they were high in the trees and wary. At the sight of him they flitted upward. He groaned and shifted weary limbs on down a path lined with palm trees. They really had to find something to eat or he was going to get too weak to carry on. Relkin could have wept for his lovely little Cunfshon bow. These fat lizards would have fed him well and given the dragon a little something to stave off the worst pangs of hunger, and with the bow the lizards would have been easy targets.

Suddenly he heard a triumphant shriek behind his back. Three of the yellow-skinned carnivores stepped out of

concealment. Another shriek came from ahead and there
were the rest of them. He was trapped.

Relkin didn't hesitate. He hurled a stone at the nearest
and scored a good hit high on the forehead. The creature
hissed and shook and he was gone, running for his life
through the conifer forest beyond the palms. The forest
was a mass of young fir trees no taller than Relkin. He
was able to force his way through and stay ahead of the
ululating pack, but they were right on his heels.

Soon he was running through larger trees. He ran
bent over low and managed to get along beneath their
lowest branches. The predators were not as agile here;
they bulled through with their heads and they were
inevitably slowed. Relkin sensed after a while that he was
gaining.

Then the firs ended and he burst out into a wide
clearing. Tall trees lined the eastern side; the scarp cliff
was visible on the other. He doubled for the cliff, his legs
extending strongly before and behind him. There were
scattered palms and a few pine trees as he approached the
farther side. Behind him he heard the first shrieks as the
pursuit emerged from the fir tree forest. They had him in
their sights. Now it was simply a footrace and Relkin was
sure he would soon lose that—he'd seen these creatures
run and they were better than any human athlete in the
world.

He burst through a patch of ferns and caught sight of
the spring's wide pool and the dark cave mouth beyond it.
Shouting for Baz, he sprang toward it. Behind him came a
dozen nightmares, their long arms held out for him, their
jaws eager to rend him to pieces.

He was still ahead by the time he reached the pool, but
he knew he couldn't get all the way to the cave. In desperation he dove into the water and swam out to the
center. It was deep there, well over his head.

The yellow-skinned killers ran up and waded out into
the water, and Relkin's heart sank. Then, when the water
was up to their bellies, they stopped. They did not swim
well and would not venture into water too deep for
wading. Instead they stood there in a pack and ululated in
frustration as he trod water in the center of the pool and

tried to think of a way out of this fix. Their eyes had an implacable gleam. They would wait for him. He could not stay out of reach forever. Even if he drowned, eventually he'd float close enough for them to eat him.

Chapter Two

Relkin was beginning to think that this really was going to be the end. Keeping afloat wasn't a problem yet, but eventually he would tire and either drop his weapons or drown. It was a miracle that these killers didn't swim, and that alone had saved him.

How long could he float? Despair was solidifying when a sudden gleam of metal caught his eye. He focused and glimpsed a movement in the palm trees. A moment later Bazil slid forth from the trees with Ecator in his hands.

Relkin roused himself to splash and splutter and moved a little closer to the edge of the pond. The predators crowded to that side, their eyes intent on the prey.

Relkin moved closer yet. They made grasping motions, and even stepped farther into the water so that it rose to their shoulders. They could virtually taste him, he was sure.

And then the Broketail dragon was upon them from the rear. Ecator came around in beautiful flashing cut and two of the beasts expired in an instant as their heads were severed from their shoulders. Their bodies fell in the water in a red froth as the rest whipped around with a weird, collective wail. Bazil swung the other way, just above the waterline, and took his third in the legs, bringing it down among the others.

The rest sprang at him.

Relkin had been paddling closer. Now his feet were on the bottom and he pushed to the shore and launched himself onto the back of the hindmost, landed on the hard backbone, reached around the next moment, and sawed its throat apart with his sword. It bucked, tried to claw him off with its foot, and would have but for the intervention of sudden death. Relkin rose from the wreck in a crouch, ready to throw himself back into the water if several of them came for him. None did.

Bazil, meanwhile, had slain his fourth beast with a backhand slice, cleaving it through the neck and shoulder. The jaws in the severed head kept snapping in rictus spasm even as it hit the ground and rolled into the margin of the pond.

The rest stood their ground, growling and shrieking, but not venturing within range of Ecator. The things had finally grown wary. They drew off out of range of that gleaming arc of terrible steel and started circling. Relkin splashed all the way out of the water and lurched up to join Baz. Together they backed toward the cave.

"Real glad to see you," he muttered to the big dragon back.

"Fool boy almost make lunch for these things."

The creatures had noticed now that their numbers had been reduced almost by half. Their pack had suffered terrible damage. They grew more cautious, but there was no sign of any slackening of interest. They continued to stalk their prey, step by step, as they went back over the rock and gravel into the cave mouth behind the spring.

Still the yellow-skinned killers hesitated, holding off for fear of the sword, until Bazil and Relkin had actually reached the cave mouth. The realization that the prey was going to escape into a cave finally overcame their caution and they thrust forward suddenly.

"Back," hissed the dragon as he swung the sword. The things had learned their lesson; they dodged and ducked back. Bazil struck a rock with the heel of his foot and he almost wobbled off balance, presenting his belly to those deadly sickle claws, but at the last moment he managed to steady himself with a hand to the rock wall. He kept his sword point between himself and the killers. They drew back again.

He edged backward into the darkness of the cave.

It was cool in there, and moist and very quiet.

The yellow and scarlet demons outside let loose with a volley of mournful ululations.

"Wish they'd give it up," grumbled the dragon.

"They're shockingly persistent."

Suddenly the leader of the pack thrust its head in and Relkin cut down and his sword sank into its neck. It jerked its head back violently and tore the sword out of Relkin's hands. The sickle claw lashed forward and Relkin felt it part the skin over his left ribs as he darted to the right. When he put a hand to the cut he found he was bleeding slightly from a gash over four ribs. But he'd been lucky—another inch the wrong way and his guts would have been around his ankles.

The pack leader was still struggling with Relkin's embedded sword when Bazil thrust with Ecator and ended it. The great sword spitted the beast clean through and it died virtually instantly. Bazil put a foot on its fanged snout and heaved Ecator free. The blade was home to a fell spirit, long ago tamed by the witches, but still implacably fierce. It seemed to glow for a moment, saturated with the equally fierce life force of the dead predator. Relkin recovered his own sword with shaking hands.

The others were reluctant to follow their leader. They remained outside, mourning the destruction of their terrifying pack.

Relkin groped his way back into the cave a short ways. The cold mustiness spoke of water in that darkness somewhere.

"Let's try the cave," he said.

Bazil agreed readily enough. There were still enough of the killers back there to be dangerous in the extreme. "Run to ground, as they say."

"I think you're right, Baz. They don't want to come in, so they're hoping we'll eventually have to come out."

Relkin led the way, feeling with feet and hands and describing the ground to the dragon as they entered it. It was smooth and moist, and there were occasional blocks of stone fallen from the ceiling that made it essential to feel one's way carefully.

"Wait a minute," said Baz.

"Why?"

"Food."

Bazil stepped back to the mouth of the cave and hauled

in the body of the pack leader. He took it by the head and
pulled it along behind them. It weighed perhaps two hundred pounds and would feed both of them pretty well for a
couple of days.

Still dragging the carcass, they moved on through a
series of limestone rooms not quite large enough to be
called caverns, until Relkin spied a light coming from
above. Soon they were under it, light trickling, gleaming
down from somewhere up on the scarp slope. To reach it
they would have to climb.

Fortunately there was a tumbled mass of limestone
blocks fallen in from the ceiling of the chamber. They
clambered up these and eventually emerged from a sink-
hole in a gulley that had cut into the steep face of the
scarp. Cautiously Relkin stepped forward and peered out
of the gulley. They were about sixty feet above their
former position. The pool was visible in the palm trees
and so were a couple of the sickle-claw killers. The predators stood stock-still facing toward the cave. Relkin knew
the rest of them would be there, too, hidden among the
palms, all watching for their reappearance.

With as much stealth as they could manage, Relkin and
Bazil slipped away up the gulley for another hundred feet.
Then they slid into the short-tree forest and worked their
way along the face of the scarp about half a mile before
cautiously descending again. There was no sign of pursuit. Once on level ground, they paused to butcher the
sickle-claw carcass. The meat was very tough, as Bazil
discovered when he bit into a thigh after cutting it free.

"It's going to need long, slow cooking to ever be
edible," said Relkin.

"Bake in hot rock oven, then. Like troll, it tough, but it
soften with long slow heat."

"Good idea, Baz."

There was still some time before nightfall. They hurried
away as fast as they could, now carrying the burden of
legs and chops and other prime pieces.

When they'd put a few miles between themselves and
the remains of the pack, Relkin started collecting all the
dead wood he could find. Since there was quite a lot of
well-cured litter on the forest floor, he soon had enough

for a good blaze. They came out upon a small clearing and there Relkin built a fire. Bazil pulled in some larger pieces, they were virtually tree trunks, and the two broke them up with their swords as best they might.

Relkin still had his pouch and a few necessities, including flint and steel for making sparks, and a small bottle of Old Sugustus disinfectant. Now he got the fire going quickly and used dried grasses as tinder to get wood chips and twigs alight. The stuff was nicely dry. Soon he had a blaze that roared on through a great pile of branches and brush. While the fire burned, they dug up dozens of large stones which they placed in the fire to get red hot.

Then they waited, virtually slavering with anticipation. Relkin took care of his wound, a slice that just broke the skin about four inches long straight down his rib cage on the left side. The sun went down in the swift tropical manner and left them in possession of the only firelight in hundreds of miles.

Later, the fire burned down to a huge mass of embers, with the rocks glowing in their midst. Relkin had wrapped the joints, ribs, and chops in palm leaves wetted in a nearby stream. These he laid out to sizzle and sputter on the mound of hot coals. Then they put more wet palm fronds over them and piled on some dirt until it was completely covered.

Separately Relkin had roasted a few slices from one thigh and a section from the shoulder. They chewed on these while they waited for the rest to bake through completely. The meat was very tough and took a lot of chewing. Bazil hardly bothered, tossing back a few fragments with a grunt. It stimulated an appetite that needed no reminding of its fierceness.

They went to slake their thirst at the stream and disturbed a small group of two-legged herbivorous beasts, each twice Bazil's size. With nervous hoots, the huge beasts looked up and then withdrew quietly into the trees on the other side of the stream. In a few moments they were gone. Relkin watched them go, awestruck by the silence in which they moved.

When they returned to the fire they found a small predator beast in possession of the site, prowling around the warm place from which the delicious smells arose. It was not a sickle-claw, but an immature member of another type which they called the "red-browns," for the earthy color of their hides. They'd grown far too familiar with these huge two-legged horrors during the Legion march across the ancient Lands of Terror. The biggest red-browns were used to attacking anything and everything. When confronted by the Legions, with their oxen and horses, the big red-browns had always attacked and had always to be slain before they would stop.

This one was smaller than Bazil, however, and at the sight of them it withdrew, snarling in frustration and some degree of mystification. Bazil considered killing it, but Relkin recalled to him the way it had been at the Legion camp in the jungle. The smell of dead meat always brought more predators, and you had to keep on killing them until they were stacked around you ten feet deep. It was better to let this one depart, since it wanted to anyway.

Stomachs rumbling, they waited until the ground had begun to cool before digging into the mound of earth and leaves and pulling out the steaming parcels of meat. They were still too hot to handle, but dragon and boy were too hungry to wait any longer and with a lot of blowing to cool pieces down, they tucked in.

The meat was stringy, but it was food. Relkin found that with his shrunken belly he was sated very quickly. As his stomach went to work for the first time in days, he grew drowsy and fell asleep for a few minutes. While he slept, Bazil continued to eat, working his way through a baked thigh, holding it up and chewing it down to the femur. When Relkin awoke from his nap, his appetite was restored and he tucked into the rest of the smaller chops. It reminded him of mutton, braised mutton.

Before they had finished, however, they were interrupted by the arrival of a much larger member of the red-brown fraternity of carnivorous beast. This one was close to full grown and since as a tribe they tended to be enormous, it was easily twice Bazil's weight. The monster refused to go away even after Bazil heaved hot rocks at it by grasping them with a wad of palm leaves. It stalked around their fire, eyeing them and sniffing the remains of their feast hungrily. Finally hunger overruled caution and it lunged forward with a mighty scream.

Bazil arose with a grunt of annoyance. He felt wonderfully full, but just a little torpid as a result of the effort to digest a hundred pounds of meat. The red-brown beast came lunging at him, snapping its huge jaws and trying to frighten him. Perhaps it was the torpor of so much meat, perhaps it was the knowledge of the power of dragonsword, but Bazil felt no fear. Bazil had dedicated his life to skill with the great sword. The red-brown tyrant beast knew nothing of such matters. It simply wanted to eat him. Bazil steadied himself, raised Ecator, and waited until the beast finally drew close enough. Bazil had observed that these brutes usually tried the same maneuver: They would charge and try to panic you. If you turned and ran, they would seize you by the back of the neck and you were done for. If you stood your ground, they would swing the huge head in from one side or the other in an effort to get in a killing bite. One bite from those heavy jaws would be enough in most cases. It came on; he refused to run, so it ducked low and tried to sink its teeth into his left side. He swung Ecator with full force and took its head off with a single, clean blow.

It collapsed in a fountain of gore and twitching hind limbs. Relkin saw the potential at once.

"You know, I think we solved our food problem, Baz. We just keep cooking these critters and we'll always get more of them. Forget the herbivores, they're too much trouble."

"By the breath, this dragon thinks you right."

They went back to feasting on the meat already cooked. When they could eat no more, they built up their fire to a blaze. They could see eyes glinting in the forest around them. The fires would frighten the forest predators away for a while, perhaps all night. Bazil and Relkin butchered the red-brown beast and threw the viscera and larger bones into the jungle, where things squabbled over them with coughs and roars and weird but chilling whines.

They each took turns sleeping, while the other kept

watch and fed the fire. The flames were enough that first night to keep the eyes at bay.

At dawn there was a changeover of hunters and one lot went to their lairs while another emerged to sniff the day. Bazil and Relkin took the opportunity to snatch a quick breakfast and then make their getaway, carrying with them enough meat for a second enormous feast.

Weighed down with meat, they only made ten miles in the whole day. The dry forest gradually gave way to wetter lands, and when they came on some small hills jutting out of the river forest, they climbed one and pitched camp. The woods here were drier than the bottomlands and furnished better firewood. Their position was also more defensible. They were set on a wide triangular ledge sticking out of a cliff about ten feet from the bottom, and attacking beasts could only really come at them along one side of the ledge.

Again they built a huge fire and burned it down to the coals, which they covered with wet palm leaves and meat before burying.

Relkin wasn't nearly as hungry as he'd been the first night of feasting, but he made a determined attack. Still, it was Bazil who really tucked in.

The cooking smell brought the usual audience, but the travelers' position on the high stone ledge deterred most attack, and when a mid-sized beast with long legs and a greenish hide tried, Bazil slew it and butchered its hind legs and tail and tossed the rest off the ledge in chunks.

The darkness below the ledge erupted with growls and struggles while Bazil proceeded to dress the new meat and Relkin prepared it for transport the next day. He had collected some palm fronds for the task and was devising ways of weaving them together to form meat baskets, a huge one for Bazil and a small one for himself. He stripped out withe from the palm stalk and used it to stiffen the leaves by braiding it through them. He reinforced sections at opposite corners by doubling over the palm fronds again and again. Then he made a fibrous rope from twining together vines which he passed through the crude baskets, exiting at the reinforced sections. His first try with the big basket was a failure. The meat was just too heavy. He reinforced it with more rope and some springy branches torn from a nearby conifer. At length it made a sort of small hammock that would hold the huge haunches of the night's kill. The smaller parts went into Relkin's own hamper along with some of the already cooked meat. From now on they would eat regularly, three meals a day. Relkin made a mental note to look for fruit. In the Legions they had all learned of the need for certain acids in the diet, to prevent scurvy. Now that they had all the meat they could eat, Relkin started to think about the medium to long term.

Later the moon rose. Various creatures wailed and roared to greet it. Relkin looked up at the moon and thought of other times he had stared at her beauty. For instance, from the dragon house in Marneri, on cold crisp nights, when the moon was a silver coin bathing the white city in an ethereal glow. Or from the camp house at Dalhousie, in Kenor, where they'd spent several years on duty. The moon in Kenor hanging above the trees on summer nights.

Most of all he remembered how it had looked from the top of Wattel Bek, with his arm around Eilsa Ranardaughter, his true love and his wife to be.

And with this thought his calm was shattered. For he was now separated by more than time and distance. He was completely out of touch with the army. It was just him and the dragon, and they were on the other side of the world from the Argonath and the lands of Clan Wattel.

Ah, the fair hills of the Argonath, how far away they seemed suddenly. Would he ever see them again? Could he and Bazil, alone, get out of this ancient jungle and back to the distant coast alive? One part of him insisted that they could. Another was not so sure.

Chapter Three

The river landscape was flat and huge, the air hot and damp, but the mosquitos were not as bad as Relkin had expected. They moved slowly along the mud flats, heading downstream. Relkin was considering building a raft.

"We could sail it up the coast."

"Good." Bazil had become monosyllabic with the gathering heat of the day. The landscape had grown wide and flat since they'd emerged from the forest. The smell of the river overwhelmed everything else, though Bazil had noticed a couple of odiferous trails as they'd moved northward. There were other animals around, but as was so often the case in this fragment from an ancient world, they weren't to be seen.

"Question is, though, what are we going to build it from?" Relkin deliberately posed the difficult point for them.

The nearest sizable trees were a quarter mile distant, up above the high tide mark. The land was very flat and the river sprawled miles wide. Cutting timber for a raft and moving it down to the river would be a slow business.

"Not good to use dragonsword as ax."

Relkin nodded. "That's true."

Ecator was all they had, though, for the heavy work. Relkin had his own sword and a dirk, but these were insufficient for cutting down trees. Dragonsword, however, was mighty enough. The work would, however, dull the great blade, and they lacked a good whetstone.

"Still, it may be all we can do."

Relkin spotted some driftwood ahead, a stranded tree trunk brought down from somewhere far away on the flood and deposited at the high tide mark. They stepped across to inspect it.

It was a mighty tree, an ancient hardwood that had come downstream hundreds of miles and then snagged. The bark had been worn away in places and the branches were broken off, but it was still sixty feet long and must have weighed several tons. It had been there for years. There was other debris, branches, dried-out mats of weed wrapped about the main trunk. Relkin despaired of ever moving it until the next high flood tide, and they might have to wait months for that. Even then it would be tricky with just his and Bazil's strength to rely on. Relkin clambered about the tree, checking its moorings in weed and sand. He came to the riverward end and just happened to look up and see a boat drifting by about two hundred feet out. It was a large canoe or similar type of craft, apparently empty, heading slowly downstream. Relkin pointed, amazed.

"Man-made boat," said Bazil.

"Yeah, but it looks empty."

Relkin ran down to the water's edge, shed his sword, but retained his dirk in case something unseen attacked him from the water, and waded in. There were no crocodiles visible in the vicinity, though he and Bazil had seen quite a few just a little farther upstream. He plunged on and kicked out toward the boat.

The water was pleasantly cool and the current was light. Relkin was a strong enough swimmer to easily master it. He reached the canoe's side but found that it was too high out of the water for him to reach up to the top. He swam around to the other side and was rewarded with a crude net slung over the side. It was a well-constructed craft, capable of carrying five or six passengers. He took hold and swung himself into the canoe.

Then came the first shock. There was a girl lying on her side in the middle of the boat.

He shifted forward carefully on the balls of his feet. Was she dead?

Her eyes were closed, but her rib cage rose and fell gently. She lived. More than that, she was beautiful, with her soft brown skin, large eyes, and a firm, generous mouth. Her nose in profile was large but handsome.

Now he noted the wound on her shoulder and neck and the big bruise associated with the long, ragged cut. The wound had begun to fester at the cut end. Relkin knew that he would have to operate on her at once and clean out the wound and dress it with Old Sugustus, or she would die.

In the next moment, he realized that the girl also possessed a tail. The shock of this revelation made him grunt and sit back on his haunches. It was a sinuous brown tail, about four feet long, that projected through a slit in the girl's one-piece garment at the base of the spine. The tunic was fine work, made from animal skins neatly sewn together. The tail was undoubtedly part of her, with the same light brown skin, and ending in a tuft of black hair, exactly like the hair on her head.

Relkin swallowed heavily and shifted back a foot or so. "By the old gods," he whispered. He stared at the tail, then tentatively reached out and touched it. It felt firm, exactly as he imagined her arm might feel. For some reason this discovery made him feel dizzy and he put out a hand to the side of the boat to hold himself steady. After a moment or two he recovered.

He touched her shoulder. She continued to breathe slowly and softly, but she did not awaken. The tunic had been cut through across her shoulder blade and there was massive bruising. Something long and hard had struck her across that shoulder. He felt gingerly for broken bones, but detected nothing. Her head fell back. Her glossy hair was cut to shoulder length and braided.

Struck by her beauty, Relkin felt a number of strange, untoward thoughts running in his mind. The tail was uncanny. It brought on strange feelings of unease. He found his palms were sweating. At last, he snapped himself out of the trance and stood up. The canoe was equipped with paddles; there were three in plain sight. He was drifting seaward, on a slow current. Time was wasting. He took up the nearest and started paddling to get the canoe's head turned around and pointed to the shore. It took a few strokes to get it in the right direction.

Bazil was walking slowly along the shoreline, about two hundred feet away. At Relkin's wave, he increased his pace to catch up.

Relkin paddled hard, first on one side and then the other. The river's current was running into the incoming tide, which was growing stronger, and this made it fairly easy to reach the shore.

At last the canoe ground on sand. The dragon came down to the water's edge to heave it up onto the drier ground. His eyes popped as he looked inside.

"Where does this girl come from?" said Bazil.

"I don't know. I've never seen anything like her."

"I should have expected it, I know. If anyone can find a female in complete wilderness, it would be you."

There came an audible intake of breath into mighty lungs.

Bazil had noticed the shocking, unusual attribute.

"She have tail!" The big eyes had gone round. He clacked his jaws. "This is very sensible. Dragons always wonder how humans can live without tail."

"She's hurt real bad, Baz."

Bazil had just noticed the wound himself.

"This dragon has eyes in the head, fool boy."

"Then help me move her."

"Where to? Where do you suggest?" Bazil clearly didn't think there was anywhere better than where they were.

Relkin looked up and realized the truth of this. They were a long ways from anything remotely defensible. The boat would have to do.

"I've got to cut those skins off and clean the wound, and then I've got to sew it up. We've got a little Old Sugustus, I think we can save her. I'm going to need a big fire, though. And we'll want to build a barrier around us, too."

"She need to eat."

"When she wakes up I expect she'll be hungry."

"What do we do first?"

"Got to make a fire. Need to heat the knife to cauterize the wound. Need to heat some water as hot as we can make it."

"There's plenty of driftwood."

Indeed, it took them little time to accumulate enough dried-out wood to get a fire blazing. Relkin pulled out some more dead branches a little farther upstream and dragged them down to the fire. It blazed high while he cut away the skin garment, revealing a slim body, nicely muscled, with a young woman's firm, round breasts. Swallowing hard, he cleaned the wound and examined it carefully. Fortunately, while the bruising was severe, the cut was modest. Her one-piece garment had taken just enough of the blow. Still there was an obviously infected place that had to be cauterized. He sharpened the dirk as much as possible and heated it on the hot coals before using it to swiftly cauterize the wound, while ignoring the stench of the sizzling flesh.

The girl moaned, struck out with her arms, and he had to hold her tightly to keep her still, but she did not emerge into full consciousness. Gradually her struggles ebbed and she fell back into motionlessness once again.

He then set about heating water. First he and Bazil trekked along the shore in search of rocks. Fortunately they found a jut of rock, much eroded and broken up, not far downstream. From its cracks they extracted a lot of good-sized pieces, which they took back and put into the fire. Then Relkin and Bazil searched for a hollow log. This sent them scouting back along the forest's edge for quite a ways, but eventually they found a suitable one, partly rotted but not entirely, and hollow for much of its length. Bazil cut the bottom part free and carried it to the waterside and Relkin washed it out as best as he might, working with a sharpened stick to rouse out all the loose bits and pieces at the bottom.

Then he had Bazil fill it and bring it back to the fire. Relkin had already cut down some tree branches with which to pick up the red-hot rocks, which he then dropped into the water-filled hollow trunk. When the water began to steam, he tore up some strips of cloth from his ragged jerkin and put them in the water and stirred them around with his dirk. Then he used them, wet, to wash down the wound area and get it as clean as possible. Next he took an end of a cloth and soaked it with Old Sugustus and went over the wound again. Then he used the strips for a field dressing, under her arm, over her shoulder, and down across her breast, which was darkly nippled. He tied off the dressing and made sure it would hold.

Relkin knew of several good herbs for poultice making, but he doubted he would find them in these ancient forests. This forest was a strange place. There were very few flowering plants; the trees were mostly conifers, and unfamiliar types to him, too. Few of the familiar herbs were visible, either.

Still, Old Sugustus and hot water would do wonders, and the worst part of the wound had been cauterized with hot steel. If they could get some water into her and keep her safe, maybe she would wake. Maybe she would even survive. Relkin thought there was an even chance of it. He had seen more than his share of bludgeon wounds, not to mention sword wounds, arrow wounds, and every other wound one could imagine, and had come to hold expert opinions about them. The girl's skull was intact, there was no blood in her ears or from her nose. That was a good sign. So was the furious twitching of the limbs when he cauterized the wound. She was not paralyzed in the least. The heaviest part of the blow had come on the shoulder behind the collarbone, which had not broken. Relkin was pretty sure that no bones at all had been broken, though he couldn't be absolutely certain about the shoulder blade. If she came around, they could find out. Until then she must be kept perfectly still, dry, clean, and supplied with water.

He brought her water in a vessel made of a gourd he had cut from a forest vine and hollowed out and dried over the fire until it was as hard as fired clay.

She drank small amounts when he held it to her mouth, but choked after a while so he desisted. Every hour or so he gave her more.

Meanwhile, Bazil gathered more wood. Some went for the fire. The rest went to build a wall of brush around their position. The tide had come up about halfway to the high tide mark, which it clearly only reached a couple of times a year. They had dragged the boat farther up until it was beside the big beached tree. Now they built a "boma" around the position, cutting out brush, branches, and masses of twisted vines, some of them bearing savage thorns. The barrier was eight feet high before they were finished, and Relkin was satisfied that it would deter all but the biggest predators and even delay those.

Here they would stay until the girl either got better or died.

Before the sun went down, they built their rock oven and laid over it the haunches of meat they'd brought down from the hills. The meat cooked while the sky darkened and the moon rose. Relkin thought of Eilsa, and tried not to think too hard about the girl with the tail, lying on a bed of palm fronds he'd made, bandaged and struggling for life.

Chapter Four

Their life by the river wasn't difficult, particularly once Relkin had the time to make a crude bow and some arrows, and then some fishing line and finally a net. These items improved their diet quite considerably. It turned out to be a necessary move, as the supply of over-aggressive reptilian predators had thinned out over the weeks as they were killed off night after night by Bazil and the sword. The lack of such ill-mannered fellows had also made for uninterrupted sleep.

From the skin of one of the largest red-brown beasts Relkin had renewed his own wardrobe and outfitted a sun hat for the dragon, with a long flap at the back that could be unrolled to cover the shoulders. Bazil had long complained of the power of the tropical sun's rays. Leatherback dragons were creatures of the northern coasts, after all.

Their camp gradually took on a more permanent look. First Relkin built a crude shelter, over the girl and thus over the boat. Around it there sprouted a palisade of sharpened sticks, and around that an outer palisade. Finally a ditch of sorts was dug and more stakes put out in the bottom.

By then there was a much larger shelter inside, in which both dragon and boy could sleep at night. Attacking animals made so much noise on the stockades that it always woke them up well in time to deal with the nuisance. Then the animals grew fewer in number and dwindled to nothing and the nights became quite peaceful.

To capture more food, Relkin tried a deadfall trap and a pit with a stake at the bottom, but neither produced any game. Bazil did manage to surprise some big two-legged critters and kill one of them after an epic chase. The bounty from this kept them in meat for a week. In all this time the girl drifted in and out of unconsciousness while her wound swelled briefly and then drained and began to heal. The bruising began to fade and the color deepened in her cheeks. When she stirred and groaned, Relkin had found he could feed her soup, and so meat soup had become a staple and was made fresh every day in a hollowed-out trunk. In time this became fish soup. He thickened it by grinding the flesh of the fish between two smooth rocks before adding it to the hot stock in their firepit cauldron. Without a pot or a kettle it was arduous work, but Relkin was used to such a life and he quickly adapted.

With Bazil's powerful assistance they examined the trees and plants in their surrounding area, searching for whatever might be useful. From the bark of a tall tree that had leathery little round leaves Relkin could extract long threads of fiber. These he wove together to make string. By various means he learned to make this fiber string stronger and more effective, and eventually coated it with pine tar and dried it in the sun and then by the fire. After some trial and error he finally had an effective bowstring with reasonable strength. These strings broke more frequently than good Marneri-made twist, but he could always make more, and they did the job well enough to give him an effective addition to their armament.

In addition he was working on softening the sinews of the beasts they had killed. When cooked they were useless, as stiff as pieces of wood. So he cut out a few while the meat was fresh, a laborious process. Then he stretched them in the sun while working them constantly to keep them pliable. Later he hardened them by the fire. However, although they were strong and had a fair degree of elasticity, they were hard to work, tending to unravel when stressed repeatedly. This sent him back to the pine-tar–shellacked string, which worked well enough.

In the meantime he had woven enough coarser thread to start stitching together his first net. That was a small one, an experimental model that proved its worth when used in conjunction with a fishing line and one of his precious collection of metal hooks, also from his waist pouch. They were good Marneri hooks bought on Foluran Hill and he had four of them, and when they were gone he would have to make his own hooks. Which had him working with the teeth of some of the larger fish they managed to catch. One monster was eight feet long and had been caught when it came out of the deeper water to take a smaller fish that Relkin had hooked. At Relkin's cry Bazil threw himself in with Ecator in hand and emerged with the back half of the fish, while Relkin pulled in the rest. The teeth were large and partly hooked. Relkin sought to accentuate the hook with the tip of his dirk. The results were not that good. The small net, however, made it much easier to land smaller fish and it became a permanent part of his fishing equipment.

As days passed into weeks his busy fingers twisted together fiber from the tree that Bazil had felled, and the bigger nets were done and they quickly made life much easier. They stretched the first around a snag stuck about four hundred feet out in the river. Bazil swam out to check it after every tide and usually found something big caught in it. The river teemed with fish.

Meanwhile, Relkin was also making rope from vines and trying to figure out how to make a trap that they could lower to the bottom of the river to see what they might catch down there. He imaged crabs and lobsters of great size and wonderful flavor. The ropes were easy, since the vines were tough but pliable and could be held together with a glue made from pine tar thinned down with hot water.

In these ways the days passed quickly and their camp became ever more comfortable.

And slowly the girl began to awaken for longer periods and even to some sort of awareness. At first it was just little cries and moans. Her body might shiver a moment during these episodes. Later her eyelids fluttered open and she stared around for a moment before falling back into unconsciousness. The next day she woke again and remained awake longer. Her face registered astonishment, fear, and curiosity in equal measures. She said something incomprehensible and repeated it several times.

When Relkin spoke to her, she screamed and tried to
get to her feet. She wasn't physically ready for anything
like that. Her legs wouldn't hold her and Relkin quickly
took her in his arms and laid her down again. Her eyes
were fixed on him. Although at first she stared at him
with suspicion, he gave her some meat broth in the gourd.
She sniffed it suspiciously, then devoured it and looked
for more. Relkin refilled the gourd from the fire.

When Bazil came back with a load of driftwood, she
screamed again and tried to crawl away, but could only
roll onto her stomach and wriggle. When he dropped the
driftwood by the fire and squatted down nearby, she
stared bug-eyed, on the point of dragon freeze. Then Bazil
spoke to Relkin. When Relkin spoke back, she fainted.

Thus began a period of mutual education. Relkin
learned that her name was Lumbee and that she was of the
"Ardu" people, the people with tails. In return she soon
managed to pronounce "Relkin" and "Bazil" clearly. It
took time for her suspicion of them to really fade, but
gradually it did and at the same time they picked up words
of each other's language so that within a few more days
they were capable of carrying on basic conversation. He
learned that she had escaped an attack by "no-tail" men
on her people. She had been clubbed in the fight, but had
retained consciousness long enough to fall into the canoe
and push it out onto the river. Lumbee spoke of the "no-
tail" men with dread and hate in her voice. She had been
remarkably lucky, because the lake that her kin were
camped beside had two exit streams, one flowing south to
the land of the no-tails and the other north into the lands
of terror. By pure chance the canoe had gone north; otherwise she would have long since fallen into the hands of
the dreaded no-tails.

Later, when Lumbee was strong enough to walk, they
moved camp several miles downstream to a small island.
It was perfectly defensible and equipped with a nearby
companion islet to which Relkin could string the big net.
The fishing was good and they built a crude raft on which
to float across the daily mound of firewood that Bazil collected along the shore.

It was at the island camp that Relkin began to seriously

learn the language of the Ardu folk. It was a process of trial and error with occasional outbursts of laughter as he mastered the pronunciation of common words and began to fashion crude sentences.

In exchange Relkin taught Lumbee some Verio, the common language of the far east, and a few phrases of dragon speech. Lumbee was a quick study for languages and learned even more swiftly than Relkin, who was trying very hard. Lumbee was not so quick to accept that Bazil was what he was, an intelligent person who could speak and be spoken to. Her own first efforts at speaking to the dragon, in unfamiliar Verio, left her weak and frightened afterward. But, as the days progressed, so she grew used to the huge, friendly presence of the leatherback wyvern.

Once, when they were attacked by a pair of green-skinned long-striders, Bazil unsheathed Ecator with that weird, shivery, ringing cry the blade made when hungry for action. Then with smooth, lethal strokes he cut down the predators. Lumbee was awed. She understood now the power of the pairing of a man and such a warrior beast. The sword in such huge hands became a godlike weapon to a simple Ardu girl. Lumbee now confronted the realization that Relkin and Bazil came from a civilization of an order beyond that of anything she knew or understood. They spoke of cities and great oceans, things that she had only heard of in legend, and of ships that sailed on those oceans. All these things churned in Lumbee's mind and she would ask Relkin questions for hours at a time as she tried to understand them. Her world was turning upside down and it was not an entirely comfortable experience.

Furthermore, she began to have the most shameful ideas about the pale brown boy that had saved her life. With his sun-bleached hair and easy, infectious smile, she felt strongly attracted to him. He was a young man, his body hardened by a life of constant movement and physical work, but she saw in his eyes a depth of experience and a sadness that she wanted desperately to quench.

Lumbee was not a stranger to love. She had gone beyond the fire circle with Konsh, until the previous summer when he had disappeared, presumed abducted by the no-tail slavers who haunted the Summer Lands. More recently she had been paired with Ommi, though she did not care for big Ommi as much as she had for Konsh.

To meet with Konsh beyond the firelight to kiss and fumble and entwine tails was an acceptable part of the courtship of marriage. The Ardu owned no property; they were hunter-gatherers with garden plot agriculture. They were relaxed about courtship rites.

But to meet with a tailless one for such activities?

Lumbee had already asked to see the base of Relkin's spine, and been amazed at the complete absence of a tail. Where her own, muscular, brown-skinned tail sprang out of her body to flex behind her, his backbone stopped abruptly, just above the buttocks.

At first she had been repelled by this lack, but after a while she found that she had accepted it. The way everybody had once accepted old Gampi, a distant great-aunt of Lumbee's, who had lost a hand in her youth and had just a stump at the end of one wrist. Nobody had thought twice about it in the clan. After a week or so she found she didn't miss the tail on Relkin anymore.

She prayed for guidance to the forest gods, the gods of wood and glen, creek and pond, that had stood by the Ardu for millennia. But she was far from her homeland and unsure if her gods could hear her prayers in this dark, ancient forest.

Still she asked questions, compelled by a frantic need that she scarcely understood. Perhaps it was just to deflect the mounting interest she felt in Relkin.

As she became more conversant, so the others learned more from her concerning their whereabouts. Relkin had been correct in his supposition that they were on the southern shore of the Inland Sea. The Ardu's knowledge of the world was limited. They knew of the sea as the northern terminator of the world. They knew nothing of the lands to the east and north. When Relkin spoke of the sea, Lumbee's eyes lit up and she gestured to the north. But when he spoke on, she grew troubled and asked many questions. Relkin was left exhausted by the effort to both learn the new words and answer the endless questions.

The general outline of the situation was clear to Relkin

by now. Lumbee's home lay on a plateau several weeks' journey upstream. There, the Ardu folk had dwelled since the beginning of the world, or so their shamans told them. They were the chosen of the forest gods, and thus they were allowed to keep their tails while all other peoples lost these precious, beautiful attributes.

Bazil was much amused by this concept. Relkin was left wondering. Could this really be true? Could the Old Gods have made this sort of bargain with the Ardu? Relkin had been exposed to too much great magic in his short life to be really sure of anything. He tended to call on the Old Gods, the deities of Veronath, like Asgah and Caymo, except in the tightest spots, and then he was likely to ask the Great Mother for her help, too. He wasn't sure, however, if the rule of the Old Gods extended here to this far-off land. As for tails and no-tails, this was a problem he had never encountered before.

Furthermore, the existence of tails on the Ardu left him wondering what other variations on the human norm there might be in the world. He had never heard of tailed people. Might there be folk with three legs, or four, and standing eight feet tall? What about two heads?

None of this bothered Bazil. The gods of dragonkind were immutable, ancient, harsh in the rule of the Egg. Humans were a comic turn, very new in the world. His amusement continued unabated.

However, amusement faded as Lumbee's story continued.

The uniqueness of the Ardu had, in fact, become their undoing once travelers from the southern cities broke into their isolated world. Lumbee was unsure exactly how long ago that had been, but thought it had been in the time of her great-grandmother. Since then slavetakers from the south had haunted the forest of the Ardu, snatching anyone they could catch and taking them away in chains to sell in the rich markets of the southern cities. Especially in the dread city of Mirchaz. Even speaking that dreadful name caused Lumbee to break into tears.

So it had been with her more immediate family. First some of them had been taken while out hunting. They knew this because Ommi, Norwul, and Uncle Durs didn't come home one day. Lumbee's father, Uys, then moved their camp to the lake of two rivers, where the honto trees were in fruit. The family ate well, but worried about the missing men. Then came the slavers, tracking them with dogs, surrounding the camp and attacking at dawn. The family had been taken, including her mother, Erris, and no doubt were soon to be sent south as slaves.

Lumbee had been left drifting down the river to the north, preparing herself for death before she lost consciousness.

Relkin and the dragon had heard many terrible tales during their time, but this struck home in a way that many had not. Their eyes met in a grim, nonverbal communication.

Later, when they went to check the nets, they spoke.

"I know what you are thinking, boy. I am thinking the same thing."

"I have been thinking about it, Baz. I know the Lady would want us to help her. The Lady hates slavery more than anything. She would do it."

"Then we agree. Question is, how?"

"Build a boat."

"Boy know how to build a boat?"

"Not yet."

Chapter Five

The next few weeks brought some surprises.

The first boat wasn't strong enough. Relkin had attempted to make rough planks by splitting a certain type of conifer. These balks of wood were then held together with wooden pegs made laboriously from a much harder type of wood. Lumbee assisted in making the pegs and scouting the forest for the right kind of trees. A few pieces were taken out of Lumbee's boat and used intact in the new one.

Now healed and fit, Lumbee came into her element in the trees. She could climb almost as fast as a monkey, and her strong, effective tail was put to constant use. Relkin found himself quite outmatched when it came to climbing trees, something that he'd always prided himself on since boyhood. It took a little getting used to, for not only was he outmatched at tree climbing, but by a girl.

Still, they worked well together. Lumbee found useful trees. Bazil hewed them down with Ecator and all three strove to haul them out and split them. The effort took a month of hard work before they finally floated the boat, a flat-bottomed scow. It was crude and tended to list a little to one side, but it was beautiful to their eyes as it floated there, moored by a thick piece of vine. Relkin spent an hour just gazing at it in slightly smug self-satisfaction. It was the best thing he had ever built.

Alas, the next morning it broke under the dragon's weight, the pegs separating, the planks coming apart, and the whole thing collapsing, leaving them swimming in the wreckage.

With frantic efforts, Relkin saved as much as he could from the wreck and started anew. The second boat was larger and cruder, a narrow raft of logs tightly bound together, with a prow stuck on the front made from salvaged parts of the first boat. This boat stood up to the test of Bazil's weight.

There was a mast, a yard, and a single sail that they made up binding together strips of bark into a square, flexible mat. This became the base on which Relkin poured layers of latex-rich sap from a tree with large dark leaves. Lumbee had exclaimed with delight upon finding some of these trees and immediately began the process of making rubber, a material that her people used extensively in mats, storage containers, and the like. The resulting latex was flexible and waterproof and their sail could be rolled up quickly to the yard when the wind became unfavorable.

Relkin had never encountered latex before and was much impressed with this material.

After experiments showed the need, they made a keel board by weaving together stout saplings into a very stiff mat. They cut a space for it to be raised and lowered through a gap between the central logs.

The effect of the sail with a wind coming directly upstream was quite good, enough to overcome the current and allow them to gain some way and move slowly through the water. By rigging the yard on the mast and adjusting the crude sail, they could also make some way on winds that were not quite directly from behind the boat. Any other kind of wind had them in trouble, however, and forced the sail to be rolled up. Bazil had to provide the motive power then, with Relkin and Lumbee steering with oars set in the prow.

Bazil's huge paddle was made from woven sapling material, with sheets of liquid latex poured over it and dried in the sun. As soon as each sheet was dry, another would be added. After a while there was a thick coating of crude rubber around the head of the paddle. The handle was a six-inch-wide tree trunk, which Bazil had cut and trimmed with Ecator.

It was the attachments that were the problem. The crudely made vine rope tended to give way under the heavy stresses of paddling. Eventually Relkin reworked it all with sinew and coated the whole thing with latex. The latex wore off quickly and Bazil complained of the smell, but it partially solved the attachment crisis and they continued to make slow but steady progress up the river.

In the mornings there was often a breeze heading inland from the sea and they were usually able to harness the wind and use it to ride many miles upriver. This wind would die in the heat of the day and they would rest, laying up and preparing food. In the later part of the afternoon they would paddle until the sun was well down in the sky. Then they would find a campsite and immediately gather all the brush and driftwood they could find, which was always considerable. No one had combed it out before themselves. This was unexplored territory, the very heartland of the Lands of Terror.

While the fire was burning high, they dug their cook pit and later filled it with hot rocks and glowing coals. They would roast fish and bake the tree fruits that Lumbee selected, mostly a greenish pod the size of a coconut but with a soft outer skin. Raw, these fruits smelled sour and almost rotten; baked, they had a pleasant nutty smell and a bland taste. They were quite common and easy to collect. Groves of these trees would appear in certain regions along the bank and the travelers would heave to beside them and collect the fruit for an hour or two.

As they moved inland, out of the district they'd previously emptied of predators, their camps were once again visited at night by aggressive beasts. Many were deterred by the improved bomas surrounding their camps. Relkin had learned to use thorn tree saplings as long spines jutting out of the main mass of twisted vines, branches, brush, and small trees that they piled up every night. But now and then a large, particularly aggressive specimen, often one of the red-brown type, would force its way in and then Bazil would slay it with Ecator. They always had good warning of these eruptions, first from growls and snarls as the heavy beast struggled with the outer part of the boma, then the crushing and crashing as it forced its way in.

As before, Bazil found that these beasts were far more aggressive than they were intelligent. They were fierce and terribly active, but their form of attack was fixed, just a few basic instinctual moves. The big head would bob, the neck muscles bunching behind it. The beast would lurch forward and bring the jaw around in a hook for the wyvern's throat or flank. In so doing, they opened themselves perfectly for decapitation with the dragonsword.

These beasts were added to the travelers' larder. Baked whole and rolled in ashes to preserve them from flies, their powerful haunches were sufficient to feed them all very well at the end of the day. The meat was chewy but satisfying and had a taste like a gamy chicken. They ate tremendous meals, and slept soundly thereafter. The starved look had long since given way to a robust good health. Lumbee's wound had completely healed weeks before. Bazil was even putting on a little weight.

As they traveled, so their exchange of languages went on, and with them descriptions of two utterly different and separate worlds: the greater world outside, from which came Relkin and Bazil, and the forest world that was Lumbee's.

Lumbee told them the names for the trees, and the wild beasts, and the birds, and various insects, and a thousand other things. Slowly the names solidified in Relkin's memory. The "chai" tree, the "medor" tree, the "chich" ants—the list was long.

Some were easier to recall than others. For instance, the big red-brown carnivores were called "pujish." In fact, all carnivore beasts were pujish of some kind, but the red-browns were the archetype because they were the largest and fiercest.

The smaller, yellow-skinned killers that hunted in packs were called "kemma wan," which translated as "deadly lizards," although Relkin was sure they weren't lizards; they were far too active and their flesh was warm to the touch when they were freshly killed. Still, he had no argument with the "deadly" designation. *Deadly* was a popular description of things, it seemed. Many other things in the jungle were "ke"—they were ke-this and ke-that, and that meant they must be avoided. Lumbee repeated these things in the same tone in which they had been taught to her when she was a little girl.

Whole regions were riddled with "ke," and were best avoided. "Ke" was a powerful force in the Ardu universe, as Relkin soon came to realize. Swampy, low-lying areas, covered in rushes, were particularly strong reservoirs of "ke," and Relkin understood that this was a reference to the plague that had felled the Legions during their trip down the great river. For days the entire army had been paralyzed by fever and delirium. They had survived only by the slimmest margin when the great red-browns forced their way in past the failing lines of dragonboys and the few fit men still able to stand. A single dragon had awoken from near-coma just in time.

All pujish were ke, of course, but in varying degrees, with the red-brown pujish as the strongest and other, smaller varieties having less ke about them, except for the yellow-skinned killers, which had almost as much as the red-brown pujish.

In exchange for these insights into the ancient forest world, Relkin told Lumbee about the cities of the Argonath, and then about the land of Kenor, with its fierce winters, where he and the dragon had served for much of the past few years.

Her eyes went wide as he described ice and snow and the wintry blasts that sent a chill right through a Kenor freecoat. She was aghast at the thought of water freezing solid and of all the trees losing their leaves and "dying" for the winter.

She had many questions, a great many.

Then there were the cities.

He told her about Marneri, the white city on the strand overlooking the blue waters of the sound, the queen of the Argonath cities. He told her about Foluran Hill, with its great houses and busy shops and the great, somber Tower of Guard that stood at the top of Tower Street and dominated the whole city spread out below. He told her of the fairs and the festivals, like Fundament Day, which was everyone's favorite.

Lumbee was familiar with the general concept of a city, a place of power where many people came from, but she had no clear idea of what a city actually looked like. The Ardu were semi-nomadic, moving about their family and

kin group ranges on an annual trek with migrations to the
land of summer camps, where they roamed as they waited
for the monsoons. Then they would migrate up to the
plains and hunt for three-horns. They would salt and dry
the meat to see them through the journey back to the
summer camp region in the south. There were only just
enough of the Ardu to live in balance with the land and
the game animals that they lived off. They had no villages, no towns, no large buildings at all.

What cities she had heard of previously had all been
located far to the south and were led by the dreadful name
Mirchaz, which stood for all that was unholy in Lumbee's
life. Just the sound of the name brought a tremor to her lip
and filled her eyes with angry tears.

At such moments Relkin had a strong urge to take her
in his arms and comfort her physically. She was beautiful
and he was attracted to her. Moreover, he had hardly seen
a woman in months. These desires disturbed him deeply.

Relkin still loved Eilsa Ranardaughter. And if he ever
came home alive he would wed her, if she would still
have him. This was a bedrock conviction, the foundations
of the edifice of the future life he had built in his imagination. However, Eilsa was thousands of miles away. He
had not seen her in almost a year and it was possible he
would never see her again.

Lumbee was disturbingly beautiful and right there in
the here and now. Moreover, they were alone, far from
anywhere or anyone else. There was nothing to prevent
him from reaching out to her, except the thought of Eilsa,
and the other thought, the one that made him cringe
inside.

The tail. The great, insurmountable difference between
them. Relkin sometimes felt a desperate unease when he
contemplated the strong brown tail. He was drawn to it as
it floated about her and occasionally brushed against
things, including both Relkin and Bazil. When it touched
Relkin he felt something like a static shock. It was the
same shock he felt when he and Eilsa held hands the first
time. He wanted Lumbee, but she was not of his kind.

And yet they shared the boat together and were constant
company. Lumbee was an openhearted person, honest

through and through. She captivated him with her generous nature and he was drawn into a desperately complex relationship, wanting her and her love, and fearing the desires within him.

More and more often he caught her looking at him with an odd expression. Those big soft brown eyes seemed almost unfocused, her mouth settled in a tiny smile. How he wished he could kiss those lips!

Despite the tremendous difference between them, he was constantly drawn to her and the feeling was strengthening. Worse, he sensed that she reciprocated his feelings.

This unleashed speculations that left him feeling guilty enough to pray to the Old Gods for guidance. Where was Caymo now that he needed him so badly?

Still the question nagged at him. What if he asked her? What then? What if she said yes? Then his guilt choked him until unworthy thoughts rose in his mind like a dark cloud.

What would it matter? Eilsa would never know. She was so far away she might as well be on another world entirely. If he ever saw her again, if he ever managed to find his way home.

Besides, how long could she refuse the demands of her clan? The clan did not want her to marry the orphan dragonboy. They wanted her to marry to cement kinship relations within the clan. When the news of the disaster that had befallen the expedition to Eigo reached home, they would have learned that among the missing was one Relkin of Quosh. Then the pressure on Eilsa would rapidly mount.

How could she conclude anything but that he was lost forever and that it was time for her to do her duty and marry for the sake of Clan Wattel?

Confusion, longing, and self-loathing competed for attention in Relkin's thoughts. He grew moody and pensive and spent as much time as possible sitting by himself at the prow of the boat.

Chapter Six

The weather continued dry and hot, and they made steady progress until the river narrowed to a half-mile width and began to curve in great meanders across its floodplain. The forest was thinning out, although it still fringed the river itself. Now they had to paddle almost all the time. The winds were rarely favorable and hardly ever lasted more than a few minutes at a time.

Lumbee was certain that her people were still in the slaver's camp. It seemed the slave raiders built a stockade at the beginning of the long dry season and used it as their base for the summer's depredations. Only when the rains began did they break camp, jam all their captives aboard rafts, and float down the southern rivers to the distant cities.

"Has anyone ever come back?" Relkin asked her.

Lumbee shook her head grimly.

"Never. The cities are far, far. Too far for our gods to call back our people. Even their ghosts are lost. Truly, it is the complete death when one is taken."

"Tell me again what we should expect ahead."

"This river flows out of the southern lake, but we will not be able to get that far—the boat is too big and the river level has fallen. We will probably have to start walking in the next day or so."

"I was afraid of that."

"It is not so far, though. We will be on the Plain of Three-Horns. We can cross the plain to the southern forests. There we will find the slaver's camp."

"But we will have to search for it, right?"

"It will be on the south river somewhere, and it will be

a big camp by now. The slavers will have taken hundreds of people there."

Relkin nodded to himself. All the more important they get there in time and put a stop to it.

"How long do we have, do you think?"

Lumbee squeezed the end of her tail with one hand, something she did when she was concerned or upset.

"It feels like the end of the dry season. See how the grass is all brown, and the vines had gone brown, too. The trees along the river are listless. There has been no real rain here for many moons."

"If the rains come?"

"The slavers will break camp and we will never catch them."

"So we're cutting it fine."

"What is this 'cutting it fine'?"

"Nothing, a figure of speech."

"You say that before." Lumbee had switched into Ardu, a sign of impatience, even irritation.

"It is just a saying. You have them, too, I'm sure."

Lumbee did not seem so sure about this.

"Well, when rains come, slavers go."

All of this had long made Relkin wonder.

"If this has been going on for a long time, why do the Ardu not change their ways? Why don't they move away from the south river? Go somewhere else in the dry season, like to this forest?"

Lumbee reacted as if stung. Her lips pulled back in disgust.

"What? Not go to Summer Lands? Then where do we go? Into old jungle? Old jungle not have good food. Only fish and breadfruit. So many troublesome animals there, Ardu people not like that."

"Better the animals than the slavers."

Lumbee's brow furrowed once more.

Relkin explained. "I mean that the animals might take fewer Ardu than the slavers do."

Lumbee shrugged. "Ardu always go to Summer Lands. The food is good, it is best time of the year for fruit. The men make wine, everyone loves the summer."

Relkin had heard this line before. The Ardu were a folk

with a rigid schedule and Lumbee often recited it. They went south in the dry season because the three-horns herds massed and then migrated north to Lake Gam. When in these big herds, the three-horns were dangerous. The bulls were very likely to charge anything that they came across. And worst of all, where the three-horns went, the pujish followed, and the Ardu always tried to avoid the big pujish. So the Ardu forsook the savanna and went south to make their ancestral summer camps. They had been doing this since the forest gods first blew the breath of life into them long, long ago.

Later, Relkin withdrew to the boat's prow and sat there brooding. Bazil was resting amidships under the sail, which billowed actively. For once, there was enough of a breeze to keep their unwieldy craft coursing steadily upstream, and this reach of the river was long and straight. Lumbee came and sat down beside the dragon. She had overcome her initial awkwardness around the great beast. She had come to accept that this huge, terrifying creature could actually speak, and could learn the words of her own language. It was astonishing, but she had been traveling with him for weeks and it was impossible to pretend anything else.

She had noticed many things about the great dragon. For one, he was not as quick at learning new words as Relkin, but once he learned them, he remembered them very well. He was not as verbal as the dragonboy, but he was shrewd and possessed an abundant sense of humor.

Now that she and the dragon were alone together, she asked Bazil the question that had been much on her mind.

"Why does Relkin fear Lumbee?"

The dragon's eyes fixed on her. Once she would have gone into dragon freeze, but now she was proof against that elemental terror. Bazil made a rumbling sound in his chest, a sound she now understood to mark gentle amusement.

"Boy fear he lose control of himself. He want to fertilize the eggs with you."

Lumbee laughed, relieved to hear that her suspicions were confirmed. The no-tail boy was interested in Lumbee, just as Lumbee was interested in him.

"Then why doesn't he?"

"He is pledged to another."

Relkin had told Lumbee about this distant girl several times and Lumbee had sensed a great tension in his words.

"But she is far, far. She will never know if Relkin and Lumbee lie together."

More rumbling in that immense chest. "I tell this to boy. It doesn't help."

"Lumbee like Relkin. Lumbee want to help him."

"Boy be happy to know this. This dragon thinks that sooner or later Lumbee will have her opportunity to help."

Lumbee giggled and flashed the dragon a look that said they now shared a secret together.

The next day the river broadened over shallows and rocks. It was much lower now than it had been when Lumbee had drifted downstream. They were forced to abandon their boat and begin the march south, through the gradually thinning forest. Clearings grew frequent and then became very large. And then they were walking through grassland, with clumps of trees scattered across it.

The land was parched and deserted. Once again food became a concern. The large animals had gone to cluster around the lake, which lay beyond the nearby hills. This meant the travelers had to skirt the hills, where the big pujish would be concentrated, and go around the lake.

The small animals they encountered were fleet of foot and quick to distance themselves from anything the size of Bazil. Relkin and his primitive bow were enough to ensure a supply of smaller fare, lizards and some of the ground birds they encountered, which kept Lumbee and himself fed well enough, but was not enough for the dragon. Nor were there fruits or much of anything edible in these grasslands except for occasional patches of tubers that had to be dug out of the rock-hard ground.

The nights were beautiful. Under crystal-clear skies, the heat of the day gave way to a deep chill. They usually camped near some small, dried-up watercourse. They dug down in the center of the dry streambeds and soon found underground water, enough to slake their thirst and give them water for a wash and for cooking.

There was enough dry brush to make good fires, though the fires had to be watched so as not to ignite the surrounding terrain, which was all dry tinder. They no longer bothered to build the huge protective bomas of brush and thorn, since the pujish were in the hills.

Still, they stood watches, Relkin the first, Lumbee second, and the dragon last. Little did they see. Their fire drew only a solitary kemma wan, somehow isolated from its yellow and scarlet kind. It fled before Lumbee could rouse Relkin and he could get his wits about him and put an arrow into it. Bazil was left with little to eat for another day.

On the fourth day, they came on an old, four-legged animal about Bazil's size. It had a large frill of bone that surrounded its head like a huge collar, plus a single, wicked horn that sprouted from its nose.

The old beast was lame and unable to continue the journey to the hills. When they found it, it was lying on its side, panting its last breaths. Small things, like lizards but running on their hind legs, were waiting.

Bazil took its head with a mighty stroke from Ecator and they cut it up and took the haunches. That night the dragon filled his belly with the stringy meat of the old one-horn.

They were camped above a dry streambed. There was still green grass growing along the center, and the trees were in leaf around it. The travelers had dug down less than a foot before hitting the wet ground. Soon they'd had a pool of muddy water five feet wide dug out, mainly by the dragon, who looked forward to a splash-down at the end of these dry dusty days.

They cooked the meat in the usual fashion, using large rocks from the streambed at the bottom of their fire pit and putting smaller ones on top of the meat. Afterward, the dragon sprawled out on a huge pile of dry grass and watched the skies for the red dragonstars. Soon he began to snore.

Relkin and Lumbee were left alone, as they had been on many occasions before. Now, however, there was something different in the air. An electric charge seemed to pervade everything and made them feel awkward together. Relkin was particularly hesitant, which was odd, since he had never been that shy around girls before.

Lumbee suggested suddenly that they stroll out a little ways onto the plain and look at the moon, which had just risen above the horizon to frost the land with tawny light.

The moon seemed huge, and while they stood there in awe of it, Lumbee slipped her hand into his. Relkin looked down, felt his throat go dry, and squeezed her hand gently. The electric tingle faded and was replaced by a warmer feeling. An overwhelming desire was rising like a spring tide through his limbs. Their eyes met.

"I . . ." he began.

"Lumbee feel the same," she said quickly.

"I didn't know—I mean, I didn't want—"

"Lumbee understand about your mate-to-be. Lumbee suggest that it does not matter here. She is far, far, you are here, here, near to Lumbee. Perhaps you go home in time. Perhaps you are reunited. Perhaps you never go home again. Either way it will not matter if you lie with Lumbee. With Lumbee it will be for the Ardu land."

Relkin took her other hand in his. The tail swished in the moonlight and no longer repelled him.

"Perhaps Lumbee is right."

Chapter Seven

The tensions between them dissolved after that night. It was as if everything had moved to a new level. Relkin had a song in his heart when he woke up in the mornings, and between himself and Lumbee there had blossomed something sweet, but deep and as much a true case of love as anything he had known previously, either with Miranswa Zudeina, Princess of Ourdh, or Eilsa Ranardaughter, his wife-to-be of Clan Wattel. Buoyed by the sweet emotions, the first in a long time, he gave scarce heed to any misgivings. It was as if he had thrown down a huge load of responsibility that had been crushing him.

For now he would live from day to day, and he would forgo thinking of the future, which had become something of a preoccupation with him lately. It was pretty obvious that the future for Relkin and Bazil was unclear and probably hazardous, if it existed at all. Relkin would live only for the present. He was a new man, or so he did his utmost to proclaim to himself.

Somewhere the other voice was still speaking; he knew that, too. His rational self would not be stilled forever, but his love for Lumbee was so sweet, so direct, and so strong that he was borne away on the tide of the emotions it aroused.

The next few days Relkin seemed to be floating on air, as was Lumbee, and the two of them were in almost continual contact, entwined together, kissing, going off on little moonlit walks. Relkin's attention to the details of existence dimmed, and meals became fewer and further between.

Bazil watched at first with a bemused fondness in his own heart. The boy and the tailed girl practically stopped speaking to him. They were in their own world, and he was just a dimly seen companion moon. After a while, he became a little more resentful. He had splinters in his right foot and Relkin did nothing to remove them all day, not even inquiring about them.

Finally he felt a strange jealousy. They were snuggling together under a protective rock set conveniently across two others while he sat beyond the fire, alone, whetting the blade of Ecator with a piece of very high-grade pumice that Relkin had found a few days before. He worked the sword's edge every night now. Against pujish that towered over him at the point of attack, and which wielded jaws capable of taking his own head in a single bite, he could not afford a dull blade. From the steel came the rasp of the pumice stone. From inside the rocky alcove came soft giggles, punctuated by sighs and kisses.

Bazil swore under his breath, by the fiery breath of the dragon gods, humans had the longest, most teased-out courtship of any creature in the world. He had seen cats in heat teasing a circle of toms; he had seen whales courting their females, but nothing came close to humans in love. They never seemed to get enough of it.

One thing was certain: Humans enjoyed themselves in this way far more than dragons. He recalled his own courtship of the green dragoness atop Mount Ulmo in far-away Kenor. It was a golden memory for the leatherback dragon, but it did not have all this endless kissing and cuddling that the humans went in for so lavishly. With dragons, the lovemaking was fierce and swift. High Wings, the mother of his young, could not be said to have ever become "sweet" at any point in her entire life. The dragon male knew well that if his teeth ever came away from the back of the female's neck, she'd rip his throat out in the next second. This was often cited as one reason the numbers of dragonkind had dwindled over the years, while those of the humans swelled.

The blade was as sharp as he could get it. For a moment he felt a strong urge to have some foe against whom he might wield this blade, the greatest he had ever known. For a brief, unimaginably savage moment he would exhaust himself in the fire of battle. His foe would fall, as all his foes had fallen since the day he took up this witch-made blade, and later, when he cooled, these feelings of jealous isolation would be purged, burned away in the heat of battle.

He put Ecator in the scabbard and then poked around in the hot coals of the fire with a large stick and withdrew the haunch of the old one-horn that had been baking there. A test with an overlong talon told him it was done.

He sucked it for a moment and then sighed. His talons were much too long. He had splinters in the foot and there was something loose in the binding holding the scabbard to the joboquin. He was being neglected. It was not a good feeling for a leatherback dragon that had grown accustomed to the best handling in the Legions.

Once he'd eaten, an unsettled Bazil pulled himself to his feet and took a stroll away from the fire. The lovers paid no heed.

The moonlit hills loomed in the west. Since the travelers were in a race with the approaching rainy season, they were passing close to the hills in their hurry to get on to the southern plains and then the forest.

Something flickered behind him and he turned. Black clouds were mounting in the north, lightning flickering amid them. Such clouds had floated over the previous two nights, too, but they had brought no rain.

These were the harbingers of the monsoon, small storms empty of moisture. Still, they told him that there was not much time left to them in their race to the south.

He walked to the top of a gentle rise and stepped up through a rather battered-looking grove of acacia trees. Something large had been eating them recently; whole branches had been torn off. The splinters in his right foot made him limp. He hoped the boy would get over the worst of this infatuation before too long. He hated to beg for help.

He turned his gaze to the tawny darkness of the plain, dappled by moonlight. Bazil's eyes widened, transfixed by the sight. An enormous herd of big, four-legged animals with heads surrounded by huge frills of horn was spread far and wide in front of him. There were thousands of the beasts. Snorts, rumbles, and an occasional groaning cry came from them. When a nearby brute swung its head in his direction, Bazil saw that it had a pair of wicked-looking horns projecting from above the eyes, and a third horn from its nose. Furthermore, it was about twice his own size and weight. Bazil thought it a most formidable-looking brute, and when he considered its most likely enemies he understood why it was armed so heavily. Only thus could it hope to survive the assaults of the red-brown pujish.

The animal's small beady eyes were peering at him. He realized he must be more visible than he'd thought, so he slid back a half step into the acacias.

The dimensions of this herd of huge animals were awesome. He'd never seen so much flesh on foot, although he thought some of the schools of whales he'd seen might exceed it in sheer mass. But so much meat would draw predators as a matter of course. He presumed he wasn't the only spectator and cast his eyes up and down the crest of the rise on which grew the acacias.

There was one, a darker outline amid the trees, perhaps a half mile away. And then farther away, he caught a glimpse of another—pujish, red-browns from the shape of the big heads.

Bazil took more careful stock of his immediate surroundings. The last thing one wanted was to be caught off guard by one of those things. The red-brown pujish were awfully quick for such hefty animals. He gazed around him intently, studying the battered grove of small trees. After a while he reassured himself that he was alone.

He turned back to contemplation of the huge herd grazing peacefully on the plain. Such a sight was something he had to engrave on his memory. He would want to recite every detail for the Purple Green, if he and his friend were ever reunited. He knew the Purple Green would be entranced by the thought of so much meat on the hoof. Bazil chuckled to himself, but then the Purple Green was just as keen on his dinner as the big red-brown pujish.

Finally he turned away and headed back to their camp. With all these pujish in the area, it was best if he didn't stay away too long. The firelight twinkled in the dark and he moved along as quietly as possible, not wanting to draw the attention of all the red-browns he sensed hiding in the acacia groves. The pujish made no move, however. They were rooted in place, their attention fixed on the herd.

After a while, Bazil relaxed and strolled the rest of the way unconcerned. The pujish were simply not interested on this occasion.

The boy was up, alone for once, taking the early watch. Lumbee was asleep.

"What did you see?" said Relkin.

Bazil lay down by the fire.

"Big herd of horned animals over that rise. Must be thousands of them."

Relkin looked in the direction of the rise; the hills rose beyond. "I don't think they were there when we pitched camp."

"Well, they are now. And they aren't alone. There's a dozen or more of those red-browns just standing there watching them."

Relkin started up nervously at the news. "Just watching?"

"You heard this dragon." Bazil pulled out what was left of the baked haunch of the old one-horn.

"They didn't see you?"

"Don't know. Just not interested, maybe."

"By the gods, I hope not. We better get away in the morning before dawn. Maybe they're trying to work out what to eat tomorrow and they haven't noticed us yet."

Despite his earlier urge to wreak violence in battle, Bazil did not relish fending off a pack of red-browns on the morrow.

"That sound like good thinking. Better turn in now, get some sleep, maybe."

"Why are you limping?"

Ah, the boy had finally noticed that he had a wounded dragon on his hands.

"Splinters in foot, from the morning."

Relkin threw his hands up in the air. "Why didn't you

say anything? I mean, you've probably worked them in good and deep by now."

Bazil closed his eyes and did his best to blank out the sudden anger. "Normally this dragon never have to report something like that. Dragonboy usually starts to work with tweezers and pick as soon as something like that happens. Nowadays, dragonboy not seem to care about this dragon."

Relkin groaned. "I should've known. Come on, put the foot closer to the fire so I can see what I'm doing."

Relkin unwrapped his kit and went to work.

"Why does it have to take so long to fertilize the eggs? You should be back to normal by now."

"I'm not a dragon, Baz. We're different. People like to be, well, intimate. We're not solitaries like dragons, not fierce, not pure carnivores."

"You seem to take forever."

"You don't understand. It's not like that. It's more . . . well, I don't know how to express it—it's what we call love. We don't have any control over it sometimes."

Bazil gave a grunt of pain as Relkin heaved out an inch-long splinter from his foot.

"That's the worst of them," said Relkin.

"Talons are getting too long."

"You're right. Sorry, Baz, I guess I've been a bit neglectful."

Relkin pulled the other splinters, then cut down the longest dragon claws and filed them smooth.

The dragon slept soothed by Relkin's attention to the splinters and overgrown talons. The lightning flickered in the north, and dull thunder beat across the land.

Chapter Eight

The dragon slept, snoring quite softly, for him. Relkin sat tending the small fire that remained while he kept his eyes peeled for any sign of those red-brown pujish. The travelers had no protective boma and were defenseless except for Bazil and the great sword. But the grassland hissed in the dry night air and no menacing shadows showed themselves, so he let himself relax.

After a while his thoughts wandered. He marveled at the strange cast of Caymo's dice of fate. He'd come halfway around the world, seen terrible battles, and faced the Doom Master Heruta on the very lip of the volcano's fire. Somehow he'd survived all that, only to be cast onto an empty shore.

Was this some ploy of destiny? Were the gods involving him again in their struggle? He shivered. Relkin had reached the point where little that happened in the ordinary turn of events really worried him. Not even battle. Events moved too quickly in a fight, and there was no time for fear. But things like the magical apparitions in the pit below the city of Dzu still scared him. They were the ones that cast the dice. They set you on these tracks of destiny, and then there was nothing you could do about it.

Relkin wondered how they fit in with the pantheon of the Old Gods. Or were they the Old Gods themselves?

In battle, if Caymo rolled your number, that was that, unless perhaps the God of War, old Asgah, intervened. If you were sufficiently brave and valorous, Asgah might save you for his own. Those chosen by Asgah, in the days of Veronath the Golden, lived long lives despite a multitude of risks and dangers.

He shook his head. He was no hero of the golden age.

He prodded the embers of the fire and tossed on another piece of wood. He just did what he had to do, and sometimes he'd been lucky. Those old heroes, they were a different breed, he was sure. But what did the golden beings do? What was their role? And why were even the great witches Ribela and Lessis afraid of the very mention of their names?

Were the golden beings a sinister force directing him toward a dreadful end? It was hard to imagine, since they had always seemed benevolent, but was it possible that he was but a kind of rabbit to them, gulled out of his natural suspicions, to be taken when they wanted and condemned to some horrible demise?

He gave up a prayer to old Caymo for his intercession in the matter. Matters of gods and goddesses seemed too complex, too fraught with awe, for Relkin to feel comfortable with them. Caymo was good enough for him. Roll the dice and see what numbers come up and play them out with whatever skill you could muster. That was the way to deal with life.

He looked up at the stars. There were new stars, that he had only become familiar with since coming to the tropical zone. High above he saw some of the more familiar constellations: There was the goat, and there the ram. He saw one of the red dragonstars was high in the sky, but the other was not. The dragon would be concerned when he saw that.

Looking at the stars was something Relkin had done since he was a lad. He'd been lucky there. The village of Quosh in those days was the home of Ruperno the Astronomer, a didactic old man who loved nothing more than passing on the lore of the stars.

Knowing just how enormous the universe of stars was always brought on a sense of humility. That surely was the Mother's Hand, just as they tried to tell you in the temple. The gods of Veronath were mere dancers on her hand, the priestesses said. Her Hand was their stage on which they strutted. He laughed and shook his head. Gods and goddess, it was too complex for a dragonboy with little education. Who knew what the gods were up to?

The green Salt Star was there, and blue-white Dex-
terbee, he knew them well. In Kenor they were prominent
summer stars. With that awe he always felt there came a
sense of peace. In the scale of things his trials were of
little importance. Just as he was lost on the immensity
of Ryetelth, so the world itself was lost in the enormity of
the cosmos.

Something flashed nearby. He looked over his shoulder. The black clouds had slid up the sky from the north.
Thunder boomed down and rolled across the plain. Relkin
looked around quickly. The plain was softly lit by
starlight, no pujish approached, but in the north there was
complete dark.

Another flash. This time lightning forked down and
struck the plain in the distance. The thunder was loud.
The fire guttered in a sudden wind out of the north.

Lumbee had awoken. She sat beside him without a
word, staring at the oncoming clouds. He could feel the
emotions running high in her. The rains were coming.

"We are too late," she said after a while.

Relkin thought she might be right. It seemed impos-
sibly unfair. They'd come all this way and they'd run a
good race; how could they be about to lose now? On top
of which they were about to get a soaking. More lightning
struck down, much closer, followed by an ear-rending
crack of thunder that brought Bazil out of his slumber and
automatically reaching for his sword.

The big eyes blinked. "Where did that come from?" he
hissed.

"We're in for a bit of a blow," said Relkin.

He proved correct in this assessment. The wind grew
fierce and they had to stamp out their fire to make sure it
didn't spread to the wildly waving grass all around.

The clouds came on. Several lightning strikes came
down around them. The crackling and booming became earsplitting. There was so much noise that at first
they didn't notice the change. Something had become
different, however. After a while, though, they felt the
ground shuddering. Relkin looked up and met the dragon's gaze.

"No volcano here," said Relkin.

Bazil's head snapped up. Relkin turned.

Along the top of the rise there was movement.

"Aiyee!"

Lumbee was on her feet pointing. The first rain came down. It was warm and was hurled by the fierce wind so hard that it stung their faces.

"Stampede!" Relkin was on his feet, grabbing his pack and bow.

"Run," said the dragon.

Almost lost in the rain was a lightning-flash glimpse of the long slope up to the line of acacias. It was rapidly filling with an endless sea of animals, all in motion.

The rain was patchy. It would come down hard for a half minute or so and then cut off. But the wind was relentless as they ran through the waving grass. Ahead of them, in lightning flashes, they could see a seemingly flat and limitless plain. The stampede was spread out on a wide front, and there was no chance that they could get around to the side and out of its way.

They were joined in this judgment by a couple of the huge red-browns, which were stalking along at a rapid clip ahead of the stampeding herd of three-horns. It seemed they knew, too, that their only hope for escape was a flat-out run. The three-horns could not gallop, but they could move quickly nonetheless, and they could keep it up for a long time, which was worse.

There was nothing for it but to run, for as long as they could keep it up. Anything else would mean death under the feet of the onrushing wall of muscle and sinew. Not even a dozen dragons, wielding dragonswords, could long hold off a panicked herd of five-ton beasts.

And then Relkin noticed that the plain ahead came to a sudden halt. They were on the edge of a canyon so deep its bottom was lost in the dark. The walls were almost sheer.

They turned. Behind them came the wall of death. The pujish had stopped at the brink and gave out great roars of fear and rage. One approached the travelers head swinging frantically as it sought for some way to get down.

Relkin was looking for the same thing. The canyon was

huge and cut right across their line of flight. The three-
horns were close. He examined the cliff line and was
rewarded a moment later when he spotted a place where a
rock shelf jutted out from the cliff about ten feet down
from the top. Farther along, the shelf ran beneath a large
outcropping that overhung the canyon.

"There!" he pointed. There was salvation. Lumbee saw
it at once, then she whirled back.

"But how can Bazil?"

Bazil stared down at the ledge. It was a drop of more
than his own height. That was a huge jump for a leatherback wyvern. He might easily break his legs or stumble
over the edge of that shelf, which was no more than ten
feet wide at any point, and go hurtling all the way to his
death below.

But, on the other hand, a glance over his shoulder
showed him that he couldn't stay where he was. The
three-horns were five hundred feet away and still coming
at full speed. They had not yet noticed the canyon. Lightning flashed brightly and he saw a forest of waving horns
and neck frills.

The big red-brown was roaring at them in its fear and
frustration.

Relkin tugged on his arm.

"Baz, watch what I do. We've got to slide down and
then run over to that overhang. You see it?"

"I see it. I don't believe it."

"Believe. Come on."

Relkin sat on the edge, facing out into the canyon, then
tossed down his pack and bow and then dropped over the
edge, hands pinwheeling, and dropped onto the rock shelf
and rolled onto his side to dissipate the force.

Lumbee had already climbed down. She pulled him to
his feet.

Bazil got down on the edge. The rock shelf looked very
small; the canyon yawned black beyond it. The approaching pujish was screaming and snapping those huge jaws
together. There was no time for regrets or recriminations.
He pushed himself off and felt himself sliding down the
rock. It was ripping the hell out of the joboquin and his
scabbard. He bounced off something hard and was in free

fall for a long moment and then landed with crunching power on the rock and pitched off his feet, to land with a bruising crash on the flat stone.

For a moment he lay there, unable to breathe. Then he struggled to move his limbs.

"You did it, Baz!" Relkin shrieked into his ear while trying to get him up. Bazil felt that it might be the last thing he did. That fall had driven the air right out of him. Still, the three-horns were coming, and they wouldn't stop at the edge, he knew. Somehow he got his heavy legs beneath him. His tail tip grabbed for a support on the cliff wall. His arms pushed and he lurched upright just as a ter- rific flash of lightning ripped the sky apart. The thunder rolled long and violent almost immediately.

He was just in time to see a red-brown pujish go flying off the edge of the cliff, just ahead of the first group of three-horns. The pujish fell with a despairing bellow into the dark, and was followed by the three-horns, five of them, right off the outcrop over the overhang.

"Run, Baz, run." The boy and Lumbee were already under the overhang. He thrust himself forward; it was hard. His feet hurt horribly, there was no breath in his body, but he knew death would be hurtling over the cliff onto him in a moment if he stayed put. He got a step and another and was on his way when he felt himself trip. He fell, sliding almost off the edge of the rock shelf, and only by luck did his outstretched claws dig into a crack in the rock, keeping himself from slipping out into the void.

Something huge smashed into the rock ledge just behind him and then went on, tumbling to its death. He pulled himself to all fours, threw himself forward the last few feet, and collapsed beneath the overhang. The boy and Lumbee danced back out of his way.

The rock shelf shuddered again and again as huge bodies impacted briefly before continuing the long fall into the canyon below. The storm lashed the land, light- ning flashed, and the torrent of huge animals continued crashing over the cliff, bouncing off the ledge and disap- pearing into the darkness. Parts of the rock ledge fell, but the part they stood on remained standing, and at last the stampede petered out. The remaining three-horns in the vast herd had stopped themselves on the brink. They milled there, groaning and crying, as the storm waned and the rain became gentler and finally ceased altogether.

Chapter Nine

Dawn found the travelers huddled together beneath the overhang. To their left the ledge had vanished, destroyed by the torrent of huge three-horns. On their right, fortunately, the ledge had survived. The cliff above overhung it farther and the doomed animals had missed it on their plummet into the depths. They could see that their ledge extended along the cliff with a downward trend. A quick look informed them that it was out of the question for the dragon to climb back up to the top of the cliff. The only way out was to go along the ledge and hope it went down all the way.

Immediately beneath them was a charnel mound of dead three-horns, with occasionally one still groaning out its death agonies. Relkin was appalled at the enormity of the slaughter. The scene was worse than a battlefield on the day after.

At first things went well. But the ledge narrowed, and progress for Bazil became difficult, then next to impossible. The dragon had to ease himself along, his belly to the cliff wall and his talons clinging to whatever holds Relkin could identify for him. For a while Relkin feared they wouldn't be able to make it, but after a couple of hair-raising passages they came to a place where the ledge itself and much of the cliff wall had collapsed, forming a jumble of stone blocks piled up to the same height as the ledge. With care and concentration, they were able to use these to descend the rest of the way to the canyon floor.

"Look," said Lumbee, pointing back. The mound of meat was already attracting hungry animals. Everything from dog-sized two-legged critters to huge red-brown pujish was converging on the carrion. The huge pujish were roaring at each other. The smaller ones were ignoring the giants and just running in for a few bites before they moved away again to safer territory where they could chew the meat a little before bolting it down.

At Relkin's urging the travelers joined the harvesting, cautiously taking claim of an outlying three-horns carcass that had fallen quite a ways from the main pile. A nearby pujish roared threats at them from a quarter-mile away, but stayed beside the much larger mound to which it had taken possession.

They detached a hind leg for Bazil and some hefty pieces for Relkin and Lumbee and then they resumed their journey. They worked their way down the canyon and came out on a wider valley. A river, still very low from the dry season, snaked along in the middle. Lumbee pointed off to their right. "The river runs to the great lake. The pujish will all be by the lake, where most of the herds are."

Giving the lake a wide berth, they headed due south. When the moon rose they walked again, for it was more important than ever that they hurry. The storm had quickly cleared. Their hopes began to build again. If the real rains held off for just a few more days, they might yet get a chance.

The night was clear and cool. The grass was a constant silvery presence, rustling slightly in the whispering breezes. Clumps of trees formed darker bulks here and there, patches of intense darkness. Above them the stars glittered, while a crescent moon rode across the heavens.

At dawn they halted for a quick meal, roasting thin slices of the tough, chewy meat over a small fire. The only water in the vicinity was a dried-up pond. Relkin dug in the ground at its center and soon uncovered a small pool of gritty water. They drank what they could, then walked until the heat grew so intense they drew up beneath some acacia trees. They built a larger fire and set their meat to slow baking on hot stones. While it baked they dozed, snacked on nutlike pods that Lumbee had collected around the trees, or visited a muddy little water hole at the center of the clump of trees. Despite Relkin's fears, no pujish visited their grove. As Lumbee had suggested, the pujish were away down by the lake, where the herds of herbivores were concentrated.

They slept through the rest of the day, awoke at dusk, and walked all night under the moon.

Relkin continued to ponder their options. He questioned Lumbee closely, trying to dredge up anything she might have heard concerning the conditions in the slave camps. Lumbee had heard a wild mishmash of rumors with a few facts thrown in. The camps were big places, of this Relkin was sure, but he was unsure just how big was big. For Lumbee, any group larger than a couple of dozen was an alien concept. The Ardu were clannish, slow-breeding folk. Lumbee had never seen more than forty or fifty people gathered together at spring festival. But she had heard that the camps were filled with hundreds of captives, chained up in pens. She had also heard that the camps stank, that they were places of terrible cruelty and disease. These things Relkin was sure were true; the rest he could not be sure of yet.

He and Bazil conferred and agreed that if the camps were small enough they would try a surprise attack, perhaps at night. One dragon with a sword could raise complete havoc on unprepared men, especially in the dark. Relkin would watch the dragon's back and let him concentrate on sword work.

For four more days and nights they marched through the singing grass until they reached the margins of the southern forest. At an oasis pool Bazil slew an aggressive green and black pujish that was about his own size, but filled with nothing but ferocious hunger. Against Ecator, however, not even two tons of agile ferocity could stand a chance.

They took the opportunity to feast and rest up for one day. Then they pushed on, into the thickening forest.

The next day clouds came up, the first since the storm. They were low, hurrying gray clouds, wispy and empty of moisture, which they had dropped long before. They were harbingers, however. The real rains would arrive any day now.

That night the travelers' progress was slowed by poor light and an increasing density of vegetation. The acacias were gone, replaced now by larger trees, and there were more and more of them. There were also pools of water amid the reed beds, and streams rather than empty courses.

They camped by a river the next day and at dusk smelled the smoke of someone else's cooking fires. Immediately Relkin and Lumbee probed downstream, before the light failed completely. They were rewarded with the distant gleam of fires, which told them they were close to a slavers' camp.

They got back to a hungry dragon, waiting by their own fire.

"Slavers are just on the other side of the next bend in the river, perhaps an hour's walk," said Relkin.

"The gods of Ardu folk are watching out for my people," said Lumbee in a solemn voice.

Relkin didn't want to start thinking about what the effect of the Ardu gods might be. How did they get along with Caymo? Or the Great Mother who was worshiped in the east? Or the other things that were interfering in Relkin's life? Theology was an endlessly complex subject and one that Relkin wished he might be spared for a while.

"We're in time, but only just," he stated. "We've got lots to do."

Chapter Ten

At dawn Relkin went out alone. Lumbee wanted to come, but he insisted on going on his own, on what might be a dangerous reconnaissance. Relkin had learned how to move quietly in the woods and he also knew how to avoid being observed. Lumbee might be quiet enough, but she might not understand how to achieve the art of seeing without being seen. Once in the woods alone, he moved quickly and quietly downstream and reached the slavers' camp in less than an hour. He stayed in the vicinity for the rest of the day, studying the camp carefully.

The camp was not as big as he'd first feared in the night. It was shaped like a figure eight with two circular stockades. In the upstream part there was a five-foot-high stockade of sharpened stakes atop a shallow ditch. Inside this was a cluster of tents, grouped on two lines that met at the upstream end. At the point where the two halves of the camp joined there was a big open pit fireplace with a cookshack built beside it. Men in cool white pantaloons strode about here on various errands; others sat in the shade, waiting for who knew what.

To see into the other half of the camp Relkin had to climb into a tree. Then he saw long, low sheds that made his hackles rise. It was from these unprepossessing structures that the hideous stench emanated. This half of the camp had a ten-foot-high stockade wall and two observation towers, fifteen feet high, placed opposite each other.

There were always men on watch in these towers, but they tended to watch the sheds and not the jungle. Relkin crept to other vantage points. He counted twenty men in the camp altogether.

In the afternoon two small boats came in carrying brush

and reeds. Each boat was crewed by two men, also wearing pantaloons, with black jackets and round hats.

A fire was lit and large cauldrons set upon the fire. Gruel was prepared and taken into the slave pens in big pails, carried in by a detail of a dozen men. The others gathered at the entrance, with clubs and whips to hand in case of trouble.

The rains were coming. The slaves grew desperate, knowing that soon the journey south would begin. Long practice had informed the slavers that they could not take chances at this stage of the expedition.

The slaves were then fed. The pails were emptied into long troughs that ran the length of the pens and the slaves ate from the troughs like animals. While the slaves were fed, the cooks prepared hotcakes and mincemeat for the slavers.

The slavers were of an unfamiliar race to Relkin: short, thick-necked men, with square-cut beards and plaited hair. They were loud of voice and very active, vigorous, imbued with much violence. Light brown in complexion, they oiled their bodies and wore baggy pantaloons of silk, with calf-high boots of stout construction. Some wore small sleeveless jackets, but all carried short swords and tomahawks on their belts. There was a cheerful bantering between them, and sometimes a little mock fighting, even some roughhousing. They were obviously feeling cocky. Behind them was a good hunting season and their longhouses were packed with slaves. If they got two-thirds of the slaves to market they would all be wealthy.

Their part of the camp was upwind generally of the slave pens, and there was also the smoking cook pit in between, which must have helped to mask the stench from the other side. They had plainly built it from a plan with much thought and experience behind it. Relkin could also see that they kept a tidy camp, their tents aligned in a V with the cook pit at the open end. This implied organization and discipline. They were not just loose freebooters. They were not Legion soldiers, however. There was a small group of young Ardu females, who were kept chained in a small tent near the cook pit. These females were kept busy servicing the slavers.

Relkin felt his anger burn bright every time he saw these pathetic creatures. They wore a mockery of the universal whore's costume, and leaned hopelessly against the wall of the cookshack. Throughout the day the men took them, leading them into the tents. Relkin had no doubt that the men took them all night as well.

There were four large boats pulled up on the shore of the river in addition to the two small ones. There were thirty men in the camp. Relkin was sure that four, perhaps five of them were permanent officers of some sort. These were all older men, who always wore embroidered shirts and small gold hats. They appeared to give all the orders. The other men also seemed to do their best to stay out of their way.

Relkin watched most carefully for signs of arms other than swords and tomahawks. He looked especially for heavy bows or long spears. He was sure the men would have such things to deal with the pujish, which, while not too common in these forests in the dry season, might still be encountered. But these items remained out of sight, stored either in the tents or perhaps in the boats. He studied the men. Most had a seasoned look about them. Even the old ones in the embroidered shirts looked capable of wielding a sword. Such a group might not be taken off guard and panicked so easily. They would know what to do in an emergency.

He measured carefully the distances between the slave pens and the rest of the camp. There was always a watch kept on the pens, one man in each of the towers and another man on duty at the cookshack, where he could clearly see the men in either tower and relay messages from them.

Relkin realized this was a tried and true system for keeping a good hold on their valuable captives. Once again he recognized that these men were professionals, and hardened to their life. The one thing he noticed that was a definite weakness was that the slavers hardly ever ventured out of the camp compound. They sat in there all day. To relieve themselves they swam out to some rocks in the river. They avoided the sullen, ancient forest. For food they had stores of grain, and fish hauled from the river.

This told Relkin that these men were not country people. They were more likely from a city. If they were defeated they would head for their boats. Indeed the boats would be the one thing they would be most protective of in a real emergency, since the boats were their link to returning to their city home. They would value them over-much. It was also plain that they had not been bothered much by pujish lately, for they kept no watch on the forest.

They were very attuned to the state of the slaves, but they largely ignored their surroundings. This was something that might be exploited.

The slavers ate, then some bathed in the river. Others swam out to check the fishing nets. Still others took the young Ardu females into their tents. Toward the end of the day Relkin's wait was rewarded with the sight of a large boat, crewed by six men, which pulled up to the shore. He observed that it was of the same style as the four boats already on the shore. Ten newly captured Ardu were pulled from the boat. Their hands were bound behind their backs and their legs were hobbled, too, and they found it difficult to move quickly enough to satisfy their captors. They were forced out of the boat with blows from a rope's end.

Even the indignity of bondage could not conceal the fact that the Ardu were a proud, handsome folk. The ten captives were all men, and they were all short but well muscled and walked with heads held high despite their bonds and the blows directed at them by the slavers. Still, they were bound and doomed to servitude. They were herded into the main stockade and thrust into the long, low sheds, where they were shackled to the common chains and left confined in stinking, pitch-black horror.

Relkin returned to the dragon and Lumbee shortly after dusk. Lumbee had a small fire going and was preparing some bristle fruit and dall pods. Their last piece of meat was grilling over the flames.

Lumbee was on her feet in a second. "What happened? Are you all right? Where have you been all day?"

Relkin smiled at the anxiety in her voice. He hugged her and kissed her to reassure her. "I'm fine. We're in time, at least with this camp. I don't know if there are others."

Lumbee's arms were around his neck the next moment and her tail was curling around his waist and hugging hard with excitement.

She babbled a string of phrases in Ardu too quickly for Relkin to catch.

The dragon stirred and extended a huge hand. Relkin clutched a massive digit.

"Boy is back. What did he see?"

"All right, listen carefully. It's a large camp, but not too large for us if we can panic them."

"How many men?"

"About thirty. Well-armed, but without shields."

Eyes intent, they hunched over as he went on to lay out his plan of action.

Chapter Eleven

Relkin's plan hinged on an attack under cover of darkness, when they might cause the greatest confusion.

Accordingly they worked throughout the following day to prepare themselves. Relkin and Lumbee moved around the perimeter of the slavers' camp, positioning stocks of flammables, dead vines, grass, and twigs in four separate locations. Along with these things they left collections of good throwing stones. This work also familiarized them with the area. Then in the late afternoon they sat up in a tree and studied the camp carefully. At dusk they made their way back to the dragon, who had waited well out of sight.

They ate a small meal, slept early, and woke while there was still three hours of darkness left. The time had come to test their plan.

They swam downstream, riding on the dragon's back. Lumbee found this a wonderful way to travel, cresting along, her legs in the water, the great tail thrusting them downstream at a terrific pace through a river dappled with faint moonlight. All too soon they were in sight of the slavers' camp and had to go ashore and move slowly through the forest, being careful not to make any undue noise. Lumbee was impressed by how quiet the dragon could be, quieter even than pujish.

Now they took up positions. Bazil remained at the upstream end, lurking in the trees just beyond the five-foot stockade that surrounded the tent area. Relkin and Lumbee went on to their caches of flammables and stones. When they were in position, Relkin gave a long, weird, whooping cry, a good old Bluestone sea-yell.

The guards on the towers stirred momentarily and

looked out into the forest. Briefly they discussed the noises of the forest and the possibility of an attack by pujish. Except that this was no pujish they'd ever heard before. And besides, there weren't pujish in these woods. Early in the days of the camp, at the beginning of summer, they'd killed about a dozen two-legged beasts of various sizes and emptied the range. Since then they'd seen hardly any pujish at all.

But if not pujish, then what? They argued, they called back and forth about it.

Apes or birds, that's all it could be, they decided.

The call was not repeated. The guards tired of staring at the forest and turned back to their normal pursuits, looking down on the slave pens and discussing the likely prices they'd get for the various top slaves they'd taken in the summer. Some of the younger males and females would fetch high prices automatically, but there were also some very robust older male specimens that would likely do well on the auction block. The guards' talk grew ribald as they discussed the question of whether they should geld these troublesome, robust males before the trip downriver or let the buyers in Mirchaz make that decision for themselves. Gelded they'd be easier to ship. It was well known that newly gelded Ardu became mute and meek and were easily controlled. They had six weeks of downstream travel ahead in crowded boats. The Ardu would get ever more desperate as the journey went on. It would be a testing time for the slavers. Terrible things had happened to slaver parties on the last laps of successful missions. Thus castrating the most troublesome males was the usual tactic.

There had been a shift in the market lately, however. Some of the female magicians of Mirchaz, a strange, reclusive clique, had taken to keeping hyper-robust male Ardu as pets and lovers. They placed them under heavy spells, addicted them to foul drugs, and made them bed slaves. This had produced a demand among wealthy females of the high castes of Mirchaz. They all wanted an ape of their own, as was said sarcastically by male critics. The price of a mature, robust male had risen enormously.

The talk shifted to whether they oughtn't to try making

cages again. They had tried it once, but the cages hadn't
been strong enough; a robust male had escaped and
almost killed Han Zonson. Leader Densolm wouldn't
allow them to experiment further. Densolm had a bias
against the idea because Densolm wanted to geld all the
mature males anyway.

They railed, quietly, against leader Densolm, who was
famous for having made nine successful trips into the
slave-hunting region. He had lost very few men over the
years, and his expeditions had always made plenty of
profit. Densolm was also renowned for his caution. He
always waited until the rainy season was well under way
to return home, to be sure the rivers would be up and so
ensure a smooth trip down.

Absorbed, the guards failed to notice the arrival of
the first torches out in the woods, small flames carried
quickly through the dark. Then a flame flared brightly,
and then another, and then another and another. Shouts
and calls in the Ardu tongue came out of the woods.
There was a moment of shocked silence. The guards
stared out at the trees. Then came more shouts from the
woods and the slaves in the pens woke up and began to
call back.

There were fires in the woods! A figure ran out of the
dark carrying blazing branches which were propped
against the stockade wall at the point farthest from the
two watchtowers.

Stones were thudding off the sides of the watchtowers.
An arrow whistled out of the dark and struck a guard in
the shoulder.

Alarm! The horns were blown.

In the other half of the camp the sleepers were already
astir, nervous as they were at this point during the trip.
The horns brought them to their feet in a rush. With oaths
and curses they tumbled out, clubs and whips in hand, and
ran to the gate leading into the slave enclosure.

Meanwhile, stones and arrows had continued to zip in
from the forest, not in great numbers, but with punishing
accuracy, so that the guards were keeping their heads
down inside the towers as much as possible.

More burning material had been brought out of the

woods and laid against the stockade wall at the farthest point from the towers. In vain had one guard thrown a spear—it was too far for an accurate cast. The other guard strung an arrow and got off a shot, but the shaft vanished into the gloom to no effect. The fire at the wall was blazing up brightly.

The rest of the men rushed from the tents calling loudly for information.

In the slave pens there was pandemonium. The guards shouted down to the slavers crowded at the gate, but the men couldn't understand them. It took a half minute before one of the guards climbed down, risking stones that whined off the tower a couple of times before he was down behind the stockade wall. He joined the throng of aroused slavers. Questions and answers flew in confusing patterns, but gradually the men got the idea. There was a fire set against the downstream end of the stockade and there were fires in the woods all around this end. More stones had come whizzing over to land among them, causing cries of pain and outrage and making them huddle up closer to the stockade wall. The damned slaves were screaming and ululating at the top of their lungs; you could hardly make out a word anyone was saying.

Some of the men opened the outer gate and moved out to explore the situation. With fierce expressions and swords in their hands, they ran along the wall. With shouts they urged each other on.

Relkin's arrow took one of them in the shoulder and produced outrage. They bunched nervously. Lumbee threw stones as fast as she could; the range was extreme for her and her accuracy was down, but still the sound of the rocks bouncing off the stockade wall was unnerving. Another arrow thudded into the stockade. Most of the men returned to the gate, escorting the wounded man. A handful of determined sorts went on and reached the fire. They found a pile of blazing pine branches that had just begun to ignite the stout wood of the stockade wall. Quickly they worked to pull the burning stuff away and throw sand onto the smoldering parts of the wall.

Stones continued to fall among them, striking occasionally and making the work most unpleasant. An arrow blew by every so often, too. They finished the job and looked out to the woods.

The fire was out; now was the time to deal with whoever had dared to attack them like this. There was a small band of Ardu out there, they could tell because there weren't that many stones and arrows, not enough to indicate a big war party.

Unfortunately, there were only four slavers left outside the stockade and they couldn't see where the rocks were coming from. They were nervous and this made them hesitate.

At this moment there came a sudden new sound, a deep roaring, bellowing call that went on for several seconds: the war cry of a wyvern dragon.

Silence fell abruptly. Even the damned slaves piped down. What in the name of all the hells was that?

Then there was the most awful screaming from within the upper camp. This time it was men making the noise. And then that huge cry was repeated again and again. They who had put out the fire started for the gate.

Voices yelled from the woods and the Ardu started their uproar again. There was a new sound as well. The robust males had broken loose in one shed and were shaking the structure with their efforts to break out. Slavers had run in with clubs and whips, but now they paused and looked back over their shoulders.

Pujish! The slavers' worst nightmare. There was a big pujish loose in the camp. It strode around the cook pit and looked them over with an oddly piercing pair of eyes.

The men reacted with cries of woe. Their spears and nets were all in the tents and the pujish was between them and the tents.

Then Bazil brought Ecator around in a wild, roundhouse slice and broke down the gatepost on one side. The huge sword whistled in the air as if it hungered for blood. The top of the gatepost flew off like a shuttlecock. The gates to the slave pen hung in the dust.

The slavers scattered except for a few crazed, but brave, souls who drew their swords and prepared to engage. Two rushed the dragon from the side. Two more thrust at him from the front.

Bazil struck with the backhand, Ecator sang as it took the heads of the men in front, and the men at the side threw themselves flat to escape the same fate. Bazil took the sword in both hands. The men scrambled up and ran for their lives.

Some men were already running for the boats. Bazil gave his war scream again.

The Ardu were shouting the words "Forest god" over and over and keeping up the volume.

The rest of the men, milling around leader Densolm, looked at the dragon and saw death, incredible death at the hands of a magical pujish that carried a sword, a sword such as they had never dreamed of. Leader Densolm was frozen. Nothing in his experience had prepared him for this. If pujish could bear swords, then no one would ever come here again!

Bazil lumbered toward them, head down, another war cry echoing off the trees.

It was too much for frayed nerves. The slavers broke en masse and ran for the boats. The men in the watch-towers abandoned their posts and legged it, too. Bazil went after them.

Relkin and Lumbee ran from the trees and made their way through the outer and inner gates to the slave pens.

There was a tremendous racket coming from one of the low, massively built sheds. Relkin slid back the bolts, even as the door shuddered under repeated blows from inside. Then he pulled away a beam holding it shut, the door blew open, and a group of massively built Ardu males burst through. They were short men, but Relkin felt like a stripling beside these big-chested, stocky men with their lithe tails lashing behind them.

Their eyes were caught midway between ferocity and amazement.

He found his voice.

"You are free!" he yelled in their tongue.

Lumbee appeared from nowhere and threw herself on one of the robust males.

"Ommi, Ommi, Ommi," she cried.

"Lumbee!"

The male caught her and hugged her and put her on his shoulders.

Relkin tore open the bolts on another shed and pulled open the door. Inside women and children wailed, still chained together.

The males had broken the group chain, but still bore their individual shackles.

"Come, help me free the females," shouted Relkin. "We must get away from this place as quickly as possible."

The men were galvanized into activity. The one called Ommi set Lumbee down, even as she was explaining that Relkin had saved her life and nursed her back to health.

They saw the headless bodies of two slavers lying on the sand. Eyes widened. What had happened here? Where were the slavers? They all had many questions.

As requested by the voices in the woods, they had all screamed themselves hoarse, ready to do anything to help their would-be rescuers. Now they were met by Lumbee and a slim young no-tail who spoke a few words of Ardu, albeit with a barbarous accent. Where was the rescue party?

Lumbee had jerked open the door to another shed, and with a slaver's sword was trying to cut the heavy chain. The robust males pushed forward and took the chain and began to heave it out of its socket.

Relkin saw that this would take time. He ran out and called the dragon. A moment later Bazil came into view, returning from the shore.

"Quickly," shouted Relkin. "We must free everyone before the slavers get over their panic."

The Ardu looked up at Bazil's approach and fear spread across their features. To be on the ground with a large pujish like this was a death sentence. The Ardu started backward.

Relkin saw them edging away. "Hold," he cried. "This is not pujish. This is forest god!"

The Ardu looked at him like he was mad.

Lumbee joined him. "It's true, my brothers, this is the forest god indeed. Not pujish. He is our friend."

The robust males looked to one another with bewildered eyes. Then the pujish opened that big, carnivore's mouth and spoke to them.

"Lumbee speaks the truth. I will help you."

He brought Ecator down off his shoulder and pressed the point to the ground and leaned lightly on the pommel.

The Ardu were mesmerized. They pinched themselves. Was this all some fantastic dream? They called out to the gods for guidance.

The women and children still chained up shrilled loudly for freedom. The Ardu men were irresolute.

Relkin called to Bazil. The dragon turned, took Ecator, and demolished the shed, tearing the roof off. Then he leaned in and, using the blade's tip, broke the main chains. The women and children freed themselves and streamed out of the shed, some still screaming with a mixture of fear and excitement. The children scampered widely, many chanting "Forest god!" over and over.

The robust males came out of their trance with a collective snap. They jumped forward to hug their females and their children.

More roofing came up and was thrown aside. Bazil tore the chains out and released the Ardu. Generally the children were the quickest to recover their wits. They resumed chanting "Forest god!" over and over.

Quickly Relkin and Lumbee worked to organize the still amazed Ardu. There were more than two hundred freed prisoners, seventy of them adult males. Among them were some of Lumbee's kin, but not her mother, Erris, or her father, Uys.

First they assembled at the cook pit, where Relkin located the slavers' tool kit. Then he showed the men how to wield the hammers and chisels to cut the shackles. While this vital work was being completed, Bazil resumed stalking up and down on the shore, letting the slavers in their boats see him outlined against the flames rising from the ruins of their camp.

The slavers had lit lamps on their boats and these could be seen out in the river where they hovered, arguing among themselves as to what they should do. Relkin gave them no time to make up their minds. As the shackles came off, he and Lumbee shepherded the Ardu out of the slave camp onto the trail upstream, with torches to illuminate the way.

When all were on their way, Bazil gave a last war scream and then disappeared into the woods himself, leaving the camp to burn down to embers.

Chapter Twelve

They marched upstream, bearing with them all the steel tools and weapons that Relkin could discover in the slaver camp. There was a good haul: seven swords, ten long spears, a dozen knives and hatchets, some hammers, tongs, chisels, and lengths of iron chain. In addition they had something that Relkin had taken for himself, a crossbow of heavy but utilitarian design.

Compared to his much-lamented Cunfshon bow, this was a crude device. To span the bow one used a goatsfoot lever built into the stock. The finishings were in bronze, however, and there was fancy work inlaid in the wood. There were also a dozen quarrels in a leather quiver.

The bow was heavy, but with it on his back Relkin felt something like himself again. The bow he'd made for himself was barely effective beyond fifty feet. That was good enough for hunting lizards and squirrels, perhaps, but with a good crossbow, Relkin could hit targets at two hundred yards and he was deadly at a hundred. No longer would they have to rely utterly on Bazil and Ecator for defense against pujish.

The slavers made no attempt to harass them. Some of the oldest of the robust males hung back to scout the rear, but they detected no sign of pursuit.

At midday, when the group had put several miles behind them, Relkin called a halt and built a fire. He and Bazil went to work breaking the shackles that still encumbered most of the male Ardu. Leg irons, cuffs, and bars were all removed, but the work took time.

While this went on, the female Ardu went into the forest with Lumbee to gather food. They returned to the fire and prepared uja pods and fresh tizzama leaves.

The pods had a nutty flavor and contained seeds with a pungent but pleasant salt-sour smell and taste. The leaves were sweet and minty. While the Ardu ate, the females continued to question Lumbee.

Who, really, was this Relkin? And the forest god, where had he come from? And how was it that a pujish could talk, anyway? And where had Lumbee met this tailless one, Rel-Kin? And how had she really survived and gotten away when all the rest were captured? There were those who, despite everything, were not entirely pleased with the situation.

Lumbee answered as best she could.

At the rock where Relkin and Bazil worked, the situation was also complex. Even while they broke off shackles and cuffs, Relkin found the men uncommunicative—but not sullen; there was simply too much joy in the air for that. Still, the men were concerned, especially big Ommi, who had always been sweet on Lumbee and determined to win her as mother of his children. Who were the outsiders that Lumbee had found? And why had they interceded so brilliantly on behalf of the Ardu men in the camp? And what exactly was the extent of the relationship between Lumbee and the young no-tail one called Rel-Kin?

These thoughts put a damper on their natural inquisitiveness, but could not snuff it out entirely. Norwul, Lumbee's maternal uncle, one of the biggest Ardu in the group, could not restrain the questions after a while.

Speaking very slowly, as if to a half-wit, he addressed Relkin on the topics of general fascination.

"Tell me this, tailless one, from where did you come, when you came into the jungle of pujish? Before you found my niece Lumbee?"

Relkin replied in simple language that Lumbee had taught him. His lack of wide vocabulary made things difficult. Bazil started to chip in words. Dragon memory was good at vocabulary. Though dragons were vastly conservative beasts, they remembered things very well once they learned them. Bazil's vocabulary in Ardu was already larger than Relkin's, something the leatherback dragon was quite pleased about.

The Ardu males found this disconcerting. The pujish continued to talk! It was astounding. Maybe the girls were right when they chanted "Forest god" at it. To think that they had actually lived to meet a forest god in person! To think that the forest god had heard the prayers of the women and come to their aid! To think that the forest god was a pujish! It was all unimaginable.

"North of the forest lies the sea, the big sea—perhaps you know of it?"

"We have heard of the sea, the boundless water. Ardu don't go there, that place. Too much pujish there. Bad pujish, very dangerous."

"We came from the sea."

"You live in the sea?"

"No." Relkin swallowed. There was a lot to explain.

"From far beyond sea, beyond ocean, we come. There was a war to be fought. At the mountain of fire. Do you know it? It lies far to the north."

The Ardu, while familiar with volcanoes, for there were several in their territory, did not know anything about one way out in the sea. They knew very little about the sea, either. They had always been content to live their lives here, in the lands around Lake Gam. In the dry season they left the hills and crossed the Plain of Three-Horns and dwelt in the southern forest. When the rains came they moved north, back to the hills. Along the way they trapped three-horns and took meat and horns and bones for weapons and tools.

They did not know of anything much to the north of the hills, for there the land broke downward sharply into the endless distances of the old jungle, haunted by pujish. The Ardu avoided that forest and shunned the northern rivers. The sea they knew of only through legends which claimed that there was a body of water in the north that made even Lake Gam seem tiny.

In their experience nobody ever came from the north. To do so meant traversing hundreds of miles of jungle filled with ravenous pujish.

The slavers came from the south, and they were worse than the pujish now. To the south there were cities and civilizations, of which the Ardu knew too well, and not at all, for their traffic with them was entirely one way. Above all the name they knew was that of Mirchaz, the city of the necromancers. That fell city cast a cruel shadow over their lives. Ardu were taken there, but they never came back.

"Tell us," said Norwul, addressing Relkin, "about forest god. Should we worship forest god? Does he need us to make sacrifice for him? Should we burn the haunch of three-horns?"

Relkin stifled a laugh. What a question to ask a dragon-boy. He hesitated a moment. Bazil would certainly appreciate a haunch of anything, roasted, broiled, or even raw.

"Forest god will be hungry soon. He needs no worship right now, for we have much work to do. Forest god will talk with you later."

Bazil looked up. "Why later?" he said in dragon speech.

"Because this is a delicate moment. There's a lot of tension here. Don't want to get them confused. You really want them to think you're a god? Think about it. I don't know. This is all confusing enough. Then again, you know how hard it is for people who don't know about dragons to get used to the idea. Maybe it'd be better if they did think you were a god."

"Humans think they are the only beings to be able to speak?"

"Well, yes, usually. Some parrots can talk, but not that well. It's just us, men and dragons. So don't make waves just yet."

"What is this 'make waves.' How can I? I'm not in the river."

Relkin rolled his eyes heavenward with a groan. "Just don't make a fuss, all right? Later we'll sort all this out, but for now let's keep it simple."

Relkin turned back to the Ardu, who were all looking at him with huge eyes. The forest god spoke in many tongues. So did the no-tail one. These revelations made the Ardu uneasy.

"What does forest god want?" said Norwul.

"He wants to talk with you all, later. There are many things you must know, but you will learn them in good time. For now, accept forest god's blessing."

The Ardu nodded slowly, rocking back and forth in place, something they did when they were thinking very hard.

Bazil broke the last set of shackles and Relkin slipped them off the Ardu's legs. The men were virtually free of slaver steel now, but for a few wrist cuffs that would require skillful cutting to get off.

Lumbee approached with a group of females, all bearing leaves and pods. The men ate happily, and then some went down to the river to bathe.

Relkin instructed the rest in the use of the weapons they had taken from the slavers. The Ardu were hunters more than warriors; there was much they needed to learn. While they were practicing spear thrusts and trying a few experimental moves with the swords and hatchets, Relkin took up the crossbow.

It was heavy in his hands and the goatsfoot lever mechanism was stiff and hard to pull up. You placed your foot in a stirrup extending from the bow end and hauled on the lever and that bent the bow and set the string. In battle it would be horrendously slow compared to the beautiful little coiled-spring workings of a Cunfshon bow.

Still, with a little practice he was soon hitting a tree trunk at a hundred paces and he knew he would soon get his eye in with the thing and be accurate even farther out. It was rather more powerful than a Cunfshon dragonboy bow, almost a sniper's weapon in terms of range.

He would need more shafts for it, and he was limited to just a handful of steel points. But he was satisfied nonetheless. He collected the shafts again, pulling them out of the trunks of trees, and then went in search of Lumbee. There was much to discuss. They had to keep moving, if at all possible, and they had to come up with a strategy for a campaign against the slavers.

Lumbee was at the fire, toasting more pods and wrapping them in tizzama. The other women had drawn off, grouping with children and males of their own kin. A babble of conversation had arisen to drown the sounds of the forest. There was a complex sorting of relationships going on in the group. In effect they were a new thing in the world of the Ardu, a tribe created out of adversity.

Groups that had known each other previously already had relationships, and these now had to be considered and subsumed into a new whole, at least temporarily. Other groups without previous relationships had to form them kin group to kin group at the same time as personal relationships were forming. This was a complex, perplexing time for the Ardu. All were overjoyed to have escaped the slave camp, but they were far from being returned to their happy normal lives.

Lumbee looked up when Relkin squatted down nearby. Since they had freed the slaves, Lumbee had been avoiding this moment. Despite her own wishes, she knew that things had changed. She and Relkin simply could not behave as before, when they had been so physically close, touching each other constantly, kissing, hugging, behaving as the lovers they had been, and still were.

A question nagged at her, though. *Were* they still lovers? Could they be lovers in these new circumstances? The females cast looks of curiosity and concern her way. Did she dare consort with Relkin, as if they were ready to become childbearers? Did she dare to flaunt such a relationship with a no-tail?

This thought sent up other questions, basic questions of tribal morality. Was this love between them taboo? And if not, then it ought to be, according to some spirits. Others were more generous; still, it was an upsetting thing. And poor Ommi, he had always been sweet on Lumbee, but now Ommi was consumed with gathering jealousy and rage. She could see it in his eyes.

There was no shaman among them, however, to give guidance. No one knew what correct conduct was in the situation and among the robust males there were those with strong prejudices. Such minds existed among the older females, too. Tailless ones were bad, like the slavers—they had to be. The slavers were no-tails. Mirchaz was no-tail. Therefore, the no-tail youth could not be anything but bad.

The result of all this pressure was that Lumbee felt suddenly very clumsy and cautious in Relkin's presence. She was afraid even to be seen speaking with him. Which was absurd, but then everyone's eyes were on her and she felt a fierce current running through the Ardu.

"Welcome to the fire," she said, as if in formal greetings. As if Relkin were a stranger who had just appeared weary from the hunting trail.

"I thank you," he said, inventing his own formality, sensing the pressures and letting Lumbee dictate how things should go. Relkin had been through this before, all his life, he sometimes thought. He was the perennial outsider. Once, in ancient Ourdh, he'd been denounced as an "animal barbarian with the mind of an ape" for daring to express his love for a princess of that fabled land. And even now, if he were to walk forth in the lands of Clan Wattel, with his affianced love, Eilsa Ranardaughter, there would be disapproval from many. Relkin had grown used to prejudice against orphan dragonboys.

Lumbee dropped her gaze.

"Look," he said quietly so that only she could hear. "I understand what's going on. Don't worry, we'll not compromise you with your people."

Lumbee looked up with sudden relief, then blushed with embarrassment and looked down again.

"Lumbee feels sad. Lumbee not like this situation. But they are all upset right now. Things will calm down, I think. We will have to be very secret for a while."

"Yes." He shrugged sadly. "And we've got work to do. There are other slave camps, and we have to reach them and free the people before they ship them down the river."

"Here, try this." She gave him some toasted pods wrapped in the soft, spongy-on-the-inside leaves. He enjoyed the blend of nutty and sour-sweet tastes.

"We've got to train people in the use of these weapons. We've got a lot to do and not much time."

Lumbee nodded toward the nearest group of robust males. "You will have to get their cooperation."

"Don't they want to free their fellows?"

"Yes, of course, but they are just getting used to each other, and now on top of all that they will have to get used to you. Then there is the dragon. To them he is pujish-that-talks. They can scarcely believe it yet. They are having trouble with his status, too. If he's a forest god, then how come he looks like pujish? This is more likely the look of a demon, some say."

Relkin chewed his lip. This wasn't unexpected, either. Neither a dragonboy nor his dragon could expect unqualified appreciation from people, even if they'd just freed them from an ignominious fate as slaves in the southern cities.

"Wait till we get into a fight. They'll know what he's worth then, I wager."

Lumbee had seen that flashing blade in Bazil's hands. The scale of this violence was beyond anything she'd known before. Not even red-brown pujish could stand against Bazil Broketail wielding Ecator. In time the men would understand, she knew. The question was getting everyone through the difficult time immediately ahead.

A shadow fell across them. It was big Ommi. His face was filled with tension. He could not restrain his feelings any longer.

"You speak in Ardu tongue," he growled. "Why you talk to Lumbee? What you talk about so quiet like that?"

Lumbee turned to face Ommi, challenging him in a way that was unusual among the Ardu. "Relkin saved Lumbee's life, Ommi. Relkin came many days journey here, just to save you from slavery. Relkin deserves full honor and courtesy from every one of us."

Ommi absorbed this and licked his lips while his eyes continued to rest on Relkin's. Relkin read the anger and the challenge there.

"Lumbee and I are friends; that's why I talk with her."

Ommi grunted, looked down, and fidgeted.

Norwul came over. He was carrying one of the captured swords. "I understand much better now," said Norwul. "Thanks be to you, Relkin, friend of forest god."

Norwul waved the sword in a friendly manner. "When we fought the slavers, we were defeated very easily. They killed many of us. They killed old Panni, and Dram, and Ki-kokoo. They killed many, many. We fought with club and spear, but they fought with sword and long spear. We were overmatched. We could do nothing against them. Now we know why."

Relkin clasped hands with Norwul. Ommi continued to frown.

"We have a lot of work to do," Relkin said. "We've got to practice working together, fighting together as a team. And we've got to find the other slave camps. I bet there's one on every river through this forest. We've got to smash this evil trade."

Norwul's eyes had gone wide as he took in what Relkin was saying. "You teach us to fight like slavers?"

"I show you how to fight better than them."

"That sounds good."

And still Ommi was displeased.

Chapter Thirteen

They camped on a bluff overlooking the river, which rushed by in a shallow torrent over exposed rock. The water level was very low, reflecting the long dry season. The men had killed a small four-legged beast and were busy cooking it. The females were preparing a variety of nuts, berries, and leaves.

Relkin worked on the dragon, who was bearing up well. The long march from the north had conditioned him to a peak level of fitness. His wounds had long since healed completely, but there were always cuts and scrapes and sometimes parasites—ticks and the like.

The sky had been growing gray all day, and there'd been a short bout of rain the day before. The rivers had yet to rise sufficiently, but the big rains were coming. Then the slavers would take to the water.

"The slavers will be camped downstream of here. Question is, how far?" said Relkin.

"What do you base this on?" rumbled the dragon.

"They like to be on water deep enough for their boats. Look at this stream. It's too shallow here for any boat."

Bazil nodded slowly. The boy was right. Bazil wondered why he hadn't made this deduction for himself; it seemed so obvious. Then he gave a mental shrug. A dragon just had to credit his worthless dragonboy. There were things that boys were good at.

"We have to move quickly. Perhaps we should swim."

"I don't know if the Ardu would want to swim. I know you would, but I don't know about them."

Bazil would have liked to swim.

"Rains are starting, tonight I think."

There was a feel of rain in the air. The clouds this time looked endless.

Relkin went to sit with Lumbee and Norwul beside the fire. The dragon took a huge piece of the roasted beast, sat to one side, and dug into dinner. A circle of astounded Ardu children watched him, a performance that happened every evening. At first they had been nervous; he did look like a pujish, but Bazil was a friendly pujish, who simply ate enormous amounts of meat, or any food that was given him. The children had quickly gotten over dragon freeze, which was not strong among the Ardu, perhaps because they were accustomed to the threat of pujish. The children's eyes widened as they watched him chomp into the roasted meat.

At the fire Relkin found Lumbee and Norwul breaking up some huge mushrooms brought in by a pair of Ardu women. These mushrooms were delicious, especially when they were roasted on hot stones. In fact, it was essential to heat them thoroughly, since this also destroyed a poison that they carried that could blind or kill the unwary.

Relkin squatted down beside them. "Looks like it will really rain soon. Our time is getting short. We have to move much more quickly."

Lumbee introduced the two older females.

"These are Iuuns and Yuns. They are grandmothers of the Red Rock people. There are many Red Rock in the group."

Relkin nodded to the two Ardu females. Their hair had gone silvery, their faces bore lines and creases, and the fur on their tails had gone white.

"Among the Red Rock is old Tummpy. He is oldest man alive," said the one identified as Iuuns.

"And how old is that?"

"He is four tens of years . . . how you say it?"

"Forty."

"Old Tummpy cannot walk so fast. He isn't the only one who wants to slow down. Many need to rest. Since we escape slaver camp we move every day, move far, far. Let us rest."

"The rains are coming. We have to reach the other slaver camps and rescue the captives."

Iuuns and Yuns exchanged a long look.

"You want to go to another slaver camp?" Yuns asked.

Relkin sensed the sudden fear behind Yuns's words. "To free the slaves."

Iuuns pointed a long finger at him. "No. You want to make slaves of Ardu yourself. That is why you came here. Why would a no-tail free Ardu people unless that no-tail planned to make Ardu his own slaves?"

Relkin was stunned for a moment by this level of distrust.

Lumbee was embarrassed and looked down into the ground. Even Norwul grunted a loud dissent.

When Relkin looked back, Lumbee's cheeks were coloring.

"Relkin saved my life." She couldn't keep the anger out of her voice. "He and the dragon saved all of you. He isn't a slaver; he comes from the north. In fact he comes from far, far away, some magic place, Lumbee not really understand, but he not a slaver."

She said this with such intensity that the two women turned away in a huff.

Norwul grumbled to himself again.

Relkin stood up, mildly astonished.

"Don't leave, Relkin."

"No, I'm not leaving. We've got work to do, and not that much time to do it. The rains will come, very soon. The dragon thinks tonight."

"Rains come," said Iuuns. "Time for Ardu people to head north. We gather ankolu and yoberry in the north woods. We hunt for three-horns on the plain."

Norwul shook his head with a grimace. "This is difficult to think about. We always go to the plain at this time. Soon the ankolu will be finished. But we cannot go. Not yet. We have to free other Ardu."

"Bah," said Iuuns. "You are a fool. You will end up in a cage going down the river. You mark old Iuun's words, now."

Norwul swallowed heavily, then glared back defiantly. "Norwul trusts the no-tail."

"Out of your own mouth you say that," said Yuns.

"The spirits of the forest will turn away their hearts from the Ardu if they follow the no-tail," chimed in Iuuns.

"We have to split up the group," said Relkin, ignoring the women.

"See?" said Iuuns. "See what the tailless one proposes now?"

"We have to split up." Relkin was determined to be heard. "Most of the people will go north, but slowly, because of those who are having trouble. The men, perhaps some of the fittest females, will go south with me and the dragon. We go down the river, find slaver camp, and free the prisoners."

"How you know there is slaver camp to find?" snapped Yuns.

"There's more than one camp. Everyone says this."

"True," said Norwul.

Relkin pointed to the water. "'This river is wide and deep farther down—so I have heard."

Norwul nodded. "This is the Black Eel River. It get wide and deep on other side of the near ridge."

"They will have a camp there, I am sure of it."

"Then we must go there and free the captives." Norwul was final.

Iuuns gave an audible snort of anger. Then she and Yuns left the fire.

"There will be trouble," said Lumbee.

"I don't understand," said Relkin.

"They don't trust you. To them all tailless are evil. They have lived a long time and that is all they have known. When the tailless came, they killed and enslaved Ardu."

"So even if I freed them from the clutches of that gang of slavers, they can't accept that I might be trying to help them?"

"Males will go with you. We know we must find all the other camps that we can and free our people." Norwul got up and moved away.

That left Relkin and Lumbee alone, for the first time in days, it seemed.

"I miss the way things were," said Lumbee.

"Oh, yes, we didn't know we had life so good, did we?"

"Lumbee thought life was very good."

"Well, I did, too. By the gods, I miss that life." He hesitated a moment. "Lumbee, I've been meaning to ask you something."

"Ask what?"

"Well, maybe I should stay here, live with Lumbee, join the Ardu."

As he said this, a vision of Eilsa Ranardaughter crossed his mind and almost confounded his tongue.

"No, Relkin, we cannot be parents of children together. You are not Ardu. And anyway you are pledged to another. You have told me that many times."

"But I might not ever get back there alive. She may think I am dead and go ahead and marry within her clan. I wouldn't blame her."

Lumbee gave him a sharp look.

"No. You say these things, but Lumbee know that you will go."

"Well, perhaps Lumbee would come with me."

Lumbee laughed, her white teeth flashing in perfect curves.

"Lumbee go out into wide world? Oh, no, I would be the only real person, surrounded by nothing but no-tails. Everywhere, you say, nobody is like Lumbee, only like Relkin. Lumbee not like that idea."

She nodded vigorously. "But do like Relkin." Her smile was back.

"Well, perhaps I'll stay."

Lumbee smiled again, and there was something mysterious in her eyes. "Good."

Relkin laughed a moment, then sobered. There were still lots of eyes on them; they had to take things very slowly, with maximum care not to upset too many of the older, more powerful people in the group.

"Good indeed," he said quietly. "But first we've got to work fast. We have to free as many Ardu as we can from these horrible camps."

"You will go downriver with men and Bazil?"

"We will. We have to get some of those boats. We can

make much better time if we have boats. Really put the fear of the forest god into these slavers."

"Lumbee will come, too."

Relkin knew that Lumbee's mother and father were still unaccounted for. Norwul, Palls, Ommi, and the others from Lumbee's kin group had been taken while out on a hunting expedition. Erris and Uys and the rest of the group had been taken in camp. That was where Lumbee was wounded but managed to escape in the canoe.

Relkin didn't even try to dissuade her. He knew that Lumbee would never be deterred from coming.

That night he went over the plan very carefully with Bazil and then with the Ardu men, all of whom wanted to come. Only two dozen were selected, however, all robust, mature males with missing family members. The rest would go north with the majority of the people. They would travel slowly. The small group going south would go as fast as possible. Five of the younger, fitter females would accompany them. There were protests against this, but the young women insisted. They had missing family, they would go! They would not necessarily fight, but they could find and prepare food. They were better at that than the males, anyway, who chiefly hunted and lived the ceremonial round through the year.

They divided the weapons. The assault force took most of them, including all the swords and metal hatchets. Some of the long metal spears and knives were left with the majority, for defense against pujish.

In the morning the rains began. Both groups set off after a hastily assembled meal under lowering skies with a steady continuous drizzle falling.

The war party had seven swords, twelve metal hatchets, six long knives, and six spears. The Ardu would practice with the new weapons whenever they could, but they were still clumsy, more used to club and arrow in fighting their occasional wars between kin groups. Since achieving freedom, each male had made for himself a new war club. The sharp steel edges of the knives were a marvel to men used to working with flint tools. Their new clubs were weighty and well carved.

The rains had really begun this time. The drizzle slowly

swelled into a continuous, heavy downpour. The clouds grew very dark; the land was wreathed in mists. Once in a while, when the rains let up a little, the mists rose to cloak the world.

The marchers were as wet as the world they moved through. Yet the ground was still soaking up the rain, the going was firm, and they made fairly good progress. The slope of the land was a steady, gentle one. The river coursed down through a rocky valley and then opened out into a wider vale with rolling hills to the east.

Occasionally they saw huge beasts, na-pujish, looming through the wet forest. The beasts were intent on their own affairs and gave the band of humans hardly a glance. They took one look at Bazil and, warned by instinct, slipped away into the sheltering jungle.

The rain intensified as the day wore on, building to a maximum in the middle of the afternoon, though the sun had been invisible all day. The rain came down in torrents. And now the ground, soaked through, began to liquefy and turn into mud.

The rivers were starting to rise. The slaver captains would be watching carefully, and as soon as they thought there was sufficient flow in the rivers they'd be loading and shipping their precious cargoes downstream, to the great cities of the south and the auction block.

The small band began to slow in the mud. Every gully was running a frothing stream now. The bigger ones were filled with thundering torrents. Crossing these was hazardous and never easy. Fortunately, the presence of Bazil allowed for the easy movement of trees and other bridging materials set to hand. But despite their efforts they still barely made twelve miles that day and they did not find the slaver camp just over the ridge line.

They did not find it until the middle of the next day.

Chapter Fourteen

They moved downstream, crossing occasional creeks that had swollen to something close to flood status during the night. The mists were so thick it was hard to see more than a hundred feet in any direction. Thus it was no surprise that their noses first informed them that they were approaching a slave camp.

The sour, excremental odor reached them quite suddenly as they pushed through a tangled stretch of jungle. Their heads went up. Relkin saw Norwul's eyes water and his hair stand on end with the strength of his emotions. The Ardu had seen hard conditions during their imprisonment, and their memories were strongly charged.

The heavy, mephitic stench grew stronger with every stride. Cautiously, they slowed their pace through the dank forests. Soon they came upon a large clearing by the riverbank. In the center was a big stockade in the shape of a figure eight, protected on three sides by a ditch and stakes to keep pujish out. Along the water's edge was a row of boats, hauled up out of the rising river.

Ardu captives were packed into the same kind of long, low sheds that Bazil had ripped open at the original camp. The stench was now quite fantastic. Relkin found himself gagging every so often. The dragon complained, too, and began to get sulky. Wyverns were beasts of the clear air and the sea margin. Fortunately, dragons could shut out sensory impressions after a while. This made them legendarily impervious to pain.

The guards on the watchtowers were more active than those at the first camp. The word about the "forest god" pujish with the giant sword had traveled quickly on the forest streams. That season, there were eight slaver camps on the headwaters in the Ardu country, all in fairly constant communication by boat. The violent end of a successful camp and the loss of hundreds of Ardu slaves was the sort of news that would spread like wildfire. The nervous guards kept calling to each other and scanning the nearby jungle, alert to every twitch of a leaf.

But the Ardu, Relkin, and Bazil were all skilled at the art of remaining unseen. They crept through the forest, always in the shadows, out of sight of those on the towers. They examined the stockade and the boats and drew appropriate conclusions. Relkin had soon seen enough. He called the Ardu back from the fringes of the clearing. They met in a smaller glade, out of earshot of the camp.

The plan was discussed, variations were offered, but in the end it was agreed that the basic idea was the best. Then they went to work collecting rocks and other missiles, which were piled stealthily around the stockade.

While the piles of stones grew, a group of the robust males prepared the ram. They found a recently fallen conifer and stripped its branches. Bazil could not heft the whole tree, of course, but they fashioned a hefty ten-foot section that he could just manage to hold on to for a staggering run of perhaps fifty yards. That, they calculated, would be enough.

As before, they would attack during darkness, to disguise their lack of numbers. This time, Relkin knew, they would demonstrate far more effectively. If they were successful and it came to a fight, the slavers would need the protection of the Great Mother herself once these Ardu men got to close quarters with them. Relkin would not have wanted to be fighting against these Ardu males for any treasure under the sun. They burned, they seethed with the urge for revenge. But the numbers were against them. This camp was big—Relkin estimated there were sixty armed men inside, too many for the rescue party to take on in careless combat. Caution and tactical skill would be essential. He hoped they would have enough self-discipline to make tactics work.

Furthermore, the slavers were getting ready to depart. They had eight large boats tethered to the shore. If the attack failed, the slavers would leave with their victims immediately.

Dusk fell. The rain came down hard for a while. It was difficult to keep the cookfires going, so the slavers made a dismal meal of it. Still, their spirits were high. The dry season was over. The waters were rising. In a month or less they would be back in civilization in the cities of the southern plain. After the long season in their stink-ridden camp, the men were eager to be away. Their conversation was bright with hopes and jokes and friendly banter.

There was virtually no warning. The first thing anyone heard was the sound of a big body running in the woods and then a tremendous thud as something shook the whole stockade. Angry shouts came from the watchtowers, followed by sharp cracking sounds from the southernmost part of the wall. Nervous as deer, the men sprang to their posts.

At the southern end they found the wall stove in, with timbers broken askew and a massive tree trunk thrust through the gap. With considerable unease they examined the breach in the wall. Some men hurried back to fetch fresh timbers while others sought to repair the damage as best they might.

At that point a rain of rocks came out of the forest, forcing them to keep their heads down. Rocks slammed into the timbers or splattered the mud of the compound. A couple of men were felled, one slain. The slavers took positions close behind the wall and readied their weapons. The tension was palpable.

Then came a roaring of Ardu voices from the woods, dozens of them. Then within moments, the slave sheds awoke with a shattering roar. The females made a constant, insane ululation that was deafening, the robust males roared like lions, the children's high shrieking cut through the rest. It was an ugly sound, and frightening to the sixty slavers, who knew that if the slaves got out of those sheds, they'd tear their captors limb from limb. And everyone had seen that tree trunk, seemingly thrown through the wall by the giant pujish they'd been warned about. If the wall could be breached like that, what were they going to do when it came again?

The uproar continued and the rocks kept zinging out of the rain-splashed darkness. The defenders could see nothing and hear nothing except that hellish shrieking from the Ardu females. In vain the slavers screamed threats at the slaves, who would not be silent.

Upstream, the dragon finally reached the water's edge, where Relkin, Lumbee, and the other females tied themselves to him with a length of twisted vine rope. Together they pushed out into the river and let themselves be swept into the strongly flowing current. They floated out behind the dragon, who swam through the floodwaters with his usual assurance. Within a few minutes they were hard upon the camp. Bazil pushed himself and hauled the people behind him up to the side of one of the larger boats.

No eyes were turned toward the river. There was only a handful of men left to guard the boats. Everyone else had gone to the stockade. The uproar from the slaves was enough to wake the dead.

Bazil trod water with the use of his powerful tail, and with one arm hoisted Relkin up to the rail of the boat. Relkin slipped over and dropped to the decking silently.

There was a single guard, standing at the waist hatchway, looking over to the stockade. Two other guards were standing on land, halfway down the line of boats. The noise from the slaves covered any sound Bazil might have made in the water. Relkin slid quietly across the deck, sword ready in his hand. The man sensed him at the very last moment and turned suddenly and Relkin ran him through. The man was so shocked he barely made a sound as he slumped over the blade and started to fall over the boat's side. Relkin pulled him back from the brink and slid him to the deck and took his sword. The men on the bank were still absorbed in the drama of the stockade, giving Relkin time to investigate the cables holding the ship to the bank. They were well made, the product of civilization. He slipped back to the far side and leaned over. The dragon was waiting. The Ardu females clustered at his side.

"Two men on the riverbank," Relkin hissed. "Three boats over. The rest are at the stockade. The boat is secured with three cables at either end. We'll want to free them and then connect them together."

Bazil lofted the Ardu women to the rail so they could climb aboard and hide themselves. Then the dragon slipped back into the water and swam ashore. With Ecator he cut two of the cables at the downstream end of the boat. Relkin carried one of them over to the second boat and secured it fast at the bow. Bazil was already cutting through the cables securing the second boat. Lumbee and the other females were arming themselves with whatever they could find aboard the boats, which included some long spears for pujish. The spears were heavy, but the women hefted them nonetheless. At the signal, Relkin cut the cables at the bow of the first boat, which was now all that held two boats to the bank.

When the second boat began to leave the side of the riverbank, two guards whirled to confront an astounding sight. Their largest boats were drifting out into the stream, cut free from their moorings and propelled by some unknown force that was tugging them upriver, against the fast-flowing water.

With hoarse cries the guards sprang into action, running along the side of the river, pacing the boats, trying to think of some way of getting aboard. But neither cared to dive into the dark waters, so the boats continued to drift upstream and shortly faded from view into the murk.

The guards ran back to the stockade, but their cries of alarm went unheard by the rest, who were preoccupied with the bellowing slaves and whoever it was that kept hurling rocks from the dark.

Bazil hauled the boats to shore about two hundred yards upstream from the slaver camp. Relkin and the Ardu women tied the ropes fast to trees above the flood line. The first part of the plan had gone perfectly.

They gathered themselves. Now for the real test. They had to frighten the slavers into stampeding in a panic to the remaining boats and fleeing downstream, without bothering to search too hard for the missing ones.

Bazil hefted a rock some three feet across and lurched forward, bursting out the forest, running toward the upstream end of the stockade. Relkin and the Ardu females came behind, Relkin taking pains to keep everyone out of the range of Bazil's tail, which was likely to lash around wildly.

When Bazil was a mere six feet from the wall, he hurled the rock forward, giving it the impetus of his forward motion and then some. It slammed home as if hurled by a trebuchet and burst through the timbers with a thunderous crash. Bazil reached into the breach and tore out another timber or two and forced his way inside. There was no one in sight in this half of the camp. He drew Ecator and moved on. Relkin and Lumbee slipped in behind him.

A man stepped out of the nearest tent, holding a spear. He looked up, saw Bazil and uttered a wavering little scream, than took to his heels. Relkin carefully investigated the other tents, which were all empty. The men were in the lower section defending their treasure in slaves.

On they went. There was a cluster of men at the central cook pit, where they'd gotten a fire going just before the attack began. They looked up as the fleeing man came up. At his words of alarm they turned, ice in their hearts. The pujish loomed out of the mists a few moments later. The huge sword glittered in the red firelight.

The slavers wavered on the brink of panic for a moment until one or two of the bolder souls rallied them with harsh cries. They were men, adventurers in a dangerous trade. They weren't about to run from some mad kind of pujish.

Grimly they prepared to defend themselves.

The dragon halted, threw back his head, and vented an appallingly loud roar-scream, the wyvern dragon battle cry. This scream cut through the uproar and produced a shocked silence that hung over the entire camp. Then the Ardu in the forest rushed the wall as planned and the slavers' worst nightmares were realized.

Bazil crunched into the men by the cook pit. Ecator flew and three of them were cut in two in the wink of an eye. There was a scattering, then others thrust at the dragon with spears, seeking to get in behind him. Relkin and the Ardu girls came running up to engage. With curses the men drew back. Afraid of being taken in the flank, they danced backward a few steps. Before they could gather their wits, Ecator whistled among them once more and another man's head flew away.

The power of the blow and the thin sound it made turned the slavers' resolve to jelly. At first just two, then four more, then the rest, fled for the boats, unmanned. En route they barged into a pair of their officers, who laid about them with the flat of the sword but could not stem the flight.

Then the officers looked up and saw the dragon bearing down on them. The poor men went into dragon freeze and found themselves rooted to the spot by primordial fear.

Bazil swung and sent their souls to hell, with the cry of triumph from Ecator ringing all the way. The sword seemed to grow lighter in Bazil's hand; it was an uncanny thing. But then the dragon had long since grown used to the sword's ways. It was an elf-made blade, with witchly magic buried in its heart. A spirit inhabited the steel, a fierce spirit that longed to feast on the deaths of the enemies of the light.

Now there were only the slavers concentrated inside the main stockade. Most of the Ardu were attacking the breach at the far end, and that was where the defenders were gathered, too. Bazil surged in through the interior gate, snapping it off its hinges. The men in the watchtowers saw him come with mouths gaping in horror. Ecator flashed in the light of the few torches still burning and fear overcame them. They scrambled out of the towers and ran gibbering into the woods.

The dragon paused to rip open the roof of one of the slave sheds. The slaves screamed at the sight of him, but he tore open the shed, reaching in with a huge hand, and ripped the main chain out of its anchor with a heave of enormous muscles.

Then he was gone, and Lumbee was there instead, explaining that they were free, and that it was time to kill the slavers. The robust males went wild. In moments they were bursting out of the shed, some of them still shackled, but nonetheless ready to take revenge on the slaving no-tails.

They found themselves with plenty of opportunity. Bazil's arrival on the scene had produced a convulsion in the mob of slavers gathered at the breach. As Ecator thinned their ranks, so they broke back, away from Bazil in an expanding ring. Immediately, Ardu males from outside thrust their way in and threw themselves at the nearest slavers. Other Ardu, just released from the sheds, took the slavers from behind. The fighting grew general and quite desperate and dreadful deeds were done in a medley of screams, grunts, and hard sounds made from steel stabbing home into men's bodies. Then the slavers broke and ran, unable to withstand the fury of the assault from both directions. Bazil hewed down another pair who lingered too long and the rest fled for the boats, the Ardu in hot pursuit. Bazil tore open more slave sheds while Relkin, Lumbee, and the other women worked to break the main chains and free the slaves.

The boats pushed off and the surviving slavers withdrew hastily from the shore, along which stalked the dragon, his sword resting on his shoulder. Behind him the camp was in the noisy process of being completely torn asunder by the Ardu.

Chapter Fifteen

The Ardu celebrated their sudden freedom with wild rejoicing, and indeed there was a lot to be joyous about.

Lumbee, for instance, had found both her parents, alive and as well as might be expected after spending so many weeks confined within the stinking horror of the slave sheds. Her parents, Erris and Uys, were astounded when Lumbee came to them. They had long thought her dead, lost in the northern forests, devoured by monstrous pujish. At first Erris was convinced that Lumbee was a ghost, and it took quite some persuasion to change her mind.

Around the fires they made from the stockade timbers and the slave huts, the Ardu danced. They gorged on the stocks of food they recovered from the slavers' pantry. Then someone found the brandy cache and some of the males became frenzied under the influence. The bodies of the dead slavers were cut to pieces and hurled into the fire.

Bazil was regarded with a mixture of awe and intense curiosity, as befitted his status as forest god. Once it was firmly understood that he was not a dangerous pujish, the children gathered around him in a devoted clump. The females brought him offerings of food, which he gladly devoured. He sat on a log, Ecator in its scabbard lying beside him, a ring of bright little Ardu faces surrounding him. He pondered occasionally the bizarre twists and turns of the world of humans. Here were the tailed human people. They seemed fine vigorous specimens to a wyvern dragon who was very familiar with human beings of the no-tail type. They had been enslaved, a difficult concept for a dragon mind to really understand. But now that he had seen the way they had been confined in those sheds, chained up like domestic animals, he understood better. Of course, no dragons would ever dream of making other dragons into slaves. What wyvern had the time for such laborious concepts? Who needed to work anyway? One scoured the shoreline and the shallow waters. One took whatever one found and ate it then and there. One slept in contentment and awoke to the sound of the waves.

Alas, that life of wildness was something Bazil had never really known except as legends. For him there had been nothing but service to the war against the great enemy. Since he first hatched from the egg, he had been primed for that war. In the beginning he was indoctrinated, but later he saw for himself the nature of the conflict. He saw what that enemy had done to the Purple Green of Hook Mountain, the wild flying dragon that was Bazil's great friend and colleague in the 109th fighting dragons of Marneri. He had fought that enemy's creatures—trolls, imps, and even the giant ogres—and laid them low by the score. He knew that though he had been indoctrinated as a spratling, the cause he fought for was a just cause. Furthermore the alliance between wyvern dragons and men was necessarŷ, because in the world imagined by the enemy, there would be no dragons, they would all be slaughtered for the making of death magic. And so he fought willingly in the Legions. His great love, High Wings the green dragoness, had called him "slave" and he had not understood the term. He served in the Legions and obeyed orders. Did this make him a slave? It was an issue sometimes chewed over by the wyverns, whose natural disposition to wild, individual activity made military discipline hard at first to acquire. Bazil did not think he was a slave. He had fought battles of every scale during his period of service. He understood the whys and wherefores of command and combat and he knew how important Legion discipline was for the battle-field edge they maintained over all foes. They were not slaves, and even though they were not volunteers, except perhaps for the Purple Green, they were volunteers in spirit. They would always be ready to take up the sword against the enemies of the light. Bazil angrily rejected the idea that he was a slave. He was a battledragon, and woe to those he fought against.

The Ardu, of course, knew nothing of this interior dialogue. They simply gave him awestruck worship, and hot food. A wyvern dragon had never been known to turn down the latter.

Relkin, on the other hand, was not so well received. He seemed to come under the general cloud of suspicion that fell over all no-tails. After receiving looks of frank dislike from many of the older Ardu who had just been rescued from bondage, Relkin withdrew to a small fire of his own, which he built behind Bazil's log. He took over one of the smaller slaver tents, set close by. Its former occupant had abandoned all his gear. Relkin had liberated a couple of good leather belts, a long knife and a hatchet, plus a stoutly made pack. The Ardu had taken everything else.

Lying down out of the rain, he, too, mused upon the oddities of human behavior. This ingratitude from the Ardu should have shocked him, but after his years in the Legions, he found that it didn't. People always had their own agendas and they saw events through a prism distorted by those agendas. He wondered if he'd been coarsened by his long military service. Was he a cynic now? Despite his relatively tender youth, Relkin of Quosh had seen war in all its shapes and forms. Many were the horrors his eyes had recorded. Many the death screams his ears had absorbed. In between he'd witnessed all the chicanery that people were capable of. He expected the worst. Maybe he *was* just a cynic.

Then he chided himself. He'd seen some of the best as well. The people of Clan Wattel, for instance—they had been magnificent in the war of the great invasion. Ordinary shepherds, they'd come to the call from their leader and marched off to fight to the death to preserve the Argonath. The common soldiers of the Legions were an inspiration as well. People had their faults, you had to expect it, and there was often a good reason behind poor behavior. These Ardu, for instance, had been subjected to horrifying captivity in those hellish sheds. All their woes had come from no-tail people. It was no surprise that they were still smarting from it and looking to lash out at someone.

He mopped up some gruel with a chunk of the slavers' unleavened bread. It had been a long day. He put all thoughts of the Ardu and the slavers from his mind and slept soundly with the soldier's ability to sleep no matter where or when.

His dreams were unremarkable.

In the morning he awoke to find the rain reduced to a mere drizzle. Crawling out of the tent, he decided to examine more closely the boats they'd captured. His plan called for them to use those boats to move rapidly downstream and intercept the slavers who had been hunting on other parts of the river system in the forest. Where the other branches of the main river joined, there, if they were quick, they might ambush the slavers and rescue more Ardu.

The camp had been severely used. The stockade was largely flattened, much of it already burned. The hated sheds were completely destroyed. The stench of the open latrines had been obliterated beneath a mound of fresh dirt. The people were sorting themselves out, aligning with familiar kin groups where possible. There was an endless jabber among the females, who directed much of this activity.

The males were standing around the central fire in angry groups. Many of them were decidedly red-eyed, the aftereffects of the brandy. They were mean and looking for someone to take it out on.

The sight of a no-tail, even if it was Relkin, brought growls from some throats. Relkin whistled softly to himself as he made his way past them. He could feel their eyes burning into his back. There was nothing to do but to go about his business. They had to get over this. They were all going to have to work together.

Suddenly a strapping young male named Jusp stood up in front of him. Jusp's eyes were filled with hatred. His nostrils were flaring. Relkin could smell the drink on him. A torrent of abuse poured out of the youth. Relkin understood little of it, except for the cardinal fact that the young man was angered by Relkin's relationship with Lumbee.

"You don't understand," Relkin said several times in his most careful Ardu. Relkin reflected that it was a good thing the youth didn't understand. Relkin didn't understand, either, except that he'd been lonely, as had Lumbee, and they had felt a strong mutual attraction. Then he tried to ease his way past. The last thing he needed was a fight with this youth, who was wide as a door and covered in sculpted muscle. They had to learn to get along. He didn't want to begin that process with a bruising battle with someone twice his own weight.

The young Ardu put out an arm to stop him. Relkin sighed inwardly. On the other hand, he knew he could not refuse a fight if it was forced on him.

Relkin shifted sideways to go around the arm. Other Ardu had gathered around them, hot-eyed, wanting something to happen, something to offer them a catharsis to help excise the terrible sense of humiliation and rage.

The youth snarled something unintelligible and swung at him, a huge roundhouse blow that would have taken his head off if it had landed. Relkin slipped away on the balls of his feet. The youth hurled himself at him. Relkin dodged out of his path, but drew no weapon, even though he was carrying his dirk. The young man stumbled and fell to his knees. There was harsh laughter among the Ardu.

The youth was beside himself with rage. He unlimbered a club and came at Relkin in homicidal fury. Relkin drew his dirk and made ready. The club swung, Relkin pushed forward under the blow, the youngster's arm came down on his shoulder, and Relkin drove his left hand into the other's solar plexus.

The youth took no notice of the blow. Relkin avoided, barely, being clutched by the other's free hand, and moved back in a crouch. The youth charged him once more, cheered on by the Ardu men gathered around them now in a tight, hot-faced knot.

Relkin anticipated the next crude, flailing blow with the club, evaded it easily, and kicked the youth in the crotch with all the strength he could muster.

This did have an effect and the Ardu doubled up with a gasp of agony. Relkin didn't hesitate, moving now on well-learned lines of combat. His next kick laid the boy out, slamming against the side of his head.

Relkin pulled back and sheathed the knife, relieved enormously that he had not had to use it. Spilling blood would have been a disaster.

There was a raging mix of emotions in the faces surrounding him. On the one hand there was respect. The boy had been strong and wild, and Relkin had handled him with a minimum of fuss. On the other hand there was still the rage and the hatred of no-tails.

"I am not one of them," said Relkin slowly while clearly gesturing to the slaver tents. "I come from far, far, beyond the mountains of the east. Beyond the great water."

They stared at him with expressions of sullen rage and incomprehension. To some of them all no-tails were the same, they hated all with equal ferocity. Others were less obdurate. Still, Relkin felt the tension of the moment. The wrong word and they might tear him to pieces on the spot.

He looked down at the fallen youth. Then he bent and felt for a pulse, just to make sure. That final kick hadn't been that hard, but you could never be sure with such things. There was a throb beneath his fingers. The boy lived.

The Ardu were staring at him with furious suspicion.

Suddenly the dragon's voice buzzed through the muttering.

"Where is boy Relkin?"

"Over here." Relkin was impressed with the wyvern's sense of timing.

"What are you doing?"

"Well, I had to lay this lad out when he came for me with his war club. They're upset with me because of, well, Lumbee, you know."

"Because you fertilize the eggs?"

"Yes, basically."

"Be interesting to see what spawn Lumbee produces. My own were both winged. I was surprised by that. I would have thought that at least one of them would have been wyvern kind."

"And then what the hell would you have done? Quit the Legions and gone back to Quosh to be a farm animal?"

"Never."

"Anyway, enough of that. These fellows are madder than hell at me and yet we've got to work with them if we're going to free the other Ardu."

"We free them, no more slaves. This dragon hate those who would take slaves. Ecator hates them, too."

Relkin thought to himself that this knowledge alone would make a lot of slavers give up their trade if they but knew it.

"Yeah, and if we have the chance we'll educate them in that fact. But first we have to keep the Ardu from killing me."

"They want to kill boy?"

"Well, look at them. What do you think?"

Bazil looked around at the circle of hot-eyed Ardu.

"Mmmmm." He stretched himself to his full height, dominating the mass of Ardu. There was that familiar awe in their faces, a sense that almost verged into dragon freeze in some of them. They had seen the forest god in action. They had seen that incredible ribbon of steel cut slavers to pieces.

Then, speaking careful Ardu, very slowly, with dragonish accent and pronunciations, he announced, "This is my boy. He is not enemy. He has been mine for many years. He never had time to become slaver."

Round-eyed, the Ardu absorbed these words in silent astonishment. The forest god spoke to them in their own tongue, quite clearly.

With some regrets they put aside all thought of slaughtering the no-tail. Relkin decided to take advantage of the dramatic shift in mood.

"Listen to me. We have much work to do. There are other slave camps. Now the rains have come. The slavers will be heading downstream. We must use these boats to catch them and free the Ardu."

"How we do this?" said one grizzled veteran with a massively muscled belly.

"Go downriver. Get to where other rivers enter the

main river. Wait there until slavers go past. Then follow and attack at night. Kill slavers. Free Ardu."

He sensed broad agreement surge through the Ardu. Then there came that wave of suspicion. As before, with Iuuns and Yuns, there was that elemental distrust.

"You want to go downriver? To go south?" said another elder.

"To rescue the other Ardu. There are more camps like this one. We have to stop the slavers wherever we can."

"South is where the slavers go."

"I know. But I am not a slaver. I want to free the Ardu."

Did they dare trust him? There was a shiver of indecision among them. A couple were helping poor Jusp to his feet.

"Look. I'm going to the boats. Come with me. We have a lot of decisions to make."

Carefully Relkin started off. Bazil fell in just behind him. He didn't look back.

The Ardu looked around for a moment and then followed. They would have to trust the no-tail. After all, he was the property of the forest god.

Chapter Sixteen

The war party was set to leave that very afternoon. The rain had resumed, and Relkin had misgivings about the boat-handling skills of the Ardu, but there was absolutely no time to waste and thus no time to train them. The Ardu men were used to their own canoes and small boats; they would have to learn how to work these larger craft as they went along. Like the rain, like many other things, Relkin would just have to live with it.

They had already decided that the dragon would have to swim—he was simply too large for these boats. Relkin was much more nervous about this prospect than his dragon was. Bazil actually liked the idea. The river flow would make it unnecessary to do much swimming. He would hardly have to exert himself and it would be blissful to stay in the water for day after day. Nor was he much worried about pujish in the water. There were creatures with predatory dispositions, he was sure, like crocodiles, but none that would trouble a two-ton wyvern dragon. Relkin, on the other hand, could imagine all sorts of terrible things happening.

Under a cloud of these concerns Relkin sought out Lumbee to say farewell. She was going north with her family and the surviving members of her kin group. She and Relkin had been virtually separated anyway, since the discovery of her parents.

He found her standing in front of a small shelter of leaves and branches, the sort of thing the Ardu could put up in a matter of minutes.

He greeted her with a hug. She seemed stiff in his arms and after a second he stood back. Her eyes were clouded. She avoided looking at him.

"Lumbee . . ." he began. Then he saw her father emerge from behind some nearby bushes. Uys wore a fierce scowl. A war club dangled from his belt now, along with a hatchet liberated from the slavers' camp.

"What you want here?" said Uys truculently.

Relkin was a little surprised by the tone of Uys's voice. He had assumed that Uys knew and understood that Relkin and Lumbee were attracted to each other and had formed an intimate relationship under the pressure of living completely on their own in the deep forest. They had traveled hundreds of miles together, braving everything from starvation to ferocious man-eating pujish. Alone, they had drawn on each other for the strength to carry on. He had assumed that Uys had managed to accept what had happened and to forgive.

Now he realized that Uys had succumbed to the kind of jealous rage one had to expect from the fathers of beautiful daughters. Relkin supposed that he'd been foolish to think that Uys wouldn't have reached this point. The only wonder was that he hadn't shown this side of himself before.

"I came to say good-bye, for now. We are going south."

Uys's face compressed itself. The Ardu was obviously in the grip of emotional turmoil.

"What you do with Lumbee? Out there?" He waved an arm angrily to indicate the wide-spreading forest.

"I know what you want and I'm not going to tell you. It is a private matter between Lumbee and myself."

Uys's face seemed to bulge with anger.

"Father," said Lumbee in a sharp voice.

Uys opened his mouth but said nothing.

Relkin spoke softly as if he might cushion the words somehow. "You have to remember that we were completely alone out there. We did not know that we would find you and free you."

Uys swallowed hard. "True. You come and free Ardu. We all grateful. But . . . it is not easy. I am Lumbee's father. I."

"I wish to return and live among the Ardu. I will be the father of Lumbee's children."

At this there was a scream from the doorway of the shelter. Erris appeared. She laughed bitterly.

"You cannot father children among the Ardu. Ardu and no-tail cannot mate successfully. No children."

"How do you know?"

"Slavers tell us. They say that is why slavers always have to come back to our land and steal more Ardu. They cannot breed Ardu enough to give slaves to all who want."

Relkin's and Lumbee's eyes met. There was an infinite sadness in the Ardu girl's eyes.

"Farewell, Relkin. I love you, but there is too much difference between us. It is better if you not come back, I think. Go with Bazil. Go back to the 'oceans' and the other lands."

Relkin was lost for words. He felt he owed it to Lumbee to come back and live with her and give up the other world.

Lumbee came close, defying the outrage in her father's eyes. "Relkin, you were very good to Lumbee. All Ardu are in your debt. My father and my mother would have been taken to slavery if you hadn't come here to rescue them."

Both Uys and Erris were stilled by these words. Uys looked down, torn by conflicting emotions of great strength. Erris began to sob.

Relkin was holding Lumbee close. She had her head buried in his chest. He could feel her tears running down inside his ragged, worn-out shirt.

It felt as if the ground itself had been pulled out from under his feet. Over the past weeks he had slowly accustomed himself to the thought that he would stay here with Lumbee. He and Bazil were effectively retired from the Legions and lost to the world. They would live out their lives in the lands of the Ardu.

There were two large question marks that always arose when he thought this way, however. The first was his love for Eilsa Ranardaughter. It was not her fault that Relkin had stumbled and betrayed their love with this new love for Lumbee the Ardu girl. Relkin was not worthy of one as fine as Eilsa. Relkin was just an orphan kid from a rural village. How could he hope to aspire to the hand of the daughter of the chief of Clan Wattel? Eilsa would marry someone else, someone within the clan, just as she was destined to do from birth. Relkin would be forgotten. The problem was that Relkin, in his heart, didn't believe this. He knew he wouldn't forget Eilsa and he didn't think she would forget him, either. Therefore, he would be doomed to grieve for the rest of his life with some part of his heart.

The other problem was the wyvern dragon. If they stayed here, Bazil would never be able to fertilize the eggs—wyvern eggs, that is. No one to mate with at all, unless he wanted to try the pujish, but Relkin doubted that. He knew that the wyvern regarded the big two-legged pujish with considerable distaste. They were warm-blooded like himself, and descended from some common ancestor, but they were viciously stupid and incapable of anything beyond violence. To mate with them would be like mating with wild beasts. Relkin knew that in the end old Bazil would grow very lonely here.

"I don't know what to say," he mumbled. "This is so painful."

"If we can't have children, then you will not be happy in the Ardu land."

"I can be happy if I am with you."

"But Lumbee cannot be happy if she cannot have children."

Ah, of course. Relkin understood completely at last. "See," said Erris brightly, "Lumbee is a good daughter."

"Yes," said Relkin quietly, "she is, and more than that, she is a brave one, perhaps the bravest of all."

He left them then, and later he went downriver with the men and the dragon.

Chapter Seventeen

For a month the Ardu warriors hunted slavers on the forest rivers. Word of their ambushes and of the terrifying power of the forest god quickly spread to Yazm and the other slaver towns on the river. For the first time, the Ardu had proved themselves capable of active resistance and it was alarming. Stories about a forest god were not taken seriously in the towns, of course. The men had been too long in the deep woods, it was said. But something was running amok up there. Altogether at least five expeditions had been struck and two virtually annihilated. The word went south. Prices for prime slaves were already soaring. The rulers of the slave markets in the south sent back demands that something be done about it.

"Do it yourself," growled the slavers who'd made it out of the Ardu forests in one piece with their booty. Those who'd had the misfortune to encounter the forest god were even less inclined to listen to the words from Mirchaz. An atmosphere of fear and surliness engulfed the rough-and-ready small towns of the upper river. Messengers sped downriver in swift canoes powered by a dozen slaves.

One thing was certain: The slave hunting season was over. No more expeditions remained above the portage at the great cataract.

For a week the Ardu waited beside the river, but no more slaver boats appeared. One morning, with common consent, they turned their fleet of captured boats northward and beat their way upstream. Eventually they beached the boats, which on Relkin's advice they did not burn. Instead they carefully hid them in the forest.

In the future, the Ardu would fight the slavers with all

the slavers' own weapons. They had learned much in this hard season of fighting short, vicious battles, either in midstream or ashore. One of the most important lessons had been the effectiveness of modern weapons over simple war clubs and spears without metal heads. The Ardu men who made boats had studied the slavers' craft with care. They, too, had learned much that they would introduce into their own boats.

Now the Ardu war party marched north. In ten days they reached the Plain of Three-Horns. Across the plain beckoned the hills around Lake Gam. That was where they would find the other Ardu, including the large group that had first been freed by Bazil and Relkin.

There were now seventy men in the war party, accompanied by a further two hundred women and children. They were growing into a tribe. Kin groups were forming friendships and rivalries, marriages were taking place with new kin groups, orphan children were being adopted into other new kin groups. A great social melding was taking place and it was producing a new entity in the Ardu world—the tribe, a grouping far larger than even the largest kin groupings like Red Rocks. The Ardu males had felt the power of numbers. As their strength grew, so their attacks had grown more effective. Equally important were the new weapons taken from the slavers, and the training in their use provided by the no-tail Relkin. They had a confidence now that they had never had before in their fights with slavers.

They found the other big group of Ardu by tracking the smoke of their cooking fires. They were camped in the river canyon, not far from where the three-horns herd had run itself over the cliffs. Protected by a thick boma of thorns and stakes, their camp was on a bend, surrounded by deep water on three sides.

Stationed by the boma were some older men and some youths, armed with a handful of slaver-made spears with the heavy steel heads. When they saw the advance party of warriors appear out of the forest, they gave up a shout. Someone recognized Norwul. In moments, the women gave up a wild ululation that echoed off the cliffs above the river gorge, startling huge animals in the thickets and sloughs.

Out of the forest came the warriors and the two hundred or so women and children they had freed. They passed through the boma's gate and a milling scrum began as the two groups came together in a frantic search for kin. A roar of shouts, inquiries, curses went up. Soon cries of joy echoed up the canyon along with wails of woe.

The results were widely uneven. The Red Rock kin were crying in joy to the Gods, giving praise for their mercy. The Heather Hills people were also filled with gladness, though this was sadly tempered by some losses. The small Swan's Lake clan were left weeping. Half their numbers were missing.

"Mirchaz!" they wailed, raging at the southern enemy who hovered out there, vague and shapeless, a malign presence that sent its cruel trawls sweeping through the Ardu regions to steal the people away. It was more remorseless than the pujish and far more effective.

The summertime had once been a time of pleasure, a bountiful time when the Ardu folk lived in the forest as they did of yore. They lived on fruits and monkeys and several large lizards that made good eating. They fished the streams and hunted for small pujish when they came to drink. That was the ancient way of summer. The Ardu could no more change the way of summer than they could shed their tails.

Recently, the summertime had become a grim time of fear and foreboding

In the summer came the slavers, with nets and steel swords and arrows that made them invincible. They had turned summer to a time of sorrow and loss. So many had been taken over the years that the Ardu numbers had dwindled to perhaps only half of what they once had been.

Mirchaz! Evil queen of the southern cities, dreadful moon of malice casting her shadow across the peaceful world of the Ardu.

But despite the grief for their departed kin, the folk were surprised and pleased to see Bazil return to them. To most of them he was still the forest god. The people in the camp built up their fires and roasted three-horns meat for

him. Others brought him water from the stream and
mounds of toasted bean pods, which he found very tasty
between mouthfuls of meat.

A debate went on among the women. A few had previously disparaged the forest god and the no-tail boy. Some
had seen them as tricksters, probably just slavers in disguise. There had been a lot of complaining from some
people, especially during the hard days on the long march
across the plain. Now these people were discomfited. The
forest god had returned and brought more free Ardu. The
complainers had been wrong and now they were forced to
admit it, or at the least shut their mouths.

The forest god had few complaints, other than sore feet,
some scratches, and thorn pricks and the bites of assorted
insects. He ate and he drank and he listened with amusement as the Ardu people said prayers to him, asking for
help in their daily lives. Bazil's grasp of the Ardu tongue
had become quite broad and he understood most of what
anyone might say to him now. Still, the Ardu were too
much in awe of him to accept that he was a "person" like
themselves and not a god. Bazil had to admit he didn't
care. The food was good and now that the march was
over, he wanted to relax a bit and get the ache out of his
legs. It had been a long campaign. Not much fighting, but
lots of swimming and marching. The marching had been
long at the end and Bazil was glad to get off his feet.

He accepted a huge haunch of roasted three-horns with
a cheerful smack of his immense jaws and started in on it
with a thrill of pleasure.

Relkin came into the camp with Ium and Wol, two
young men from the Yellow Canyon kin group with
whom he had struck an instant friendship. Relkin had
helped break the chains that bound them and they had
accepted him completely. Among the Yellow Canyon
group, he was universally popular.

Relkin's position had changed. Even Ommi and his
friends gave grudging admiration of the no-tail friend. He
not only spoke with the forest god and gave them the
forest god's orders and exhortations, but he fought better
than any of them and had personally saved many an Ardu
life. The robust males were unused to the melee. When

they fought among themselves they always fought in stylized combat, one on one, as champions for their kin groups. Thus they settled boundary disputes, woman-stealing, and inheritance fights. The slavers had them at a grievous disadvantage, not only because of their steel weapons, but also because they came from an advanced society accustomed to war. They understood how to organize small combat between groups.

Relkin and Bazil had changed the equation, however. Relkin was constantly teaching the Ardu new tricks with hatchet and sword, spear and knife. He had instructed Ium and Wol in the use of crossbows and they had quickly become first-class shots. As he worked with them individually, he promoted the ideas of discipline and group action. Most of the Ardu were ready to listen. They had been on the receiving end of the techniques of the slavers. They knew they had to adapt or perish.

At night around the campfire they talked of nothing but how to organize for ambushes and small battles in dense woods. They practiced working the boats until they could maneuver them with reasonable proficiency in the fast-moving water of the swollen rivers. Relkin had witnessed a transformation in some of the Ardu men. They were learning soldiery. Relkin had great hopes for them.

But Relkin's ascendancy was not welcomed by many of the people in the camp. These people had been grieving and grumbling even as they moved across the Plain of Three-Horns. For all they had gained, still they agonized over the vast dislocation their lives had received. Many now hated all no-tails with a passion.

Iuuns and Yuns had spoken poisonous words about Relkin. Lumbee had tried to stop it, but she was ignored and finally ordered to be silent by her mother, who feared the family would be ostracized.

Iuuns had put it about that Relkin and the so-called forest god had abducted the Ardu men and sold them to the slavers. Many folk laughed at Iuuns, but a few listened, and the story was spread and embellished. The sudden reappearance of Relkin and the forest god had overturned all of this, but though they willingly fed a hungry dragon, there was no love to spare for the no-tail among some Ardu.

Relkin tried to take no notice. The month had been exhausting, exhilarating, but also frustrating. They had captured two camps and set three ambushes. Two had succeeded brilliantly and they had taken whole slaver expeditions, killing most of the slavers and releasing a hundred slaves each time. The third ambush went awry, however, when some of the Ardu men moved from concealment too soon and the slavers were warned. In the confused fight that followed, casualties were heavy on both sides and few slaves were freed, while the slaver boats swept away into the gathering darkness. And after that there had been no more boats. The slavers had gone, taking their booty to the south.

The war party was now the nucleus of a tribe, the beginnings of a nation. Welded together in battle, the men had forged new, deep bonds, tying together ancient kin groups that had always functioned independently. They could not go back to the old ways living in small groups vulnerable to the slavers. Now they were something different, something new for Ardu folk.

In the war party, Relkin was no longer distrusted. The memories of Lumbee and his relationship were gone. The fighting robust males saw him as their general. He was confident that given a little time and some basic goodwill, he could win over the rest. Even the most intractable, like Iuuns and Yuns, would come around in the end.

Chapter Eighteen

The making of a tribe is a noisy business. Arguments constantly arose, and there was a great need for judgments. Lumbee had suggested a council of representatives from the kin groups. The big kin groups had balked at first. But then as disagreements arose in everyday dealings with the rest of the slowly coalescing tribe, there came crises that took up everyone's time and tried everyone's patience and all groups came to accept the need for such a council.

Several times groups threatened to leave and return to the old ways of life as a kin group alone. Each time, Relkin made an impassioned speech to them in his crude Ardu and persuaded them to stay.

Outside the tribe they were all vulnerable to the slavers. They knew that either they would have to stay in the north in the dry season and forsake the easy living in the forest, or they would have to remain in the tribe for safety. To miss the season in the forest would be tantamount to cutting the near-religious feeling the Ardu held for the old ways of the forest life long ago.

So they stayed. But the disagreements remained and squabbling provided a constant supply of crisis.

The saga of Pumo was one of the worst. Pumo was a pleasant-faced youth of fourteen with a very strong tail. Originally he was from the kin group of the Yellow Canyon. His parents and sisters had been taken by the slavers that season. Only he had escaped, breaking free when the camp was struck and the slaves loaded into the boats and taken downstream. Pumo had lived wild in the forest until he ran into the scouts of the Ardu war party and was taken in.

He had been with the tribe ever since. There were only

a handful of Yellow Canyon folk in the tribe. Pumo had
been taken in by the motherly Wulla of the Red Rock
group, which was the largest in the tribe. Pumo was good
at wrestling and swimming and had a gracious way about
him that endeared him to the other youngsters in the tribe.
He was mischievous, but without malice, and thus was
even regarded fondly by the older folk, who were usually
critical of the young.

Now a delegation of the matriarchs of the Yellow Canyon group, who were camped nearby, had come to
demand that Pumo go back with them and live with his
kin group.

Pumo did not want to go, however. The other folk from
the Yellow Canyon group within the tribe were upset.
Some were saying that they should all leave the tribe and
go back to the kin group. And that Pumo should be
brought, by force if need be. The primacy of the kin group
was at stake. Others opposed this and demanded loyalty to
the tribal idea.

Still the Yellow Canyon matriarchs would not go away.
They insisted that the law of the kin group had primacy. Pumo must come with them. Wulla, on the other
hand, had exerted her own claims to Pumo by calling on
all the notables of her large and sprawling kin group, the
Red Rocks, to come out and support her. A long, loud
argument had broken out at the water hole and spread to
the campfire and kept going for hours.

Over the past two weeks Relkin had had several conversations with young Pumo about his problems. Pumo
was straightforward about his preference for Wulla's
family. Wulla had been better to him than his own
mother, and he got along better with her children than he
did with those of the Yellow Canyon group. He was determined to stay.

Relkin grew concerned about the rancor that was setting in. There was the potential for grave trouble, even a
war of sorts. Things like this had happened before in Ardu
history and often led to fatal consequences. Even though
they were outnumbered, the Yellow Canyon males would
be expected to challenge the Red Rocks to fight. Blood

would be shed and blood feuds initiated that might go on down the generations for years and years.

Relkin went to see Lumbee. The two wandered away from the camp, on a bluff overlooking the canyonland. They looked down into a forest of purple buttes and narrow ridgelines soaking in the orange light of evening.

Since Relkin's return, Lumbee and he had been careful to keep their time together to a minimum since they knew it excited the worst fears in old Uys and Erris. Moreover, Lumbee had emerged as a new force within the tribe. Using the fact that she had known Relkin the longest, she had occupied a place in the early tribal councils and hung on to it by virtue of her skill in speaking and a certain innate wisdom. The older people had given her respect. Recently Relkin had felt a subtle shift in their relationship. Lumbee had grown, maturing into a new person almost.

It wasn't that the sweet Lumbee he'd known before had gone. It was just that she was busy with serious matters and was less inclined to look at him with adoring eyes. There was business to be attended to. The tribe was growing, but it had to be nurtured.

"How goes the dragon?" she said when they were out of earshot. She liked to use the Verio she'd learned from Relkin to keep it fluent in her mind, but she didn't like the other Ardu to hear her using it. She knew they would think it outlandish. The Ardu were a conservative folk, accustomed to the old ways. They knew nothing of other languages and didn't want to know, either.

"He sleeps well, but he's putting on weight. He needs more exercise." Relkin hesitated. But Lumbee was dragonfriend and would understand. "I think, perhaps, that he is getting lonely."

She looked up, surprised.

"I mean he is lonely for other dragons."

Her face opened in understanding and compassion. Relkin felt his heart melt, as it did so often with Lumbee.

"See, we've been away from our unit for many months now. I think he misses the others."

"It must be amazing to live among many dragons like Bazil. Lumbee would like to see it someday."

Relkin thought it would be even more interesting to see what sort of effect Lumbee would have on his own friends in the 109th fighting dragons. What would Swane and Jak and Manuel make of this gentle girl with a tail?

He changed the subject to what was really on their minds.

"Have you see Pumo today?"

"No, I think he's lying low. I expect he's not enjoying his life right now."

"Poor Pumo. And the threat to the tribe is great. Something will have to be done, and soon."

Lumbee's jaw had set. Relkin knew she had something she thought was important to say.

"Look, Relkin, I think Pumo must speak to the gathering at the campfire. Let him tell everyone what he wants to do. Everyone has been arguing above his head, as if he were a child unable to make his own decisions. These are extraordinary times; the tribe grows and Pumo believes in it. Let him announce what he wants to do. The grandmothers from Yellow Canyon will not be happy, but they will have to accept his decision. And everyone will see that belonging to the tribe is a decision we all make, individually. We are choosing to be in the tribe, and that is our greatest strength."

Relkin nodded. She was right. He grinned.

"Maybe we should ask the Yellow Canyon grandmothers to join us. Bring all the Yellow Canyon folk in." He paused and pursed his lips.

"Except I don't know if that would be popular with the groups already in."

Lumbee thought about it for a moment. It was not a big problem. "They'd see it after a while. We need numbers. The more fighters we have, the stronger we'll be. We must stop the slavers. Next season we will keep all slavers out of the forest."

Relkin thought it was quite possible.

"Won't all this put a lot of pressure on Pumo? He'll have to stare down the rest of the Yellow Canyon people we have."

"I have spoken with him. Pumo will be strong."

Suddenly Relkin saw that in her eyes was a visionary shine that he recognized for the first time.

She saw his eyes upon her and read his look. "Yes, Relkin is right. Lumbee know what Ardu must do. That is why Lumbee cannot marry Ommi even though Uys would be happy. Lumbee must marry Chasen of Red Rock to cement groups together. Chasen agree with Lumbee. He knows we must build the tribe. Otherwise all Ardu will be taken as slaves."

"And what should a dragon and a dragonboy do, Lumbee?"

Lumbee looked him steadily in the eye. "I love you Relkin, but we cannot have children. So I must wed within the Ardu. I cannot wed a no-tail. Nor will I wed Ommi, though he wants me to. He is in Heather Hills kin, and that will not help tribe. I will wed Chasen. But I will always love Relkin."

Relkin could not hold back. He held her tight and kissed her. For a few moments they were together again. Then she pressed him back, easing herself away a half step and wiping her eye. When she spoke, her voice was husked by emotion.

"But we can't do that anymore. We have to put aside our own feelings."

"No, Lumbee, we don't have to do that. We can be together, somehow."

"You cannot stay with tribe. You have to go back to Argonath lands. You have to go back to Eilsa."

The sudden mention of Eilsa's name sent a flush over his skin. Relkin was instantly confused, embarrassed, and ashamed all at once. He had not been faithful to lovely Eilsa, and now he could not live with Lumbee, after all. Would he have to live with guilt the rest of his days, or would he confess to Eilsa what he had done? He didn't think he could face that. For a moment he was frozen in place.

"Yes," he said softly. "Lumbee is right. We will have to go back. You will lead the Ardu tribe and your tribe will be a strong one, I know this in my heart. Bazil and I have to go back to our own world. But before we go, I have things I must teach your fighters. They need all the training I can give them. They have much to learn yet."

Lumbee reached out to touch Relkin's elbow. "The Ardu will always be thankful to Relkin of Quosh."

They parted and made their own ways back toward the fire.

Behind them, in the dark, eyes glittered angrily.

Chapter Nineteen

The rains slowly died down until they became occasional downpours, and all-day soakings were a thing of the past. Still, the sky was obscured by clouds most of the time and the stars were invisible at night.

The Ardu tribe moved stealthily across the plain, avoiding pujish. They camped by ancestral pits, staked them afresh, and caught three-horns on which they feasted. When the rains were finished, they would leave the plains and go up into the northern hills, where the berries were beginning to burgeon. Then they would cycle southward again, into the southern forests, where they would be at risk from Mirchaz slavers once again.

The kin groups were slowly settling in together. Three more marriages across kin lines had helped. Other marriages were planned. There was much speculation concerning who Lumbee might marry, since she was old enough now. She had become a voice for the younger people in the tribal council and had gained authority in the tribe. Many older Ardu, even the robust males, gave her great respect, far more than they would any other girl of her age. This only gave greater point to the discussions of whom she might marry, since every kin group wanted her on their side.

One day, the first with a completely clear sky since the beginning of the rains, the peace of the camp was broken by a ragged shout from the western hill. It was Mogs of the Sunny Bank kin group. He staggered into the camp. There was trouble at the new pit they'd dug for three-horns out west in the acacia groves.

The pit was a success, too much of a success. Like nearly all the pits they used, it was an old one, but this

was one that had not been used in decades. They had
cleared out brush and stones that had fallen in and
replaced the stake with a new one, freshly sharpened and
hardened in the fire. Then they had woven a new mat of
grasses to cover the hole and sat back to wait.

The very next night a three-horns cow had come wandering by with another and fallen in. She had died almost
instantly when the stake impaled her through the throat.

At once the Ardu had begun to butcher the carcass,
working quickly while messengers were sent back to
camp for all the able-bodied to make a meat run to the
butchering site and back. There was a lot of meat on a
mature three-horns.

It was important to cut the carcass up and remove it
entirely, bones and all, for if it ripened even by a day,
pujish would catch the scent and come swarming to the
site. The Ardu would lose the pit to the pujish, as well as
the remains of the carcass. In fact, the whole tribe might
have to move, because pujish would discover the camp
and then linger nearby in the hope of catching children or
others out alone.

By enormously bad luck, Mogs and Eep of Swan's
Lake had run into a pair of adolescent red-browns, each
weighing perhaps a ton or more and standing five feet
high at the shoulder with a body length of almost twenty
feet. The red-browns had attacked at once and killed old
Eep. Mogs escaped and made it back to camp.

A rescue party was formed at once, arming itself with
long spears, bows, arrows, slings, and a good supply of
stones. Relkin offered to wake the dragon and ask him to
accompany them, but Ommi, who was prominent in the
group, said that they would go alone, they were not afraid
to face pujish.

The rescuers left and Relkin went to see Bazil at once,
bringing the dragon some water and meat from the fire.
While Bazil ate, Relkin told him what had happened and
what was likely to follow. Bazil grunted softly, drank
deeply, and then exercised briefly with Ecator. In truth, he
was quite keen to see some action. The last few weeks had
passed in relative peace and quiet.

He strode up and down the riverbank, rushing huge volumes of air in and out of his cavernous lungs, stretching his arms, and whipping his tail back and forth to shake off the sluggishness of camp life. Then he drew the magical blade. As always he felt the vitality within it, the magical other life that somehow inhabited this piece of steel. The sword, too, was ready for action.

As for poor old Mogs, he lay by the fire, worn out from running five miles at top speed. The kin of Eep from Swan's Lake gathered round, peppering him with questions. It was painful to answer, bringing back the most appalling memories. The young pujish were quick and deadly. They had caught old Eep on a flat place with no cover and no hiding places. The only mercy had been the speed of his death. They had torn him apart and devoured him in the matter of a few moments. The women from Swan's Lake gave out wails of lamentation. Already Swan's Lake kin had been hammered by the slavers and now the pujish were adding to the toll. The women bent their heads together and spoke of ill luck and curses and the doings of gods and demons. Yuns and Iuuns of the Red Rock group spoke darkly of hidden things and evil designs against all the Ardu.

Soon afterward the others began trickling in from the west. Their news was dreadful. The young pujish had caught the scent of the three-horns in the pit and soon tracked it to its source. Then they'd started roaring with a mixture of triumph and anticipation. The Ardu males slung stones with punishing accuracy and power and this kept the young pujish at a distance while they worked themselves up for an all-out assault.

It never came. Instead things got worse. Their stupid, boastful roaring attracted another of their kind, an old male with scarred skin and a pronounced limp. Although not enormous by the standards of his kind, he was far too large for the Ardu to deal with. Everyone had been forced to depart, fleeing across the plain for the main camp, while behind them the young red-browns squabbled with the old male for the rest of the three-horns carcass, which was hardly touched. The day, which had begun so well, had become a complete disaster.

There was nothing the tribe could do but pack up and

move on as quickly as possible. There were other pits that could be quickly refurbished and pressed into use. The Ardu survived on the plain by their wits. Normally they were able to avoid the pujish almost completely, and of course in the northern woods the pujish were very rare, having been hunted out by the Ardu over time. Every so often though things went wrong and lives were lost. With the red-brown pujish there was little room for error.

Bazil took up Ecator and strode up the boma. The Ardu muttered and bobbed their heads at the sight of him balancing a great swath of gleaming steel naked on his shoulder. The tales of what Bazil had done with that sword had been many and most wondrous and had gone around and around the campfires ever since. Everyone felt vastly safer with the forest god watching over them.

Scouts moved out carefully at dusk and returned to say that the pujish had gorged and were lying up near the pit. They would gorge again the following day. During the night other small pujish would descend on the carcass, of course, but a three-horns was an enormous amount of meat; there would be still be some for the red-browns the next day. During this period the tribe would move, while the pujish were occupied. Other scouts went north to investigate the next set of pits that might be used.

The next morning further scout parties went out before dawn to keep an eye on the trio of red-browns by the pit. Relkin, Ium, and Wol made up one such group. As they were leaving, young Pumo attached himself to them, attracting outraged glares from the women at the Yellow Canyon campfire.

All three of Relkin's friends had left the Yellow Canyon group for the wider identity of the tribe. They faced strong criticism from the elders of the kin group. Their closeness to Relkin was constantly remarked upon.

Outside the boma they headed west and soon reached the area of the pit, which lay behind a long sloping hill, almost bare of vegetation. On this open terrain they felt vulnerable. They traveled slowly, bent over in an effort to be as inconspicuous as possible.

They had gone this way for a few minutes when Wol suddenly raised a hand and whispered urgently. About two hundred yards ahead, laid out low along the ground, were two sinister shapes. Relkin felt the breath tighten in his chest at the sight.

There they were: a pair of young red-brown pujish sleeping in the sun. They had squatted down on their massive hind limbs and laid their bodies out on their bellies with their huge heads flat on the ground. Eyes closed, they snored softly, confident that nothing would care to trouble them.

Ium looked to the sky. The morning was well upon them.

"They are slow to wake. They must have gorged heavily yesterday."

"They will wake up hungry. Their kind always does."

Relkin realized just how dangerous the humans' position was. There was no shelter anywhere around them. This was where old Eep had died.

"And the other one?"

"Don't see him."

Relkin didn't like the sound of that. He did his best to crouch even lower.

"We should move back. We're too close to them," said Wol.

They found it easy to agree on this and so reversed direction back along the hillside, until they reached some thornbushes about a half mile distant. There they could observe the pujish while remaining hidden. They would watch until they were assured that the young red-browns were going to return to the pit and the three-horns carcass.

"They'll wake up soon," said Ium.

"And they'll be hungry," said Wol.

They watched and waited. Flies buzzed in the hot air. The sun moved slowly

"In your land, Relkin, do you have grandmothers who are so much trouble?"

The Yellow Canyon grandmothers again! They just would not leave poor Pumo alone. Relkin chuckled sympathetically.

"No, I don't think so."

"Grandmothers like ours are a real pain in the tail," said Ium.

Relkin knew that Ium and Wol were also under pressure from the Yellow Canyon grandmothers.

"In your world, Relkin, far, far, do you have grandmothers with so much authority?" said Wol, who was an inquisitive sort.

"I never knew my grandmothers," said Relkin. "I only ever had the dragon for family. But I have heard that some grandmothers are like yours. They fear the new thing we are making, the tribe. I know it's hard, but you've just got to stick it out. You made the right decision, and in time they will see it, too. And they have virtually joined the tribe already. I mean, they haven't shown any signs of leaving us, have they?"

All three young Ardu nodded vigorous agreement. Pumo's eyes clouded, however.

"Still they blame you, Relkin. They say you cause all our troubles. They are crazy. You saved many, many Ardu from the no-tails."

"They think that everything they stand for is in danger. In the kin group they are very important. In the tribe they will be less so. We have to take their feelings into account. I guess I'm not the best to do that, being a no-tail myself."

The Ardu all twitched their tails in unconscious dread.

"But I have to do my best. There's still a lot to teach the Ardu about war and you'll need to know those things before next year if you are to defeat the slavers."

"Mirchaz come to Ardu lands, we kill Mirchaz," said Ium hotly.

"But why they deny that you save the people, Relkin?" said Pumo.

"I don't know, Pumo. Sometimes people just can't handle the truth. It's too painful perhaps."

"Ium know they tell lies. It hurt Ium to see that grandmothers tell lies, because lies are weak. Ium had always thought that grandmothers were strong. Now Ium know this: Only the truth is truly strong! The tribe is what we must be. All kin groups must come together. Then we will kill Mirchaz."

Relkin nodded, used by now to Ium's casual savagery.

Mother help the slavers, he thought, if they ever faced the Ardu nation in battle.

"The pujish are moving," grunted Wol.

It was true. The distant shapes were stirring. Within a few moments Relkin saw the huge heads lift from the ground and shift this way and that as their owners took in the world around them. Then the young red-browns rose to their feet, pushing themselves off from the ground with their diminutive front limbs. Immediately they were in motion. At this distance Relkin was reminded of the way birds move, active, light on their feet, taking quick, precise steps. It was chilling to think how huge the brutes were that were walking so quickly over the hill, and these were not even half grown. Relkin was enormously relieved that they were heading away from him, back to the pit. Then they were gone from view.

Though not from earshot. A few minutes later there came a series of great roars from the direction of the pit. The young red-browns were contesting possession of the remains once again with the lame male.

The scouts had seen enough. There was little to be gained by going any closer. The pujish were awake and they were gorging on what was left of the three-horns cow in the pit. Back along the hills they trailed, heading for the camp. The Ardu would have to move north as quickly as possible to be sure of avoiding these pujish.

Near the camp they ran into another scout party, led by big Ommi. Big Ommi greeted them cheerfully enough, but there was always something in his eyes that told Relkin he would never be forgiven for what he and Lumbee had done. Uper of Black Lake and Bunad of Red Rock clasped forearms with Wol and Ium and even with Relkin. Pumo they merely nodded to, since he was not yet fully adult.

Ommi's group had been around to the far side of the pit, where they had seen the old male wake up. They confirmed that he was full-grown, but had a pronounced limp. One foot had been crushed at some point in his life. He remained enormously dangerous, of course, and best avoided.

Wol gave their group's report while they marched. The

pujish would be busy for the rest of this day cleaning up
what was left of the three-horns cow. Then they would
probably lie up for a day or so, and then they would hunt
once more for meat, either fresh or carrion.

They found the camp already half dismantled. Everyone worked with great dispatch. Before the morning
was very far advanced they were on the move, heading
north in a ragged column, with scouts in front and on
either side.

Bazil marched near the center of the tribe, to one side
of the column, with Relkin beside him and several Ardu
youngsters bouncing along around them, peppering them
with endless questions.

The day's march was uneventful. The scouts reported
only very distant herds of three-horns, and no sign of
pujish at all.

That night they camped on an island in the midst of the
stream and made no fire, to avoid attracting pujish.
Everyone had to be content with a small meal of nuts and
berries, except for the dragon, who ate the last of the
three-horns meat they carried.

Bazil slept the early watch. Relkin stayed awake and
was kept company on watch by Wol and Pumo. They
asked him many questions about the outer world and he
did his best to satisfy their curiosity, worrying now and
then how good a picture he was painting for them.

During the night they heard distant bellows from a herd
of three-horns that appeared to be moving from west to
east across their trail a few miles to the south. This was
regarded as excellent news, since the passage of such a
herd would obliterate any trail they might have left. Even
better, it would divert the attention of the red-browns and
lead them off into the east as well.

Relkin let the dragon sleep on. If there was an emergency, he'd be awakened soon enough. The wyvern
needed a good night's rest. They all ultimately depended
on him and the great sword.

When men from the Red Rocks and Heather Hills took
over the watch, Relkin went and sat beside the recumbent
form of the wyvern. Bazil slumbered easily enough.
Relkin looked him over with the concerned eye of a

dragonboy, however. In recent days there hadn't been time for adequate care of the dragon. Relkin made a note for himself to check Bazil's feet the very next morning. He had no skin toughener, no liniment, in fact none of the usual lotions and tonics that dragonboys depended on. On the other hand, Wulla had told him how to crush certain berries to get a juice that would ease swellings. Lumbee had shown him how to prepare a dozen other plants in order to obtain active juices and poultices. Some of these things had worked pretty well on Bazil's cuts and bruises.

From a piece of hammered three-horns hide, Relkin had made himself a wrap in which to sleep. He had been surprised at the way the hide, initially stiff from curing in the sun, had softened when the old women beat it with clubs. He had rolled this wrap up tightly, bound it with thongs, and wore it over his shoulder when they marched. Now he loosened the thongs and unrolled the wrap. Inside, a long piece of bone glowed slightly in the moonlight.

Feeling the hairs crawl on the back of his neck, Relkin picked the bone up. It was undoubtedly human, the upper part of a femur. It was yellowed with age and worn smooth. The break was clean, as if it had been cut with something very sharp.

Relkin was sure this was not a good sign. After a moment or two of calculation, he put it aside and lay down and wrapped himself up. How long had it been in his roll? Who had put it there? What did it portend? It was obviously some kind of Ardu magic, but what was its purpose?

He sighed deeply. Relkin of Quosh had been exposed to a lot of magic in his young life. So far nothing had either crippled him or managed to kill him.

What could it all mean? What did the bone symbolize? He shrugged and pulled his wrap around him and set himself to sleep. Whatever it was, there was nothing he could do about it at that moment. Soon, with a soldier's ability to sleep anywhere, anytime, he slid away into dreams.

In the morning, he saw Lumbee and asked her what it was.

She blanched.

"Show me," she demanded.

He pulled it out.

" 'Tis the death bone," she said grimly. "They have marked you for death. It is the grandmothers from Yellow Canyon, we can be sure of that."

"What does it mean?"

"Ardu folk cannot have anything to do with one who is marked with death bone. He ceases to exist for them. Even if he strikes them down, they take no heed and accept the blow as a thing from the gods. They cannot see him. They cannot hear him."

"I was afraid it might be something like that. What can I do about it?"

"Nothing," Lumbee said. She was as forlorn as Relkin had ever seen her. "You cannot even get rid of the bone. If you throw it away, they will fetch it and put it back with you when you sleep. If you bury it, they will dig it up. If you throw it into the lake, they will swim out and find it. You cannot escape the death bone."

Chapter Twenty

Over the next few days the tribe was riven into a majority that obeyed the law of the death bone and ceased to take any notice of Relkin, and a minority that was sufficiently brave to defy ancient custom and continue to associate with the outland no-tail.

As one result, the military training program was crippled. It had reached the level of small group tactics, and Relkin had seen the Ardu make great advances, but now the men stopped coming and he was forced to admit that perhaps his time among the Ardu was at an end.

Bazil was ready to move on. Though the food was good and plentiful, the wyvern was growing bored with the soft life he had been living on the plains. In addition he missed the company of his own kind. There was no company to be had among the flat-headed pujish with their tiny brains and vicious ways. He missed his friends in the old 109th fighting Marneri dragons. He missed the Purple Green and Alsebra. He even missed Vlok, though he would never have admitted it.

In a desperate bid to break the spell of the death bone, Relkin ostentatiously burned it in a special fire of his own. With elaborate ceremony he built the fire high, using only the driest wood so that it burned splendidly. He made sure that nothing was left. He strode around the camp telling various men what he had done, even though, of course, they had known all along. He sat openly with Ium and Wol at the evening fire and ate roasted three-horns meat.

That night, as he slept, a new death bone, almost identical to the old one, was placed by his head. When he

awoke, his eye fell at once on the top half of a human
thigh bone. A chill spread through his heart.

His incineration of the other bone did not produce any
converts, either. He was still a nonperson to more than
half the tribe.

Relkin knew the source of the venom, and so did poor
Pumo, who came to Relkin's fire that night and confessed
that he felt he had to give in and go back to the tutelage of
the Yellow Canyon grandmothers. Until he did so, they
would not cease their campaign to drive Relkin away.

Relkin persuaded Pumo not to surrender. Pumo
belonged to the tribe now. He loved Wulla as if she were
his real mother. He liked all the Red Rocks children. It
was not as if he were without family and friends. To go
back to the Yellow Canyon grandmothers would hurt the
tribe. Relkin confessed that he and the dragon would be
leaving soon anyway. It was time for them to head north.
They had a long journey ahead of them and they needed
to start soon. They had to return to their own world.

Pumo wept the open, unselfconscious tears of the Ardu
at this news, for he loved Relkin as a brother. Wol and
Ium were also saddened, but they had expected this for
some time. They could sense the dragon's restlessness
and Relkin's feelings of futility as the death bone took its
grip on the folk.

Still, Relkin struggled to complete the training course
he had begun. There were a few men, including mighty
Norwul, who would still listen. They came and sat a short
distance away from him so that they would not be seen
befriending the no-tail, but still close enough so they
could see and hear clearly while Relkin demonstrated,
with the help of Ium and Wol, how the Argonath Legions
trained men to fight in small groups. Combinations were
the key to success. Every man had to be looking out for
the welfare of every other man. Every fighter had to be
flexible in approach and prepared to give his life for those
around him. When these fundamentals were accepted,
then came training to proficiency with sword, spear, and
shield.

The Ardu were only just now learning the value of a
good shield. Relkin and Wol had made a few, using

flexible green wood and sections of three-horns hide. Relkin and the young Ardu sparred with clubs and shields and sometimes with blunt spears, and Relkin passed on all he knew of feints and blocks, kicks and rolls, and all the other maneuvers of close-order combat that he had assimilated in his life as a dragonboy in the Legions of Argonath. He'd been gratified to see shields passing around among the men, who were already experimenting with design and decoration.

He felt that he'd done his best and that if they stayed together and continued to train as he'd taught them, the Ardu men would be able to give a good account of themselves in any fight with the slavers. The Ardu people would have a fighting chance at survival.

One day Relkin, Ium, and Wol went out to hunt for small hopping beasts the Ardu called yoosh. These were smaller than a man, but very speedy, running on two legs and capable of leaping into the branches of trees at a moment's notice. To hunt them successfully took good coordination among a group, and good spear throwing.

They headed east, toward the big river. There was good yoosh country there, with open grasslands dotted with small forests. The yoosh fed in the grasslands and retreated swiftly to the treetops when pujish appeared.

The men hunted, always with an eye out for pujish themselves, through the heat of the day, but discovered only a wugga, a squat, four-legged brute covered in armored plate and with a pair of horns on the end of its tail. The wugga ignored them and though they briefly considered it, they moved on. Wugga were very hard to kill, and surprisingly dangerous for such sluggish-looking beasts. They could whip those horned tails around with lethal speed. Besides, the request from Wulla was for yoosh. She intended to roast yoosh and have it with a sauce made from apples. Fresh jungle apples were appearing now on trees scattered through the forest. Everyone in the Red Rock group maintained that eating Wulla's roast yoosh with apple sauce was one of the great gustatory experiences in the world and not to be missed.

The appearance of the jungle apples was another sign of the turn of the seasons. Soon the tribe would head into the northern hills for the second quarter of the year, the lush time of the light rains. The berries were ripening there and young, fat shmunga and untishmunga would be on the trails. The Ardu would stake the pits once more and feast on the young shmunga.

Relkin had made up his mind to leave the tribe at that point. He and Baz would make a boat and go downstream on the same river that he and Lumbee had ascended. They would return to the Inland Sea and then head east. With luck they would find the kingdom of the Kraheen and rejoin the Legions. They had been out of all contact with the Legions for almost a year. Relkin knew that they'd been given up for dead by now. What a shock everyone was going to get! He looked forward to seeing friends' expressions when he and the dragon showed up alive. The Purple Green, in particular, would be a treat to see when Bazil came back!

By late afternoon they'd reached a bluff with a view across the river. To the east the hills glowed purple. Some huge shmunga had plowed through the forests here not long before leaving a trail of broken trees and mowed reed beds. Long-necked shmunga, the enormous critters that had almost done in Relkin and Bazil once, were too huge to hunt, or even to stake a pit for. The Ardu regarded adult shmunga as sacred beasts and would never kill them. The fact that big shmunga killed pujish, usually by smashing their skulls with the tail whip, made them seem godlike to the tailed folk. Young shmunga, however, were fair game, but hard to hunt, since they were usually protected by their elders.

Suddenly Relkin stiffened. Out on the river, which was swollen with runoff from the rains, bobbed a small boat, single-masted with a big white bellying sail. Relkin's blood chilled. The Ardu did not use sails in their canoes and dugouts.

"Slavers," said Ium beside him in a whisper.

"Early in season for slavers," muttered Wol.

"They are searching for the tribe," said Relkin with complete certainty. "The damage we did them must have set off a reaction. I bet there are parties like this all over the plains, hunting for the Ardu."

"They want to find the tribe and take all Ardu back as slaves."

"They have to stop the growth of the tribe. It's a direct threat to them."

Ium and Wol saw the point of this instantly.

"We have to tell everyone. Tribe must move north early. Stay away from slavers."

Relkin nodded slowly. Another idea had occurred to him. "We could take them as prisoners. Find out why they're so far up country so early in the year."

As the boat tacked in close, just below the bluff, they could clearly see the three men, brown-skinned, massively built. They turned perhaps a hundred feet from the shore and then tacked back toward the opposite side of the river. After a while the boat disappeared around the next bend.

That night they camped on the bluff. The dark came quickly, as it always did in the Ardu land, and soon after they observed a light burning off in the canyonland, some miles distant. The slavers had put in to shore for the night. Relkin watched the distant glitter for a long time. He wondered just how strong a response the slaver cities would make.

These were scouts, most likely, searching for the tribe. Maybe they had already mounted a punitive expedition. Tales of the forest god must have been a shock. The Ardu could not be allowed to progress to nationhood.

The question was, what should the tribe do in response? Fade into the hills? Or take the initiative and capture these slavers and interrogate them? Find out just what they might be receiving in the next summer season. Then with better intelligence on their enemy's plan they might fade into the hills if need be, or else try to come up with a more aggressive strategy. Aggression might cost lives, however, and it was inherently risky. Relkin wondered if a resumption of ambushes on slaver groups would reduce the slaver presence in the Ardu territories or spur yet further expeditions. The Ardu needed to raise a small army, several hundred strong. And that army had to be trained, at least in Relkin's view, if it was to have any chance of success. The slavers would bring mercenary troops, well

armed, seasoned with years of warfare. The Ardu, still virtually Stone Age in culture and technical skill, would have
no chance unless they had learned how to fight together in
a large group. They were used to one-on-one combats and
very occasional melees between two kin groups, but not to
battles between forces with several hundred on either side.

He wrapped himself and lay down to sleep for a while
as Ium took the watch. Who could he call on for help?
They might need ten men to be sure of success. They had
to be sure of capturing all three and getting their boat.
Apart from Ium and Wol there was Norwul and probably
Uper of Black Lake and Mogs of Sunny Bank. That gave
them six, a minimum number.

At dawn they moved out, heading upriver in pursuit
of the slavers. The bottomlands were covered in a forest
of gloomy conifers that shaded out the ground. They
made good time, therefore, unimpeded by brush. Relkin
had some hope that they might catch up to the slavers.
What they would do then would depend on events. If they
could take them unawares, then he and his two young
friends might capture them. If not, then at least they
would learn more. A larger party would have to be called
up back at camp.

Their pursuit was fruitless, however. They cut across
the ridgeline, passed a trail where shmunga had cut a
swath through the forest, and came down to the river
again. The slavers had already broken camp and moved
on. Relkin glimpsed the sail, far down the next reach of
the river.

"We must head back. No point in trying to catch a boat
on foot."

Wol and Ium accepted this. The Ardu were swift of
foot, but had less endurance than Relkin, who had long
ago been hardened to long marching.

They climbed the nearby bluff to fix their bearings
before heading back to the main camp. Relkin was preoccupied with thoughts of who he would try to recruit for
the ambush party. They reached an outlook where white
limestone broke through the green and gained a view out
over the land to the west as well as the east.

Far away loomed the mass of the northern hills known

as Gunja Luba, the "Safe Land," where the slavers had never been and where the pujish had long ago been hunted out. There the Ardu would spend the next season until the land began to dry out and it was time to trek back to the southern forest for its fruits and fibers.

They ate some dried sausage made with three-horn meat and drank from a small stream spattering down the bluff.

Relkin surveyed the distant river reach once more. He wondered if they should cut across the next bend. This reach was perhaps five miles in length—they might save themselves almost that many by going across the ridge. Of course, once they were up on the ridge the undergrowth would get thicker and their progress would be slowed. Once over it, though, they would be on the edge of the plain and could hope for better speed for the rest of the way back.

Relkin turned back to ask Wol his opinion, when he heard a cry followed almost instantly by a thud. There followed a confused mélange of images. Ardu men were beating Wol and Ium with their clubs. Big Ommi was there. Big Ommi swung a massive fist into Relkin's face and Relkin found himself on his back the next moment, dazed and bloody. He shook his head to try and clear it, to little avail. His jaw felt like it might be broken.

Ommi and another Ardu hauled him up to his feet and dragged him to the edge of the bluff. Below was an almost sheer cliff falling straight to the river.

"Good-bye, no-tail, we don't need you here," said Big Ommi.

The next moment Relkin was in midair, arms pinwheeling to keep himself upright. Was the water deep enough?

He barely had time to pose the question before he went in feet first and drove deep into the river and sank up to his knees in mud. The shock jarred every bone in his body, but his legs didn't break. He rolled out of the mud, kicked frantically to free his legs, and rose in a huge cloud of mud to the surface, rising just in time to fill his collapsing lungs with air.

He lay at the surface, coughing a little, gasping,

treading water. Looking up, he saw nothing but the tawny walls of the bluff, which already seemed to be dwindling as he drifted slowly downstream.

The shock, the pain in his jaw, and the luck of surviving that fall combined to leave him stunned. He drifted. He prayed that they did not kill Wol and Ium. That could start a blood feud between the kin groups. By the gods, his face hurt. Ommi could really land a punch. Relkin didn't think anyone had ever hit him so hard before.

He let himself drift, with an occasional kick. He felt for his sword and found it was gone. He had only the knife.

Nor did he have his little hunter's bow; he'd set it aside when they stopped to eat.

Old Caymo had rolled the dice pretty damn badly there. Relkin prayed that they would spare Ium and Wol. Ommi, damn him! Of course it would be Ommi. Relkin had expected some kind of blow from Ommi for a long time. Ommi had seethed for weeks.

After floating for a while, he kicked slowly toward the far shore, trying to keep an eye out for crocodiles, which infested some reaches of the river, but not others. It seemed that this was one of the latter.

It seemed to take a long time, but at last he staggered out of the water and onto a pebbled beach. The bank was lined with gnarled and twisted roots, and small trees hung overhead. He hauled himself up and crouched, listening carefully. You could usually hear large pujish approaching, even though they were very quiet for their size, but it was best to be absolutely sure.

Nothing stirred except insects. The coast seemed clear. He left the cover of the small trees and started up an open slope toward the higher ground. There was further forest there.

He was perhaps halfway across when there came a dismaying roar from the trees ahead. Relkin flattened himself to the ground. It was devoid of cover here, and a footrace to the river with a big pujish was out of the question; the pujish were much too fast.

There was a tremendous crunching of trees and undergrowth and a series of enormous roars and then a huge red-brown burst out of the forest. It was full-grown, bigger than any wyvern, bigger even than the mighty Purple Green of Hook Mountain, with a vast head filled with teeth like daggers. Relkin was both awed and terrified. Caymo had sent some bad dice Relkin's way in his time, but never anything quite this bad. Old Gongo was going to get a pretty chewed-up dragonboy when he came to take him to the halls of the dead.

But then the dice wobbled. There came another terrifying roar that made the ground shudder, and then the monster stepped forward with that curiously precise, almost mincing gait, which seemed incongruous in an animal this large. It stepped past Relkin, taking no notice at all of the small prone form on the ground.

Amazed to be alive, Relkin dared to peek up. The pujish went past, downslope toward the small trees that fringed the river. It had its great head cocked, as if it were listening for something. In a moment it came, a distant roar, followed by another and then a string of them. Relkin understood—there was a rivalry. They were marking out their territories. They probably did this every day.

As Relkin watched, the huge monster threw its head back and emitted another roar. The stiff tail and low-slung carriage of the body was more accentuated than it was in wyverns, and the head was all wrong, with the flatness of the forehead, where wyverns bulged with intelligence. The first roar was followed by more, a long series of satisfying bellows aimed at warning all others of its kind that this was its territory. Then it moved again, stepping down to the water, where it roared again.

It was time to move while the creature was preoccupied. Relkin scrambled to his feet and bolted into the forest. He turned upstream and kept going, ignoring the aches and pains in his legs following the jump. One place you didn't want to be, if alone and virtually without weapons, was on the ground close to active pujish.

When he paused for a breath, listening with every fiber of his being for nearby sounds in the woods, he was struck by the power of the death bone. The grandmothers had laid the death bone by his head and he'd been unable to shake it. And now it was hunting him. That damned death bone was coming for him.

Chapter Twenty-one

Relkin awoke in the crook of a tree, sore in far too many places. When he shifted position, his back went into spasm and he nearly fell out of the tree. And on top of all the aches and pains, he'd slept badly, waking in sudden fright at loud sounds in the jungle. At night some pujish were very active, which wasn't conducive to a sound night's rest.

He prayed to Old Caymo to stop rolling those dice for a while. Relkin was having trouble handling the results. He consoled himself with the thought that at least nothing had tried to eat him in the night.

He started down. More aches and pains informed him that he had not escaped unscathed from that fall from the bluff into the river. Nothing was broken, but a lot of things were tender, from the ankles to the knees to the hips.

He repeated the sobering inventory from the previous night. He had a long knife and some of his tool kit, which had survived the river. He'd lost his boots, stuck in the gluey mud. Relkin shrugged; those boots had been pretty well played out anyway. His feet would harden up pretty quick. He just had to watch out for thorns from now on.

The first necessity of the day was to find something to eat. Armed with only a knife, he would have to content himself with fruit or nuts for the time being. Once he'd made himself a new hunting bow, then things would improve.

He looked around for the trees that Lumbee had made him familiar with, the eem and the pik-o-pok in particular, since these were in season. At first he saw nothing but pines; then he saw a grove of pik-o-poks and headed that way.

He was in luck. These pik-o-poks were filled with nearly ripe pods. In a few minutes he'd cut enough for a breakfast of sorts. Then he split open the pods and ate the large, tasty beans inside. They had a sweet, nutty flavor and a coarse consistency. He filled up on them and then drank from a clear-running stream. He rose refreshed, his hunger sated at least in part, and after stretching exercises he reduced the soreness from the long, uncomfortable night in that tree.

He went slowly, ears alert for the slightest sound that might indicate pujish. Without Bazil on hand to wield mighty Ecator, or even a bow, Relkin felt decidedly unsafe in these ancient woods.

He searched for a place to make a quick crossing of the river. He decided it would be better to cross on a log rather than swimming, because of the risk of crocodiles. He'd been very fortunate the day before. Caymo was rolling some weird dice these days, that was for sure.

Then, as he often did, Relkin fell to wondering if the Great Mother was still guiding his steps. Did her presence pervade even here, in this wild land beyond the back of nowhere? Perhaps things were getting kind of shaky because she could no longer protect him from the effects of Caymo's dice play. And he knew that the strands of fortune were subject to wild shifts. There were levels of understanding that existed far beyond the world Ryetelth. Relkin had seen this, had heard the strange singing of the golden ones.

By the gods, but his legs hurt! That impact in the mud had come close to breaking his ankles.

He confronted the next problem in his mind: how to extract Bazil from the tribe without them realizing Relkin had survived.

Of course, he didn't have to do it that way. He could just go back to the camp publicly and accuse Ommi of trying to kill him. He could get justice for Wol and Ium if they'd been killed.

And he would also split the tribe irrevocably. The Ardu would fragment and be left virtually defenseless against the slavers once more. If they followed the natural round and went south, the slavers would get them. If they stayed in the north, they would starve. Even their gardens would fail them after a while. They could hunt three-horns by the lake, but that would mean competing with full-grown red-brown pujish, who were too much for Ardu spears and stones. The Ardu would be scattered and devoured and all Relkin's work would be wasted. Whatever they did they would be doomed, unless they banded together into a tribe and learned how to fight with their numbers to completely destroy the parties of slave raiders.

Relkin doubted that Caymo had ever thrown him more of a difficult play. For it went without saying that Relkin would go back to the camp and find the wyvern. No force in the world could keep a dragonboy from finding his dragon.

But how was he going to sneak a wyvern dragon away from a camp full of Ardu hunters? There was always someone on watch. Relkin thought about suppressing the watch. He did have the knife. It was a grim thought, but if he had to do it to free the dragon, then he would.

On his own, Relkin knew, Bazil would be lost. He might try heading north alone—and if anything could live in this jungle and prosper it was probably a two-ton battledragon armed with the fell blade Ecator—but without a dragonboy there would be problems with little wounds, split talons, parasites, and many other things. Relkin imagined the wyvern hunting for him up and down the land of Ardu suffering from a host of misery-inducing ailments.

No, Relkin had to go back. And then they'd have to sneak out of the camp with no one seeing them. Not an easy task, even if wyverns were naturally sneaky and capable of moving very quietly. And then they'd have to leave, with no good-byes. Anything else would only cause trouble and split the tribe. And Relkin was determined not to split the Ardu people. But it would be sad to leave without saying farewell to Lumbee.

He just prayed they hadn't killed Ium and Wol.

He finished the pods, then moved on. Intending to investigate the shoreline, he moved closer to the river,

where he caught the smell of woodsmoke. Faint, but
unmistakable, a fire was burning nearby. The rains were
too recent for it to be a natural fire. Relkin felt impelled to
investigate. The slavers must have hauled up their boat
for the day. Perhaps they were in trouble? Sickness, or
damage to the boat, whatever, Relkin knew he had to take
a look at them.

For the next hour he moved stealthily toward the source
of the smoke. As it grew stronger, he slowed his
approach, eyes searching the way ahead for any hint of
man. Eventually he looked out across a wide sandy
clearing in the brush. The river loomed down below the
beach. In the center was the smoldering remains of a fire.
There was no one in sight.

Cautiously he approached the smoldering embers. The
slavers were long gone. They had camped here the night
before. Relkin could read the signs of disturbance in the
sand. They had done a poor job of putting out their fire
when they left.

He scuffed sand to smother the embers, then walked
down to the water's edge to scan the water. No sail
showed itself on the river. It was irrational, he knew, but
he was disappointed. Some part of him had half expected
to see that triangle of white. He had just started to turn
when he felt something whir around his head and drop
past his shoulders.

In the next instant it tightened into an expertly thrown
lasso and his arms were pinned to his body. The shock
was considerable, the surprise total. He braced himself
and dug in his heels, but was still pulled off his feet and
drawn helplessly across the sand by a powerful pull from
the edge of the trees. A man appeared in his peripheral
vision. A club was swinging. Then came the impact and
the light went away in a blaze of sickening pain.

When he woke up, it was to a thundering headache and
a regular, rhythmic motion. Wind soughed over him; he
glimpsed the sky above and a billowing sail. He felt distinctly nauseous and for a few moments lay there just
breathing, hoping the urge to vomit would subside. At last
it began to ebb and finally left him, but he was weak and
felt cold sweat running down his back.

He shook his head to try to clear it, not altogether successfully. For a moment the nausea threatened to return. He made some more unpleasant discoveries. His wrists were bound behind him. His ankles were bound as well. The bonds had an expert feel to them, tight but not so tight as to cut off circulation.

Deliberately he looked up. Sitting watching him was a man with the coldest eyes Relkin had ever seen. Under a black topknot oiled and skewered with red lacquer needles, the eyes regarded him for a moment with cold humor.

The man spoke, over Relkin's head. Relkin heard a sour chuckle behind him. He noted the man's heavily muscled chest and arms, the leather vest and leggings and the brass-handled cutlass stuck in his belt. The man had the air of someone used to violence in all its forms.

There was more laughter behind Relkin and a big hand grabbed his face, which sent a flash of pain from his sore jaw, and turned it so he was looking into that of a fat man, red-faced, head shaved, with a big round nose and close-set brown eyes. He exuded a malicious glee. The red-faced fellow said something in Ardu that Relkin didn't catch, then repeated it in another tongue to the one with the topknot.

The red-faced man let go of his face with a laugh and Relkin caught a glimpse of a third man, tall, gray-faced, with stringy hair, but then his gaze dropped back to fall on the first man again.

The man said something in the slaver tongue. It was meaningless to Relkin, who shrugged. The man laughed. He had a cruel laugh. The man switched to crude Ardu. The pronunciation was off, but it was intelligible. Relkin was not surprised; of course the slavers had learned a smattering of the tongue of the people they preyed upon.

"You are No-Tail. We search for No-Tail. You just drop into our laps. Very good."

The man had the most unpleasant smile.

"Caught you sneaking around. Easy. One of the oldest tricks."

Relkin felt a hot flush creeping up his cheeks. Of course, just leave the fire burning a little, the Ardu would come to investigate, and then you took them captive with the rope and the cudgel. Damn! He hated to be thought of as "easy."

"Who are you, then?" said Relkin angrily.

"I Katun. Of Mirchaz. The slave city only. I take you there. You fetch a record price. Ardu No-Tail. Already the game lords seek you. You attract a lot of attention. You regret this."

Again the merciless smile. Relkin suspected the scarlet skewers indicated some kind of caste or elite status.

"Who them?" Relkin indicated with his head.

"That is Bilj, and Eidorf. Bilj, he want to take you like a woman. That is Bilj's way with boys like you."

Relkin's alarm must have showed, despite his effort to betray no emotion, because Katun smiled again, a little softer this time. "Katun kill Bilj, he touch hair of your head. You safe from Bilj while Katun alive."

Relkin swallowed. And Eidorf? Eidorf didn't seem worthy of a mention to Katun, at least in this context.

"We go south now, quick, quick. Get to Yazm City in few days. Then big boat to Mirchaz. We sell you in a moon."

This seemed to really amuse Katun.

Chapter Twenty-two

For a week they followed the same routine. The rains had dwindled to occasional downpours, followed by blue skies and a burning sun that soon dried them out.

Nights were spent on small sandy beaches, usually with a fire blazing and a strict watch kept for pujish. The slavers were very nervous about the presence of pujish which they called kebbold, the name in the tongue of Mirchaz. Kebbold were always called "bloodthirsty" or "man-eating" and were spoken of with special loathing. Relkin understood better why the slavers had always limited their raids to the southern forest, where the pujish were few and far between.

Days were spent in the boat, always bound at wrist and ankle. Katun himself made sure of Relkin's bonds. He was released briefly, to eat and relieve himself in the evening and in the morning. Calluses grew on his wrists and ankles.

On one occasion when a big green pujish showed itself at the campfire and began to make threatening advances, the slavers ran for it. Katun simply grabbed Relkin and threw him over his shoulder, sprang nimbly to the boat, and shoved it off in the next moment with an incredible heave. Relkin now realized that Katun was an unusually strong man. Combined with his speed and undoubted prowess with weapons, he was a deadly combination. Relkin wondered what some of the other great fighters he had known in his time would make of Katun. He also realized that any attempt to escape would have to be well planned. If he had to kill Katun, he would have to strike without warning and be successful with his first blow. Relkin knew that in combat with Katun he would have little chance, and Relkin of Quosh had fought in many battles and faced all manner of opponents. Relkin suspected that Katun was a gladiator, a born killer of swordsmen, and beyond Relkin's own power.

He also understood why surly Bilj obeyed Katun's strictures and avoided contact with Relkin. Bilj and Eidorf kept to the other end of the boat. For this Relkin was grateful, but he did his best not to seem so. To Katun he had to maintain a front, a mask for his emotions. At no time could he reveal the despair he was beginning to feel.

Between Katun and Bilj there existed a constant undertone of dislike and unspoken violence. Relkin sensed that Bilj would have killed Katun in an instant if he dared, but understood that Katun was the better man.

Eidorf, an older man of few words, barely seemed to associate with either of the others. Relkin learned that Eidorf had once been a soldier, a man of honor, and now felt much reduced in the world. Eidorf received little but contempt from Bilj, while Katun hardly ever spoke to him, though Relkin noticed that Katun did not treat Eidorf with contempt.

No opportunity to escape ever presented itself. The Mirchaz slavers' techniques for restraining a captive were foolproof. And in his case they were making a special effort. Relkin learned that there was a reward out for him. He had been identified during the summer battles as a leader of the rebel Ardu and freed slaves. The Slaver Associations had offered a brick of gold called a tabi for him. Katun was determined to collect that tabi and retire from the slave business.

That was not the end of it, however. Beyond the reward was the price that might be obtained by selling him to the lords. Apparently there were lords who would pay a fine fortune for Relkin. Between the lords there was strong competition to win such prizes as were represented by occasional freaks like Relkin. Such prizes might be displayed at social gatherings, sometimes in cages, and they might also be used in darker, more secret ways, for the lords were magicians all, and both old and very wicked.

Relkin's mental picture of the city they were going to had become clearer over the course of some conversations with Katun. It was a large place, and very old. Katun said the Lords Tetraan had come from the far north, at the end of the Old Red Aeon. They had been led by a great prince, Zizma Bos of Gelderen. Under Bos and the Arkelauds the lords had set to building a great city of marbled streets, great public buildings of white stone, palaces, libraries, concourses, and huge monumental structures that were used for the Great Game of the Lords Tetraan.

This had become the Upper City and it was enclosed within high walls and mighty gates. Outside the walls there was a "lower" city, known as the City of Slaves because the bulk of its population consisted of former slaves, many of them elderly and worked out, who were no longer useful and were simply ejected from the city and left to their own devices. Most died within a year or two, but while they lived they formed a lumpen mass of gray-faced white-hairs who formed the bottom layer of the society of the Slave City.

One thing Relkin learned early on was that most slaves were no-tails. The Ardu, in fact, were unusual and highly sought after for their physical beauty. Most of the slaves came from tribes in the western interior of Eigo. Large organizations dominated the slave trade in those regions. It was in the more dangerous Ardu trade that buccaneers like Katun could hope to make some gold.

Beyond the lumpen mass of elderly slaves was another population of drifters, adventurers, merchants, and cutthroats. Laws were enforced by the Upper City. Relkin gathered that there was a kind of legion which served to protect the Upper City from physical attack. This legion was recruited from all over the world. Katun had once belonged to it, as had Eidorf.

The Upper City was a complicated place. There were several levels, of increasing exclusivity as one approached the City of the Temples and the Game Board. In addition there were eyries set high above the city called the Overlooks. These were occupied by the leading lords as ranked in the Great Game that was played in the Pyramid of the Game. Every mention of this Game brought a tone of reverence into Katun's voice, though to Relkin's questions concerning it, Katun gave few answers. Relkin felt that Katun was acutely aware of his loss of social status. He had been ejected from the Upper City when he'd been kicked out of the Guardians, as the protective legion was called, and he yearned to return to that life. He regarded his sojourn in the Slave City as an aberration of which he was ashamed.

Of Katun's life before he'd migrated to Mirchaz, Relkin learned much less. Katun was evidently not proud of that era, either.

Toward the folk of the Slave City Katun had little but contempt. For the Lords Tetraan, who competed in the Great Game, he was filled with conflicting emotions. Relkin detected envy, desire, and a kind of hate. Relkin came to understand that Katun felt he should belong to the lord class himself. He despised both the slaves and the thieves in the outer city.

The frontier town of Yazm City appeared one day as they rounded a bend. It was a mean little place, huddled along the bank of the river. Most of the buildings were of logs and rough-hewn timber. There were a dozen jetties and some dilapidated docks. Beside the docks were large cages, now empty, but Relkin knew they had been full just a few months earlier, jammed with Ardu slaves.

Katun didn't care to waste any time in Yazm City. Bilj protested, but got nowhere. The whorehouses and saloons would have to do without their business. They took their small boat into a jetty. Katun negotiated briefly with the jettyman and sold the boat for pretty close to what he'd paid for it. Then they went across and boarded the big river brig that was tied up at the longest jetty. It was single-masted and schooner-rigged and well maintained from the look of it.

Relkin was taken below and chained up in a dark closet. His wrists were cuffed to a single chain attached to the ceiling. This chain was long enough to leave him some freedom of movement—he could scratch himself, for instance, a relief from days of torment—and the lack of restraints on his ankles was another great relief. Not that there was enough room to move around or anything. Friendly rats came to investigate his clothes and hair, but

found nothing to seriously interest them and eventually
left him alone.

While he was asleep the brig slipped her moorings.
When he woke up he felt the different motion of the hull
and the slap of waves against the bow and knew they were
on their way. Mirchaz loomed ever closer.

The routine was quickly established. Meals were
simple, basically just bread and water, with one small
piece of fruit a day. Exercise was taken on the deck, with
a long chain running from his wrist cuffs to a belt around
Katun's waist.

As before, Relkin could see no way of escaping except
by somehow overpowering Katun. However, Katun was
an experienced slaver who understood the wiles of desperate captives all too well. Relkin saw no opportunity.

Of the others, Relkin saw little. Bilj seemed to sleep
most of the time, and Eidorf sat up in the bow all day,
alone.

Relkin had time to study the crew. There were five
sailors and the captain, a burly brute with a missing eye.
All were capable men and their ship was trim and well
handled. They made good time on the long reaches of the
river. None spoke enough Ardu to converse with, however, which limited Relkin's inquiries.

The country changed as they passed through it. The
dark-leaved forest of the Lands of Terror gave way to a
forest of palm trees and then a forest of many different
kinds of trees, but with a lighter green than that of the
realm of the pujish and the mighty shmunga.

As the days went by, Relkin sank into a deep depression. Escape seemed impossible and he had come a long
way from the land of the Ardu. How was he going to get
back and find his dragon? How was his dragon going to
manage without a dragonboy?

His faith in the gods had sunk to a new low. He caught
himself whispering the prayers he'd learned as a child, to
the Great Mother, who was said to hear all, see all, feel
all, and know all. Relkin had never really believed this;
now he hoped he'd been wrong all these years. If ever he
needed her help it was now.

In an attempt to keep his spirits up he questioned Katun

as much as possible. Sometimes Katun would allow himself to be engaged. At other times he would be irritated by something and would fall silent before dragging Relkin down below and chaining him in the dark closet.

Katun disliked owning up to the fact that he knew so little of the outer world. He knew the interior of the continent Eigo, but he had never seen the oceans, not even the inland ocean the Wad Al Nub, from which Relkin had come to the land of the Ardu. Katun had heard of their existence and he soon came to believe some of the things Relkin told him about the rest of the world, but he hated the thought of his own ignorance and made up for it by denigrating Relkin's intelligence whenever possible.

One day Katun mentioned Bos while talking about the northlands. Katun knew very little about the north except that Bos came from there, accompanied by the Lords Tetraan.

"Who was Bos?"

"You know nothing, just like Ardu. Stupid as pigs."

"I just don't know who Bos is."

"Bos founded the great city. He come from the holy lands, long ago. You will see very soon now."

Katun got to his feet. "Come." He hauled on the chain and dragged Relkin down into the dark.

Another time Katun asked Relkin about the faint scars on his back, acquired from the lashes given him by dwarves in an underground city in the magic forest of Valur far away.

Relkin tried to explain, but at the mention of dwarves, Katun snorted and refused to listen to any more. Dwarves no longer lived in the world. On this point he was adamant. He accused Relkin of lying about his wounds.

"Probably caught thieving. Don't want to admit that you're just a little thief."

And then one day the forest gave way to cultivated land. The river broke out of forested hills onto a wide alluvial plain that was dotted with villages, crisscrossed with roads and tracks, and at night speckled with the lights of man.

That day Bilj appeared on the deck. Katun seemed

much more lively than usual. Relkin understood that the
journey was approaching its end. This was civilization.

Ahead appeared a line of wooded hills punctuated by a
canyon cut by the river. They wound through the hills and
emerged into a long lake, flanked on either side by steep
slopes. Trees grew up the slopes. On nearby hills there
were meadows with flocks of white sheep. There were
lines made by stone fences and small stone houses.

It soon became apparent that this was only an extension
of the main lake, for the water ahead broadened and the
far side of a bigger body of water began to come into
view. Relkin saw distant buildings, large buildings, and
there were gleams of gold, which at this distance told him
that fairly immense objects were catching the sun and
reflecting it to him.

Katun tugged on the chain and pointed upward to the
hill to their left. Relkin looked up and gasped. Atop the
hill was a statue, a huge work. Carved in white stone there
stood an enormous figure, a man, with arms stretched out
in benediction over the lake below, toward the distant
shore.

"Bos!" said Katun with adoration in his voice.

Bilj looked around and said something that made Katun
spit before answering with a curt negative.

Bilj's eyes rested momentarily on Relkin's. Bilj giggled. Relkin gave him a hard stare. With a knife in his
hand, Relkin could take care of Bilj all right. Katun . . .
now, that was another matter; but Bilj was just a fat bully.

The lake opened out now and Relkin looked out to the
east across a wide stretch of water, two or three miles
across north to south and many times that on the east-west
axis. All across the southern shore there were buildings, a
mighty city. Far across the water in the east there were
some enormous structures that bulked up into the air like
hills. One was a pyramid and it reminded him at once of
the enormous pyramids to Auros in the ancient land of
Ourdh.

Eidorf had drifted back. Relkin studied the lean features. Eidorf looked at him and for a moment Relkin felt
pity from the man.

"Mirchaz is there. You in Mirchaz now."

Chapter Twenty-three

They came ashore in the port at the southern end of the lake, where Relkin glimpsed briefly the splendor of the tall houses in the merchants' quarter. Then they entered a wide, cobbled passageway that sank down below high stone walls and passed out of a massive gate into the City of Slaves.

There they entered a world of tightly packed, dingy tenements that loomed over narrow, twisting alleys. Sewers ran openly and unspeakably foul ponds collected here and there. The stench was eye-watering. At corners were gangs of gaunt figures picking through piles of garbage.

They made a swift passage through the teeming warren. Visibly nervous, Katun had his hand on the hilt of his sword, leading the way as Bilj and Eidorf hustled Relkin along right behind. Relkin was ready to bolt at any time, but they kept a tight grip on the chains around his waist. Katun, meanwhile, watched for any reavers who might try to dispossess the slavers of their hard-earned prey. The City of Slaves might as easily have been called the City of Thieves.

All too quickly, from Relkin's point of view, they swung into a courtyard, climbed a set of heavy stairs over a stable, and entered a tenement building. More stairs followed and then they passed through a massive wooden door into an apartment of square, dimly lit rooms. A connecting corridor was even dimmer. A sour smell filled the air, as if the room had been shut up for a long time.

Relkin guessed that this was Katun's home. From what he could see as they hustled him along, the place was clean and spartanly furnished, with a rack of spears and swords on one wall. Then he was thrust into a small room.

The chains were removed and he was left to his own devices.

The room was small and stoutly built of brick. A tall, narrow window was the only opening, and it was far too small to crawl through. There was a heavy wooden bench to sit or lie on. That was it. Katun did not see fit to decorate the walls of his slave locker.

The window did afford a view into the alley below. A pervasive din rose from the street, a terrible stench from the alley.

He sniffed and remembered what he'd said when they pulled him through the great gate in the wall of the Upper City. "How do you stand the stench?"

Katun had laughed. "You get used to it."

Bilj had sniggered. "No-Tail be sold before he get used to it. He be going to Upper City. Castrate for the harem."

Katun had told Bilj to shut up.

Relkin stared out at the alley and the distant street. The building was crude but solidly built. Like its neighbors, it had stood for a long time. Escape seemed impossible. The future was pregnant with unpleasant possibilities. Relkin had never felt so alone in his life. He was hundreds of miles from his dragon, for the first time since they were put together in childhood. A dismal mood descended upon him.

He shook himself to break the grip of despair. Look on the bright side, he told himself determinedly. Here he was free of restraints for the first time in weeks. He rubbed his wrists and examined his ankles. Katun had been careful. The bonds were always lined with good leather, so the metal never chafed on bare skin. Slaves were more valuable if they were unmarked. Still, his ankles were sore. His wrists felt odd without that leather around them and the chains holding them together.

After examining the room, he celebrated his new freedom by doing push-ups and sit-ups and squats until sweat streamed from his body and he was gasping for breath. His shoulders and thighs were burning when he stopped. Later he slept.

A day passed. He saw no one except a harried-looking Katun, who brought him some food and some desperately needed water in the evening. To Relkin's questions there was no reply. The door closed again. In the morning there was some porridge. Katun would not speak. The second day passed in mournful lack of event. Relkin used the time to work his muscles hard, putting in hundreds of push-ups and squats. In the evening the door banged open and Relkin heard several sets of feet entering. He heard Bilj's growling voice. A door slammed.

After a while the conversation grew loud. Something was slammed or banged and there was shouting. Another loud bang and then there was commotion, a kind of rumbling sound with heavy bangs every so often. Relkin knew they were fighting. It went on for half a minute and then there came the sound of something very heavy hitting the floor and staying there.

There was a renewed conversation, but the voices were quiet. The door opened, there were footsteps in his direction, then they turned about and went back and the door closed again. The quiet voices resumed. After a while Bilj's voice returned, but in a subdued sort of growl. The door slammed again and then the outer door.

Relkin leaned against the wall of the room and chewed his lip.

Later Katun opened the door and stood there silently examining him.

"What do you want?" said Relkin.

"Katun have to describe no-tail boy to buyer. Customer have many questions."

"Who is this customer?"

"I have promised you to the Lord Pessoba. I have promised undamaged goods."

"By the gods," growled Relkin in Verio.

Katun caught the defiance in his voice and smiled thinly. "You curse all you want. Katun take you to Pessoba. You worth very good reward."

"What did you fight with Bilj about?"

Katun looked surprised for a moment. "Bilj fell hard."

It was Relkin's turn to offer a thin smile. "So I heard. But why did he attack you? I should have thought he knew better."

"Hah, it take a lot to get things through his thick head.

Bilj think he deserve a third of the reward. That was not our deal. He takes a quarter, Eidorf takes a quarter, and Katun takes the rest."

"Oh, of course, of course. I should have known that."

Katun gave him a sharp glance. "I do all the work. You think Bilj does his time with the paddle? You think Eidorf has enough strength to move a boat upstream? Katun did the work, Katun collects the reward. Katun deals with the lord. Katun belong in the Upper City."

Relkin realized he was hearing Katun's deepest wish. Katun was hoping to reclimb the social ladder back to the pleasant surroundings of the Upper City.

"Who is Lord Pessoba?"

Katun gave a surly chuckle. "Ardu no-tail boy soon find out. Lord Pessoba collect you tomorrow."

Katun left shortly afterward and did not return at nightfall. Hours passed. Relkin grew increasingly concerned. If something had happened to Katun and no one came back, he would die of thirst in the locked room. There was no way through the door or the window. He looked at the heavy bench and eyed the wall. Could he possibly ram the bench through the wall? It promised to be hard work at the very least and probably impossible. Katun had kept a good many slaves in that room before the dragonboy from Quosh.

Then he heard the front door open and shut. Heavy footsteps sounded, moving through the apartment room by room and ending up outside his door. The key rattled in the lock and the door swung open and Bilj came in.

Bilj's face bore the marks of his disagreement with Katun. Big purple bruises around both eyes, a grossly swollen nose, and abrasions on the chin and left cheek went with puffed-up lips and a murderous look in his mean little eyes.

Bilj gave an ugly laugh. "Katun cheat Bilj on the gold. But Katun not stop Bilj from having no-tail boy. Before the lord gets to him."

Relkin did not bother to waste words. He had no weapons, but he had been schooled in martial arts since childhood. Grimly, he noted that Bilj had more than twice Relkin's weight and they were in an enclosed space. The only thing he had going for him was that he suspected Bilj wasn't much of a skill man in close combat. Bilj probably relied on his mass.

Bilj did exactly that, lumbering forward with his arms out wide. Once he wrapped Relkin up in those hams, there'd be no getting away.

Relkin drove his right fist into Bilj's solar plexus with all his might. It was about as hard a shot as he was capable of. There was a dismayingly slight response. Relkin continued with knee and foot, fist and elbow, scoring stunning shots with each, but still barely slowed the giant. They bounced around the tiny room. Bilj cornered him at last. Relkin tried to kick Bilj's head off his shoulders, but Bilj deflected his foot with a massive arm. Huge hands seized Relkin's shoulders and drove him back into the wall. Bilj leaned against him, crushing him against the wall with that heavy body. Bilj's eyes were alight with a weird mix of rage and lust. Relkin felt the breath leaving his body. He kicked and struggled, but could get no leverage against all that bulk. A desperate half scream came out of him as he wrestled with the monstrous weight leaning in on him and he started to weaken from lack of air. Somehow, he pulled a hand free for a second and drove his fingers into Bilj's eyes. There was a spasm, Bilj lashed out instinctively with one hand, and his center of gravity shifted and Relkin drove him off the wall for a fraction of a second. And that was enough for Relkin to slip free.

Relkin was giddy from the lack of air. He stumbled toward the door. Had to get out of that room. Bilj couldn't see clearly at that moment, but his big foot lashed around anyway and Relkin tripped before he could escape. He was up before Bilj could reach him and spun away for a moment, but a big hand came around very fast and slapped him into the wall.

Relkin was sure his nose was broken. He could feel the blood running over his lips. His head rang, and it was hard to see straight.

Bilj fixed him with a madman's stare and leaned in, laughing.

Relkin struck desperately with the heel of his hand,

hammering into Bilj's throat. He hit the bull's-eye. Bilj gurgled, then gasped. He seemed unable to suck in air, and his eyes began to bulge in his head. Relkin staggered away, fell over the bench, and rolled to the far wall.

Bilj had gone down on his knees and was clutching his throat. Relkin crawled up the wall to vertical, leaving a bloody streak behind him, ran for the door, and almost caromed off Katun, who had suddenly appeared there. Katun wore a wild disheveled air. There were bruises and abrasions, his clothes were torn and messed. In his eyes there was a lethal fury.

Bilj was still gasping, while clutching his throat.

Katun didn't hesitate. He grabbed Bilj under the arms, hauled him to his feet, and dragged him out of the room. Relkin stared, then headed for the front door. An armed Eidorf was at the door to block his way.

Katun hauled the squealing Bilj through another room and out onto the balcony. Bilj fought back, but weakly. He was still having a hard time breathing. Katun hit Bilj a couple of times in the face and then jammed a hand into Bilj's crotch and heaved the huge man into the air. With a great effort, Katun lifted him flailing over the balcony and tossed him into the alley.

Bilj's scream was muted, but the sound of his landing, several stories below, was not.

Katun returned and spoke briefly to Eidorf, who disappeared for a few moments. Then he reappeared, accompanied by a sharp-faced little man with black hair worn up in a bun at the top of his head.

"Master Lum has come to escort you to your new owner, the Lord Pessoba," said Katun stiffly.

Master Lum was laughing. He pointed to Relkin, who was liberally soaked in blood. Katun growled ferociously, but Master Lum refused to be cowed by Katun. He snorted in disdain and fluttered his fingers in Katun's face. Katun's eyes filled with death, but he made no move against the little man.

Master Lum turned his birdlike, bright eyes on Relkin again.

"You don't look like much my little one." Master Lum's Ardu was very good. "But the lord will want you no matter what. You will come with me. Perhaps, if we hurry, we can clean you up enough to be something less than a total disgrace, before His Lordship has to rest his celestial gaze upon you. Come, we go to the Upper City."

Chapter Twenty-four

Life in the Upper City was not at all what Relkin had expected. He was greeted with effusive warmth and a tender concern for his comfort that was quite a surprise. As an orphan and then a dragonboy, Relkin of Quosh had seen little of the kindness of life and found it now a little disconcerting.

The moment he arrived at the Lord Pessoba's tall house, he was whisked away by servants for a hot bath. Food and drink were brought by Ardu females, trained from the cradle to serve. When they saw that he was unable to chew, they brought him a nourishing soup that slipped down his throat. A surgeon with exquisite skills tended to his battered nose. Relkin had had surgery before from well-trained but hard-handed Legion surgeons, and he understood the difference.

Within an hour, some of it rather disagreeable, Relkin's nose had been cleaned, set, and stitched back together where necessary. The surgeon expressed the opinion that Relkin's nose would return to something like its normal condition. The bridge would not be straight, but it would not be flattened, either.

He was left to rest in a small room muffled with heavy drapes. Astonished, he tried to take stock of his situation, but remained somewhat apprehensive. It had been quite a day, and it wasn't over yet. He examined the clothes they had given him—dark breeches, a loose shirt of fine linen fastened with silver buttons, and soft slippers of doeskin with red tassels. The comfortable, well-made garments fit him well.

He had been welcomed like the long-lost prodigal

son, but it was a little unnerving. What did such treatment portend?

At least he was out of Katun's heavy grip. Perhaps some chance for escape would offer itself soon. Perhaps he would find an open door or window. They couldn't all be like Katun.

Then came the soft summons to a late supper with the Lord Pessoba himself. The lord was very eager to see him, it transpired. Master Lum was very excited. It was a real feather in his cap that Relkin was of such interest to the lord. Master Lum had suggested the purchase of the no-tail Ardu boy from the moment they heard he was for sale. That brute Katun had no idea what a jewel he had in the boy. Master Lum had been certain that the lord would be most captivated by this treat. There'd been a battle with Shex in the budgetary office but Lum had prevailed. Now he was proven right.

Relkin followed a servant wearing a silk sarong through a marble palace. Each room was laden with such fine rugs, furniture, works of art, and fountains, that it was a marvel to behold. All was lit with unearthly glowing globes, set in wall sconces that suffused the rooms with a warm amber light.

They emerged on a larger space, opening out onto a wide veranda and a vast view of the lake and the hills beyond it. Beneath a vine-covered arbor was a table set with crystal plates and goblets of gold. Waiting to greet him was the Lord Pessoba, a wondrous creature. Relkin stared at the glacially calm, utterly symmetrical features, the blue-eyed beauty framed in silver curls, and thought at once of the Elf Lords that had rescued him from the Dwarves of Valur. Althis and Sternwall! Was this part of their realm?

The lord was small-boned, yet his head seemed large for his body, and he moved with a silken grace that was subtly inhuman. He greeted Relkin in that same magical tongue that Althis and Sternwall had used. Intharion was the subtle root language of the Elves, and understood by all who heard it, no matter what their own tongue. Relkin replied in Ardu and the lord appeared to understand him perfectly.

"Come, my prodigy, sit with me and take some supper. Try the wine, 'tis quite superb this year."

Relkin sat. On the far hills glittered a spectacle of lights, and bright avenues sprawled along the shores of the dark lake. The city of Mirchaz was lit at night like no city Relkin had ever seen. The vast cities of Ourdh were dark in comparison. Even the white city of Marneri could boast nothing like this, he marveled.

Far across the lake, the huge, illuminated statue of Zizma Bos stood atop a small hill projecting out onto the lake. To his right was another structure bathed in lights, a massively built pyramid that humped up against the night like a small mountain. Relkin had seen pyramids before in the ancient land of Ourdh. The sight brought back a rush of memories.

Servants brought him rolled pancakes with a creamy filling, served with wedges of fruit and small slices of smoked fish. They were so tender and tempting that he managed to do considerable damage, despite his injuries. An effervescent wine was poured into his goblet. Relkin had never drunk anything so marvelous. Not even the great red wines of Arneis were this good!

"I thank you for your kindness, sir."

The lord was amused. "Such manners. Who asked it to speak? But, it is grateful and that is a good sign." The lord took a sip, then discoursed upon the wine. "Charming, is it not? Urshen has become the best of the sparkling wine-makers. I think his new vineyard on the overlook of Arkelaud is responsible. Of course, one must have excellent fruit, but it is the fruit that has been stressed, that has been grown too high and with less water, which will give you such passion and precision in a wine."

Relkin's astonishment must have shown. The blue seemed to glow with golden filaments in those eyes.

"You are amazed, child. Stupefied! At least you wear the expression of an amazed dolt. Come, come, stretch your imagination. Your horizons have widened abruptly due to the activities of commerce. In short, I have purchased you.

"Listen carefully. You are no longer in the jungle.

You are now in a much more dangerous place." The lord giggled. Relkin's eyes widened.

"Oh, I do wonder what you look like under all that bandage. Will you be the pretty thing that I've been promised by Katun? Or is your beauty gone forever? Only time will tell. The surgeon says you ought to heal very well. He claims that you are extraordinarily fit, but a little bruised. You like to fight, they tell me.

"Well, now you won't have to fight. You are in civilization here."

Relkin made no response, still struggling with the changing tenor of this conversation. To this lord he was evidently somewhere between a pet and a child.

"Well, one of these days we will see you in all your glory. Until then, we must fantasize."

Relkin felt his face go stone hard. The lord laughed, a light brittle sound that verged on cruelty.

"Yes, yes, but until then we can talk, at least. And drink the fine wines of House Urshen. If you only knew what they cost." The blue and gold eyes blinked. Another expression snapped across the perfect features.

"Look at it drink," the lord said. "Look at it savor the Urshen, all those sparkling bubbles, on its tongue. We are intrigued."

Relkin abruptly stopped drinking and set the glass down.

"Tell me where did you come from? These fools thought you were some strange kind of Ardu, but you are clearly no Ardu. You have come from much farther away, beyond the jungles of terror."

The eyes were simply blue now. Some of the electricity had gone out of the curls of silver hair.

"My name is Relkin. I come from the Argonath, from the city of Marneri. I serve in the Legion of Argonath. I am a dragoneer in the 109th Marneri Dragons." Relkin decided to speak with candor. Let this strange lord know that he was a soldier and that he came from the greatest army in the world.

There was a moment of disconnection. The lord shrugged.

"None of these names is known to me. You must

forgive me, child, but I am from an earlier aeon of the world. All names change. It seems to happen with every second aeon. Thus the continent we called Reshesh became the continent now called Eigo. The lands of the Harkann became great Ianta. And in the north the seas have reclaimed lost Gelderen."

"The Legions came to Eigo to destroy our enemy, the Doom Masters. They had some deviltry going on on the big lake, the Wad Nub."

The lord was entranced. His eyes golden. "Good heavens, it's like having a talking cat. Quite extra-ordinary."

Despite the insults, Relkin couldn't seem to stop him-self from revealing everything. With growing alarm, he heard his own words spilling out. "We came from far away on the white ships, which are famous the world over because they're so big and fast. They come from the Argonath, and from Cunfshon, our friends on the Isles."

"Extraordinary." The lord reached out a slender hand and gently held Relkin's chin. Relkin wanted to bat his hand away, but for some reason did not protest. The golden eyes held his.

"Oh, I do hope it heals properly, and soon. Child, you shall be exhibited at the Investigative Society. I shall post the proclamation today. I do think they would be enor-mously appreciative of such an evening. You shall appear before Their Lordships and entertain them with your thoughts.

"Do tell me more about these ships."

"You've never heard of them? Well, we came on one of the biggest of all, called the *Barley*. It has the tallest main mast in the entire fleet. These are square-rigged ships, three-masted, with lots of sails and a big crew. Well, they brought two whole Legions and all their horses and dragons and supplies all the way from the Argonath to Sogosh. That's more than ten thousand men and two hun-dred dragons. Dragons take up a lot of room."

The eyes were very blue. "My dear child, I think the Investigative Society is in for the day of its life. Just pos-sibly my ranking will improve enough to regain the board."

Relkin was baffled.

"About your coming, my dear child, there was much speculation, but little information. We have been so desperate to find out what kind of a wonder you might be. And we have, haven't we?"

"Have what?"

"Have found a wonder. A wonder to behold." Pessoba was transfixed, and ecstatic. This boy had been worth every gold piece he'd given that thug Katun.

"Now, tell me about this kebbold you have been described as riding in your assaults upon the slave takers. Yes, you think I am an ignorant old fool, and it is true I am not in the Thousand right now. But Pessoba will be back. My game improves. And you, my little trump, you shall help me back into the league. I was a player in the ninth hundred once, I can do better than that. I just need the chance.

"But you see, I am not so ignorant. All the slaves have been atwitter about the kebbold that troubled the slaving expeditions this past season and drove them from the ancient forest."

"Kebbold . . . you mean what the Ardu call pujish?"

"Ah, yes, the ancient Ardu term! Yes, of course. Terrible creatures, enormous lizards with the energy of cats, they infest all the surrounding lands and thus fulfilled the prophecy of Zizma Bos."

Far in the distance, across the lake, stood the glowing statue of the great Bos. For a moment Lord Pessoba's eyes rested on it. Then he turned back to Relkin.

"So how in the world came you to be with one? Kebbold are entirely intractable, I understand. One of the Arkelauds raised one from the egg. It killed and ate him when it was only semi-adult."

"He is not pujish. He is battledragon of Argonath."

"Battledragon?"

"Wyvern dragons. They live wild on arctic coasts. Long ago they made an alliance with the Isles of Cunfshon, who protected them when the Doom Masters would have killed all of them for their dark magic."

"Doom Masters? Who might these be?"

"They are our enemy, sir. We checked them at Tummuz

Orgmeen, the cold, barren place where they live. I don't know how they do it, sir, but they build Dooms and use them to rule their empire."

"And what are these Dooms?"

"The one at Tummuz Orgmeen was in a huge, beautifully smooth round rock, about thirty feet across. It was just a mind, a terrible strong mind, and it had servants who obeyed its every order."

"A mind?"

"In the rock, sir, put there by the masters. Evil magic, sir."

Lord Pessoba was beginning to show signs of amazement himself.

"Sir," said Relkin, who tried, and failed, to stop himself from talking, "the dragons of Argonath are the rock in the center of our battle line. Otherwise the masters of Padmasa would have swept us away long ago, and the Argonath been lost. My whole life has been amid dragons."

Pessoba's blue eyes popped. "So, you have tamed waterkebbolds in your native land! The world has moved on from my day. A tame dragon! Such a thing was unimaginable then."

"No one who'd seen them fight would call our wyvern dragons tame. There's no other army in the world can stand against the Legions of Argonath. I was at Salpalangum, and the enemy were as numerous as an entire city, but they could not stand against the dragons. Our cavalry cut them to ribbons. And we lifted the siege of Koubha, just a year or so back. With just a few squadrons of dragons, we cut their army in half and broke them to confusion."

Pessoba's glacial calm betrayed only the occasional quiver, with a raised eyebrow or a small quirky smile. But as he listened, there came into his eyes a curiously intense interest.

What he had here was worth a fortune. That fool Katun had thought to sell him a sex toy. This youth was far too valuable for that. He was a window on the outer world, of which the ruling elite of Mirchaz was terribly ignorant. Their policy of shunning the world had lasted far too long. While the Lords Tetraan played the Great Game, the world had moved on.

Where was this child from? By the descriptions, far to the east on the margin of the great northern continent. It sounded like ancient Gazzat, the fabled land of forest, mountain, and plain beyond the cold deserts of the interior. But in those days it had been ruled by petty mage lords, each to his own small canton. It most certainly had no Legions, or tamed waterkebbolds, either.

Pessoba sighed with contentment. All would be discovered in good time.

Chapter Twenty-five

Relkin's fame in the city of Mirchaz was assured after he was exhibited at the meeting of the Investigative Society. More than a hundred members attended, and all were astounded to discover that Relkin was not Ardu, not in the slightest.

He had first become known as the "No-tail Ardu" that had been so troublesome in the previous dry season. Now he was revealed as having emanated from far beyond the shores of Eigo, which the Mirchaz elves had once called Reshesh.

His appearance stirred considerable debate among a deeply conservative folk. The golden elf lords of Mirchaz had lived in isolation for aeons.

"The world has not stood still since we abandoned the Harkann and forsook the golden land of Gelderen. We should reengage with the rest of the world."

"Never! We must remain aloof. The Game is the only thing we need. Let the world go its own way. We have more important work to do."

"Hear, hear. Leave the damned world to its own devices."

"The Game, the Game!"

And this was from the Investigative Society, a group vastly more interested in the world beyond the great board than were most in Mirchaz's Upper City.

Of course, this public devotion to the Game and isolationism did not keep members from attempting to privately interrogate Relkin. All secretly bubbled with questions they longed to have answers for.

Pessoba's social calendar blossomed suddenly with invitations to the most sought-after addresses. Zulbanides of the ruling clique, the Tendency, invited them to dine at the academy. Pessoba almost swooned with delight. This was exactly what he'd been hoping for.

Relkin was much impressed with the towering white marble building. Its broad steps, worn by the tread of illustrious feet, its wide halls and oversized doors, all spoke to him of authority. Power had designed the place and still resided there.

In the open-air refectory they sat at large round tables beneath trees of contentment, which grew flowers to order and gave off a soft jasmine perfume. A fountain played in the center of the court. Relkin's bandages had come off at last and his nose had shrunk to almost normal size. He could breathe through it quite normally.

Zulbanides was another, slightly older version of Pessoba. He had the same stiff face, without wrinkles but thousands of years old. He had the same strange blue-gold eyes and silver curls.

At first Zulbanides could not address Relkin directly. Zulbanides dealt only with his equals. All others were slaves. As Pessoba had done, Zulbanides spoke past Relkin while Pessoba translated. But the ancient elf mage soon turned withering eyes of gold toward Relkin, examining him more and more carefully. The child brimmed with mad stories. What did it portend?

Zulbanides thought to test these tales. The child might have been taught to recite these things, like a trained horse. What did he know of these fanciful places whose names he tossed off so lightly?

"Where is this Argonath you speak of?"

Relkin felt the mage lord's spell as it descended on him. His sensitivity to magic had grown considerably in the past year. No words were spoken, yet a sweet little voice spoke in his head, telling him to reply.

"Far to the east, on the eastern shore of Ianta."

"Ianta is the undermen's name for the Harkann, Lord." Zulbanides thought for a moment. "Then this must be what was once Gazzat. Do the mage lords still rule?"

"I know nothing of mage lords, sir. In the Argonath there are kings and queens, but they rule by the consent of the common folk. Men of Argonath are thought the freest in the world, except perhaps for some men of Czardha."

"Free men, you say. I fear this is a contradiction of terms. Men are born to be slaves. They were only put on the world to serve the elvish. They roam and rampage now only because their natural masters have withdrawn from the world."

Relkin wasn't sure if he understood it all correctly, but what he was hearing confirmed his fears concerning the Lords Tetraan. Zulbanides was an older model of Pessoba, and older, too, than Althis and Sternwall as he remembered them. But how could one tell the age of these creatures with their nearly identical features, all beautiful, all symmetrical, all perfect? And yet one could. There was something cold in the eyes and a sharpness in the creases around the mouth that marked Zulbanides as much older than Pessoba. Perhaps there was something about the aura. Zulbanides had lived too long.

"Tell me all," the elf lord said.

There was no obvious compulsion, but Relkin felt a strong urge to comply. "I will tell what I can."

Relkin found it hard to control the flow of words once he began. After Heruta's work on him, Relkin had learned ways to resist magical intrusions of this sort. Something had awoken in the mind of the orphan boy from the village of Quosh, some power of which he understood little. It was unformed, he had no control over it, scarcely knew it was there, but it had grown under Heruta's lash. Could he resist this sorcerer of an ancient era as he had resisted Heruta? It wasn't easy; the elf lords were practitioners of more skillful techniques than those possessed by the Doom Masters.

On the other hand, Relkin also wondered how much exactly he might tell Zulbanides without doing any harm. He had to tell him something, but he felt he'd already made the mistake of telling Pessoba too much. On the other hand, it was not as if Relkin were privy to state secrets of the empire.

"How did you really get here?" said the sweet voice.

There was no harm telling him.

"We came on the white ships. It was a long voyage

and we had a few adventures during it, all right. By the gods, we had some close shaves on that voyage!

"Then we landed on the Bogon coast, and marched to Koubha, where we fought an army of the Kraheen there. Pretty much finished them off. We weren't there long, but Baz and I had a great dinner with the king. We were involved in an incident where the king was almost assassinated, but we just happened to be there." Relkin paused; Pessoba paused. Both of the blue-eyed, silver-curled heads were turned to him with evident fascination.

"Well, to cut a long story short, we left soon after and marched west. That was the longest march I can recall, but all dead west, straight to the big mountains there, the ones they call the Ramparts of the Sun. Have you heard of them?"

The Ramparts of the Sun—Zulbanides knew well what they were.

"Ashoth Dereth," he said reluctantly.

"It was cold up there in the high passes, I can tell you. Anyway, we crossed the mountains and went west on the rivers. Built big rafts to carry the army and the dragons, and floated down. We went into what they call the Lands of Terror."

"Narga Dulachu. That shadow has never lifted. Still the monsters hold their land."

"Well, we didn't have too much trouble with the pujish, not at first, not till we came down with that plague there. That just about did our whole army in. Everyone was down with it. I was lucky, I guess, since I never got it. We recovered, but it took a long time. Then we marched north, along the coast of the Inland Sea, the big body of water up there."

"The Wad."

"That's right, the Wad Al Nub. That's what they call it in Og Bogon."

"You have seen the Wad, then." Zulbanides' astonishment was now tinged with equal parts dislike and respect.

"We fought the Kraheen there, at Tog Utbek. We beat them, but they hurt us bad."

Somewhere deep within, Relkin found the ability to keep silent about the weapon of the masters and how badly the Legions had been handled at Tog Utbek. He was determined not to tell anyone about that.

"A small group went out to the Island there, that they call the Bone."

Zulbanides stared at him coldly with golden-yellow eyes.

"Well, that was the enemy headquarters. We found our enemy and sent him to Gongo. His shade lies in the halls of the dead now. But the volcano blew and Baz and me were thrown way out to sea. We swam for a long time. Never would have made it without the wyvern—they can swim forever. We landed on the south shore of the sea, back in the Lands of Terror. It was hard, couldn't get a thing to eat for a long time, then we started eating pujish, because they came after us and made it easy to kill them. Well, it wasn't that easy, actually, they're devilish quick, but Bazil is quicker and the sword is too much for them. By the gods, it's too much for battle trolls from Padmasa, so it's too much for pujish." Relkin smacked a hand on his thigh and gave them a grin. "So we ate well enough."

The elven lords stared at him. Their eyes tinged gold on blue.

" 'Tis amazing, Lord. It claims to eat kebbolds, but has a tame waterkebbold of some kind. The whole thing is quite astonishing. The world has changed since the days of Gelderen."

"Ah, Pessoba, we must not speak of Gelderen. The world did not need our mastery, so we were told by the kings. We left and we must have no backward looks. Still, I must agree that this creature represents something most significant. You did very well in bringing it to the society."

Zulbanides turned back to Relkin. "So how did you come to be such a champion of the Ardu? Are there Ardu people that far north?"

"We found this girl, and we helped her. She'd been wounded getting away from your damned slavers."

Zulbanides' mouth wrinkled in a strange smile. "You come all the way south and cause the slave merchants no end of woe, all on behalf of some Ardu wench?"

"Slavery is wrong. No man should be owned by another."

The eyes shone intensely gold.

"It seems to think we are men, Pessoba. Astonishing impudence, don't you think?"

"Astonishing, m'lord."

Zulbanides turned his gaze to Relkin, who felt suddenly oppressed. A vast, superior mind was focused on him. "I am no mere man, child. I am of an older kind."

"And that gives you the right to own men?"

"Yes. Just as men take the right to own horses and dogs, so I take it as my right to own men. They are no more and no less a commodity than the other animals. All are there for my pleasure and purposes."

"We do not think that way in the Argonath. We give no worship to men, only to the gods and the Great Goddess. We obey our kings, for the king is the center of each of the nine realms of Argonath. We obey our officers in the Legions because discipline is the backbone of the army. We know that it works. But we do not worship kings, and we do not allow slavery."

Zulbanides, despite himself, was brought to respond. "Listen to Zulbanides, child. I was here long before the sun's rays fell for the first time on the kind known as men. Ye may deny each other the possession of one another's bodies, but what is that to me?"

Relkin stared at the golden eyes and did not flinch. They tightened, hardened their gaze, seemed to bore into him, but still he looked straight back. He felt the pressure of the golden orbs, the might of the lord was pressing down on him, but he found himself able to resist.

Finally Relkin shrugged. "I believe you would have to bring an army with you if you wanted to own slaves in the Argonath. And the army that you bring will have to face the Legions of Argonath on the field, and none has defeated us there."

Zulbanides stemmed his first, scornful response. Something in this boy's demeanor told him there was a powerful truth behind these words.

"Fascinating! I do believe you are a proud young man. I

expect that you deserve to be. Tell me more about your cities and why I should not enslave them."

Relkin recited the names of the nine cities and spoke passionately about their mission. They worked to renew the civilization that had fallen when Veronath had succumbed to evil in days of old.

This interested Zulbanides. "So you are no novice of the cycles of history. You realize that there is always decay and eventually a fall. Even your mighty cities of today will one day be leveled unto the ground."

Relkin of Quosh had had little formal schooling. But he had learned to read and write and he had read a few items from the camp library in Dalhousie, and also from the larger one in Marneri. His brush with destiny in the Arneis campaign had sparked in him an interest in history and fable.

"Veronath of old rotted from within. Veronath was already weakened when the masters sent Mach Inchbok to strike. What rotted out the old empire was slavery and the corruption that went with it."

"Indeed, child, continue." Relkin had Zulbanides' attention now. The gold had faded; pale blue filled the orbs.

"There was the dark age. And during that time only the Isles were free in all the east. And from the Isles, where all men worship the Great Mother, came the founders of the cities. They landed and they drove back the forces of dark-hearted Padmasa and in time they defeated Mach Ingbok and tore down his dread fortress at Dugguth."

Just thinking of his homeland brought on a sudden, dismaying wave of homesickness. Relkin had never wanted to see the white city of Marneri more than he did just then. His voice grew steadier as he harangued the elf mage as if he were drawing strength from the idea of the Argonath itself.

These elf lords, related in some way that he did not understand as yet to those golden elves that had rescued him from slavery to the dwarves, lived amid a splendor of gold, white marble, red silken hangings, and the marks of high civilization, and yet they operated under the regime of slavery. For this Relkin felt a natural contempt. It strengthened him. He spoke on for some time, surprising himself with this sudden oratory.

Zulbanides and Pessoba listened intently, eager to hear everything he told them about the outside world beyond the mountains that ringed them in in southern Eigo.

Suddenly Zulbanides came awake with a jerk. He realized with astonishment and some chagrin that he had fallen under the youth's spell. Time had slipped away while he listened to incredible stories of these nine cities far away. No one in Zulbanides' circle could have achieved this effect with plain speech. Perhaps it was something to do with the complete uninflected conviction in the youth's mind. In Mirchaz they had long since lost any vestiges of the simple, of the uninflected, even of convictions.

The sun had definitely declined in the sky. Zulbanides realized the day had almost passed. He waved a hand to Pessoba.

"This has been fascinating, dear Pessoba. I must speak with you again, very soon. However, I have some moves to make today. I'm due to play at the sunset switch. I have engaged Pitz as my player. What do you think of that? Old Pitz will play today for the Tendency."

Naturally, Pessoba was thrilled to be asked to discuss matters of the Game with a member of the first hundred, indeed one of the top ten. His head bobbed up and down.

"Turns the record books quite upside down," he said.

"I've got a flank on Yermst of the Hawkbishops. Old Pitz is the one to exploit it in board play, don't you think?"

"He's had a very good year, I believe." Pessoba struggled to recall Pitz's statistics.

"An extraordinary season, but all for the Cabal. Now I've secretly recruited him for the Tendency. Wait till Cabalatu and the others see him in Tendency blue! Now, that will be a sight to see!"

Pessoba sighed. He ached for the prestige of a high rank on the Game board. To have the opportunity to wield the top board players would be perfection. One would think of strategies, but leave the tactics to the aces with the pieces. One's energies could be devoted to the social and political side of the Game. One could enter the true heart of it, the rulerships of far-off places, both probable and improbable worlds.

If he wanted to witness the sight of Pitz in Tendency uniform, he would do so from the public seats, far above the booths of the Thousand. Once he had had a booth himself, so he knew how fabulous it was for watching Game play. There was such a sense of belonging, of being central to the great mysteries of the Game. Of course, as a Game lord of the nine hundredth quality, Pessoba had been forced to play his own board moves, very hard work, and to eke out an existence at the edge of the great swirls of Game play. A cautious Game, much concerned with survival and given to frights. The lesser hundredths were natural prey for the powers in the top hundredths. The pieces were hard to concentrate, and scattered pieces were easy targets for such killers as old Pitz, or Swalock or Gamutz.

Indeed, it was to a combination of bad luck and a sudden attack by three strengths moved by Swalock that had destroyed Pessoba and driven him from the Great Game on a day of personal infamy that he would never forget.

Zulbanides left them in the court outside and headed for the looming pyramid that housed the hall of the Game. This rested above the mind mass of the slaves that provided the psychic energy that powered it all.

Pessoba's hired bodyguards, men who reminded Relkin somewhat of Katun, formed up around them and they strode back to Pessoba's house through the marble-covered plateau of the Upper City.

Once safely within Pessoba's walls, Relkin took a light meal and exercised on the open rooftop. At his request a punching bag, some weights, and a skipping rope had been provided, and he soon worked up a sweat. He pondered his predicament and plotted an escape.

So far no opportunity had presented itself. Pessoba took no chances. There were well-armed guards around Relkin at all times. He slept in a windowless room with a pair of guards at the door. There were guards at the front door, on the roof, and covering the back garden. There had hardly ever been a moment when he was completely out of sight of the guards, except when he relieved himself in the morning, and even then he was in an escape-proof chamber.

The best chance to make a getaway would therefore come during one of their social visits. For example, this very evening they would attend a dinner given by Lady Tschinn and Lord Rasion, the current heads of the Arkelaud clan. This would be a larger occasion than previous dinner dates when the bodyguards had been oppressively close all evening. Several pairs of eyes had followed his every move. Even an attempt to palm a small fruit knife had been spotted. With any luck, there would be a little more chaos at this evening's dinner. Certainly Pessoba had described the place they were going as the zenith of society in the Upper City. That promised a good dinner in glamorous surroundings. Perhaps there would be a crowd, and perhaps some opportunity for escape would present itself.

Chapter Twenty-six

While Relkin worked up a sweat beating hell out of the punch bag, Lord Pessoba sipped invigorating nectar on the terrace and pondered his options. Since the exhibition at the Investigative Society, Pessoba had received many offers for the No-Tail Ardu, as he was still known, despite the evidence to the contrary.

Already, as one result of these offers, Pessoba had begun negotiating for a review of his Game. If he passed the review, he could compete for a chance at reinstatement in the ninth hundred. The last ten positions were always changing. Ten went down at the end of each lunar cycle, and ten from outside the Thousand were raised up and given places in the ninth hundred. There were other, easier ways to get back into the ninth hundred, but they required influence with the councils of the high.

The offers varied widely. Mot Pulk had offered seven tabis of gold. Mot Pulk was a fading star, now in the sixth hundred. He needed help with his Game, he needed a new piece, something fresh and very different. The no-tail youth might be just that thing.

However, Pessoba had never given Mot Pulk's bid much thought. Mot Pulk offered more gold pieces, but Pessoba was already wealthy. What Pessoba needed was influence in the councils of the Game Lords. Vastly more interesting to him were offers like that from Cabalatu of the Cabal, the major opposition group to the Tendency. Cabalatu, working through his friends in the Arkelaud clan, had offered twelve hundred keppox of gold and precious assistance in regaining Pessoba's rightful place in the Thousand. Twelve hundred keppox was equal to perhaps three tabis. Even better, they offered the services of

the Cabal's top contract player during his first week of
Game play once he was back in the ninth hundred. That
first week was the most dangerous; often a new player
lost all his pieces within days as they were hunted down
by the predators from the higher hundreds. Such an offer
was more valuable to him than gold in almost any
amount.

There was also an offer from Red Elk of the Tendency,
and it was wise to listen carefully. The Tendency had
become the top clique by ruthless group play. If crossed,
they might launch a lightning assault with two or three
top players at once. Such assaults often destroyed a player
in the lower hundreds and drove him from the Game.
Unfortunately, the Tendency offer was for a thousand
keppox of gold and just a vague promise of "help" in
regaining Pessoba a place in the ninth hundred.

Pessoba was offended. He'd given Zulbanides a free
audience with the boy and this was the response from the
Tendency? He reined in his anger. It might be the result of
politics within the Tendency. What if other leaders, like
Red Elk, were trying to undermine Zulbanides? Perhaps,
if he contacted Zulbanides and complained discreetly
about the paltriness of this offer, he could get a better one.
And there was always Cabalatu's offer in the background.
If the Tendency wouldn't improve their offer, then he
would take his chances with the Cabal. One way or
another, Pessoba was determined to ride his success right
into the ninth hundred. Once he won his way in, then he
could use his new techniques, learned from the Arkelaud
school. His rise would begin, and this time it would not be
stopped!

He finished his nectar and summoned Lum to set in
motion their departure to the banquet at Lord Rasion's
quarters in the fabulous luxury of the Arkelaud. Lum
barked orders and within thirty minutes Relkin had been
bathed, shaved, and clad in a suit of black silk with silver
slippers. A squad of five guards surrounded them as they
rode in a horse-drawn carriage up a zigzag road,
ascending the flank of the ridge on the city's southern
margin.

At last Relkin glimpsed the Overlook of the Arkelauds,

perched on a crag high above the city and suffused in a blaze of lights that cast a fantastic jumble of shadows across marble surfaces.

The road worked its way up the crag. As they went, they were afforded further views of the Overlook and of the city spread out below. Past the city was the dark mass of the great lake. On the far side of the lake could be seen more lights, with the statue of Zizma Bos blazing in the west.

Eventually they drove through a great gate and entered a huge courtyard. Servants, some of them Ardu slaves, were there to assist them. They entered through enormous doors and passed down a long, gloomy entry hall until they emerged into a wide space, covered by a ceiling of glistening scarlet lacquer. Pillars covered in gold leaf held up the ceiling. A long table covered in white linen took up the center. Around it were seated two dozen or so of the high and mighty of the city of Mirchaz.

Relkin and Pessoba were introduced, to a round of applause. Lord Rasion, a ruddy, well-fed version of the Mirchaz elf mage norm, stood to welcome Relkin to a place beside him. Pessoba, after a moment's hesitation, was detached and seated on the further side with Lady Tschinn and her friends. Relkin understood that this was not Pessoba's wish. Relkin also warned himself to be careful. There were many threads to this situation that he did not yet understand or even know about. The ground ahead was littered with traps, of that he was certain.

Lord Rasion sat at the head of the table, Relkin on his right. Beside Relkin was another beefy, silver-haired elf mage introduced as Red Elk. Next to him were Repadro Toba and across was Lord Kyenn. Relkin saw the same reddened, coarsened elf face on each figure. The hair was still the glistening silver curls, virtually lacquered into place, and the chin was still the same strong, square chin, but the jowls had swollen, the nose had reddened, and the skin had sagged all in individually different ways.

"You are not Ardu at all, are you?" said Lord Rasion, who seemed to finally be coming to terms with this truth.

"That is correct. I am a soldier from the land of Argonath."

"Yes, yes," rumbled the beefy Red Elk. "So we have heard. That and much more."

"Some kind of Ardu, but from the east," said Repadro Toba.

"No. I am not Ardu."

When Repadro Toba spoke, the heavy jowls wobbled. Relkin thought of the martial visages of Althis and Sternwall and shivered. This was virtually the same face as theirs, but buried beneath rolls of fat and wrinkled skin.

"There is the prophecy of Zizma Bos," said Lord Kyenn. "Is this the one they will call Iudo Faex?"

Repadro Toba gave a sour chuckle. "Of course not. He is mere human flesh, the clay of Ardol. The Iudo Faex must be of elven kind."

"That is not necessarily so," commented Lord Rasion. "Nowhere in the text of Zizma Bos does it say that."

"Perhaps not explicitly, but there can be no other reading of the text of Zizma Bos."

"Bah, there is no such thing as the Iudo Faex. 'Tis all but a tissue of lies put about by the faint-hearted, who grow weak at the thought of the grim lives of former slaves," growled Red Elk.

"Does that mean Rasion is one of the faint-hearted?" said Kyenn.

Repadro Toba's lips narrowed into a nasty smile. "Lord Rasion is one of our greatest warriors. All who know him must admit this! 'Faint heart' is no phrase for such as Lord Rasion!"

"Yet Rasion clings to his generous notions of society." But Kyenn's attempts to draw Repadro Toba on this subject did not succeed.

Red Elk suddenly leaned forward. "Rasion, one day you will wake up to our danger."

"Red Elk, the only danger I face is on the board. I had Pitz making sharp moves against my flank man this evening. We had the devil of a time extracting some strengths from the trap."

Eagerly, the ancient elf mages turned to discussion of the Great Game.

"These were the Jumping Strengths that Zulbanides was boasting about?"

"Was he boasting, the dog? Why the arrogance of Zulbanides knows no bounds. Pitz threatened the Strengths, but all he actually took was a Leaper and a Pawn."

"I maintain forty Leapers," sniffed Lord Rasion. "I will have a new one within the week."

"Old Pitz was sharp tonight. His first session in Tendency blue."

"His defection was noted. The Cabal will take measures. Pitz will have to be careful in coming weeks."

"Pitz will be running forty strengths, half of them Jumpers. I think Pitz will have sufficient forces for any struggle."

Food and wine were brought. Relkin drank water. The wines of Mirchaz were delicious, but he needed to keep his head clear. If there was to be a chance of escape, it would come on one of these sorties from Pessoba's house. He had been examining his surroundings carefully from the moment he'd sat down.

The room was enormous. The walls were lost behind pillars, statues, and clumps of servants standing beside trolleys and service tables. Dozens of servants were in motion at all times. It was hard to tell where the doors to other rooms might be.

He noticed that there were pairs of burly men set on either side of the table, about fifty paces distant. These men seemed to watch him closely the entire time.

An escape bid would have to be made very carefully. Finding his way out of this place while evading pursuit might be taking on too much at one go.

No worthwhile plan had formed as yet.

The elf lords were still discussing board play from that evening's session. Relkin had already gathered that it had been unusually active. Something called the "Ninth Gold" was in play. This Gold was a position of some sort that was held by the Tendency, the group that Red Elk and Zulbanides belonged to. The Ninth Gold was, however, almost surrounded now by a force of pieces belonging to the Cabal. The Tendency pieces were in great danger. There was a chance the Tendency would lose so much matériel that the Cabal would take the lead position. Zulbanides had already unleashed Pitz in merciless attack play; the Tendency would not give up without a bitter struggle. Red Elk promised as much. Relkin listened politely with half an ear while continuing his surreptitious examination of the room. Suddenly he noticed that Lord Rasion was watching with an amused smile on the perfectly proportioned lips.

"You are admiring our lovely dining chamber, I think."

"Yes. It is the largest I have ever seen."

Rasion's smile dipped for a moment, then brightened. "And as we know, you have traveled the world."

"I have seen some of it. A soldier of the Argonath goes where he is ordered to. That has been my lot, and my misfortune."

"Hardly that, child, for it has brought you here, to Mirchaz, where the glory of the Old Red Aeon still lives on. Can you not feel it? Can you not hear the sweet singing? This is the marbled heaven that we ascended to when we abandoned Gelderen."

"I'm sorry, I don't know these things."

"Of course you don't, child. You know nothing. You are as evanescent as a moth. But we, we are still alive, and we were alive in the Old Red Aeon, too. Think of that. Think of all the centuries that have passed as we have walked beneath the stars of Ardol here in our sacred vale."

"It is magnificent," said Relkin judiciously.

"And you will live here. You will take a place of honor among the Lords Tetraan."

"Will I see the Great Game?"

"You will see it. Oh, I expect you'll be in it up to your neck." Rasion chuckled soundlessly and in a way that was both cruel and mysterious.

Through the dinner the lords talked mostly about board play. There was a long argument about moves from standstill and which openings were currently the best. Occasionally the lords would focus on Relkin and he would be quizzed again about the Argonath, or the monster kebbold he was supposed to have in the forest. Relkin's replies were controlled and as brief as possible. The lords would probe a little, but then they would happily return to their argument over the new openings from standstill.

The main courses were at last completed. Relkin ate modestly and drank little, so his head remained quite clear.

A hot beverage was served in small pink cups. It turned out to be kalut, scented with cinnamon and sweetened with honey. Then a troupe of Ardu dancers, oiled and naked, performed a wildly sensual dance while an orchestra of twenty men filled the air with thundering music. The performance was not the Ardu's native dancing; this writhing and suggestive motion was more like something from a brothel in old Ourdh. The Ardu male dancers worked their tails between the legs of the female dancers, much to the merriment of the elf lords. Relkin felt only a mild disgust.

When Relkin asked to be allowed to relieve himself, he was escorted from the dining hall by two of the Katun lookalikes. These men hadn't touched a drop and they were alert and ready for anything. Relkin saw no opportunity for escape.

Back in the dining chamber a sweet dessert was prepared for them. With clashing cymbals a team of cooks, small men with yellow skin and shaved heads, worked over a huge metal pan that spanned perhaps ten feet. A mixture of nuts, raisins, dried fruit, and sugar was cooked in the pan and served in small bowls, drenched with a sweet concoction that conferred a floral bouquet.

Two of the men-at-arms approached with a message.

With a certain amount of ritualistic grumbling, Lord Rasion allowed Relkin to be escorted to the ladies' end of the table to be introduced and looked over by the elf ladies, clad in long gowns of silver, blue, and green.

As their names were announced—Lady Ansalld, Lady Shej a Goot, Lady Iaruka—Relkin was struck by how different and yet how similar the ladies were from the mighty lords. They all shared the same face, but the ladies were so thin, and with such prominent elfin cheekbones, that their faces bore the mark of the skull. The lords had grown more humanlike with age and increased weight, but the elf ladies had become distinctly inhuman. It wasn't just the star patterns in their eyes, where gold blazed amid the blue, but the odd upturn of their mouths, which formed an eerie permanent smile, like some foxlike grin, laden with cunning.

Relkin quickly realized that the elf ladies were not responding to his bows and polite salutations even though he was sure they understood enough Ardu. They gazed at him with gold in their eyes and treated him without respect, as an animal, an object. They discussed him in the lewdest terms. Of course, they spoke in quicksilver Intharion, the magic tongue, and he understood them perfectly. He felt his face burn as he heard himself compared unfavorably with a prime Ardu bullboy, bought for the bedchamber. Another voice promised to have his ears pierced for little chains, the better to guide him with in bed.

Relkin blushed, then growled with fury. They were looking at him as if he were no more than some kind of rooster.

"Bring it closer," said one. "Let's have a better look."

There were harsh giggles.

The men-at-arms shoved him forward three steps.

One lady, the golden stars glowing in her eyes, put her hand on his hip and caressed him. There was mocking laughter from the others. Angrily, Relkin pushed her hand away and drew back a step.

"I am not your plaything," he said in furious Ardu, "I am a soldier of the Legion of Argonath."

The ladies hissed, and one called loudly for him to be whipped. The nearest of the heavyset men-at-arms reached out to grab Relkin by the shoulders.

Relkin's temper broke asunder. He exploded, pivoting and driving the heel of his fist into the fellow's midriff. The guard doubled up and Relkin rammed a knee into his face. One down, sang the war spirit in Relkin's brain. He looked around for a weapon, the fallen guard's sword. With a blade in his hands, Relkin swore he could do something about this shameful disrespect.

At the very moment that he began to reach for the sword, his legs were swept out from under him by the other man-at-arms wielding a heavy spear butt with practiced skill. Relkin hit the floor, rolled in desperate haste, and started to rise, but the spear point hovered half an inch from his face and there was no way to evade it.

Slowly he raised his hands, palms forward in surrender.

The elf ladies were still screaming, in a mixture of excitement and fear. Many voices were raised in loud command. Elf lords came running. Some had drawn short stabbing swords and seemed ready to throw themselves at Relkin.

"I am here!" bellowed one tall figure, identifiable by the silver patch he wore over his left eye. It made him instantly recognizable in a population of almost identical folk.

"Have no fear," said a caustic elf lady, "Mot Pulk is here."

"Mot Pulk, do not embarrass us all with your overeager pronouncements," said another.

Ignoring them, the one with the eye patch pushed through to confront Relkin, who still had a spear point at his throat.

"So what have we here? Some kind of young rogue who has caused our ladies distress. You must be more careful. Men have been banned forever from the Upper City of Mirchaz for less."

"I did not ask to be brought here," said Relkin coolly.

"Oh-ho, listen to the creature." The single eye burned gold. "It shall have to be gentled, lest its lusts overwhelm us."

"It is not my lust that's a problem," said Relkin.

Several ladies screamed in rage at this.

Mot Pulk was amused. "Then even greater threat is posed to our civilization."

The fallen man-at-arms had made it back onto his feet. There was a murderous glint in his eyes. Relkin hoped he didn't end up alone with the fellow or he was going to pay.

Help was on its way. With loud calls against violence, the Lord Pessoba finally broke through the throng to reach the scene.

"Do not hurt the child. I'm sure there has been a misunderstanding, nothing more." Pessoba's own guard shoved through and pulled Relkin away from the spear wielder.

The one nursing his sore face growled angrily and reached for his sword, but other men-at-arms moved in around him and disarmed him.

"Put up your weapon. There will be no need for it," said Pessoba angrily.

Lord Rasion approached and harangued the ladies, chiding them for their lack of good manners.

Pessoba's eyes were deep blue with concern.

"Child, what have you done?"

"I am no plaything." Relkin nodded at the indignant elf ladies.

"You should be honored to receive their slightest attention. They are the highest ladies of Mirchaz, veritable queens of elven chivalry."

"If they are ladies of chivalry, then your chivalry has forgotten all decency."

Pessoba sighed. "They behaved badly, it is true. You must remember where you are, though."

Relkin knew very well where he was. He nodded toward the tall elf with the silver eye patch.

"Who is that?"

Pessoba's face seemed to freeze for a moment. "That is Mot Pulk."

"Who is he?"

"An inconsequential person, a comet."

"What does that mean?"

"Oh, he burst upon the scene for a while. His game had some new tricks and he rose to the sixth hundred for a moment. Now he declines toward insignificance. I believe he will fall from the seventh hundred at the end of the moon's cycle."

Relkin felt a grim smile hover momentarily on his lips.

Lord Pessoba, of course, was struggling desperately to get back into the ninth hundred.

Chapter Twenty-seven

Pessoba's first mistake, perhaps, was in not withdrawing at once from the Overlook of the Arkelauds. Relkin was ready to leave. He'd had his fill of these strange, ancient creatures and their elaborate game. Pessoba, however, was still hunting for some trace of favor from the high and mighty.

"Hush, child, we have been invited to an audience with the Lady Tschinn herself."

Relkin was in no mood for it, but his feelings were not important in the scheme of things. Thus events were set in motion that might otherwise never have stirred.

Relkin was relieved that at the least they would get out of the banquet hall and away from the elf ladies and their angry eyes and accusations. Pessoba's guards formed up around the elf lord and Relkin so they moved in the midst of a formation ten strong. They moved down huge, echoing halls past enormous white marble bas-reliefs, where ancient elven heroes were engaged in wars, love-making, and the business of raising a great city.

They came to a large door, passed more guards, and moved inside to a small door. It opened onto an intimate room paneled with dark burgundy velvet and lit with tiny pinprick ceiling lights. A scent of sweet spice hung heavy on the air.

Seated on a black throne was the Lady Tschinn. She shared the universal appearance of these golden elf folk, but in her eyes there was something akin to kindness, and perhaps a farsight that he had not noticed in the others.

"Welcome, young sir. I thank you for coming."

Relkin's face must have showed his surprise, unused to being thanked for anything by the elf lords of Mirchaz.

"Your name is said to be Relkin."

He nodded.

"Do I pronounce it correctly?"

"Yes."

"Good." A hint of a smile played briefly across the lady's elfin face. The huge eyes were blue, with tiny gold sparkles in their center.

"I am sorry for your mistreatment at the banquet. I am afraid the ladies had overindulged in wine. They will be most grievously embarrassed when they recover their wits."

Relkin was further taken aback by this apology. "I thank you, Lady, for your concern. Perhaps I over-reacted."

"Yes, perhaps, but those men have to earn their keep, and fortunately no one was really hurt."

She examined him frankly. The tiny gold pinpoints had spread suddenly into visible stars.

"Well. After all the talk, I have finally seen you for myself."

Pessoba leaned forward. "The child has a remarkable tale to tell about his origins, my lady."

"Yes, Pessoba, I'm quite sure. Let's allow him to tell it himself, shall we." Pessoba retreated.

"Now, child, I am sure you're tired of repeating it, but for my sake tell me how it is you came to be here among the Ardu folk in the land of kebbolds."

Relkin took a deep breath. The gold stars in her eyes faded to pinpricks as she listened to his tale.

"We came on the white ships, a whole fleet of them. Landed at Sogosh. From there we moved upcountry, to a place called Koubha." The gold stars had faded away. She seemed to be listening intently as he told the story of the campaign that had taken him and his dragon from the eastern coast all the way to the heart of the continent. Then he told of how they had found Lumbee and nursed her back to health before ascending the river to the land of the Ardu. He went on to the campaign against the slavers and Lady Tschinn nodded during this part, for she had heard it before in one form or another.

When Relkin was finally done, she put her hands

together and sat back on her throne with an astonished expression.

"Child, you have lived a most adventurous life. This is the stuff of legend."

Relkin shifted uncomfortably. "Legend" was getting dangerously close to "destiny," and Relkin of Quosh had found out to his cost what that could lead to. The elf lady stared at him for a long moment in silence.

"I would ask you to humor me, child. I must test you. I sense something about you that makes me think you are not quite what you appear to be."

Relkin's eyebrows rose.

"No, do not think to try and escape. If you are some wizard, sent here to spy on us for the overlords, as I think you may be, you will not escape our fury. The doors are blocked, my guards are protected against sorcery."

"Lady," said Relkin, "be assured I am no wizard, just a dragoneer, first class, in the Legion of Argonath."

She waved a hand in his direction to silence him and tinkled a little bell.

At once a slave, a man, oiled and shaved, wearing just a loincloth, appeared from behind the throne. The lady whispered something and the slave disappeared. Within a minute he was back, accompanied by two others, who helped him manhandle a large crystal globe, held in an equatorial mount and supported on a stand the size of a heavy chair. It was moved on little rollers attached to its feet and positioned between Relkin and the lady. The crystal globe was pale yellow and more than two feet across. The brass mounting that held it around the middle was in the shape of a beautifully rendered serpent.

The lady reached out and spun it in its mount. The crystal glowed. The slaves had vanished. She gestured to him.

"Come closer, child, I will not harm you if you be only what you appear to be." Relkin hesitated.

Pessoba stepped forward instead. "My lady, may I speak?"

Lady Tschwinn turned to him with a frosty look. "What is it, Pessoba?"

"The boy is valuable to me. That is, I must beg you not to damage him in any way."

"I will do nothing to harm him if he is what he says he is. But I detect more here than meets the eye. The aura is strong, too strong for a simple-hearted youth, as he claims to be. Have you considered that all this might be no more than a front? That behind the youthful facade there might be lurking some wizard, some wight sent here by our ancient enemies to undo us?"

Pessoba blinked. He had not considered this possibility. Relkin had seemed to be exactly as he described himself. He glanced at the boy. Could all this be a deception? Pessoba's skin crawled at the thought. Could it be? But what about Katun? How could the slave taker have been fooled? Could he have been under some sorcerous spell? Pessoba shivered a little.

"Place your hand on the crystal ball, whoever and whatever you are," said the lady.

Relkin considered for a moment, then did as he was bid. There was nothing to hide. He felt the smooth crystal, strangely warm to the touch, slide by beneath his fingers.

The lady purred.

"Now, empty your mind and look into the crystal and we shall see what we shall see."

We shall see what we shall see. . . .

Suddenly a sensation of extreme cold spread up his fingers, then his arm, and flashed over the rest of his body, like a gust of icy wind. Relkin pulled away with a gasp.

There came a flash of light from the crystal that threw shadows leaping across the walls. When their eyes had recovered, they saw that within the crystal an image had formed of a green circle criss-crossed by gray lines. For a moment it made no sense, then Relkin saw that it was an aerial view of a piece of countryside. A forest grew away in one direction, and long fields, bounded by stone walls, led down to it. A village of gray stone was laid out atop the slope, surrounded by vineyards.

The picture seemed to gain focus all of a sudden and they became aware that the village was the scene of an enormous battle. Up the long slope marched a huge host beneath black banners and skull-topped pikes. At the top of the slope, among the stone cottages of the village, sprawled the battle, spilling into gardens, jamming up in heaps of dead in the streets.

Relkin shivered a little. Terrible memories were stirring. At the same time, he was amazed at this sorcerous image. It was tiny but so clear, as if seen through the purest mountain water.

Within the crystal the scene shifted. The struggling figures could be seen clearly now. Men, imps, trolls, and great battledragons were engaged in a swirling, smashing conflict of sword, ax, shield, and armor. The violence was unending and horrifying.

And then the scene cut off abruptly. The crystal cleared for a moment and slowly the yellow coloration returned.

The lady had pressed her hands together tightly while her eyes fixed on Relkin in spangled gold.

"So, there's a great battle in your past. The ball does not lie. You have been a soldier. That much is true. Lay your hand on the ball again."

Relkin was reluctant. She pointed to the ball. He realized that if he refused, she would order guards in and they would force him. He decided to avoid that humiliation. Once again he experienced that unnerving shock of iciness. A moment later there was another flash of light, though this time it was not as bright. A new image slowly coalesced within the crystal ball. A pyramid towered up into a clear night sky. Abruptly Bazil Broketail appeared in the view, as if he were walking out of the pyramid. He came with the predatory lope of his kind and he bore Ecator in one hand and the great shield in the other.

"And this is the kebbold that's been running amok in the Ardu forests."

Relkin bit back his angry denial. There was no point in lying, just as she was coming to believe him. He kept his hand on the ball.

The scene shifted to a bright, brilliant day at sea. Plowing through medium-sized waves beneath pyramids of sail came a fleet of immense ships, with white-painted hulls, trailing the blue pennon of the Empire of the Rose.

Lady Tschinn's eyes widened.

"Such beauty, such immensity," she murmured. "So this is the ocean great, of which I have heard." She stared at the ball for a long moment and then turned him a glance, with new respect in her eyes.

"And this, too, you told the truth about, it seems."

Lady Tschinn was close to a conviction that Relkin was just what he said he was, a simple soldier from a faraway empire, albeit a soldier with a giant kebbold for a mount or a companion, if you could believe his fantastic story about the beast being able to speak and march with an army. Lady Tschwinn could not understand why such a kebbold would refrain from simply eating the men in such an army. The concept of intelligent kebbolds was still too much for her to accept.

The young man was still telling some kind of untruth, but probably it was of a more ordinary variety than she had earlier suspected. So ... a young soldier, lost in the heart of the great continent, and in need of friends. She considered him carefully. In truth he was shapely. Slender, but already muscular in an adult way. She had already noticed the calm in those young eyes. She recalled the speed with which he had moved in the brief fight in the banquet hall. Presence and speed, she liked that combination. Perhaps she would take the boy if Pessoba would sell.

And then came a flash of light from the great crystal ball and the image of the ocean and the white ships disappeared. For a moment the ball went black, and then a bizarre scene occupied the crystal. First there was a flat plane, purple and without texture. Across the plane ran a silver wall, at right angles to it, which continued off into the distance, where the purple plane ended in a flat horizon beneath a pink sky. A group of small silvery clouds was moving across the sky.

Floating overhead came a pair of dusky orange toroids, their surfaces puckered like waffles. From their central holes came beams of light that struck down onto the purple flatness.

The view changed again. There, floating in the crystal, was a face. Calmly it seemed to look back at them from enormous green eyes framed in a face that was like both that of a man and that of some huge insect. The features were jammed up beneath the great luminous eyes. The ears supported growths like antennae that curved up and forward in front of the face.

Relkin shivered uncontrollably, it was one of *them*. . . .

The things he had seen floating above the pit in ancient Dzu. The things that had dogged his step from that moment, or so it seemed.

Lady Tschinn gave a terrible cry and slammed her hand down on the sphere to halt it. The image vanished. The crystal became yellow and opaque once more.

"What are you?" The long finger pointed at him. She was shaking. "Where did you see the Sinni? You, a mere soldier, have known the Sinni? This is simply impossible."

"I don't know them. I don't even know what they are. But I have seen them. At Dzu, when we killed the Meso-master in the pit, they were there. We all saw them."

"What?" Her perfect forehead creased with confusion. "Are you some golem made by Althis and Sternwall? What are you really?"

Althis and Sternwall! Relkin was rocked. Those were the very names given to him by the golden elves, in the hidden city of the dwarves beneath the forest of Valur.

"Answer me, or else I will order you destroyed."

"I have seen *them*, or things like that, but not that place. I've never seen that particular image. Don't you see? That didn't come from my mind."

He clenched his fists in frustration. "Those other things actually happened. That first one was the fight at Sprian's Ridge. That was the worst fight I've ever been in. I never want to see another one like it. The other thing was at Dzu. You saw my dragon, the Broketail. Those things are from my life. That last thing we saw was different. I have never experienced it."

"Maglaea," she said to herself. "Maglaea's warning has come at last. The prophecy will be completed."

"I don't know what they want."

"So, you are a messenger. You bring us the death knell. You are the Iudo Faex."

"What is that?"

Her face had grown pale and hard.

"You are the harbinger of doom. The one who will end the Game."

Chapter Twenty-eight

For a long moment there was silence, and then Lord Pessoba let out a shriek of rage. In a moment things became very confused. Pessoba's guards burst in. Pessoba yelled that he was being victimized and he would not give up his property.

The lady's guards engaged Pessoba's in a shoving match. She invoked the authority of the Arkelauds in an equally loud voice. Pessoba denied that it applied to him. The Arkelauds no longer ruled the Game, or the city, he cried. They had no right to steal his property. He had paid good gold for the youth. He had all property rights in consequence.

The lady commanded Pessoba to obey the authority of the Arkelauds. He disagreed violently and broke for the door, propelling Relkin ahead of him. Relkin, confused and alarmed by the open display of weapons by the guards, moved with Pessoba. There were blows, grunts of pain as the guards jostled. Shouts of alarm went up. One guard was knocked down and they scrambled over him and burst out of the small room. They ran through the huge corridors, with the cold stone faces of dead elven lords staring down from the walls.

Relkin was elated and busily calculated his chances of getting away. This was exactly the sort of chaotic situation he had hoped for. He looked back over his shoulder. Their pursuit was coming, but it was still around the last corner. Was there a door anywhere here? A window? He felt a tug at his elbow, turned, and found Pessoba pressed close to him, almost eyeball to eyeball.

"If you run away from me here, you will not escape,"

he puffed. "They will catch you and kill you. Just in case you really are the Iudo Faex."

Relkin reflected for a moment. He didn't know his way around this vast place. And if he was caught by the Arkelauds, he'd probably be slain out of hand. Perhaps this wasn't the moment to be making a break for freedom. It was a hell of a pity, but Relkin had a strong suspicion that Pessoba might be right.

They passed through the main gates of the Overlook of the Arkelauds and found their coach ready and waiting. Moments later they were moving swiftly down the road leading back to the city while the sweating guards ran alongside, their weapons and armor clinking in the darkness.

There was no pursuit. The Arkelauds dared not move that openly. Even though Pessoba was a relative nobody, they could not wage war within the city walls. Their Game position was weak. The Tendency might crush them completely if they drew down unwelcome attention. Thus the coach zigzagged down the mountain road and then sped swiftly through the streets with no immediate pursuit. The guards gradually fell behind, despite their best efforts and glares from Pessoba. They arrived at the house with no guards except the driver. Once again Relkin thought of escape, but as the coach slowed in front of Pessoba's house, the door swung open and four fresh guards sprang out to surround them. Biting back a snarl of frustration, Relkin left the coach and walked back inside the prison of the lord.

Mulled wine was brought them on the terrace. Relkin ate a handful of glazed fruits and stared gloomily at the night view of the dark lake and the distant light around the statue of Bos.

He felt as glazed as the bonbons in his hand. The perfect moment had come and gone and left him a prisoner still. Worse, he was now marked for death. He had been named the "Iudo Faex." Legends and myths were in play. Relkin knew to his cost that such things could be dangerous.

For once the bossy tones of Pessoba were absent. Relkin glanced at the elf lord and saw a face frozen in immobility as the mind behind it performed furious calculations of the odds facing various efforts to sell Relkin for a good price.

Relkin understood a little of what Pessoba was thinking now, and he could see that the lord was dithering, unable to choose. He knew he was damaged goods. Pessoba was probably thinking of a way to unload him as quickly as possible. How long Relkin survived after that was unknowable, but after his visit to the Overlook of the Arkelauds, his chances had definitely declined.

Relkin looked at the dark lake and the distant lights in silence. He thought of his dragon, lost somewhere in the land of the Ardu. Then he thought of the ruins of his life, and of Eilsa Ranardaughter. Bitter self-recriminations came easily to the surface.

He should never have gone out hunting that day. He should have remembered the prime rule of the dragonboy's life: Always keep your dragon in view. That way they could never get in serious trouble. And he'd broken that rule and thoughtlessly gone out hunting in a foreign land, mostly because he was bored in camp. And now he was lost.

Pessoba suddenly stood and swilled down the last of his wine.

"To bed with you, child," he said. Pessoba's eyes had turned golden. He snapped his fingers at Relkin with an angry gesture. The guards came in and formed up around Relkin. He was escorted to the secure room in which he slept. The door shut behind him and the bars thudded home.

There was just the ventilation slit, and little light came in from that. In the dimness Relkin groped his way along the wall until he found the hard little pallet they'd given him to sleep on.

He had a vision of Bazil's joboquin broken in several places, the cinch strap giving way, the equipment falling and being lost. No one in the Ardu land knew how to take proper care of a leatherback wyvern. Nails would break, cuts would turn septic, what was left of the equipment would be lost. And what would that dragon think of his dragonboy, who had left him one day and not returned? Relkin didn't think he'd ever faced a bleaker time than this.

Eventually, after staring into the dark for a while, he offered up a perfunctory prayer to Old Caymo. At the back of his mind he also offered up a small one to the Mother just in case she was listening.

If these were the best dice the god could come up with, then maybe Relkin would have to abandon the old gods and subscribe full-heartedly to the worship of the Great Mother.

Later he slept and endured evil dreams. Occasionally he tossed and moaned.

He did not notice when the air in the center of the room began to shimmer strangely.

There was a faint hissing, as of water dripping onto a hot iron.

The shimmer in the air increased. Small sparkles of light flashed momentarily. A dark thread appeared, blacker than the darkness. Slowly it grew to a sheet. Something was thickening in the darkness. It grew from the thread, bulging, wobbling, slowly shifting into existence.

In time it became the figure of the elf lord Mot Pulk.

For a moment Mot Pulk gazed down through the dark on the sleeping figure of Relkin, then he crouched beside Relkin. From within his robe he produced a dark crystal, cut with many facets.

He played the light on Relkin's face. Relkin awoke with a startled grunt and his eyes fell on the dark crystal. He froze. The crystal shimmered strangely, and he knew that some devilish magic was at work. Then he found he was unable to control his limbs.

The crystal moved, the light shone on him, and he got to his feet, without willing it himself. A face floated there, an elf lord with an eye patch, the one they called Mot Pulk.

Chapter Twenty-nine

Mot Pulk himself stood there, breathing slowly, trying hard to keep from shouting out in triumph. He, Mot Pulk, had done it! The most dangerous ploy in the Game, some said. Full materialization within the enemy's fortification! A process that took hours, during which one was completely vulnerable as the life force was poured, slowly, across the subworld of chaos and back into the real world of Ryetelth, only in a different location. For long periods during the spell there would be two copies of he who attempted this feat of the magic of the Old Red Aeon. Either copy would be weak, virtually helpless. Of course, one would be the primary, safely lodged in secure surroundings. The other, however, would be projected into a place of danger where it might be destroyed, or worse yet, captured at any point. The results would be fatally weakening to the primary.

Materialization was rarely used now. Once, when the Game was ruled by buccaneers and adventurers, it had been more frequent. But the buccaneers had died out with the age of the Arkelauds, in large part because more cautious players had killed the wild men. The Great Game rewarded the cautious players and thus had come about the era of the great cliques, like the Tendency and the old Cabal.

But Mot Pulk was a throwback to the great days of old. He was a buccaneer, a jackbooter ready to seize any opportunity. The higher-ups sneered at him, of course. They had always sneered at the adventurous. Now they all thought him finished. Unable to break into the settled ranks of the first three hundreds, he faced inevitable decline, they said. They carped about the lush beauty of the worlds he invented. They sneered at his voluptuaries, at his love of flesh and pulsating life. The probable worlds of the Tendency were bijou works of art, small and tasteful, controlled and dead. Mot Pulk worked in older genres, and was glad to see life spurting and leaping, while growing in its own direction.

Mot Pulk had no time for the controlled environments preached by the Tendency rulers, Zulbanides and the rest. They were timid souls and thus they had outlasted the greater talents of the game. Mot Pulk was younger, born late in the cycle of the elves. He was something the older generations could not comprehend. They held him in contempt and refused him entry to one of the higher cliques.

And so Mot Pulk had decided to act alone. He would take advantage of the situation while others were frozen with indecision. Pessoba, that mouse, would be huddling in drugged sleep within his fortress. Mot Pulk had bribed a servant to get a layout of the place. He had studied it from without and traveled its halls by astral projection. He knew where to materialize. And he knew it would be relatively safe. Pessoba would not have mounted adequate defenses against materialization. Since Pessoba would not have dreamed of trying to materialize inside a hostile environment himself, he could not conceive that anyone would try to do it inside his own house.

Mot Pulk calculated that he could get in and out in a single night and take the youth with him. Lady Tschinn had apparently identified the youth as the Iudo Faex, which immediately made him very valuable, far beyond even his worth as a curiosity.

Ha! His spirit reveled in his triumph. Pessoba was such a no-hoper, forever doomed to struggle outside the Thousand. Compared to Mot Pulk, Pessoba was a donkey!

The materialization was finally complete. His body was no longer in his own house. Instead, he was free to move within the heart of Pessoba's domain. For a moment Mot Pulk considered all the possibilities. Then he shook his head. This would be enough for now. He stepped forward and brought out the crystal Mydroja, to which he murmured. In a moment a green light pulsed forth from it and bathed Relkin's face.

Relkin awoke with a startled grunt. He began to rise, but then his eyes filled with the bewitching radiance of Mydroja and he froze as completely as anyone first seeing a dragon and going into dragon freeze.

Mot Pulk beckoned with his hand. Relkin rose unsteadily to his feet and stepped forward as if he were in a dream. Mot Pulk halted him with a hand to the chest. Relkin stared, eyes glazed, his mind numbed by the power of Mydroja.

Mot Pulk permitted himself a soundless laugh. The guards were right outside the door, standing somnolent in the dark with hands on their spears. And inside the room they guarded, Mot Pulk stole away the treasure!

Mot Pulk laid a hand on Relkin's shoulder and began the spell that would dematerialize both of them. The jewel Mydroja flashed brilliant green as the power went forth. Once more the slow process of movement across the subworld of chaos began. Slowly the vitality drained out of both figures, as they stood there frozen, unable to move.

And elsewhere, the first shimmer appeared in the pergola at Mot Pulk's lovely manse of Ferlaty.

Chapter Thirty

It was like a dream, and again it was not a dream. The green light from the stone lit the elf lord's face from below. The one eye was frozen, staring back at him. Relkin felt a thrumming in his blood, a galloping in his temples, but the world was frozen still and he was unable to move a muscle.

Questions poured through his thoughts like syrup, slowed to a crawl. The greatest puzzle was how this interloper had gained entrance to the cell. The next was, what could he want? Relkin knew he was damaged goods now that he'd been labeled as the Iudo Faex. It was all so mad, so utterly crazy. He knew nothing of their Game, and yet they claimed he would destroy it. And now this one-eyed elf lord, whose name Relkin could not recall, had broken into Pessoba's fortified house and abducted him.

And what was happening now? Why was he frozen in place? What did it mean?

So slowly that the process was undetectable the elf lord's face in front of him lost focus and began to blur. The features grayed out, the face blanked. At the same time Relkin felt curiously lightheaded. Even the darkness of the room had changed, turning gray and vague.

And then there came the unutterably strange sensation of suddenly seeing another place; as if through the view of the gray darkness he could see another place. Shapes wild and disorganized surged in gray twilight. He was seeing two places at the same time. It was disturbing. Nausea racked him for a moment. A second later he felt something like a ring of fire draw across his left foot, and then across his right and travel slowly up his legs. It was as if he were being dipped in molten metal. He wanted to scream, but could not even open his mouth. The ring of fire traveled up his body to his waist, then his chest, and finally to his head. It wore across his mind like a searing flash of blue light that left him dizzy and nauseous again.

The riotous forms were taking shape and color. The darkness of the room was fading to nothing. The brilliant viridian of unimaginably lush vegetation had taken its place. The air bore a rich, spicy scent. Relkin understood that somehow or other he had left behind the room in Pessoba's house.

This was like nowhere he had ever seen before. A soft purple sky, streaked with pink clouds, looked down on a world of fantastic plant life. Enormous bull's-eye flowers loomed overhead on ten-foot stalks. Other, smaller blooms ran riot around the bases of these huge flowers, and a lawn of brilliant green filled the foreground. In the center of the lawn was a statue, a creature, vaguely humanoid. Beyond the lawn in one direction was empty space, and beyond it a waterfall that pitched off the gray rock and arced out and down into mysterious green darkness at the bottom of a canyon. In the other direction the ground rose in a series of hilly bumps, each covered in trees. Beyond the trees was the uncanny purple sky.

In that sky burned a small sun, too bright to look at even for a moment, a sun not much bigger than a star.

Relkin knew in his heart that something very strange had happened. Either the world had changed or he was no longer on the world he knew. This madly verdant place was alien in every way. This thought brought on the grim realization that he had no idea how to get home.

He felt a warm wind blow across his face. The smell of the place was strangely sweet. The elf lord stood beside him, in the same position as before. Neither of them could move a muscle. The wind soughed in the round-leaved trees.

Time passed with infinite slowness. The pink clouds were blown slowly across the sky, a process that seemed to take hours. All the while Relkin was immobilized, as frozen as someone with the worst case of dragon freeze.

And then, when despair had begun to grip Relkin with the thought that perhaps he would be like this, a living statue, forever, he found he could swivel his eyeballs. To his right he could see a wooden wall, a vine-covered roof above it. To his left there was more lawn, and beyond, more flowers, in deep blues and purples. His lips opened and he took a breath.

At once he felt his body come to life. Feeling surged through him.

He turned at once to the elf lord.

"Where is this? What do you want?"

But the elf lord made no answer; instead, the figure suddenly softened and lost definition. In a matter of seconds all facial feature was gone and then so was the rest of it. Relkin was alone.

He took a careful look around himself. Suddenly he was breathing hard, as if he'd run a mile at full stretch. His eyes watered. There was nothing to see but jungle, and these huge flowers, and the wooden pergola, roofed in vines. Around the pergola the lawns were smooth, well tended. It was beautiful, overwhelmingly so.

There was something alarming about the scent in the air. A hint of a spice that was just a little maddening. Enticing but also frightening, for some unknown reason. The pergola appeared to be the only structure around. To one side the ground broke down steeply into the grotto, or canyon, into which arched the waterfall from the far side. To the other the clumps of trees thickened into wild, fantastic forest.

Relkin took several deep breaths and tried to get a grip on himself. He took stock. He had no weapons, wore only the bedclothes given him by Pessoba, his feet were bare.

He looked around in the immediate undergrowth until he found a fallen branch that he could trim until he had a four-foot length of wood that gave him a crude club. He felt absurdly better for this armament, although he was aware that it was completely inadequate if there were pujish in this fabulous forest. The thought of pujish worried him into seeking out a climbable tree.

Fortunately, there was a massive, thick-boled tree, configured like an ancient oak but with almost circular leaves, that stood right outside the pergola in the midst of thick-grassed lawn. It was easily climbed and offered a better view of the surroundings. This confirmed his initial suspicions. There was no sign of any other structures or people or anything except verdant forest.

In the tree, equipped with his crude club, he felt more secure. If there was even a chance of pujish in this forest he didn't want to be on the ground with them.

Darkness fell, and then began the procession of the three moons. One after the other they rose above the horizon and threw their silvery glimmer across the forest. Each was subtly different in tone from the others. The first was a pale ocher, the next was umber, almost pink, and the last had a green-gray shade to it. On the faces of the moons were a few marks and visible craters, dark places and lines connecting them. The moons rose at different rates and so their arrangement slowly changed as they swung around each other through the sky.

When all three moons had risen, new life began to stir in the magical forest. On soft wings, moths of mythic size flitted through the dark. One particularly large one came to rest on a nearby leaf. Relkin estimated it was the size of his hand. Then he noticed with a start that when it folded its wings the pattern produced across its back was unmistakably the face of the elf lord with the eye patch.

At last the name came back to him—Mot Pulk, that was what Pessoba had called him. An ambitious elf lord, in trouble, his ranking dropping in the Game they were all so obsessed with. He recalled that mocking voice, as it had questioned him while the spear point hovered by his throat.

What did Mot Pulk want with him? Was it anything to do with his being named the Iudo Faex?

The night wore on. The air remained soft and warm, and the moons swung around each other as they rose to the zenith. Nothing disturbed the night but the soft breeze and the fluttering of enormous moths.

When the moons reached their highest point, Relkin noticed with a thrill of unease that they were aligned, with the pink and the yellow ones uppermost and the green-gray below. The features on the moons now formed the face of Mot Pulk, as if it had been carved in portions on all three.

Relkin swallowed hard. These signs were clear marks of creation. This, then, was a magic world of some sort, completely dedicated to Mot Pulk. These elf lords were like the gods of old. They could create entire worlds, using the power of the slave mind mass that drove the Great Game. This was powerful magic indeed.

What could this elf lord want with him? He was tainted, cursed as the Iudo Faex. That would surely hamper a sale. Or was there to be a reward for him, and Mot Pulk hoped to collect it?

Relkin thought that it seemed an unholy amount of attention to pay to a dragonboy from Quosh. By the hand, he thought, it would have been better for all of them if Katun had never brought him to Mirchaz.

For a little while he fell into despair again and thought of his dragon, lost and no doubt in agony of despair. He felt enormous guilt. No dragonboy should ever lose his dragon, it was the absolute rule of the craft of tending to a wyvern battledragon. Boy and dragon were inseparable and were meant to be that way. Relkin had done a pretty bad job of it if this was anything to go by. He was no longer even on the same world as his dragon. Sick at heart, he stared sullenly at the whirling moons which rotated further and obliterated Mot Pulk's features.

After a while the moons began to sink down the far side of the sky. Relkin was no longer watching, however, for he was sound asleep, his head resting against the side of the entrance to the pergola.

After perhaps a quarter hour, as Relkin gently snored, a short, eldritch figure detached itself from a nearby tree and approached. A thing with the head of an insect and the body of a skinny monkey, it examined Relkin briefly and then returned to the tree. From the darkness at its base it hauled out a large black sack. What was in the sack was almost too much for the monkey mantis to carry, but it staggered across the lawn and laid the sack close to Relkin's feet. Then it extended a razor-sharp claw and slit the bag open to reveal a glistening, pale purple pod the size of a large melon. After a moment's gaze upon the pod, the creature tiptoed back into cover.

Relkin slept on, oblivious. After a while the pod began

to swell. It grew enormously, and its surface began to writhe. Sinuous shapes surged across the smooth, plump purple skin. Clefts appeared, then deepened and darkened and eventually formed separation of limbs and head, until it became visibly a woman rolled up tightly in a fetal ball. The ribs rose and fell; she breathed.

Now the pale tissue lost its purple tone and became pink. Hair grew out on the top of her head, dark and lustrous, and continued to grow until it was long enough to reach her shoulders. At last she broke out of the fetal ball, slowly straightening, then sitting up, then getting to her knees, and then standing with her arms outstretched to the three moons. She was a beautiful girl, as ripe and lush as the verdant landscape that had produced her. There was a birthmark on her hip that looked very much like the face of Mot Pulk.

She implored the moons to stay; she gave thanks to the lord who had allowed her to be born. Firm-breasted, wide-hipped, long-legged, she was the voluptuous fruit of Mot Pulk's imagination and she was happy to exist.

She knelt beside Relkin and studied him in the shifting light of the three moons for a while. At one point she raised a hand, and it seemed as if she might touch him on the mouth, but then she thought better of it and stood back and moved away into the garden.

When Relkin awoke a few hours later, she had pulled flaxen anthers from some of the giant blooms and made herself a simple but sensuous skirt. Still her breasts were bare and when she saw Relkin, she smiled in a way that was both simply happy and openly seductive.

Relkin could scarcely believe his eyes. Out of nowhere he had been graced with the company of the most beautiful young woman he had ever seen. A dark-haired beauty with green eyes, smooth skin, and generous breasts. Relkin felt his pulse quicken, just looking at her. Where the hell had she come from? And she wore nothing but a grass skirt, and that barely covered her to the knees. Relkin was aroused despite all the questions pounding in his brain.

"Who are you?" he said, and thought how stupid he was to think she would understand Verio.

But she nodded that she understood and she replied

in that amazing elf tongue, Intharion, which all could understand.

"I am Ferla," she said.

He gulped for air. His mouth had gone dry.

"Do you know where this place is?" he croaked.

"No."

"Ah." Well, then, there were two of them in that boat.

"I am Ferla. I have not been alive very long."

"Do you live here?"

"Yes. I have always lived here."

"I was brought here, from the city. Do you understand?"

"No."

There was such a vast certainty to that no. Relkin saw that she would know nothing of anything beyond this leafy grove.

Ferla came and sat beside him. "Ferla is alone. Ferla like you. What are you called?"

"Relkin."

Ferla had taken his hand in her smaller one. She took his hand and put it on her breast. Her mouth was turned to his, her full, young lips desiring to be kissed.

Relkin could not resist such temptation. Ferla certainly didn't want him to. The first kiss led to another and then another, and then passion overwhelmed him.

Later, much later, Relkin found himself sitting on the sunny side of the pergola, letting the rays of the small white sun warm his skin. Ferla came from the forest and slowly swayed across the green lawn. In her arms she carried a bounty of food pods, yellow, brown, and red.

The pods had a taste that reminded Relkin of strawberries, and they were satisfying, too. He ate a couple and felt full. Then Ferla came and sat in his lap and they made love again.

And thus it went, for days.

At nights, sometimes, in his dreams Relkin heard other voices. They were of many different kinds. On one level was the tiny voice that was trying to break in, as if someone were standing outside a heavy door and could scarcely be heard. On another level was the dream voice of his dragon, complaining about problems with the joboquin and sore feet. And then there was the other thing, the enormous presence turning slowly beneath him like a whale in warm water, the thing that knew everything and knew nothing at all.

Chapter Thirty-one

When no one returned from Relkin's little hunting group, the new tribe was split down the middle. Half felt their suspicions had been confirmed. The death bone had been dealt and the outsider was gone, killed by pujish, no doubt. The other half were alarmed and immediately sent out search parties. Not a trace of the missing trio was found, although there were some confused tracks found near the river bluffs. By the end of the first day the unpalatable truth was hard to avoid: Relkin was gone.

In this land, when someone abruptly disappeared like this, the usual cause was large pujish. It was just a fact of life. Lumbee was selected to tell the dragon. It came as a terrible shock to Bazil. He heard the words but could not connect them to reality. Then it sank in. Boy was gone. Forever.

Bazil felt his eyes dilate and his breath seemed to freeze in his throat.

Then came a crushing wave of guilt. He cursed himself for letting boy go off on his own. Bazil had broken the cardinal rule for battledragons: Keep dragonboy close at hand. Always know where dragonboy is. And what had he done? He'd let Relkin go off hunting, with just a couple of Ardu striplings for company into this wild, desolate landscape which he knew was haunted by huge predatory animals, creatures that not even a leatherback dragon would have wanted to meet unless he was carrying dragonsword.

The guilt trended down into a depression. He could eat nothing. All night he sat out by the edge of the camp and stared up at the stars, his heart arching with sorrow. He watched the great red stars rise and recalled the ancient wyvern teaching: *When the red stars ride high, destiny swings in the balance.*

Sure enough the red stars Razulgab and Zebulpator were high in the sky.

In all his life, boy had been a constant, the one thing that was always there. Even when all had seemed lost back in Tummuz Orgmeen, the boy had found a way to get the dragonsword to the dragon, in time to drastically alter the situation. Relkin had survived everything; even when they thought they'd lost him at the battle of Sprian's Ridge he'd survived and been found in a field hospital. Now boy was truly gone?

Impossible!

Bazil immediately rose and stomped out of the camp, dragonsword over his shoulder. Fortunately for them, no pujish ran into him that night, or they would have had their heads separated from their shoulders by Ecator's fell steel.

For several days Bazil tramped up and down the land, sweeping all the territory between the camp and the river. He walked and waded up every creek and swamp. He investigated caves and potholes. He found not a trace, not even scattered bones. But then, he reasoned, if the party had been devoured by red-brown pujish, which were so large, there wouldn't be any bones, no mess at all since they'd have been swallowed in just a couple of bites.

Puzzling, though, was the absence of any sign of red-brown pujish. They left a characteristic, heavy, three-toed tread that Bazil knew well. There were none to see. This part of the range had not been visited by red-browns in months. Indeed, there was very little pujish sign at all, perhaps a track along a stream by a small three-toed animal, something no larger than a dragonboy itself, and that was it. There was plenty of three-horns sign; all the trails were ancient three-horns trails, worn smooth over the ages. Three-horns came through here often, usually in small groups and usually moving fast.

Eventually, Bazil went back to the Ardu camp. He was starving to death and he knew it. There was nothing to report, no trace of boy to be found.

The lack of evidence of anything happening to Relkin

and the others disturbed some of the Ardu. Old Iuun tried to start a rumor that Relkin had taken the other two captive and gone south. Big Norwul spoke out loud at the cooking fire and denounced Iuun and anyone else who would believe such a vicious lie. Some of the women of Yellow Canyon stood by Iuun.

The Heather Hills kin group men all joined Norwul. Then so did males from other groups, and in time a majority were behind him. At this show of male solidarity Iuun turned away and hid herself in her tent.

The tribe stepped up patrols. Still no big pujish were seen. One reason the Ardu had come to this campsite was because they knew the area was not favored by the big pujish. The pujish preferred the more open parkland that lay to the south. Still, red-brown pujish were the most dangerous beasts that lived. Everyone recalled the fate of old Eep. Some had gone so far as to say that Eep's death was the fault of their traveling in a large group, namely the tribe. These voices maintained that the tribe could not work, since it drew too much attention from red-brown pujish. Without Bazil's sword they would have faced a desperate plight on several occasions.

Supporters of the tribal idea pointed out that those who'd been killed by pujish had been out of camp, sometimes alone, when they'd been ambushed. No one had been hurt by pujish attacking their camps. The boma and fire combination had been enough to deter the great beasts whenever there had been a serious problem. Pujish were not stupid and could easily see that the cost to themselves of penetrating huge tangles of cut brush, with sharpened stakes worked in as well, would not be worth the meat to be had from the Ardu. Throw in flaming torches tossed against red-brown hide, and the pujish would hiss roar and then move out to the edges of the forest and roar some more before moving off to hunt three-horns. No, the tribe could survive pujish.

Lumbee reminded them that there was still no sign of red-brown pujish tracks and that it was possible Relkin and the others were alive. Perhaps they had been taken by slavers. Perhaps they were in a camp in the south jungle.

Lumbee suggested that a party go back to the jungle and search for Relkin and the others there.

Lumbee's suggestion was ignored. Lumbee's stock had fallen abruptly now that the no-tail was gone. Now she was just another girl. A very pretty one, and one who should be wed soon.

The tribe was split and spent the days arguing. Patrols went out, but nothing was found. Bazil lost heart. He slept most of the time. When asked, he would lend his strength to help the Ardu move something. On one occasion he had to wield the sword on a foolish young red-brown that dared to harass the camp. This red-brown wasn't much bigger than Bazil himself, and yet it charged him at once with a snapping roar and hiss. Indeed, if he hadn't had Ecator in hand, Bazil would have thought twice about tangling with this monster, young as it was. As it was, though, he was armed with the great blade that had felled hundreds of trolls, and several ogres. The young monstrous pujish bounded in and tried to get a bite to Bazil's right flank. Bazil swung Ecator up from under and clove the red-brown from neck to belly.

It was dead in an instant, but the big body thundered on, the massive legs still driving the carcass on, and Bazil had to dodge smartly out of its way. Then it fell in a tangled heap; the tail thrashed briefly and was still.

The sight completely destroyed Bazil's appetite, for once.

The wiser heads in the tribe were getting really worried. They knew they needed the dragon—he was invaluable as a protector—but if he didn't eat, then he would waste away. Already he seemed gaunt and his ribs were showing. Inevitably they came to Lumbee, who was the only one who could converse with the dragon now. To everyone else he had turned silent.

Lumbee brought him food, platters of roasted ground fruits that she knew he loved. A haunch of three-horns, roasted to perfection. He ate, but not with the hearty gusto of yore. Lumbee tried to get Bazil to talk, but he was uncommunicative. She noticed a cut on his forearm that was becoming inflamed. The wound needed to be cleaned and bandaged. She noticed that he was favoring his other hand and when she looked closer she saw that the middle finger was swollen, especially at the end around the talon. Bazil had split the talon and it was infected and starting to get very painful. The potential was there for a serious problem. Many a wyvern lost a finger or toe to infection. Sometimes it could even be fatal, especially to the older individual.

From the gaunt face, the hollow neck and the downcast eyes Lumbee saw a dragon in desperate need of attention.

"Let me help you, please!" she blurted out, unable to contain herself any longer. "I can do it. We have Relkin's kit with his tools and ointments. You mustn't just rot away like this."

Bazil lifted exhausted eyes to hers. "This dragon feel so weary."

"Let me help. You can't give up hope. There's no evidence that they were killed. If they've been captured, then they're in the south."

Gingerly Bazil flexed his hand. The pain from his swollen digit was a constant thing now, and occasionally it flared up like blazes. "Then we must go south and find them."

"But first I've got to do something about that talon. It's split, correct?"

Bazil said nothing. Lumbee took his big hand in her small brown ones, lifted it up, and inspected the damaged talon and the inflammation at its base.

"What would Relkin do?"

"Boy would lance the infected area to let out the pressure, then dress with the white cream that stings."

"What about the talon?"

"Boy would cut that back to nothing. File it down."

"Then Lumbee will do these things."

Lumbee's presence brought about a turnaround in Bazil's spirits. She lanced the infection and filed down the talon. As she worked, she talked to him, telling him that all was not lost and that there was yet hope. The depression steadily lifted as he regained a sense of purpose. They would go south. That was all he needed to know.

A few days later, the talon was much better, the pain

had subsided, and the nail had been filed smooth and flat. The work was good, just about as good as that of a dragonboy. Bazil and Lumbee went for a last look at the river from the bluffs. The tribe was going to leave in two days for the northern hills. Lumbee and the dragon, on the other hand, were going south, back to the jungles with a small party of men, led by Norwul.

The river was wide and serene when viewed from these heights. Beyond it was a sea of green where the forest clung to the southern bank of the river for many miles. In the distance hills rose up to block off the horizon.

Bazil stepped back and looked south. And saw Ium and Wol standing unseen on an outcrop of rock. Bazil's eyes widened. Instinctively he slid into hiding, pushing Lumbee ahead with a huge but gentle hand.

"What?" she said.

"Silence. I see Ium and Wol."

Her eyes went wide. Incomprehension followed by understanding and amazement came in swift succession.

"Relkin?" she whispered.

"I don't see boy."

"Where have they been? What does this mean?"

Bazil was in motion, though, circling around to come to the next outcrop through the forest and thus to cut off any escape from it. Lumbee followed in his footsteps. As always she was amazed at how quiet a dragon could be as it moved through the forest. It was something he shared with the pujish.

If Ium and Wol were alive, then so might Relkin be. But where was he? Lumbee's head was buzzing with questions she wanted answers to, and soon.

Chapter Thirty-two

Bazil suddenly stepped out of concealment behind the two young Ardu, who were still standing there, staring into the east from the top of the bluff. His shadow spilled across them and they whirled around in panic, expecting pujish.

"Greetings," said Bazil in his best Ardu.

Ium and Wol stared at him, dumbfounded.

Lumbee emerged from the woods and stood beside Bazil.

"Where have you been?" she said. "Where is Relkin?"

Wol and Ium exchanged a long look.

"Tell us!" she fairly shouted at them.

"They will kill us if we tell you."

"You may not live if you don't tell," she replied.

One glance at the dragon was enough to confirm what she was saying. His big eyes were blazing.

The young Ardu hung their heads shamefacedly.

"We were afraid. They told us to go to the Yellow Canyon and stay there."

"Who is they?"

"Ommi and Pilduk, mostly."

"Ommi?" Lumbee was incredulous. "He wouldn't."

"Ommi and Pilduk threw Relkin off the cliff. We saw him fall to the river."

Lumbee was stunned by this news.

"Boy dead?" growled the dragon, who drew Ecator in a swift, fluid move. In Bazil's eyes Wol and Ium saw the imminence of death.

"No!" said Wol. "He swam across the river. We saw him step out on the far bank."

"You lie," rumbled the wyvern.

"No, he tells the truth," said Ium. "They beat us and told us to go to the Yellow Canyon. That's where we've been. Ommi said he would kill us if we told anyone what we had seen. He said they would kill Relkin if he came back."

The dragon head swung around to Lumbee.

"Lumbee, dragonfriend, do you think they tell truth?"

Lumbee was acutely conscious of the fact that she held the lives of the two young men in her hands. Fortunately she was also sure they were telling the truth.

"I do."

Bazil looked up and over to the green on the far bank.

"We were afraid," said Wol, his lower lip trembling.

It took a moment for Bazil to accept this and internalize it. That was a long moment for Wol and Ium, as they looked at the dragon and expected death. Finally Bazil gave a soft snort. These were just boys, not even dragonboys. Dragonboys were different—they were hardened in war, the hardest school of all. The drop from that bluff was a long one; only the toughest could have survived it.

"Then possibly boy lives, but somewhere on the other side of the river."

Bazil was in motion the next moment. The Ardu had to trot to keep up with him as he headed south, where the bluffs fell away and the river wound through meadowlands.

As soon as he was able to, Bazil climbed down to the water's edge and slid into the river. He called Lumbee and the others to join him.

"Hold on," he told them, and when they were attached to joboquin or scabbard, he pushed off into deeper water, propelling himself with smooth strokes of his long tail.

It was wonderful to be in the water again. He had avoided it since he'd first heard of Relkin's disappearance; now he surged forward into the glorious coolness of the river like some enormous crocodile. His flesh rippled in the water and his heart sang with renewed hope.

Boy might be alive! He had lived long enough to cross this river, anyway. Boy might have been afraid to come back, since it had been Ardu that had thrown him off the bluff.

Bazil ignored the unlikeliness of this thought in his newfound joy in living. He drove himself furiously through the water, terrifying fish and other creatures all around him, and rose up on the far side and strode ashore. He paused and took careful stock of the situation. Important to come up with a plan. Alas, boy was usually responsible for planning. Bazil had to admit to himself that over the years he had become accustomed to letting Relkin organize life. It was the usual way in the Legions. Battledragons were intelligent, but they were unsuited to the minutiae of daily life among human folk, things like schedules. It was easier to let dragonboys take care of those things. But now it was up to him to come up with a plan, and for a moment he couldn't think of a thing to do. It was overwhelming. The vastness of the land here was frightening. The eastern side of the river was a flatter landscape, more heavily forested in the north, more open in the south. Boy might be anywhere.

For a few moments his jaws moved angrily as he tried to grapple with it. There had to be a way. How would boy do it? For that matter, how would the dragon himself do it if he were hunting?

These thoughts set his jaws together and he thought harder. There was a lot of space to cover, and time and energy were at a premium. It was best to look first by tracking up and down the riverbank. For a few miles in each direction at first. Try to find some sign of where boy came ashore.

Up and down the shoreline they went, searching for some sign of Relkin. It had been some time since boy might have passed here, but there had been little rain, and it was possible some track might have survived, some scrap of information concerning a dragonboy's fate.

Nothing presented itself. No tracks had survived. Regretfully, Bazil turned north again and retraced their steps, carefully examining every inlet and beach. They found tracks, including several trails left by big pujish, but nothing that looked like a human footprint.

They reached the northerly point where they'd given up earlier and turned back south. He pushed on this time, and this time he was rewarded. They emerged onto a sandy area, where the beach was very wide, and there they found the remains of a reasonably recent campfire. Coals, ash, and pieces of burned wood littered the center of a ring of blackened cook stones. Excited by this discovery, Bazil checked the shoreline, and sure enough he soon detected the long straight mark left by the keel of a heavy boat.

It had been hauled out of the river, right up onto the sand, and there was still the imprint of the boat's keel.

"Boat was here," he grunted. Ium and Wol agreed.

"Slaver boat was here," said Wol.

Lumbee found a scrap of leather, a foot-long piece of thong.

"Slavers were here."

"Slavers take boy."

Bazil was certain now. To him all the pieces of the puzzle had fit together. He knew in his heart that if boy were alive, boy would have come back. Dragonboys always came back.

"Have to go south to find him. There are cities there. Boy will be there."

"We will go south, but we have to tell the others. Some will want to come with us."

"We must go with you. Ommi will kill us otherwise. Our kin folk hate us and will not come to our aid."

The dragon snapped his jaws together. "Ommi not kill you."

Lumbee grew frightened for Ommi. She was still not sure she could accept that Ommi had done this, despite Ium and Wol's certainty; despite the fact that she believed them when they said Relkin had lived to swim across the river. But if he had committed this crime, then the great dragon might kill him, and Ommi was kin of Lumbee's and one to whom she might be wed. If the dragon killed any Ardu, it would make him a kind of pujish. He would cease to be the forest god. But she knew that nothing would stop Bazil if he decided to slay Ommi, and if the Ardu got in his way he would kill them, too.

Bazil was silent as they set off, moving alone in a very grim mood. The Ardu followed him at a respectful distance. This was to save their lives.

Senses clouded by strong emotions and fragile hopes, they headed back down the riverbank to a point where they stood on a bank about ten feet above the river level. The top was flat and open, with a dense thicket of small trees about a hundred feet inland. The ground was rock-hard and hot beneath their feet. The river was a blue-gray mass to their right. Bazil was thinking of how much he would like to swim forever in that water.

Suddenly, with explosive swiftness, the thicket of small trees erupted as a huge red-brown pujish lurched out of concealment and charged them with an earthshaking roar. The beast was on them in an instant. There was no time to deploy, no time to even draw Ecator. The Ardu ran for their lives and so did the wyvern dragon. Against this monster, easily three times his own weight, with a head jammed with serrated teeth like knife blades, Bazil knew he had no chance at all unless he had a weapon in his hands, preferably Ecator.

Bazil dug his big feet into the ground as he accelerated. Each stride might be his last, for he could feel the closeness of the red-brown. Some sixth sense made him duck, and he heard the massive jaws snap shut just behind his neck. The fishy stench of the great predator's breath enveloped him for a moment. The river was ten feet straight down and no telling how deep it might be. But it was his only chance. There just wasn't time to reach up and pull Ecator from the shoulder scabbard. To stop for a second was to invite sure death when the monster's jaws slammed shut around his head.

He ducked low, desperately; there was another loud snap just behind his ears. The next would surely have him, and then Bazil was launched in thin air, all two tons of him hanging for a split second in nothing before he hit the water with a tremendous splash, went to the bottom, and sank into a deep bed of mud. For a moment he floundered there, and then surged out into the river in a vast cloud of disturbed sediment.

Another ear-shattering roar-scream came from the top of the bank. The massive red-brown did not fancy a jump of ten feet. With weird delicacy for a brute of its huge mass, it spun about and stalked downslope, where it thrust into the water at the earliest opportunity from lower ground.

Fortunately, the red-browns were so well adapted to hunting on the plains that they were not nearly as good swimmers as wyverns, who were predators of shorelines and inshore seas. Bazil had a huge lead, big enough that he was able to detour to pick up the young Ardu, who had hit the water first and swum out quite a ways. Still, the red-brown did not give up until it saw Bazil step up the beach on the far shore. It realized then it had no hope of catching him and it turned and swam back to the other shore.

In the meantime, of course, Bazil had pulled Ecator from the scabbard, and had the big predator pressed his attack, he would have paid for it with his head. A wyvern dragon with dragonsword in hand was still too much for any pujish, no matter how massive and mighty.

Together, shivering a little, they watched the huge red-brown stride out on the far side. It gave its great scream-roar and marched off into the forest. For a long time afterward their pulses were all still pounding hard.

Bazil, in the meantime, kept Ecator in hand and insisted that they all keep a keen eye for any more such monsters. The red-browns were acknowledged masters of ambush and could hide their mountainous selves in very modest clumps of vegetation.

The western side of the river remained peaceful, however, and they made their way back to the camp without any further excitement. The sun had just set, the cooking fires were going strong, and soon there was food. Wol and Ium crept into hiding—Lumbee brought them some food in secret—while Bazil ate a hearty dinner and then settled down to sleep well, for the first time in weeks.

The next day, in the late afternoon, Ommi came in from yet another hunting trip. Since Relkin's disappearance, Ommi hadn't been around the camp much. He had chosen the wrong day to return.

Bazil spotted him as he came through the boma. Ommi always seemed to take evasive action when he saw the dragon, and sure enough, as soon as he saw Bazil looking at him, Ommi slipped away into the tents of the Red Rock kin group.

Bazil gave no sign of further interest, but that night when Ommi was in his own sleep skins, the tent flap was suddenly pulled up hard and the whole tent rocked and almost collapsed as the dragon shoved its head inside.

Ommi yelped in fright, and would have bolted out under the side of the tent but for a big hand that shot forward and pressed him to the skins.

"Why you try and kill my boy?" growled the dragon in the dark, a vast menacing shape that promised death.

Ommi quailed. "I never—"

"Don't lie," snarled the monster. "I know truth. I found Ium and Wol."

Ommi gasped. Then the monster knew everything. Ommi doubted that Ium and Wol could have kept the truth from Bazil.

"He lay with Lumbee!" he said with sudden rage. "How can Ommi wed Lumbee, now that she has slept with a no-tail?"

The jaws snapped. Dragonish pragmatism came to the fore. "You are stupid. Lumbee and boy cannot fertilize the eggs. Too different. She unfertilized. You take her and fertilize her if she accept you. So you lose nothing."

Ommi purpled. "He defiled her!"

Dragons found it difficult to comprehend the jealous passions of mammalian beings. Dragons only mated when females were ready to fertilize eggs. It was a brief time, soon done with, and afterward females wanted little to do with males. Men and women were so much more intense in their possessive passions. Dragons thought they were mad.

"Boy meet Lumbee far away from here. Nurse her back to health. They feel the thing you call 'love.' You cannot blame them. They did not think they would ever see anyone else again. Lumbee not fertilized, though, so no harm done."

Ommi was unmoved. "She is ruined forever."

Bazil gave a dangerous snort. "Lumbee is dragonfriend. You be careful what you say about Lumbee."

"She would never have done this if he had not forced her."

"Stupid lie. She not forced. Ask her!"

Ommi swallowed. This was the uncomfortable part, for he had asked and been told the truth. It was just that he could not accept this truth. It was inconceivable that Lumbee could prefer the no-tail stripling to Ommi. Lumbee was for Ommi—that had been the unspoken agreement in the kin group. For Lumbee to choose Relkin as a potential mate was so horrible it was unthinkable to Ommi. Therefore he had blacked it out of his mind. Now he was forced to confront this awful truth.

"I cannot! I cannot accept this!" He broke into deep sobs.

Bazil relaxed his grip. "I understand. You weak. Problem is strong." In an absurd gesture the dragon patted Ommi down onto his sleep skins.

"Sleep. I not kill you. You too weak, unless"—the big eyes glared again—"you hurt Ium or Wol. Then I kill you, certain."

The dragon departed, the tent partially collapsed around Ommi, who lay there quivering for the better part of an hour.

Chapter Thirty-three

It was the quiet season in Yazm City. The rains had tapered off, but the dry season had not properly begun. Now came the growing season of the plains. As lush grasses and ferns sprang to life, the huge herd animals scattered far and wide, leaving a denuded region around the lake. In pursuit went the giant predators. At this time the Ardu left the plains completely and went up into the northern hills, where the berries would be ripening.

Since the Ardu were in the hills, there was no easy way to get at them, so the slavers didn't bother. The Ardu would come back to the southern forest when the dry season intensified in a few months.

Yazm's dock cages were virtually empty, and the bars and whorehouses did a desultory business. A few free-booters came through, along with a steady trickle of frontier merchants selling steel tools and good weapons from the weapon shops of Mirchaz. The boat builders were active—they needed to have new boats ready for the return of the slaving parties later in the year—but most other craftsmen had little work to do.

Yasoob the butcher virtually shut up shop at this season and spent his time fishing by day and gambling by night at the Three Seasons Saloon, which also doubled as an extensive brothel in the slave taking season. The owners always brought up women from Mirchaz to work the rooms upstairs. Sometimes there would be Ardu females, too. In the off season, though, there were just the regular girls, mostly.

On this night, however, there were a couple of young Ardu girls being heavily used upstairs. A trader named Noron had brought them in from his last swing through

the bush. His men had captured the girls after killing the
rest of their family in an isolated part of the forest. The
girls were completely wild and had to be broken in before
they could be worked as regular whores in the brothels.
So Noron had put them on the house in the Three Seasons,
there for anyone who wanted to take them now, while
they were still wild.

Yasoob had been thinking about it for a while now.
Tuts and Boo-whit, who ran the boat depot store, had
been first. Tuts had a fat lip and some bloody scratches on
his face when he came out, but he also had a bg grin.
Those Ardu girls were famous fighters! Which made
raping them that much more satisfying.

The boat men had crowded in then: Rylok, Clope and
Clanth, and then all their workers. Yasoob thought the
Ardu girls would be getting pliant by now. Yasoob preferred them that way himself. Wrestling with a squalling,
tailed bitch was not his idea of fun. It was better when
they were physically broken but still had some spirit left.

He took a swallow of mint beer. He'd had a good
supper. Baby monkey, cooked with lemons and served
with a mash of putcheems, had been the main course, and
very tasty, too. He belched contentedly and the sound
echoed in the room. Yes, it was another quiet night in
Yazm City, except in those rooms upstairs where the
Ardu girls had fought their desperate battle and lost.

Outside the mean little town, straggling along the bank
of the river, the forest was quiet, too. It was the quiet of
the grave, usually, since most wildlife had long since been
hunted out around the town. There was no game within
five miles of the place.

Light from the moon spilled over the forest. The dark
masses of trees were broken in many places by clear-cuts
where men had taken wood for fires and construction.
Yazm City was a hungry place, busy devouring the forest
around it. This was a night like any other, except in one
remarkable aspect. For while it was very quiet in the
ruined forest, it was not empty.

Silent figures moved through the night. Two lines, each
of fifty Ardu men, moved toward the flickering lamps of
the town. And with them came the dragon, stalking for-

ward like the ghost of the ancient pujish that had once roamed these devastated woods.

One of the Ardu girls being raped in the rooms above the Three Seasons let out a bloodcurdling scream as she was beaten by a man whose mouth she'd just bitten. The eyes of the Ardu men seemed to glow a little in the dark. They hurried their step.

The dogs of the town sensed something was up when the party was at the town outskirts. Soon they caught the scent of Ardu, and then of pujish, and began to bark. No one took much notice at first. The Ardu trotted down the street, clubs and battle axes swinging easily in their hands. A man stepped out of a warehouse and was struck down almost instantly. Two more came out of the River Inn, arguing about a bill, and found themselves confronting six armed Ardu. They barely managed a scream before the Ardu clubs were thudding home, driving them to the ground.

That scream did bring a few heads to windows, and at last Yazm City awoke to its peril. Dozens of strapping Ardu bucks were sprinting through the streets whirling their war clubs over their heads.

Shouts of alarm, the rumble of boots on floorboards, a hoarse bellow from someone on Pangler's Dock as he was clubbed and thrown into the water for the fish to eat, joined the general barking of dogs.

In the Three Seasons, Yasoob the butcher heard the news as he set down a fresh mug of mint brew. It was really hard to accept. He was feeling good and was looking forward to going upstairs and having one of those Ardu girls. And now there were Ardu bucks out there killing folk? It was incredible. It had never happened before. It wasn't likely to be happening now. Yasoob refused to believe it. He was going to stay put.

Then a rock came smashing through the big glass window of the Three Seasons. Following it came an arrow and then another rock. The arrow sank into the pillar beside the stairs. Everyone looked at it stupidly for a second or two and then they leaped to their feet.

Converted to instant belief, Yasoob ran for the back door.

He found a scene of intense confusion. Outside the door
a dozen Ardu bucks were waiting and their clubs flashed
in the moonlight as they struck home. Tuts and Boo-whit
had already been brained and were lying on the ground.
Old Meldrom joined them there the next moment, as he
was hit with a tremendous blow across the side of the
head delivered by a mountainous Ardu male.

Yasoob ducked and turned around and ran back inside,
elbowing boatmen aside. He heard the screams and blows
continue. This was serious! The town had to react with
discipline. They had to organize, get swords and shields!
Call out the guard. Yasoob found his voice.

In fact the guard, four sleepy fellows who were usually
to be found fishing off Pangler's Dock, were responding
to the call. They ran out into the street with spears and
shields and immediately came under ferocious assault
from a dozen or more Ardu youths. They shouted for help
at the top of their lungs.

Yasoob sprang out into the street, armed with a trun-
cheon taken from behind the bar in the Three Seasons.
Rylock and Clope joined him; they had big watermen's
knives in their hands. They moved to join up with the
guard. Their arrival drove the Ardu bucks back and now
they had possession of the main road and the front of the
Three Seasons all the way down to Pangler's Dock.

But now rocks were being lobbed at them from all
around, some coming right over the buildings and
plunging down into the street. Several other men had
joined them by then, including big Sturjon, the slaver,
who had taken command. He was a huge man, heavily
armed and greatly feared in Yazm City. Sturjon told them
to move down to Pangler's Depot, where they could get
inside out of the hail of rocks.

There they found more men who'd gathered from the
other beer halls down the street. Uat the little Nadrosi
weapons merchant came up with two men toting a box
laden with swords and tomahawks. They handed these out
to the rest, who took them eagerly. Yasoob grabbed a
heavy cutlass and swished it through the air. It was sharp
enough to take someone's head off with a single blow. As

a butcher, Yasoob was wise to the ways of meat and sharp implements.

Now let the Ardu come!

He and the others let out war whoops and yells to get their courage up. The Ardu had pulled back. Flames licked up from the stables across from the River Inn. A man and a woman ran from the building next door to the stables and were pursued into the dark by a pack of Ardu youths.

Upstairs in the Three Seasons one of the rapists, too drunk to make it out the windows, was caught with his pants down. Norwul picked him up bodily and dropped him over his knee to break the man's back. The man's scream was the loudest of the night so far. Then Norwul hurled the man bodily off the top floor balcony into the street, where his screams cut off abruptly.

The Ardu girls were cut free from the beds to which they were tied. Fire was set downstairs. The Three Seasons would be no more than a hellish memory in less than an hour. In the kitchens, Ium and Wol smashed the cages holding monkeys, birds, and little pigs and drove the animals out to their freedom.

More men were coming: Lagzul the carpet seller, Herme the boat builder, everyone was turning out with weapons. The first unbelievable story had turned out to be true. The damned Ardu were actually attacking the town. This was unheard of. After last season's war in the forest the Ardu were getting outright dangerous. The men of Yazm were united. They'd show the brutes some cold steel and then they'd take them for slaves. Damned Ardu would regret their temerity in attacking Yazm City.

The situation was already out of control, however. Parties of Ardu were running up and down the alleys, killing anyone they came across and starting fires in the sheds behind Pangler's Depot.

Tuts's place was blazing. His hunting dogs came raging out of the blaze and were killed by the Ardu with terrible blows from their war clubs. Next to slavers the Ardu hated these dogs more than anything in the world. They showed no mercy.

There were twenty-five Yazm men now, and they

formed a big circle and moved down the street toward the blazing Three Seasons. The Ardu attacked suddenly, ten of them leaping out of the shadows of the alley between Pangler's and the fish sheds. Ardu clubs and Mirchaz steel clashed. There was a melee; the men struck home with their spears—swords drove in against unprotected bellies. Lagzul was down, but so were three Ardu bucks. The others pulled back.

The men gave a great cheer. They could do it! All they had to do was get everyone together in a group and they could kill or drive off these damned Ardu. And now two stable hands ran up, terrified after crouching in the hay while the Ardu killed Bonship the horse handler and set fire to the hay. Poor Bonship had fought hard, and they'd killed him slowly. Everyone had liked Bonship and the news of his death was greeted with roars of displeasure.

After the two squeaking stable boys there came a group of six men, in from Shayt's Saloon at the southernmost part of the town. They'd heard nothing until that scream from the Three Seasons when Norwul broke Porrity Banbup's back. They'd pulled weapons from their shacks as they came and had even chased a couple of Ardu youths in the alley briefly before reaching Pangler's.

Boats were going over the river to the houses on the far side. There'd be reinforcements from there, too. Pretty soon they'd have a hundred or more and then they'd really go on the offensive.

More screams came from Poke's Alley, where Madame Hanek and her daughters lived. Some men were tempted to run up there in response, but were harshly told to stay with the main group. They couldn't afford to get all separated and broken up. It was important for them to stick together and draw everyone in. Besides, Madame Hanek was a pain in the ass and her daughters were too expensive for Yazm City. Someone joked that Madame Hanek had only to let her daughters screw the Ardu and everyone'd be fine. The Ardu would all die of the pox, too!

They roared at that and waved their weapons above their heads.

No one noticed Bazil slide out of concealment in the shadows behind the warehouse that stood next to Pangler's Depot. He took a long step forward and raised Ecator high.

Suddenly he was there, towering over them. Men screamed at this apparition. The sword flashed in a crimson-stained arc and six men were cut in two in the twinkling of an eye.

This was truly the unimaginable, the nightmare of nightmares, a giant kebbold from the forest loose in the town. Ecator whistled in the air as Bazil struck again and again.

Yasoob had the presence of mind to duck inside the depot. Most of the other survivors broke and ran in all directions. The Ardu chased them, barking like dogs and swinging their heavy war clubs.

Broken up into little groups and singles, the men were hunted down and slain. Clubs thudded into heads, knives slit throats and bellies. The Ardu men had built up an enormous charge of hatred for men like these, exploiters and slavers alike. None would live long in Ardu hands.

Yazm City was soon engulfed in flames, and what did not burn was smashed and thrown into the river.

Yasoob the butcher, along with a couple of boatmen, escaped clinging to a piece of driftwood. When they dared to, they kicked to shore and then ran downriver along the banks as if hell were at their heels.

Chapter Thirty-four

Relkin awoke, eyes staring in terror. The voices were calling, the dream voices that came more and more frequently now, making sleep hazardous. They wanted something from him, but what it was he did not know. They called to him like distant metallic gnats from far across a misty meadow. He could not understand the tiny, high-pitched voices.

It was still deep night. A sliver of moonlight came in through the door and it frosted faintly the graceful outline of Ferla's shoulder and side. Her breathing came soft and easy. Her long hair, bunched in a ring of flowers, covered the pillow.

His breath, sobs virtually, was the only sound. There was sweat on his brow and all down his back. He put his head back and gasped. His nose itched and he had to fight down the urge to scratch it. It was still healing and touching it would only make it itch more and hurt a lot.

Normally Relkin simply wanted Ferla. Whenever his eyes fell on her, he desired her. That had been the way of it for days and days. Time had stopped having much meaning. He slept, he ate, he made love to Ferla, that was about it.

But now, disturbed again by those tiny metallic voices calling to him from across the fog, he felt cold and uninterested in Ferla's immediately beautiful arm and hip. He hated waking up terrified like this. He hated this vague, insistent pressure in his mind. They wanted him to listen. He shook his head irritably. Why did they need to call to him now? Why couldn't they just leave him alone?

He pushed himself out of the bed and walked out through the other rooms to the balcony overlooking the grotto. The moons were descending to the horizon, the features of Mot Pulk scattered on their surfaces. Relkin felt as disorganized as the features on the moons.

He was no longer really sure who he was or what he wanted from life. His plans and dreams seemed far away. And yet, life had never been so paradisiacal. He had food and water and Ferla. Why would he want to go anywhere else? And still the nagging questions would surface out of some deep well of self-preservation.

What was he doing here? What did the elf lord want with him? And where was this place, this grotto of hedonistic luxe? He had no answers and, increasingly, no desire to learn them anyway. He was shedding the need to know anything. All that mattered was Ferla, and food, or sometimes food, then Ferla. For drink they had the crystal-pure water that came from the spring. Food was pods and fruits that Ferla brought from the forest and prepared in simple, easy ways.

Ferla was Ferla.

Most days Relkin took walks on the hill above the grotto. At other times he exercised, working his muscles hard to retain condition. Sometimes, especially after a meal of food pod, he would just sit in the pergola and stare into space above the grotto, until Ferla came and took him back to bed.

Relkin was not a novice to the arts of love. Not after that summer in Ourdh, when he and Miranswa Zudeina, Princess of Ourdh, had been lovers. They had lived together during the crazy period after the end of the great siege of Ourdh. From Miranswa he had learned much about love. And with his beloved Eilsa Ranardaughter there was another kind of love, a love so pure and central that he could not bear to think of it now.

But with Ferla there was an oceanic sense of peace and emptiness in the act of love. With Ferla it was as if he had dived off the world itself into the deep, smooth waters of oblivion.

During these times he thought of anything but Eilsa, or a certain leatherback dragon of legendary repute with dragonsword. With Ferla he thought of nothing except Ferla and physical pleasure. Guilt and loss, disorientation and fear, even the weird little voices from far away, all were banished in the glow of Ferla.

He wanted Ferla in so many ways he couldn't count them. He wanted her when she came back from the forest, when they had eaten food pod and fruit, when she laughingly tore away her garments made from woven flowers and jumped into the warm bathing pool.

At other times he would sit by idly and just watch as she wove flower stalks or sliced food pod and marinated it for breakfast. The way she moved, her shoulders, breasts, and buttocks all had a soft, sensual grace that was so perfect that it went beyond the merely human. She rarely spoke, but when she did, her voice was always light and soft, sometimes husked with desire, sometimes tinkling with laughter.

Most of the time, though, they said nothing. Words seemed superfluous.

He went out on the balcony from the main room. The grotto below was dark, but the trees on the hill were still silvered with light from the moons. His mind was blank now. The fear brought on by the dream had faded; the sweat had cooled and was evaporating from his skin. He stared into the darkness and thought of nothing. He was drained, emotionally empty.

At that very moment there came a feeling as if something were knocking on a door in the center of his consciousness. He blinked, but had barely begun to react mentally when there was a blinding flash that ripped across his senses with a burning smell and the sound of molten metal hitting water. An image, an amorphous shining thing, rose up in his mind. It grew and distended.

"You!" It said to him—as if a whispery voice had spoken in a silent room. The surprise was mutual. Confusion reigned. He sensed that the entity he felt was not really aware of its own existence.

"Are you the one?"

Recognition blossomed. He had felt this before in the city of Mirchaz, where he had seen it in dream, lying below the city, a great whale of submerged mentality.

"What do you mean?" he said aloud.

"The one!"

And then the blinding flash was repeated, but in reverse, and left him gasping on his knees on the balcony, holding his head.

It was gone.

His mouth had gone dry, his nose tingled, there was a weird discomfort in his stomach. He had seen it. For a single moment he had glimpsed the great mass of human minds, enslaved into the mindless service of the Great Game. Endless rows of them. Lying silent in the dark marble galleries while their minds were ruthlessly used by the elf lords to give power to their Game of power and ego.

Relkin now also saw that underlying the existence of Ferla and the grotto of love was a vast magic of a complexity beyond understanding, created by the great elves in their decline. The magic was powered by the slaves, ten thousand at a time, stacked in the stalls below the pyramid of the Game.

Relkin of Quosh had seen far too much sorcery in his young life and some of the things he had seen had amazed and horrified him. But he had never experienced anything like this. The sense of mental contact had been so absolute, so complete. It had stunned him at first and then left him hungering for more.

In that moment of contact, Relkin had seen into its heart. It did not know what it was, so distracting was the multitude of mental tasks that the component minds were engaged in. It was too busy with the roaring torrents of detail to glimpse the vaster picture, using the wholeness of the gestalt consciousness that it had developed. Those minds, boosted to constant, massive effort by the magic of the elf lords, were keeping the whole vast edifice of the Game in being. All the magical pleasure worlds, all the palaces floating in air, all the moves and pieces, were given life by these slaves who would be burned out within a year and thrown into the street, witless, suddenly aged by sixty years and left to die of starvation, disease, and exposure.

The slaves did not know their power. They had but to awake and they would shake down the worlds and bring the Great Game to a halt.

This is what they meant when they said he was the Iudo Faex. And for a moment he felt a premonition of death. To be the Iudo Faex was to be the destroyer of the whole empire of dreams built up by the evil lords of Mirchaz.

To be the Iudo Faex meant being the killer of Ferla.

For a moment he stood very still. He could not kill Ferla! But he could not leave this evil edifice standing. The forces warred within him. He had to awaken the mind mass. Yet if he succeeded, then Ferla would cease to exist, along with this entire worldlet, with its moons of Mot Pulk.

His throat had gone dry. He went up to the spring and splashed some cold water on his face and then climbed to the pergola above the grotto. The moons tumbled slowly toward the horizon. The stars were beginning to show. Soon the stars would be visible, forming Mot Pulk's features in the same broad strokes as seen on the moons. There was only one constellation, and it was Mot Pulk.

He slipped into the pergola and found to his surprise that Mot Pulk himself was inside. Mot Pulk came here sometimes, to sit and think. Relkin wasn't certain of this, for Mot Pulk did not deign to speak to him on these occasions. He was protected by the demon statue, which came to life on his command and prowled around the pergola. A glance out at the lawn showed the demon on its pedestal. Mot Pulk had chosen to be without its security.

"So, there you are, the prodigy, the sought-after object of desire. I hope you have been enjoying the lovely Ferla I made for you."

"Ferla . . ." At the mere mention of her name, Relkin wanted Ferla. And a sudden rage blossomed in his heart at the thought of Mot Pulk doing anything to Ferla.

"Yes, child, my Ferla. I made Ferla to entertain you. This is my world, and Ferla is a construct of my own design. Did you know this world takes the power of five strengths to hold, and yet it is completely hidden?" The elf lord seemed immensely proud of this.

"All the power of a full node is concentrated here, but they can't find me. Hah! So much for the Cabal, and even for the Tendency. They disparage my game, call my gambit a fault, but is there a world more lushly beautiful than this, which I made and they have never found?"

Relkin stared stupidly at the elf lord, whose single eye glowed gold.

"Why?" he managed.

Mot Pulk frowned, caught despite himself. "Why, what?"

"Why do you want me here?" Relkin mumbled.

Mot Pulk stared at him for a moment. "Everyone wants you, child. They're harrying me to find you. But none of them know the route to this place. My Game is too good for them."

"Why do they want me?"

"Because you're the Iudo Faex, child. Or at least that's what the fools believe. It only takes one weak-witted ancient to come up with that label and that's it, mass panic ensues. 'Iudo Faex,' indeed!"

"I still don't understand."

"Of course not. You're just a young soldier, I know that. All of this nonsense just sails over your head. But you have been happy, haven't you? You have been enjoying Ferla, I am sure."

Just the way Mot Pulk said Ferla's name made Relkin's teeth go on edge.

Relkin closed his eyes to shut out the thought of Ferla. "Stop that. I know what you're doing."

The elf face cracked into a perfectly symmetrical laugh, all but for the eye patch. "Such a creature! I do not regret it. It was sitting there to be taken. That fool Pessoba is as ignorant as a cow and half as intelligent. He took no precautions against entry on the psychic plane. And so now everyone hates me and they pursue me through the worlds."

Relkin's eyes had widened.

"But they shall not find Mot Pulk!" A crazy triumphant smile flitted across the perfect features.

"Why do you play this game that uses so many slaves?" said Relkin suddenly. "What right do you have? You burn up their lives like so many candles."

The lone eye of Mot Pulk was gold, with a small blue center.

"Do my ears detect a complaint from you? Here you are in the very concept of paradise and you are complaining. What is wrong? You don't want the luscious Ferla in your bed at night?"

"Don't talk about Ferla," husked Relkin.

"The arrogance of it, the sheer unmitigated gall. Child, you appall me."

"Leave Ferla alone."

The elf face broke into a weird leer. "Oh, I see. Well, you better be good or I'll have Biroik attend to her in front of you."

"No." Relkin was irresolute, unsure.

"Biroik!"

The statue demon had come to life and descended. It advanced on the pergola, snorting fiercely.

"That is Biroik," said Mot Pulk evilly. "You had better not let him catch you in the pergola."

Relkin slipped out the far side and outran the demon to the invisible perimeter of the area it patrolled.

Chapter Thirty-five

Halfway around the world from the evil city of Mirchaz lay the blessed isles of Cunfshon, green and healthy beneath the summer sun. In Cunfshon City's great harbor, a mass of ships rode at anchor or were winched into the docks. Dominating the rest was the white ship *Barley*, her side catching the sun with blinding glare.

Across the waters of the estuary frowned the harsh walls and granite towers of the imperial city of Andiquant. Here beat the heart that gave strength to the Empire of the Rose. Here also was waged the constant struggle familiar to bureaucracies everywhere. The empire was a benevolent system, run by astonishingly few bureaucrats, for it relied on local rule in all but a few functions of government. Still, the functions quarreled over scarce resources. Wily servants of the state intrigued constantly.

These struggles ran from the lowliest of concerns, such as the ongoing battle between the city sanitation service and the office of shipping over the matter of the excess paper waste, to the highest levels, where concerns involved the entire world.

From the outside, Andiquant appeared at peace. Ivy grew on the walls of buildings, and carefully tended quadrangles of grass looked verdantly cool in the warm sun. The imperial gardens were flush with flowers and the horse chestnuts were in bloom.

Inside the gray stone buildings, it was a different matter entirely.

Outside, the sun shone brightly on the walls and windows of the Tower of Swallows. Inside a room on a high floor, behind heavy drapes, two towering figures of authority confronted each other in semidarkness, lit only by a pair of candles.

The Emperor of the Rose, Pascal Iturgio Densen Asturi, sat in his favorite chair, an old, comfortable navigator's chair, that he had favored for many years.

Across the map table sat the Greatwitch Ribela of Defwode, Queen of Mice, dressed in a black velvet gown trimmed with silver mouse skulls. More mouse skulls glittered on the ends of silver skewers in her long black hair, which was pulled back behind her head. Ribela exhibited her usual chill, lean-faced beauty, ageless but not young.

Emperor Pascal had sat his throne for more than a decade. He had weathered many storms and seen great victories for the empire. Still, these meetings with the witch were difficult. They were essential but hard to bear. At least with Lessis there had been a comradeship, a sense of mutual respect. With Ribela there was just the chilly contempt that she exhibited for all men.

In truth, these were difficult times with hard decisions to be made, but the poor chemistry of the relationship between emperor and Chief Officer of the Unusual Insight exacerbated problems and made life even more exhausting than it had to be.

Pascal had known Lessis of Valmes for most of his life. She had been an odd, occasionally glimpsed aunt who popped in and out at critical periods, observing him. Rarely had she given him advice. Ribela, on the other hand, had always been a creature of legend, an undying thing that lived in a coffin while her mind explored the vastness of the Mother's Hand. He had never expected that he would have to deal with that creature in her eerie physical form on a regular basis.

Or to put up with her insolence and contempt!

The basic problem was that Ribela was used to communicating only with inferiors. When she spoke, she gave orders. Only with Lessis and the other greatwitches would she speak in any other form. She also came from the most matriarchal and conservative of all the provinces of Cunfshon and was ill disposed toward men in general. This made a deadly combination in someone who was an adviser to an emperor.

An emperor did not take orders, especially not the Emperor Pascal Iturgio Densen Asturi. As a result, they were constantly butting heads. There was no sense of collegiality.

For the thousandth time, he regretted the loss of Lessis. She had resigned her office and gone into retirement after the campaign in Eigo. No one understood her reasons for doing so better than Pascal himself, who overnight aged ten years when she gave him the final casualty list. That night, it was said, his hair went white. Thereafter he found sleep a torment and avoided the light of day.

With Lessis lost to the mystic, there was only one other choice to head the Office of Unusual Insight. This office was the most secret part of the imperial government, completely hidden within the much larger Office of Insight. The "Unusual" ran spy networks in dozens of countries around the world and combined the efforts of many greatwitches, bringing the emperor the most vital intelligence. The office had always been headed by Lessis, the second oldest of the greatwitches of Cunfshon. She had advised the emperors, and emperors frequently followed her advice. Now she was gone, however, and the only mind that could hope to replace hers was that of Ribela, the oldest of all.

Ribela had definitely not sought this appointment, but she accepted the judgment of the other greatwitches. Ribela was the only one of them who had spent long periods of time with Lessis on certain highly important missions. Lessis had run the office for so long, and affairs had grown so complex in far-off theaters, that only Ribela had enough overall information to understand it all.

Ribela grasped Lessis's thought more clearly than any other person alive. She had also grown to realize how important to the Empire of the Rose was the witch Lessis. Filling those plain little shoes had turned out to be an enormous job. Somehow, without appearing to do so, Lessis had run a tight little bureaucratic ship that maintained several hundred spies and informants, plus networks of contacts and safe houses and friendly shipping firms, and on and on, and Ribela was just amazed at how much work there was to keep it all in motion. She had never given these matters much thought while she pursued her own agendas, in her own department within the Office of Unusual Insight. Ribela had covered the astral planes and undertaken the arduous and hazardous investigation of the higher planes.

Harried and anxious, Ribela, too, had found sleep a difficult matter. Not that she needed much sleep, but every so often it was essential. Being physically exhausted made her irritable. It was all too easy to clash with the emperor.

In particular, she found his newfound caution in military matters most irritating. It was the source of constant flare-ups between them. He couldn't seem to grasp the strategic point that risks had to be taken!

Once again she pulled back from her own harsh words.

"I am sorry, my emperor, I did not mean to impugn your motives. But this is the moment to strike. We have our great enemy on the defensive. Axoxo is the last fortress between our forces and the Inner Hazog. If we can dominate the Hazog, we will be threatening the heart of their realm. We can force them to battle and destroy them while they are still weak, still recovering."

Pascal nodded, controlling himself with an effort, having been virtually called a coward a minute before.

"Well, Lady, are we not besieging Axoxo? We have four Legions in place there, with elements of a fifth covering the supply route."

"I know, my emperor, but it is not enough to simply lay siege to Axoxo. Not with only four legions. We must capture it. Axoxo must fall, and soon."

"I cannot risk more than four legions at any one time. As it is we have called up the reserves all across the Argonath. This is a delicate time. Here in the isles we still grieve, you understand. The losses in Eigo will wring bitter tears from every village in these islands for years to come. Some will never recover. Think of Tel Delf; they lost all nineteen sons in the village."

Ribela knew the sad story of Tel Delf, and those of a dozen other small villages that had been overrepresented in the Legion of the White Rose that had gone to Eigo. She refused to allow sentiment to color her judgment.

"The generals think they can do the job with what they have. They say you must cut them loose. At present they sit in front of Axoxo and run occasional interdiction patrols behind the city. Smuggling goes on night and day and Axoxo is not completely cut off. Reinforcements have even gone in."

"The generals hope to win reputations. It is rare that generals die on the field of battle these days. Though we lost our great Baxander that way, in Eigo. Those men at Axoxo are recruited to my standard! I am their emperor and I am responsible for their lives. I will not waste them."

The word "waste" caused Ribela's hackles to rise. She knew that it referred to the Eigoan expedition, which had resulted in so many casualties. Ribela knew that the expedition had ended with the resounding success of the primary mission. She was also aware that Pascal had never really accepted the mission to Eigo. He had gone along with it on Lessis's plea, but he had never really believed it. The horror of the casualty lists, thousands and thousands of dead, thousands of maimed and crippled, had confirmed him in his dislike of the advice of witches. As Emperor of the Rose he was obliged to consult with them, but he feared their manipulations and was set against them in his heart.

The problem was that after long and careful consideration, Ribela had grown certain that the long war could be ended within a decade if they could but capture Axoxo. This fortress, deep in the White Bones Mountains, was the key to the inner Hazog. By a stroke of good fortune they had already captured the other eastern bastion of the enemy, Tummuz Orgmeen. Thus if they took Axoxo they would open up the outer lines of defense. The path to Padmasa itself would lie open.

She swallowed her anger. "Heruta was destroyed in Eigo. Our enemy's counsels are clouded. The four divide, two on two, and cannot easily make decisions without Heruta's lead. Gzug Therva thinks that he should now lead. Gshtunga disagrees. The others are indecisive."

Pascal shook his head in dismissal. Reports of this kind were always hard to accept. How could the witches have such quality of information? His own networks were unable to penetrate the Square in Padmasa.

"There is no hard evidence that Heruta was destroyed. Padmasa still has great strength. Axoxo will be hard to capture outright."

"You doubt the word of Lessis? Why would Lessis lie? It would hardly be like her. But whether you believe her or not, now is the time to strike, while they still reel from the Czardhan success in the uttermost west. If we hit them hard enough, they will have to weaken themselves in the west. The Czardhans will press hard. Padmasa itself may fall to us."

"I would welcome it with all my heart, but for now I will not risk five thousand men's lives for this dream. We will besiege Axoxo and we will bring it down. The engineers are working steadily enough."

"They will undermine the south tower of the citadel in two years' time! That is too long. That will give the enemy time to recover. The loss of their great army in the invasion weakened them throughout this theater. We have the initiative. We must not be afraid to use it."

Pascal Iturgio Densen Asturi had had enough. "You are the greatest of our mages, Lady, and you have delved deeper into the secrets of the world than any other, but you do not bear the responsibility. That falls to the emperor."

And this was the rock-solid heart of the Empire of the Rose. The greatwitches could advise, but they could not rule through magic. Ribela could easily have over-whelmed the emperor's mind with one device or another and planted her wishes there. One suggestion or another would do the trick, but it was forbidden, absolutely and utterly. Any suggestion of sorceress rule and the people of the Isles would rise and begin to build the burning pyres once again. They had freed themselves in long-distant times from the rule of wizards and would not endure it again.

Ribela thought, with regret, that Lessis would have been capable of moving the emperor without magic. She would have found some way to salve his psyche in the matter of the casualties and get him to see the need for swift, decisive action. Ribela hated this job. She took a deep breath and tried to be as deferential as possible. It was very difficult to do this with a male.

"My emperor, I know that you find me difficult. I accept that I am not the right person for this posting. I know that you were much happier with Lessis, but, alas, she is not here. She has gone into the mystic, leaving me as her unworthy successor."

Lessis had been the mentor of every emperor. Pascal Iturgio now demonstrated that he had learned something from the Gray Lady along the way, and spoke in his most gracious tone.

"We must overcome these differences, Lady."

"I agree wholeheartedly, my emperor."

"Good. Then we will take further advice about these ideas. Perhaps a sortie into the enemy's rear territories will be recommended by all, and other ideas may surface."

Ribela could not help herself; the words slipped out without her control.

"No, this is wrong! Time is short in this interval. You waste it at your peril. Attack now—we can capture the place!"

Pascal Iturgio Densen hated the Eigoan disaster, and feared to lose ten men more to add to those thousands that haunted him in his dreams. His name would go down in history as a figure of grim tragedy. The witch kept rubbing him raw on this place and would not give way. With a great effort he controlled himself.

"We will take it in good time and without unnecessary slaughter."

"My emperor, may I repeat the elements of the problem?"

She was talking to him as if he were wet behind the ears. He ground his teeth but refrained from exploding.

"First, the Czardhans are unified. They have defeated Padmasa in one campaign and are poised to begin another."

" 'Tis true. Even Hentilden has joined them. The Trucial States are at peace with all their neighbors."

"And with our siege of Axoxo we have largely cut off

the trade in Ourdhi women for the slave pens in Padmasa. The supply of fresh imps for their armies has dwindled dramatically."

"For this we give constant thanks to the Mother, morning and night."

"And now we besiege Axoxo, while already holding Tummuz Orgmeen. The door is almost open to our enemy's heartland."

"Ah, that is true, but opening that door all the way might cost ten thousand lives, Lady. Our edge in battle is our trained infantry and our dragon force. If we lose those, we lose everything."

"We are the weaker force. We have to accept risks."

"Up to a point, but that point has been reached. The foolishness in Eigo has used up our reserve and with it a lot of our goodwill from the folk of the isles. Remember Tel Delf, Lady! The folk will not stand for suicidal attacks."

Pascal had good reason for his concern. The fortress of the Doom of the White Bones Mountains, Axoxo, was a peerless keep of adamant built atop frowning cliffs on three sides. An easily defended route into the mountains behind was covered by two small forts. All works were on a tremendous scale and were equipped with the heaviest catapults and trebuchets. To besiege it completely would take an army of two hundred thousand, kept in the field for perhaps a year. They had perhaps a tenth of that number.

In addition the supply line for the besiegers was long and frighteningly tenuous. A long passage across the grasslands of the Gan. The nomad tribes were always out there, waiting to pounce and take their toll. To keep it all going was enormously expensive and the empire was already stretched to the limits of its financial resources. Only levies on the Enniad Cities of the Argonath could produce the necessary funds to keep the siege going, and the cities were already balking at the additional taxation. To risk heavy casualties by adventurous soldiering in this situation was too much for the emperor to consider.

Ribela had heard the simmering anger in the emperor's voice. Her own teeth clamped against the rage, and she backed off. Lessis would never force the emperor into an argument, for he would become immovable. Turning aside from her own natural inclination, Ribela bowed her head and became silent. She could not move him with words alone. The temptation to cast a spell and force her way was very strong, but she could hear a warning voice in her ear, that calm, gentle voice that Lessis always used.

Ribela tried to appear attentive as the emperor turned the conversation to a subject more dear to his heart, the building of new grain chutes at the Darkmon Breaks in Kenor. The new lands coming under the plow in the high country were producing such an abundance of grain now that the existing chutes had become a bottleneck at the end of the harvest. Pascal Iturgio had taken a personal interest in the problem. He believed firmly in encouraging the agricultural boom in Kenor. The populations of the cities were swelling, and the grain magnates of the older provinces, along the eastern shore, were becoming a political and social threat. It was the emperor's job to cut the grain kings down to size. No individual city-state could deal with them, and they already ruled the councils of the King of Kadein. Pascal Iturgio had put his own personal money into the project. He produced a map and a series of watercolor renderings of the new chutes.

Ribela nodded and smiled at what she hoped were the appropriate times. When he was done, she made her excuses and left, returning to brighter light of day, blinking after the gloom of the emperor's chamber. The sense of frustration ruined the otherwise pleasant effect of looking from the Belvedere at the base of the Tower of Swallows, out into the lovely green dell of the Upper Garden.

Feeling old and defeated and even misused, Ribela trudged through the city to the drab-looking block that housed the Office of Insight. There she went to the second floor and passed through the quiet rooms of the Office of Domestic Insight. Few people were about; Domestic was a small service, and most of its work was actually done by the provincial officials of Cunfshon.

At the back of the Office of Domestic Insight, a short passage and a right-angle turn brought the knowledgeable person to another blank door. Beyond that door lay the small, musty rooms of the "Unusual."

Here worked a dozen or so people, the faceless functionaries chosen by Lessis to pull together all the strings of networked information from around the world.

Here also Ribela kept a cell for her own personal use. It was austere, with nothing but a lovely red Kassimi rug on the floor and a simple cot cut from Defwode oak and made in the Crafte Way. She hung her robe on a hook by the door and placed the silver skewers from her hair onto the small Crafte chest of drawers on one wall. She took up a hairbrush from the same small chest.

Wearing just her hose and tunic, she sat on the cot and took a series of deep breaths to calm herself while she brushed out her long straight hair.

Gert, the housemaid, brought her some hot tea which prompted her appetite. Gert then brought her a tray of boiled rice flavored with toasted sesame seeds and salt, some seaweed, and a few segments of orange. It was enough.

She decided to meditate on the difficulty. She knew what Lessis would have done, and she felt humiliated that she could not match Lessis in this dimension. But diplomacy and manipulation were not her strengths. She would seek guidance in the Mother's Hand.

Ribela finished her austere meal, washed it down with tea, and performed some stretching exercises.

Sleep in her current state was out of the question. But she could achieve a restful meditative state. She crossed her legs beneath her and closed her eyes and composed her mind for the shift in modes. Her breathing became deep and regular; a count of seven through the left nostril and seven through the right was her favorite pattern.

There came the familiar dislocation, the feeling that the surrounding world was receding and growing silent. Darkness and peace entered her soul, and with them came a spreading relaxation.

She murmured a prayer to the Mother and the centering presence of the universe for which she dedicated her life. Once more she floated in perfect solitude in the emptiness. At this point she was ageless, connected in a heartbeat to the young woman, Ribela of Defwode, who had first explored the great powers of the white magic of the witches. It was she who had codified it and taught it to the Defwode coven, and from there to the world. She had located its secrets in this dark, solitary place in her mind. Here lay the essential Tao of existence and with it the ways of altering the vibrations of being and mastering the subtle energies underlying them.

For Ribela this was a blissful state.

And then quite suddenly she was aware of another presence. A horrifying intrusion, something that had never happened before. She recoiled in shock, but before she could even open her eyes and disengage, the presence exploded across her inner horizon like a vast thundercloud, lit from below with flickering lightning. And from the cloud came communication.

It was unintelligible. Like tiny voices shouting far away, the noise of the insects. Ribela knew at once that it was the High Ones, the strange, mercurial beings known as the Sinni.

Suddenly the voices of angels were singing around her, and perfect alabaster-white faces, elven faces, appeared to float in front of her eyes.

The most bizarre images flickered in her mind.

The white angel faces metamorphosed into the faces of insects with huge green eyes. A glass globe, with the continents of Ryetelth upon it, spun slowly and then fell from its cradle to smash in slow motion upon the floor, pieces flying in all directions, spinning, whirling, lost.

And then all went black, and in lightning flashes she glimpsed a vast edifice, walls that were miles long, towers and battlements beyond assault, huge gates that frowned over a precipice. Ribela shivered. Surely this was the Heptagon of the dread Lord Waakzaam, the largest single structure in the universe on the dead world Haddish. But what did it mean?

Then the oppressive sight was gone and was replaced by a scene of flat savanna upon which burned a hot sun.

Enormous monsters of antiquity placidly grazed in the thickets. Their huge heads were surmounted by frills of bone from which two deadly horns projected above the eyes, while a third horn stabbed up from their nose. They were the most dangerous herd animal that had ever existed, a river of enormous life, eating its way across an ancient continent.

Eigo, this was a view of the Lands of Terror in the heart of the southern continent. And then the monsters were gone and were replaced with a view of a city of white marble, seeming to float above a blue lake. A pyramid faced in marble dominated the rest. Out of that pyramid floated a face, all alone, and she realized with a start that she knew that face. It was a certain dragonboy from the Marneri Legions, a boy she had known quite well during the terrible struggle in Ourdh several years before.

The Sinni could not communicate easily with humans. It was as if thunderclouds wished to speak to ants; there was no basis to even begin. But Ribela understood.

They wanted her to find Relkin of Marneri. There was a message that he must hear, and things he must do, but they, the High Ones, could not contact him themselves. Ribela must do it. At once. There was not a moment to lose.

At last the shock struck home.

"But he is dead!" she said, breaking the silence of her cell.

Relkin's image remained vibrant.

"But the volcano . . ." she began, and then fell silent. They believed that he lived, though how he had survived the events retold by Lessis was hard for Ribela to grasp.

Somehow he had survived; that was all that mattered. She recalled what the dragons had said about Relkin. That he was harder to kill than a ratbug. If anyone could have survived the inferno, it would be Relkin.

"That little rascal is still alive. Well, well."

Ribela had a moment of fond feeling. She sighed. That's what came from this constant exposure to people. Then she had another thought. She must be sure to tell Lessis.

"But where is he?" she whispered.

The image returned of the savanna, and in the distance a great range of snowcapped mountains. A shoreline on which a warm sea beat endlessly.

"Eigo, of course, but Eigo is a big place."

The marble city floated above the blue lake. The view had shifted to show a steep-sided peninsula that jutted into the lake. Atop the hill was a turret bearing a massive statue of a man with arms extended.

Ribela knew at once what it was.

"The statue of Bos. He is in Mirchaz."

Ribela gave a nervous shiver. Alas, what dreadful mischance had lured Relkin to that nest of evil? There, locked away in isolation, dwelled the fallen lords of Gelderen. Long ago they had forsaken the world and hidden themselves in their fastness.

Since then they had been known only for their perversities, their massive population of slaves, the vileness of their imagined universe. They had grown fell and evil and ignored the world outside their savage realm. For Relkin to have landed among them did not bode well.

The final image was mysterious; three moons tumbled through the sky, their surfaces cratered in an interesting way.

Abruptly the thundercloud in her mind shrank to a sphere and then to a pinpoint and was gone in a clap of psychic thunder that left her shaken as she emerged from the remains of her meditation.

She put out a hand to steady herself. This was not the way one usually came out of meditation mind.

But already she was thinking through what she would need. The first thing would be a couple of dozen prime young mice.

Chapter Thirty-six

The Ardu fleet now consisted of five longboats, a dozen smaller ones, and the raft, on which reposed the dragon. The raft was a crude affair. It sagged beneath Bazil's weight and was devilishly difficult to steer. Frequently it snagged. As the days went by, the front became waterlogged and began to dip. Some of the bindings were coming apart and the logs shifted every time he moved.

Bazil realized that the Ardu were not nearly as good at building rafts as the imperial engineers that he was used to. He recalled with sad fondness the huge rafts on which the Legions had floated down the great River Chugnath on their way to the Inland Sea. Those rafts had been tight, their bindings taut and their upper surfaces dry. The Ardu raft was soon halfway waterlogged and Bazil's feet were wet the whole time.

This wasn't a problem at first; wyvern dragons were designed to swim. But he had cuts on his feet that began to fester. Nothing Lumbee could do would stop it, since they were in the river water all the time.

Finally they had to call a halt and let Bazil's feet heal in the sun while the Ardu men did their best to rebuild the raft. After two days the cuts were mending and the raft was much reinforced. They resumed their progress downstream.

Along the way they had picked up some Ardu who had been abandoned by slavers spooked during the campaign in the forest. They'd been wandering in the forest for months and joined the expedition, eager to kill slavers any way they could. They were happy to throw in their lot with the forest god and his little army.

Towns were few and far between in this region of

steep-sided hills and dark, primeval forest. But whenever the travelers came across one, they liberated a few more Ardu, acquired more swords and spears, and left columns of smoke threading the skies above the slaver mansions. In front of them went a swelling tide of fear-stricken fugitives and a growing rumor of terror and war.

Town militias were incapable of dealing with hundreds of Ardu warriors and a battledragon armed with dragonsword. There was a notable slaughter at a place called Calzac, where a force of about a thousand men gathered, confident in their numbers. They found the Ardu line hard to break, and before it could they were beset by the dragon, who suddenly appeared whirling a huge blade that cut through men by the half dozen in a tight press. The men panicked. A few armed with long spears tried to rally behind their leader, but the Ardu threw war clubs with lethal accuracy and then the dragon broke them up and sent them running.

The Calzac brigade was forced to swim the river after a third of its number had been hewn down or taken captive by the Ardu. In the river, other predators took their toll. Scarcely half the brigade made it to the farther shore. The tale of the Battle of Calzac soon spread down the river and helped to empty the frontier settlements.

In between fights and some fishing, Bazil had little to do. He kept the sword sharp and performed exercises with it at every landfall, to keep his muscles in shape. A good long swim at the end of the day when he went fishing was enough to keep him healthy. The rest of the time he sat silent, trying not to worry.

His overwhelming concern was that he would be too late and that the boy would be dead before he could get there and find him. If boy was dead, he vowed to take a grim revenge on Mirchaz, whatever it was.

In the mornings before they pushed off into the river again, the Ardu practiced the arts of war taught them by Relkin. They formed squares, at first of four men, then of eight, and then of sixteen, and practiced defensive tactics. In actual battle they still lost all cohesion very quickly and became a line or a mob. Still the drills were performed enthusiastically and they were steadily getting better. The Ardu had the sense that this was magic of a high order brought down to them by the forest god and that they must learn it well.

Then they practiced fighting in threes, two men in front armed with newly acquired swords and a third behind them, ready to assist or to stab over their shoulders with the spear. All carried spears now, as well as swords and war clubs. No matter what, they would not give up their war clubs. They had become reasonably proficient in this style of fighting, and with a single commander they might have gone far. As it was, they argued a lot of the time about who should be saying what to whom.

They practiced with the sword, but they had much to learn, and in actual sword combat had taken quite a few casualties in some of the earlier battles. After Calzac, however, few militia groups would stand against them and they passed almost unmolested.

Lumbee had tried to fill the place of the dragonboy. She had tiny amounts of the Old Sugustus antiseptic from Relkin's big pack. She had Ardu poultice lore and herbs and guidance from Bazil himself, who insisted on cleanliness. Water had to be boiled, bandages cleaned. He knew these things from endless lecturing in the Legions. One reason the Legions stayed sharp in the field was that they paid attention to details. Cleaning wounds and using antiseptic was one of the most important of those. They avoided dozens, even hundreds of unnecessary deaths to the deadly infections that could take hold from the smallest cut. Between Lumbee's efforts and Bazil's memory of how things were done, they had cured his feet and kept him in fighting shape.

At night he sat a little apart from the Ardu, by a small fire that they made especially for him. Lumbee brought him food, usually roasted tubers and baked fish. Bazil ate heartily, as always, and felt no shame, since he usually contributed a big river fish to the pot. Sometimes these fish weighed more than two men and were ten feet long. When he had eaten, Lumbee would go over him for cuts and ticks.

As she worked, Lumbee practiced her Verio on Bazil. This always meant she wound up asking the dragon for new words. Nearly always, he was able to supply them. Bazil was surprised at just how much of the human tongue of the Argonath he had absorbed over the years. Indeed, he knew it as well as any man.

On the tenth night on the river, Bazil watched the dragonstars creep above the hills. Lumbee put some more wood on the fire.

"We cannot be far from Mirchaz now."

"How do we know that?" Bazil was depressed. Lumbee did not know it, but she had a sulky dragon on her hands.

"I just feel it. We have come a long way. Mirchaz must be close."

"Bah! This dragon does not feel this. No signs yet of larger towns. In fact there have been fewer of them these last few days. Perhaps we are going in the wrong direction."

"Oh, no, this is the right way to go. Ardu know that much."

"Ardu know too much for own good," rumbled the wyvern.

"We have never been in these places, either, Lord Dragon."

"I am not Lord Dragon. We do not have lords among dragons."

"Yes, uh, Lord Bazil."

He growled in dragonspeech, Lumbee went on blithely. "We know the slavers come up the river. That is all they have to do to reach the Ardu summer land from their city."

"We are lost."

"Lord Bazil, we just have to follow the river."

"You not understand." Bazil seemed on the verge of an outburst. Perhaps he would get up and plunge into the river for a swim, if only to get away from all humans, Ardu and otherwise. He'd done that before. He'd also taken Ecator and savaged some vegetation, even though he knew it would dull the blade. Lumbee didn't know the tricks required to stir the sulky dragon out of his mood and help him settle.

But this time he got a grip on his emotions without any

help and slowly damped down the anger and fear that were causing such turmoil in his heart.

"Sorry. You good friend to dragon, Lumbee. This dragon just anxious. Just have to find boy."

Far away, in the city of Andiquant above the harbor of Cunfshon, the Greatwitch Ribela made preparations for great magic.

First she asked Gert to get her some mice. Old Gert knew what that meant and set into operation a well-oiled system of mice procurement. Soon she had a half dozen stable boys at work with traps and scraps of cheese. Within the hour she would have the two dozen requested.

In Ribela's cell there was a small altar stone made of Defwode marble that stood by the wall. Ribela had lit cubes of lapsulum incense and the heavy musky smell filled the room. As it thickened, so Ribela went over the Birrak and assembled the patterns of declension and volumata that she would require. She practiced a few tricky volumes. It was a spell she had used many times before, but there were more than a thousand lines of declension and some of the shadings were very fine. Ribela had always believed in the memory drills and exercises of her sorcerous craft.

The curious sounds of the volumata and the hushed incantations hung in the still air, vibrating in the incense smoke. Elsewhere in the crowded rooms of the Office of Unusual Insight the workers felt the hair stand up on the backs of necks and hands, or tears suddenly start from their eyes. They, too, knew what this meant and made their own preparations for the coming squall.

In her kitchen, a small, comfortable room at the rear of the offices, Gert set herself down on a stool with a sack of bread and a gallon jug of olive oil. She broke bread into chunks into a tub, soaked it with oil, sprinkled on a little salt, and chopped parsley and stirred it together with a big wooden spoon.

There came a knocking at the back door, leading to the service stairs. There was young Will Wisk with a sack of mice.

"There's thirty in there," said Will.

"If we use more than the two dozen, I'll compensate you." Gert handed over two imperial shillings. Will bobbed his head, thanked her, and darted away to join his comrades in a long afternoon of spending on sweets and small beer.

In Ribela's room, the mice were unceremoniously dropped to the floor, where they streaked for the corners. Gert had to resist an urge to stand on her chair. She had never accustomed herself to the scurrying business at this part of the rites of the Queen of Mice.

The mice ran hither and thither about the chamber, seeking a way out or a place to hide. There was nothing. They milled in the corners and the bigger males started fights with the smaller ones out of fear and tension.

Angry squeaks and yips of pain came from the corners. A few straggled along the walls, one or two were still exploring the base of the bed for a hiding place. But Ribela blew into a set of tiny silver pipes and out came a fragile sound, a high-pitched elfin song, lilting and gliding through a golden meadow far away. The mice froze in place and stared upward with eyes like glossy black pearls.

"Thank you, Gert. Be ready with the food. They will be very hungry after a while."

Since Lessis had hired her as a young girl back in Defwode, Gert had taken care of these rooms and the witches within them. She had done a lot of strange feeding exercises. She had fed bird seed to Lessis, one grain of millet at a time. She had fed any number of dazed seagulls that had been impressed into the witch system of transoceanic message transmission, and she had fed Ribela's mice.

The spellmaking was begun and Ribela caused the lapsulum incense to glow. The room filled with a shimmering power. Now Ribela was indeed the very Queen of Mice. She gathered them to her and they came willingly, running in a circle atop the altar, tail to mouth, tail to mouth until they were a blur of little bodies. As they sped up, so Ribela began a passionate declension from the Birrak and the thing was in motion. The cadences rose and fell as the spell was woven. As it went, Ribela fell into the deep trance state, but even as she did she

continued to manage the mice, releasing those that tired
and allowing them to feed, but always keeping at least a
dozen in motion. This spell would need a great amount
of power, as much as she ever used. She intended to project her astral self halfway around the world. Such a
journey would require great energy from these mice.
Ribela shuffled the mice with practiced skill, but without
conscious thought.

The spell progressed and Ribela's declension was fault-
less. As it took effect, so one part of her mind continued
to recite the words in her little cell and manage the mice
while another detached from her body and rose above,
floating through walls and ceilings. When she was free
and clear of anything solid, her astral projection collapsed
to a point and sank into the subworld of chaos.

The mice went in and out of the ring and Gert refilled
the fuel bowl again and again as they devoured bread
and oil.

Ribela now flew through the familiar realm of chaos.
Gray backwash swirled in endless vortices through the
ether. Patterning erupted from wave collisions, and heavy
crackling of lightning sent jagged blue flashes searing
away into the pixellated fog. The Queen of Mice had
spent much of her life traversing this dread region.
Now her astral self arrowed away through the gray murk
past black-patterned confusions of waves toward distant
coordinates.

Such an energetic presence in their realm inevitably
drew the predators, the Thingweights being the most
notable. One by one they swung in alongside her,
matching her pace, thrusting tentacles into the place they
felt she must occupy, but they found nothing there.
Baffled, they fell back, and some began fighting one
another. Others attacked the smaller predators that had
also been drawn to her trail. She left a wake of horrid
struggles, twisting tentacles of fire, monstrous feasting on
the dead.

As she progressed, so her scale shifted and she seemed
to rise above the sea of whirling vortices and to see farther, to a vast horizon. As she sped on, she began to sense
a presence there.

It grew as she approached and eventually she saw the first whirling lights over the terminator. Then the whole cluster appeared, thousands of blue lights all racing around an unseen center. They completed an orbit of that center once a second, and as they went, their light flickered, producing a wild, maddening display.

Ribela had seen this object before from a distance and knew well what it was. This was the pocket realm of the Lords Tetraan, fugitives from the world since the days before the Old Red Aeon. This was the product of the Great Game they played in their hidden city, Mirchaz. The lights blazed furiously in blue and purple white, thousands upon thousands of them.

That was where she must go. Ribela sent her astral self directly toward the center of the cluster. The lights rapidly grew in size and became a vast whirling shell that occupied half the universe. Then she dropped through the outermost shell and flashing teardrops, vast as worlds and flashing blue fire, were hurtling past her at the rate of one or two a second. She fell farther and entered a lower shell, where even more of these teardrop bubbles were active.

A vast churning of bubbles is what the whole thing was, but these bubbles were worlds, forced out of the ether of the Hand of the Mother by great sorcery. Each of these self-contained bubbles was a world, complete and unto itself. Each could only be entered through the Game portal, which was controlled by the lords who faced each other across the Great Game board in the Pyramid of the Game in the city of Mirchaz.

The predators could not enter here; these hurtling juggernauts produced waves that would have torn them to pieces, since they were nothing but organized energy themselves. But Ribela dodged the oncoming worldlets and continued to sink toward the center. The closer she came, the faster and more energetic were the worldlets. Here she sensed grandiose dreams had been raised up. Some of these worldlets radiated on an emotional wavelength that could be sensed to a degree by Ribela in her astral state. The information was faint, but her acuity was very highly developed.

One passed and she felt a great pulse of lamentation. A

world of woe lay within, ruled in capricious cruelty by a mad czar who enjoyed inflicting pain and suffering on a gargantuan scale.

There came another, and Ribela's heart was chilled. Such foulness she felt here that it made her spirit tremble. Here were great worlds, stuffed with creatures that were tormented, driven to war and social madness, cannibalism and slavery. Their bodies piled up in heaps beneath the feet of the laughing lords. Cruelty had become their single greatest pleasure in some cases.

Directly ahead was the Game center, a swirling sphere of psychic energy that pulsed slowly through the red part of the spectrum, oscillating between a dark dim red and brilliant ruby.

And then she sank into the sphere and entered a place of powerful mental currents. A vast spell was in place and the fused minds of the ten thousand in the mind mass provided all the energy that was required. But Ribela sensed that no ordinary mind could maintain that level of output for long, and thus she knew that this was a systematic abuse of human slaves whose lives were shortened dramatically by it.

And then she felt something else slide over her astral mind. It was not something she could perceive in a physical manner—she saw nothing—but she felt it all the same, as if a mist had arisen suddenly around her in the forest. She realized with a sudden shock that this was a mind of vast proportions, but a mind that was asleep. While its physical components were locked into the aspects of the Tetraan spell that they powered and made real, this gestalt consciousness floated above, empty and without self-awareness. This gestalt was a great engine, and a prominent object even on the scale of the Sphereboard itself, but it knew itself not and therefore was nothing but the plaything of the lords.

Ribela's heart wept for the cruelty and horror that it represented. Here was cruelty laid upon cruelty, for on Ryetelth the native peoples in all the lands around Mirchaz were preyed on to provide slaves for the mind mass. Then in the worlds they created for the Lords Tetraan, there was often nothing but hedonism or, worse, a calculated cruelty that satisfied a dark spirit among these faded elves from Gelderen.

She sank down into the space where the Game grew from the board itself, stretched out in the Pyramid of Mirchaz. There was a strong disorganizing field here that would have disrupted any Thingweight that had survived thus far. Ribela felt it as a sharp astringence, but it did not apply to the astral vibration, which slipped through unscathed. In truth, no other sorcerers had ever matched the greatwitches of Cunfshon in the arts of astrality and animancy. In these, they were the absolute mistresses.

Billions of computations pulsed around her. The mind mass was there, stacked above and below the Game board, ten thousand poor souls kept in marble troughs, fed, watered, and sluiced daily where they lay, lost in the trance state that was their lot. The scale of the magic was enormous.

Ribela was confronted with the sheer majesty of what the Lords Tetraan had done. She understood that they were great magicians, sorcerers far above her in their knowledge of the deepest arts, but she also saw that they were weak and capricious. They were the losers in the war for Gelderen, forced out by the golden elves and driven into exile for their crimes against the holy light.

Then they had fled to the southern continent and dwelled among savage monsters and primitive peoples. They had no contact with the rest of the world, disappearing beyond the mountains into the Lands of Terror. There they had grown inward and fell and their spirits had become dark. And they had created a tiny facsimile of the Sphereboard of Destiny for themselves, where they were the absolute rulers. Through this, they had sunk into a dreadful evil. They grew bored with their paradises and turned to cruelty to satisfy their need for fresh sensation. In some cases cruelty was a limited thing, in some it went to grotesquely horrible heights. Imitations of the reign of Waakzaam the Great, the dread sauronlord of twelve worlds, existed in some of the realms of Tetraan.

And so their great and majestic achievement had been turned into a vast degradation with such foulness at its heart that these lords and ladies were damned evermore.

And there, taking shape "beneath" the eye of her astral self, she perceived the Great Game board spread out. A grid of one thousand squares to a side, one million squares within. This plane of activity was studded with clumps of pieces. The clumps represented zones where the players contested with opponents. From piece to piece flew energies, determined by control of surrounding space. Small pieces were in constant motion. Occasionally a piece under assault by overwhelming power would explode into flames, collapse, and be absorbed by other pieces.

Thus did the Tetraan pass the centuries in tedious battle over access to their pleasure worlds. On this diabolical loom they wove the magic that controlled the entire process.

Ribela let her astral mind flow out and grow tenuous as it formed a film over the board. Relkin of Quosh was here, the Sinni had given her specific images to locate him with. If any outsider could penetrate this maze, it was the Queen of Mice.

She let her consciousness float as soft as down, as insubstantial as spider silk, slipping into the pieces, reaching out to the Game players hunched over their positional boards in their Game chambers above. None felt her subtle presence, so absorbed were they in their own activities.

She avoided contacting the great gestalt which underlay all of this activity. That would be to risk madness. She might be destroyed in an instant if it woke up. And she had a mission to carry out.

Through the chambers filled with gaming lords her consciousness seeped, probing so softly that she was undetected. And then quite suddenly she found what she sought. In an instant she concentrated her attention. There in that chamber, the one who called himself Psithemedes was focused on the problem of finding the world that the one-eyed lord had hidden. The one-eyed lord who had taken the boy! The boy with no tail who came from the Ardu land.

And there, another lord was thinking of the same one-eyed Game lord. A name floated up, Mot Pulk it was. And here was another, Zulbanides, who sought the impious Mot Pulk. They were all seeking the same Game lord as she and they all sought him because he had possession of the boy Relkin.

The Sinni had not prepared her for this. What was going on here?

Chapter Thirty-seven

Relkin and Ferla sat in the pergola taking the late after-noon sun. It was their favorite time of day. The air was warm, the land itself was content beneath the sun. They relaxed in each other's arms. Soon, when the sun went down in the riot of orange and green yellows that was customary at sunset, they would go back to the apartments and make love. Then they would eat. Then they might stare at the moons in a drowsy, dreamy way. Then they would sleep.

Relkin hugged Ferla close to him. She responded by turning tender hips toward him and putting her mouth up to be kissed. Their lips met and they held the kiss for a long time. Soon they would go downstairs to the wait-ing bed.

The familiar warmth spread through Relkin's loins. He held her more tightly. Never had he known such generous beauty. Not even Lumbee had been this enticing, this overwhelming as a sexual partner.

And then something very strange interrupted the normal sequence. Ferla's lips pulled back; she gave a little gasp as if stuck with a needle while sewing. Her eyes shot wide open and she pulled away with a shriek like a scalded cat, and ran to the door rubbing her mouth.

Relkin looked around him, but saw nothing that might have frightened her so. There was nothing there except the flowers and the view and the warm breeze.

From outside came a gagging sound. He looked back. Ferla was on her hands and knees being sick.

"Ferla?"

She did not look up. He went down and knelt be-side her.

"What is wrong, Ferla? Can I help?" He put his arm around her shoulder.

She shrieked and shrank down and rolled away.

"You called me Ferla?" she screamed in a harsh voice that was quite unlike her.

"Ferla, what has happened?"

"Ferla?" She put her hands to her face, distraught. The harsh voice continued.

"What has happened? Oh, by the love of the Mother's Hand, I have lost the thread to my own body. I am cut off here. But how? What magic has done this? And this body belongs to . . . who?"

She looked up at him with narrowed accusing eyes.

"Ferla?" he said blankly.

"Who is Ferla?"

"You?"

"I am not Ferla, you fool boy, I am your friend Ribela. You remember me, child, we met in Ourdh, as I recall."

Relkin began to seriously question his own sanity.

"Ferla, what is this?"

"I am not Ferla!" hissed the witch. And indeed, Ferla's lovely open face was now shrouded with concern, disgust, and other unknown emotions. Her generous, loving spirit was gone. The eyes worked differently, the body was carried in a wholly new way.

"I do not understand—" began Relkin.

"You are not alone in that. I was seeking you, and I tracked you here, but in a subtle form, on the astral plane. Something broke my hold on my own body. I had to take shelter in this mind; it was almost empty anyway. I sense that it was not a real person's mind. There are no memories—it's truly as if it were born yesterday."

Relkin swallowed hard. His worlds were crashing violently together.

"Then . . . I . . ."

"You are a prisoner in this most devilish of world systems. The Lords Tetraan have transgressed against all decency here. They have done monstrous evil."

"Evil? Ferla?"

"The girl herself is not evil, but she is not real, either. Oh, these Lords Tetraan, they have become most foully corrupt. And they have unwittingly created a new force. They do not even suspect its existence, I surmise."

This last remark was not directed at Relkin, but to the empty air above the lovely little grotto. However, it triggered a chord in Relkin.

"You sensed it, then. It lives in the Game itself!"

"Ah, you have a streak of the eldritch in you, child. Lessis said you had the luck of a wizard. Maybe you would have been one in another life. You detected the thing that they have made. It sleeps, but when it wakes, it will end all of this."

This new Ferla, with the aggressive look in her eyes, was examining him minutely. Relkin felt himself blush. He realized he was naked and he was suddenly ashamed of the fact.

He backed away and found his clothes, the lovely garments given him by Lord Pessoba. Ferla followed him and watched him while he dressed. Indeed, Ribela's initial disgust at the intimate contact with a man had given way to an odd flutter in her ancient heart. She actually found herself studying his lean young body. Relkin had picked up some scars in his time in the Legions, but he was now in the flower of his youth.

"You have changed, young man, since last we met. There is a mark on you that I did not perceive then."

Relkin swallowed. That damned thing about destiny again. But where was Ferla? What the hell had happened?

Ribela had detected the mark of the Sinni themselves. She was moved to pity for him.

"Relkin, this body I inhabit. Where Ferla lived. It is not real, child."

"Ferla is gone?"

"She sleeps, that is all. I reside in her centers of higher intelligence. She maintains the body and its functions. She will come back, but her existence is tied to this place, and this is a world of magical illusion."

"Ferla is lovely," he said, feeling a strange, terrible inadequacy. He wanted to protect Ferla from this harsh truth.

Ribela resisted laughing. The disgust that had so overwhelmed her had faded. The shock of losing contact with

her own body and of awakening in this one had also
dissipated.

Now she felt a distinct unease when she contemplated
the body of Ferla. Ribela's own chest and hips were distinctly slim and unfeminine. Ferla was a voluptuous girl
in the full flower of nubility. It had been centuries since
Ribela had touched another human being or been touched
by one. Ferla, on the other hand, was a being made for
love, with the breasts of a goddess and long hair and
what, Ribela was sure, was a beautiful face.

"Ferla is lovely, Relkin, but she will have to remain
here on this world. She cannot exist anywhere else."

Relkin became stonyfaced as he considered this.

"And you are still a dragoneer of the 109th Marneri.
You are still on active duty. You cannot rot here in this
pocket of corrupt hedonism. You must awake and escape
this place."

"But Ferla?"

"You have to leave, Relkin. You are needed elsewhere."

It was hard. It took a long time for him to accept it
fully. At times he came close to weeping at the thought
that he must lose Ferla.

"No!" he roared into the grotto, and would have done
himself, or others, harm except that Ribela calmed him
with a subtle spell.

At length he slept and when he awoke he was more or
less aware of who he was and what his responsibilities
truly were. He knew he had another life elsewhere and
that if he could escape this dream world of Mot Pulk's,
then he must try.

"How can I get out of here? Mot Pulk brought me here
with magic. I know not the spells that are needed to
escape."

"I can teach you one. It may work."

And then Relkin realized something else.

"But, Lady, if Ferla cannot leave this place, neither can
you, for you are now in Ferla's mind."

Ribela had considered this aspect of things. It did not
bode well, she had to admit.

"I will teach you a spell. As to the other thing, well, tell me this: Are there any mice here?"

"I don't know. I haven't seen any. There is only what Mot Pulk wants here. It is a simple world."

The western sky had become an orange glowing mass with pink and green clouds.

"If there are no mice, then I will have to be ingenious. But now, mind me and try to memorize my words. You will have to learn several hundred lines, and some volumes."

And as the sun set, Ribela began the task of instructing him in a great spell. Relkin sat in the pergola and did his best to learn the lines as the moons tumbled up the sky.

He was doing well enough until it came time to learn volumates. These were a delicate act, and he had none of the training going back to childhood that girl novices learned before trying to enter the sisterhood of the witches. He floundered here and after a while grew too tired to continue. Ribela gave up and let him sleep.

While he did so, she contemplated her plight. There were indeed no mice, and without them she would have to attempt a complex spell that would lift her back into the astral plane and perhaps allow her to return to herself, far away there in the cell in Andiquant.

She was sure that her body there must have slipped into pure unconsciousness. The mice would have ceased to run; there would be no power from that source. If this world were eliminated, she would die; her mind would be lost and her body would die soon afterward.

She observed the culmination of the moons' nightly show. The sardonic features of Mot Pulk loomed above. These elf lords had taken undiluted egoism to new heights. Not even the Doom Masters of Padmasa had reached so high!

By first light she was more confident. By careful dredging of her memory she had come up with some sections from the Birrak that would give her a good basis for an astral spell without mice. She went down to the apartment and stirred Relkin to life. There was no time to lose.

Chapter Thirty-eight

The Ardu flotilla emerged from the river gorge into the flat lands that lay just north of Mirchaz. Here there were villages and lush green fields, the breadbasket of Mirchaz.

Bazil understood all this with a single look. He told Lumbee they must halt and pull ashore here. It was time to go to war.

The Ardu men were puzzled. This was not Mirchaz, surely? Why didn't they go to Mirchaz and defeat it, like they always defeated the slavers? The slavers would break and run if they pressed them hard. They always did.

Bazil explained. "We need to plan this carefully. We are close to Mirchaz now. We need to know how close. If this farmland feeds the city, then this is a good place to attack if we want to draw the enemy out of his fortresses."

The Ardu were new to war; indeed, they were new to the whole world outside of their savage realm in the Lands of Terror. Norwul had come to understand that the dragon was as intelligent as any of them, and far more knowledgeable than they in the arts of war. He led the progressive group, about half of the Ardu men. The other half were uneasy. They found it difficult, in their hearts, to accept Bazil's intelligence. Now they argued. Some wanted to go on and attack directly, before the enemy could prepare its defenses. Others preferred to trust the forest god.

Bazil was sure that the enemy had been alerted some days ahead by the fugitives the attacking party had driven downriver from the upcountry towns. He was forcing himself to try to think like boy. He had been around that boy all his life. He had seen boy in every possible mood, from jubilation to deep sorrow. They were brothers as if born from the same egg, so how did boy think? Because Baz also knew that, while dragons were intelligent and quite able to converse, they were not as wily as humans, not nearly as good at planning ahead.

The argument grew heated. Bazil finally pushed men aside and regained their attention. "Stop argument," said the dragon with a massive finality. "You are men of the forest. I am a dragon of the battlefield. I see how the men do these things. You listen to me."

All the Ardu stared at him with stunned eyes. Receiving direct orders from giant pujish was an extraordinary thing. The pujish had to be a god—there was no other way. Had to be. Maybe not the forest god himself, but some kind of roving god of the forest. Ardu gods were all strictly territorial, spirits of heath and grove who did not try to affect events anywhere but in their territories. A mobile god was almost as difficult a concept for them as a talking pujish.

"The men in Mirchaz will come in much greater numbers than any force we have faced before. That means we have to take precautions. We need to draw the enemy on to our defensive positions, or we need to hit and run and try to panic him. So first we require knowledge of the area."

"Why do we not just go there and kill them?" said one of the most conservative of the older Ardu.

"Because they know we're coming. They will be ready for us. We would have to fight our way in through a high wall. The men who make cities always put up these things."

The obvious truth of this sank in. Even the conservative Ardu could see that Bazil was right. They hunkered down and began to talk.

Later they hauled the raft up a shady creek and pulled the boats into the trees. Scouts went out in three directions and returned after an hour. They were about a mile from a village upstream and two miles from another downstream.

It was decided to capture someone from the nearer of the two villages. To question him they had the Ardu from the upriver towns who spoke the tongue of Mirchaz. A party went out in search of a likely victim at once.

Bazil and Lumbee sat with Norwul and a few of the other robust males and discussed what they had to do. Bazil laid out the ground rules for a swift campaign of guerrilla war.

"First, we must keep our actual numbers a secret. We must make them think we have many more with us than we have."

The Ardu nodded carefully at this thought.

"Second, we have to make them fear us. We attack the villages, burn them, drive the people to the city."

"Do we kill the people?"

"Not necessary. Better they go to the city and spread fear. We make many fires every day, let them see plenty smoke. That help, too."

The search party came back with a villager whose eyes almost bugged out of his head when he saw Bazil loom over him. He went into dragon freeze at once and had to be pinched and slapped repeatedly to get him out of it. Then the Ardu from the towns began to question him. The poor man was so frightened he held nothing back. Their picture of their surroundings rapidly filled out.

They were in the Beharo, the "outside towns" of Mirchaz. The city itself lay ten miles farther on, through the hills to the south and across the lake that was hidden there. The Beharo was a fertile region of farms and small villages. The nearest were Yump and Passter. Their victim had been to visit a money lender in Yump and was on his way home when he'd been nabbed.

They questioned him carefully about the villages, and then about the rest of the region. There was a small detachment of guards in the town of Behar, about ten miles south. And there had been some excitement in the area after refugees from the upriver towns passed through. There had been all kinds of rumors, most of which had been dismissed as pure moonshine. Now, he could see, they were not.

Meanwhile, Norwul had organized the Ardu to move around in the brush, appearing briefly so they could be seen and then hiding again, to give the captive the idea that the raiding party was far larger than one hundred men.

Bazil also put on a demonstration with Ecator, whipping the huge blade around him so that it hummed in the air.

Then they released their victim and told him to go home at once to his village. As soon as he was gone, they moved upstream toward Yump, which became the first of many villages to burn in the Beharo.

Over the next few days this pattern was repeated. They moved quickly through the farmlands, burning villages, haystacks, fields, and anything else that would catch fire and send up a plume of smoke. The roads south filled up with refugees and rumors.

There were few casualties. The villagers were far from warlike and inclined to flee at the first sign of smoke and flames in their neighborhood. At the town of Woot, a small group of guards tried to make a stand, but the Ardu killed them to a man and hung their bodies from the trees. The entire town emptied southward and the Ardu burned it to the ground.

The conservative Ardu who had questioned Bazil's understanding of war were won over now. They enjoyed this relatively easy and painless work, and from burning these places they derived a degree of revenge for all they had suffered.

At the campfires, Bazil tried to make them understand that harder fighting lay ahead, that all this was merely the opening gambit.

"We upset enemy. They come out to find us. We ambush them unless they outnumber us too much. Eventually we have to find a way into their city. That will be the hard work."

Chapter Thirty-nine

Relkin's instruction in declension and volumata proceeded quickly. Despite appearances, and her prejudices against males, Ribela had to admit the young man was a quick study. The volumes were difficult, of course; they were hard for anyone to master. Like playing a viol with one's vocal cords, after all. But even there he made progress.

Yet even Relkin's attention could finally fail. His eyes dulled. He grew listless.

Ribela noticed eventually and was forced to stop. "Whatever is the matter with you?" she snapped.

"I haven't eaten anything today."

Ribela bit off the first thing that came into her mind. It was far too harsh. She swallowed and murmured a prayer to the Mother.

"Yes, of course." She had to admit that nutrition was essential, even to her. The body of young Ferla had been hungry for a while.

Relkin arose and went down to the larder in the kitchen. There was hardly anything in the cupboard. Ferla had brought fresh fruits and pods from the forest every day. Ribela, of course, would not know which fruits were edible. Relkin shrugged. The easy life was over, it seemed, whether he liked the thought or not. He took himself off to the trees. When he returned, he had a fair selection of the fruits he had seen Ferla collect. He sat in the pergola with a knife and some bowls and peeled fruits and pods and broke out ripe purple beans.

Ribela brought a jug of water. Relkin ate in moody silence. The purple beans weren't as good as when Ferla picked them. She seemed to know which pods were ripe.

It was hard for him not to keep hoping that Ferla would somehow reawake in her body and oust the witch. When that body moved, he saw only the grace and beauty and his emotions were aroused all over again.

Ribela recalled Lessis's voice and her strictures on handling men, especially young ones. "Be understanding, sister"—that is what Lessis would always say.

By the breath, but sometimes it was hard. She finished some pieces of fruit. The entire process of digestion had always seemed gross and disgusting to Ribela, never more so than at this point. Still, this was what duty had brought her to.

"I'm sorry, young man. You have been living in an idyllic dream that has suddenly ended. I can see that you're unhappy, and I think it's quite understandable. But you have been summoned back to duty. You remain a soldier in the Legions of Argonath. You have work to do."

Relkin shrugged wearily. "I don't know, Lady, sometimes it just seems impossible. We were trying to get back to the Legions. It wasn't our fault we were separated in the first place. I mean, the volcano blew us so far out into the ocean that we never saw the island again. We landed and we headed east. We were in the jungle. Way north of here."

He slapped his knee and gave her a bitter smile.

"There I go again. I keep forgetting I don't know where this is."

"This is an illusion, child, a fantasy world created by the Lords Tetraan."

"Then are we in Mirchaz?"

"Ah, no." And Ribela realized at last that she didn't know where this was any more than Relkin did. Her astral spell had maintained a constant link with her body in faraway Cunfshon. That had sundered, and now she was lost.

"Then we aren't in Mirchaz?"

"It would be more accurate to say that the only way to escape from this place will be through passage of the Game nexus, where the lords focus their energies. That nexus lies in Mirchaz."

Relkin chewed his lips while he digested that.

"All right, I get it. The only way out is through Mirchaz, so in a way we are in Mirchaz because it's the only other place we can go."

She nodded.

"Well, we were way north of Mirchaz. We were trying to get back to the mouth of that big river the Legions used to reach the lands of the Kraheen."

Ribela nodded again. This was an improvement.

"But we found this other river, which ran from south to north. So we followed that, just in case it joined the river we were searching for. We went downstream a ways, and then we saw this boat, and in the boat we found Lumbee."

"Lumbee?"

"An Ardu girl, in a bad way. Wounded in the shoulder."

"You found a girl, alone in the Lands of Terror?"

"An Ardu girl, the tailed folk. We took care of her and fed her and after a while she recovered."

"The tailed folk. Oh, my, they are real?"

"Oh, yes."

Ribela was amazed. Even at her age there were fresh things to learn about the world.

"How had this girl survived alone?"

"She'd floated downriver for weeks. At first she had some food, but it ran out and her wound sapped her strength. It was starting to rot and it would have killed her eventually. I had to cauterize it and then use a little disinfectant. Mainly she was dehydrated and very hungry."

"She survived."

"Oh, yes." Unconsciously Relkin expressed something in the way he said this that told Ribela a great deal.

As Relkin told her the story of Lumbee, Ribela sensed there had been a sexual union and that Relkin still thought of Lumbee with love and affection. This brought on dizzying thoughts for Ribela of Defwode, who, to her own self-disgust, found an odd excitement in the thought of the dragonboy as a sexual being. He was young, fresh-faced, but not bland. And his lean body had the hardness of youth and an innate muscular appeal. All of this made her weirdly nervous when she looked at him. What was going on? She never had these base urges. She was far above such gross, corporeal matters.

Then she recalled that, after all, this was Ferla's body,

not hers, expressing its own crude, animal desires, not hers. And yet there was that excitement. It had been half a millennium since Ribela had allowed a sexual thought to cross her head, but now it was happening.

"And so, the girl survived and then begged you to go to her country with her. Did you plan to live there happily ever after?"

Relkin spread his hands out and told her of the campaign against the slavers.

"I see." Ribela shook her head. And in the meantime, what had gone on between Relkin and this young Ardu female? Ribela shuddered as she realized that for a moment, she had wanted that for herself.

"You have had a wild old time of it, I can see."

Relkin had to agree.

"And yet I still do not understand why I find you here. This is Ferla's body, not Lumbee. Where is Lumbee?"

Relkin was about to explain when Ribela saw something behind him and went rigid. She stood up and muttered some words of power that ended with a crack like that of a great whip. She raised her hands and held them in front of her and from out of the undergrowth beyond the pergola stumbled a nightmarish creature with the head of an insect and the body of a skinny monkey.

Step by step it approached, dragged by Ribela's spell. Relkin stared at it, horrified.

"What is this thing?" she said.

"I don't know. I've never seen it before."

Ribela brought the thing to a halt just outside the pergola. She held it steady with her spell while she strode around it, examining it. It stood about three feet high and looked like a mantis crossed with a gibbon.

"It has a black mark on the top of its head, I think it is the same face that shows on the moons at night."

"That is the elf lord that rules this place."

They were interrupted by a sudden laugh from right behind them. They whirled around and found Mot Pulk staring at them from the other side of the pergola.

"What do I find here?" said the elf lord, whose eye showed golden as he came forward. Relkin felt yet another tread on the ground and saw that Biroik had been summoned down from his pedestal.

Relkin turned to confront the huge demon. Not even Katun could have fought this demon and hoped to win.

"Do not involve yourself, child," snapped Mot Pulk. "Or I will have Biroik chastise you. My interest is all in my lovely Ferla. Something has happened to Ferla and I want to know what it is."

Ribela muttered the words of a freezing spell. Mot Pulk drew back in alarm.

"What! You dare sorcery on my person?"

He clapped his hands as he ran back. "Biroik!"

The demon, with huge eyes flaring, lurched forward on massive thews.

Ribela threw her freezing spell on Biroik. He shuddered to a halt. She murmured more lines and raised her hand again.

Mot Pulk was stunned. The magic that powered Biroik was very great. What sorcery might this be? What had gotten into Ferla? Was it another player? Was this some master stroke by the Tendency or the old Cabal? He would show them!

Mot Pulk summoned power from the Game itself. Here in his own magic world, his connection to the power was strong. He reanimated Biroik.

The purple hide came alive. Biroik stepped forward.

Relkin attacked with fists and feet.

It evaded his strike and swung back at him with a heavy foot, but lazily, and Relkin scrambled out of the way.

Ribela tried to freeze it again with her spell, but it was resistant, with Mot Pulk's magical will enlivening it. Relkin sprang at its back, but it was ready and caught him a glancing blow with another whirling foot. Relkin was sent tumbling into the wall of the pergola and through it to end up outside in the flower bed.

Ribela's voice screamed words of power from Ferla's throat, but to no avail. The demon seized Ferla, lifted her high. The scream shifted to one of terror. Biroik looked to Mot Pulk, who was still quivering with fear and rage. He nodded. Biroik pitched Ferla into the grotto.

For an incredible moment, Relkin saw Ferla twist

around, her mouth open in a soundless scream, and then she was gone, falling, turning, disappearing into the dark at the bottom of the grotto. Relkin realized that Ferla was dead. A second thought struck him—that maybe this was the death of the Queen of Mice as well.

Relkin spun around and launched himself at Mot Pulk. The next moment a tanned brown fist connected with elfin chin and lip. It connected several times in the next three seconds. Mot Pulk's screams brought Biroik, and Relkin was hauled off the elf lord by a huge hand that wrapped around his head and neck.

He struck at the demon and connected enough to annoy it. It responded by slapping him almost senseless. He spun around and fell to his knees. He saw Mot Pulk was lying on the ground, retching. Blood and a tooth came out of the elf lord's mouth.

Relkin tried to get up and after a second or so he got his legs under him and started for Mot Pulk again, but Biroik grabbed him and lifted him off the ground, where his legs kicked futilely. His arms flailed but could not make contact.

Slowly Mot Pulk pulled himself off the ground and stood up. His elfin visage had been transformed. The pale skin was massively cut and bruised. Blood had caked on the chin. The lips were swollen beyond recognition and the nose was swelling enormously.

"And to think how well I've treated you," he growled. "Such ingratitude."

"I will kill you," sputtered Relkin.

"Biroik!"

Chapter Forty

The message came to the city of Marneri on the wings of a swift ocean gull. It entered the harbor just three days after leaving the Tower of Swallows in Andiquant, and flew to the roost above the Novitiate. The Mistress of Animals, Fi-ice the witch, was sent for. She retrieved the message from the bird's foot and gave it a bucket of herring, for it was very hungry.

The seal on the message sent a shiver through her. That "R" stood for only one person in the world, the Queen of Mice. The message was addressed to Lagdalen of the Tarcho.

It was midsummer, but there was a cool breeze coming off the Long Water. Fi-ice paused to pull out a shawl before taking the message herself down to Water Street, to the narrow building where Lagdalen had her office.

As she went, the witch prayed that the poor girl was not about to be torn from her normal life in the city and sent off on some terrifying witch mission. Lagdalen was still only a child, but already she had the reputation as a Lessis in the making. They said she was gifted in the magic arts.

Fi-ice knew they were wrong about that. Lagdalen was less than proficient in the arts of spellmaking. Her years of service to the Gray Lady had exposed her to sorcery on the grandest scale, but she had learned little of it herself.

In Marneri, Lagdalen had discovered her own natural skill. She was a dedicated attorney of law. In fact she was the Crown Attorney in the case against the Aubinan grain magnate Porteous Glaves. It was a torturous case with heavy political overtones. It had consumed Lagdalen for years now and had become her life's work. Or so it seemed.

Fi-ice knocked at the door. A young volunteer opened it, a girl from another of the upper aristocrat families, the Bestigari, and ushered the witch in. The message was delivered.

Lagdalen seemed haggard. Fi-ice knew it was the misbehavior of the queen that was responsible. Without the firm backing of the crown, the Aubinan case was extremely difficult to move through the courts. The Aubinans were very powerful.

The sight of the seal on the message caused Lagdalen to tremble visibly.

Not again. Not another mission for the Office of Unusual Insight. Lagdalen had been promised that that was over. Lessis had gone into the mystic and taken retirement. The wild days of the Unusual were behind them. Or so she had thought. But what else could bring a message to her from Lady Ribela, the new, shadowy executive of the Unusual?

"Thank you, Lady, for bringing this so promptly." Fi-ice heard the lack of enthusiasm in Lagdalen's thanks.

"I pray it has no significance for you, child. You have given enough."

Lagdalen nodded briskly. "And I am needed here. We have such a task in front of us." Lagdalen went into her small, private office, cut the seal, and read the message.

Her wild whoop shook the building a moment later.

"They're alive! It's incredible news. They're alive!"

She was holding hands with Fi-ice the next moment and dancing a jig.

"They survived the volcano. Don't ask me how, but the lady sends word that the Broketail dragon and his dragonboy are alive. They're somewhere in Eigo, which is a pretty big place, but they are still alive."

"Wonderful! Thanks be to the Mother."

"Thanks be. Oh, my, we must tell the dragons. Come, I've got to see the dragonhouse when they get this news."

Fi-ice chuckled. "They'll hear it in Seant."

Which turned out to be an accurate description of the hullabaloo that broke out when Lagdalen spread the news through the dragonhouse. As it happened, the 109th Marneri Dragons were in residence in the city that summer. They had spent the half year they'd been back from Eigo as a reserve unit based in the Blue Hills and had just completed a rotation into the city.

They had recovered from their experiences in Eigo, to an extent. But the dragon corps as a whole was still shaken by the casualties. The grim battle of Tog Utbek would always be a red memory, drenched with the blood of dead men and dragons. But the 109th had survived the campaign better than the other dragon squadrons, except that at the very end they had lost the Broketail.

This had been a hard blow, the worst in years. It left old Chektor as the only survivor of the original 109th. And Bazil Broketail had been the heart of the unit for a long time, a leatherback with speed and skill with that dread blade that made him the natural sword champion of the Legions. All the surviving dragons of the 109th were still in deep sorrow for the loss. The Purple Green of Hook Mountain, the only wild dragon to ever serve in the Legions of Argonath, had never felt such sorrow in his life, except perhaps for the misery he felt at the loss of his ability to fly. Even Alsebra, the caustic freemartin, had been subdued ever since the loss of the Broketail leatherback and his worthless dragonboy, Relkin. Those two had been in some scrapes before, by the fiery breath, they all had, especially the battle at Sprian's Ridge, but fate had finally caught up with them. There was a big empty space in the middle of the squadron and the new dragons, young Churn and Gryf, had been shut out socially by the older members. The unit was still not functioning well in battle drills. The new dragonleader, Cuzo, was inept with dragons, but wonderful at organization. He certainly couldn't motivate the dragons into more than halfhearted concern with his drills. They ran and exercised, but their hearts were not in it.

The Broketail had been their heart, and now it was broken.

Thus when Lagdalen sprinted in with the news that somehow those two had survived the volcano's blast, the roof almost came off with the collective roar that went up.

While enormous beasts cavorted in the gym and plunge pool, Lagdalen found herself cornered by Swane of

Revenant, little Jak, and Manuel out by the door. The noise was still loud, but they could just about hear each other speak.

She showed them the message. Bazil and Relkin were alive. They were also lost.

"Well, that was what I figured," said Swane.

"Course, Swane," said Jak. "You've always got it figured out."

"Watch it, Jak. Stands to reason. If they survived, they got lost; otherwise they'd have been back long ago."

"If I was them, I'd never come back. Just to get away from you."

"Trust those two to survive. Even a volcano!" said Manuel.

Another boy came stumbling in, his skinny frame bent under a bale of hay.

"Uh-oh, here's Curf," said Swane.

"You all right, Curf?" said Jak.

Curf merely gasped under his burden.

"Old Cuzo came down pretty hard on you this time, kid," said Manuel.

"Cuzo wants to kill me," said the bent figure under the hay.

"Put the hay down, Curf, we got some news."

Curf shed his load and straightened. Lagdalen had never seen a more handsome youth. Straight chin, fine nose, level brown eyes, and short black hair—he was almost perfect.

Swane told him about the Broketail and Relkin, and Curf whooped. He'd never met either of them, but he'd heard all the legends about the Broketail dragon when he was growing up. The loss had been a blow to the entire Legion.

"You'll have to write us a song, Curfy," said Swane.

"I'll try."

Lagdalen's interest was piqued.

"Are you a musician, Curf?"

"No, Lady, but I play guitar a little."

"I'm sorry, Lady Lagdalen, this is Curf. Curf, this is the very honorable and most high Lady Lagdalen of the Tarcho."

Curf bowed.

"Honored to meet you, Lady."

"And I, to meet you, Curf."

"Curf's dead modest, Lady," said Jak. "He's really good with the guitar."

"I should like to hear him play. Perhaps when the song is written. We'll all sing together."

"Be like old times, eh, Lady?"

"Yes, Swane. Like old times."

"Have to buy the dragons some extra beer. That'll get them singing."

"Haven't had a sing in a long time," said Manuel.

"Well, Cuzo don't know nothing about dragons," groused Swane.

"Well, let's do it soon."

"Hear that, Curfy?"

"I heard, Swane."

"Just think, those two are alive, and probably living like emperors among some bunch of natives."

"Of course, they'll be living in the palace."

Manuel snorted. "It says they're south of the Inland Sea. That means they're in the Lands of Terror still. You know what that means."

Swane and Jak knew. Carnivorous monsters bigger than wyvern dragons, twice as big in some cases, and capable of eating a horse in about three bites.

"I hope Bazil has his sword," said Jak.

Swane brightened. "As long as that leatherback has his sword, they're safe. He's deadly, is the Broketail."

"We'd better pray for them," said Manuel.

Lagdalen nodded. "You're right, Manuel, we must all send our prayers to them."

Chapter Forty-one

Relkin awoke in the house of pain. It was still night, and he was still bound to the wall of the pergola by heavy bracelets around his wrists and ankles.

His situation remained hopeless. Biroik stood nearby, as still as the statue he really was. Mot Pulk probably lurked within the pergola, nursing his hatred for an orphan boy from Quosh.

Then Biroik noticed that he was awake and clapped his hands.

There was a slight shuffling sound from the pergola and a moment later Mot Pulk was there.

"Ah, child, you are back among the living. Worse luck for you, eh?" The elf lord strutted up and down in front of Relkin, whose face was so swollen, his left eye was almost closed. There was blood caked round his mouth. "I think you remember where we had bogged down," Mot Pulk continued. "All you have to do is tell me what I want to know. Who was it that infiltrated the lovely Ferla?" The elf lord's face still bore the effects of Relkin's blows and seemed weirdly misshapen.

"I told you already," Relkin croaked. "I can tell you nothing more."

"You think I can be taken in by such ridiculous stories?" Mot Pulk said scornfully. "A witch woman from the far east somehow invaded Ferla's mind, such as it was, and supplanted her? Someone from outside the Thousand? Such nonsense. I know it was someone from the board, and I have to know who it was. It could be very important to my—even to our—survival. I should emphasize that whereas I wish to keep you alive, they will kill you."

"You killed Ferla."

Mot Pulk's eye showed a blue center for a moment.

"A regrettable lapse, I admit. No one regrets that moment of rashness more than I, for if I had her here I would have gotten the truth out of her by now. More than this drivel you give me about witches. Listen to me, child, you stand on, breathe, eat the very stuff of the magic power of the Lords Tetraan. No other magical system is as powerful as ours. None of your Doom Masters or metal lords would ever dare to challenge us. They flourish out in the lonely wastes of this desolate world because we are invested here. Stop trying to tell me that some puny heathwitch, some ignorant old hag, would have been able to penetrate my secret world. Not even the best players in the Tendency and the Cabal have been able to do it, or else we would not be here now! So it must have been some independent, some wild fellow from the second or third hundred. Someone with a new system. I must know who it was. You must tell me everything!"

"I have told you everything. You are mad, all of you."

"No, fool, we are gods. Biroik! Fetch the irons and the charcoal. I can see that we will have to move to sterner measures."

Relkin stared sullenly out to the dark pool where he knew the grotto plunged.

At that moment he would have given anything to just be able to run out and throw himself into that darkness. An end to the pain, and Biroik, and the broken heart and the sorrow and all the rest of it. Poor Ferla. Thrown to her death. That such fear and agony should ever have afflicted Ferla made him writhe inside. It was far worse than what they were doing to him. At least so far.

Biroik pulled a charcoal grill on wheels out of the bushes on the other side of the pergola. The charcoals were piled high on the grill pan. They ignited on their own, or so it seemed to Relkin's fuddled senses, and burned down very quickly to a hot glowing mass. Relkin could feel the heat they cast from five feet away.

Onto the grill went a number of long metal irons.

"Now, child, shall we begin?" said Mot Pulk in his mildest voice.

Relkin tried to grit his teeth, but that hurt too much. Biroik brought a hot iron down on the skin of his forearm and he leaped in his bonds and let out a sharp scream. In part it was the terrible surprise of it, for the iron hurt far more than he had imagined it would. His whole body was shaking from it half a minute later.

When he could speak, he begged Mot Pulk for mercy.

"Listen to me, I'll tell you anything you like. You don't have to do any more. What do you want to know? Just tell me what you want me to say."

"Good. So who was it?"

"I told you, it was the one they call the Queen of Mice."

"Stop! Consider your words carefully, you little fool. You were there; you spoke to whoever it was. You must be able to tell me more."

"I have told you, don't you understand? I'm no hero! I don't have anything to hide from you. What can I give you, what can I tell you? I don't know anything about your thrice-damned Game!"

Mot Pulk nodded to Biroik, who proceeded.

Relkin blacked out again after a while and Mot Pulk had Biroik douse him with a bucket of cold water and leave him.

Mot Pulk was troubled. The boy had resisted to a point that seemed unimaginable. Whoever had infiltrated had done a wonderful job on him. He was completely convinced of his improbable tale. Nothing would shake him.

The only way to get at the truth would be the hard way. Mot Pulk would have to cast the mind magic and probe the boy's thoughts directly.

The next time Relkin awoke, he was seated on a bench inside the pergola. Mot Pulk was seated close by. Biroik loomed in the doorway. Relkin groaned. The burns on his arms were very painful. He was still well shackled.

"Ah, there you are. Back with us again."

"No more," said Relkin. "No."

"I agree, child. Biroik will not torture you any further. Come, look up, look into my eye."

The elf lord took his chin in one hand and lifted his head. Relkin's mouth throbbed. There was a loose tooth on the left side. The pain from the burns was so bad, though, that he scarcely noticed the agonies from his battered face. His eyes met Mot Pulk's single orb and froze. The golden orb was glaring down at him; he felt himself shriveled and naked to it.

Mot Pulk pressed upon Relkin's mind. The pressure grew greater minute by minute, as if a great constricting snake had wrapped itself around his mind and was crushing it. He resisted with every bit of willpower he could muster.

It was not such a surprise this time, either. In some undetermined way, Relkin found that he was ready for the challenge. Once before he had suffered something like this, when great Heruta, leader of the Padmasa Five, had tried to enslave him. But this was a subtler, deadlier pressure than anything Heruta had summoned up.

Relkin struggled to awaken that infant power he had felt within him—one side effect of the bruising Heruta had given him. Something had shaken loose that day and had not returned to normal since.

Mot Pulk pressed in on his mind like floodwater, rising inexorably into the village that was Relkin's mind. Relkin could not keep him out forever; he just didn't have enough sandbags. There was further frustration in that Relkin could sense that there was power there inside him, something that might be able to turn the tide, but it hovered just out of reach.

Mot Pulk had mental fingers sliding into his brain, Relkin shuddered with the loathing of it and fought back with everything he had left in his heart. Still the elf lord bored in, his thought blaring brazen questions. Relkin struggled to deny the mental contact. Again and again he jerked at the nebulous power he felt was there, but still it would not respond.

It was too late, anyway. Mot Pulk's mental claws were now well embedded and they seemed to swell, crushing his own mind between them. Mot Pulk's strength was vastly augmented because now he drew on the power of the supermatrix of ten thousand interconnected minds that gave the Great Game its life.

An involuntary sob escaped from Relkin as he sagged in the shackles for a moment under the weight of the attack. Still he did not quite give in. When the forces clashed again, Relkin's lines were steadier, and he repulsed Mot Pulk once again.

Mot Pulk was amazed. There was something so determined in this impudent little wretch that it was quite uncanny. Relkin had survived beyond what any individual should have been able, even individuals like great Zulbanides. Mot Pulk himself was still shuddering from the huge effort he'd just made to control the flow of power from the mind mass.

And still the boy was defiant!

Mot Pulk ground his perfect teeth together. He would crush this wretch and he would crush him now. He gathered his strength and came on once more, grinding over Relkin's defenses, crushing all opposition. This time he would win and Relkin would be his puppet.

Relkin stiffened against his bonds. His head was pressed back against the wood. Backed to the wall, pressed down from every side, with no strength left in his body, facing the rape of his mind and utter enslavement, he gave a little scream and reached out into the void and let go, abandoning everything he'd clung to all his life. And in that moment the power in him awoke. Mot Pulk's mental claws were blown asunder. It was as if he were an arrow released. He soared too fast too think and then a lightning bolt seemed to go off in his mind and he felt something huge give way in the universe for a moment. It was as if reality had swung open on unseen hinges. For a second perhaps there was terrible disorientation, and then a sensation as of a freezing fog surrounded him in a marsh, and then he was pitched forward onto his hands and knees and found himself sprawling on a polished wooden surface.

The pergola of pain was gone. He was no longer on Mot Pulk's little world.

He was on a chess board for giants. Each square was two feet long on a side and the pieces were on an equal scale. Relkin stared up in the carved eyes of a white wooden Leaper, a three-foot winged elf in polished oak. Beyond the Leaper were a squad of Pawns, carved wooden soldiers in the same white wood.

Relkin got to his knees with a little sob of effort and pulled himself upright.

He had arrived. He didn't question where he had come to. He knew at once. This was the board on which the elves built their magic patterns. This was the very heart of their realm, the Game board of the Lords Tetraan.

He knew what he must do. Now he would summon up the servant, the trapped servant that made all this insanity possible. But how?

He had no idea. He gasped and clenched his fists and tried to recall what he had done when he'd suddenly translated from the pergola of pain to the board. How had he come here? What was that power that he had tapped?

Bemused, he called out in a hoarse croak. "Awake! Awake the sleeping dead, for their time has come!"

Awake the ten thousand immured in their tombs beneath the pyramid!

"Your time has come," he called.

But they had no ears and only eyes. They knew nothing and they knew everything. They could not feel his cry, let alone react.

And still he sensed them, sensed the huge gestalt, which in this place was spread out beneath him like a glowing sun. It hummed, it whispered, but it paid n attention to him.

Chapter Forty-two

Relkin tottered, unable to form cogent thoughts, let alone a plan of action.

Figures were approaching from all directions. He had to do something, but what? He could scarcely move after suffering from Biroik's attentions.

Suddenly into his mind floated a strange little verse.

> *Ripeness! Listening to the bell.*
> *Evening air.*
> *Above the hills.*

He opened his mouth, but only a vague croak emerged.

Something was terribly wrong. This was the wrong place. The time was not ripe.

The gestalt being that he sensed all around him would not respond and he did not know how to awaken it.

Men with drawn swords were approaching. Among them he saw several elf lords, with their silver curls and perfect features.

There were many voices raised in anger.

Two tall men in brown leather came up, seized him under the arms, and lifted him off his feet. At the harsh contact with the burns on his arms, he fainted with barely a scream.

They hurried him away, past the Strengths and Leapers, past the board players and the elf lords with drawn swords. Any would have liked to kill him, to slay the dreaded Iudo Faex, except that he was clearly not that fearsome demon. He was some pitiable wretch that had been scraped off the board after falling from the ceiling.

Or so it was said. The Iudo Faex would have been a

flame-breathing monster ten feet high, at the very least. This half-dead youth was hardly worth the fuss.

The huge men carried him into a suite of rooms high within the pyramid, and placed him on a white table under the light of three lanterns. Around the table gathered the lords of the Ten.

"It's the same one I spoke to. The one Pessoba bought from the slaver Katun."

"That damned fool Pessoba."

"He wants reinstatement. To the ninth."

"He can't hold that place. He hasn't the skill. Worthless oaf."

"The child, fools, the child. Forget Pessoba."

"Forget Pessoba? What about Mot Pulk? He had him."

"Mot Pulk has tried to pull his secrets from him. The marks on the arms are sure sign of that."

The jowls of Repadro Toba quivered. "If this is the Iudo Faex, then I am a donkey."

There were murmurs of amused support for this idea from others.

"By the greatness of Zizma Bos, I declare an end to this foolishness. Put a sword to that wretch and end its misery and let's get back to the board. We have a gold to defend, gentlemen. We must get to work."

Finally Zulbanides came forward and raised his hands. "We obviously need not fear the Iudo Faex in this child. But before we dispose of him, we should question him. There is much we could learn. Then, when he is an empty vessel, we can dispose of him."

"There is also the matter of how he came to be on the board. I have an eyewitness that says the youth simply appeared there from thin air. He materialized, in other words."

"What the hell is Mot Pulk playing at?"

"He must be punished."

"I'd have him flayed."

"Where'd he keep the boy?"

"He has a hidden world, a minor hedonic."

"At a time of emergency like this, with an enemy at the gates? He deserves serious punishment."

"Oh, not so bad. There was nothing to fear from this so-called Iudo Faex, after all."

"We will revive the youth and question him. Then we can discuss the matter again."

"Can we stop wasting energy hunting for Mot Pulk?"

"He must be punished."

"We have our backs to the wall on the ninth gold and you're worrying about Mot Pulk."

"There's smoke all over the horizon. Haven't you looked?"

"Some Ardu robbers out in the fields? While the ninth gold is under siege?"

"The Game comes first!"

"By the strength of Zizma Bos, you are right. Let us forget Mot Pulk. He is of little consequence now."

The elf lords departed, leaving only Zulbanides and Lord Rasion.

Zulbanides indicated the prone form to the guards in brown leather. "Take this away. Tend to its wounds, revive it, and bring me word when it is capable of answering questions."

The guards put Relkin on a stretcher and bore him away.

Zulbanides turned to Rasion. "What is happening out in the Beharo?"

"Complete chaos, from what I understand. And there's trouble brewing in the slave city. Patrols are being attacked again."

"What has our response been?"

"We have mobilized fifteen hundred men to form a task force to go out and find these Ardu and slay them."

"The quality of these men?"

"Good troops, but in this situation, it is impossible to say. We know these Ardu rebels have a tame kebbold of some type in their midst. They have used it to terrify the militias up the river."

"Mmm, a tame kebbold could be a problem. But they are stupid things that would as soon eat their handlers as anything else."

"Indeed, which is why we have never bothered to try and employ them in any way whatsoever."

"What can be done about it?"

"We are making a new class of super-length spear, with heads larger than the conventional spear. They're being cast shortly. Then we equip a unit of pikemen with these and they will drill in kebbold killing methods."

Zulbanides was still obviously troubled. "This is a rare confluence of events, don't you think, my Lord Rasion?"

"You mean you think this is part of the prophecy?"

"The beast in the prophecy. What is it?"

"A kind of kebbold, I believe."

"Well, it is probably just a coincidence, but nonetheless we shall have to watch our step here. This child is probably nothing of consequence. It's all Lady Tschinn's fault for stirring up this Iudo Faex business. Really, those females are a meddlesome, troublesome lot."

"They have not improved since we left Gelderen."

"By the greatness of Zizma Bos, we left Gelderen two aeons ago. And still we are saddled with them."

"This is our nature, Zulbanides. We were made male and female, like all the other forms."

"It was completely unnecessary. We have never needed them. We are immortal; why should we need to breed? We have never given them any power or any work. They have been a mere ornament for our glory."

"Damned expensive one, too—heh, heh."

"Well, we'll interrogate this youth and you'll see to dispatching this troublesome kebbold."

"We should speak again tomorrow."

"Same time?"

"Yes."

"Then here, for I will be at the board all day tomorrow. We must hold that gold."

"You don't think he is the Iudo Faex, do you?"

"No, of course not, Rasion, but there is something strange here. He appeared out of thin air right above the board. No one is capable of projecting like that. One moment he wasn't there, the next he was. We can do that in the Game worlds, but not here, not on this world. Before he dies, I will find out how this happened. If my suspicions are true, then great treachery has been unleashed on the Sphereboard of Destiny."

Rasion nodded very slowly, considering the possibilities. They parted and went their separate ways.

Chapter Forty-three

Mirchaz was built on an awesome scale and defended with massive walls and towers. Bazil understood that direct assaults were out of the question for a force of one hundred Ardu and one battledragon. As they learned more about the city through reconnaissance, so Bazil became pensive and withdrawn. No good plan seemed to offer itself. All options were speculative and dangerous. Chances of success seemed very slim. During the day he sought the hilltops, the better to survey the walls and structures of the city of the lords. Sometimes he stared so hard, it was as if by mere intensity he might stumble on a plan to unlock the gates and recover his dragonboy.

One thing was soon clear. While the place was built on a huge scale, the population was not commensurate with the size of the buildings and avenues. Two structures dominated everything else. The statue of Zizma Bos towered over the western promontory. The Pyramid of the Game, faced with white marble that shone in the afternoon sun, filled the eastern end of the lake.

Around the pyramid were clustered other huge buildings. Clearly that was the ceremonial center of the city. Along the southern shore of the lake was the bulk of the city, laid out along straight east-west avenues and protected by the ridgeline that ran parallel to a lake a mile inland. All of the populated part of the city was surrounded by defensive walls thirty feet high.

At the southwestern end of the lake, the grand city of the lords confronted another city, fenced in by even higher walls and a massive gate complex. This other city was the City of Slaves, a warren of tenements and shanties packed with the mentally damaged survivors of

the mind mass, escaped slaves, ferals—the children of
slaves who had avoided enslavement themselves—and a
polyglot population of slave takers, thieves, gangsters,
and even honest merchants from the south coast cities.
This last group were a distinct minority, since Mirchaz
was cut off from the southern coast by two mountain
ranges, the Mindor Ath and on the coast the mighty Ath
Gahut. Few were they who were prepared to travel that
arduous route to risk trade with the strange city of the
Lords Tetraan.

From that densely packed world of tenements to the
distant white palaces glittering on the ridgeline above,
there was a seeming infinite distance. And yet they
were inseparably linked by the evil of slavery. The few
who inhabited the palaces consumed the many, burning
their minds out like candles in the magical furnace of the
Great Game.

The Ardu reconnaissance soon showed that the north
side of the lake was rocky and sparsely populated. Here
were several monuments and cemeteries, but none were
enclosed in a protective wall. The western end of the
water was open and lightly populated as well. A series of
round hills filled the plain. There were winding roads
with vineyards and olive groves and just a scattering of
villas and small farming villages. Along the western shore
was a promenade interrupted only by a few warehouses
and manufactories built by the waterside.

Around the Ardu campfire in their hideout just north of
the city, they exchanged the day's information with all the
other scouting parties. They were close enough to see
through the northwest passage to the lake and the city
beyond. The looming statue of Zizma Bos held out its
huge arms to the city while the setting sun turned the
walls of the pyramid into triangles of gold. Bazil listened
to all the reports and, over many days, built up a com-
posite and detailed picture of the situation.

Several Ardu had gone into the slave city. They had
spoken with Ardu who dwelled there and passed on the
word. The forest god was come to Mirchaz, to seek an end
to the tyranny of the Lords Tetraan. They brought back
rumors of some sort of panic that was currently gripping

the High Lords Tetraan. It was called the Iudo Faex and was of terrific importance in the Great Game. They had also brought back some representatives of important groups in the slave city.

Bazil heard all this and judged that conditions favored swift action. They were a small group, but they had a big reputation. Terror filled the farmlands around them. It would not be too long before the city sent out a large force to find and destroy them. If it was large enough and well enough armed, Bazil knew it would eventually kill or maim a certain leatherback battledragon and annihilate the Ardu men. They did not have sufficient force to undertake a successful guerrila fight. One mistake and they would be undone. He had been forced to abandon his first plan, which had been to arouse the countryside, draw the enemy out, and ambush them. Now that seemed futile.

Therefore they needed to act while the initiative still lay in their hands. Confirming him in this belief was the word that the Upper City was tense and volatile. The City of Slaves seethed with complex tides of emotion, but all were assured that it would rise if given sufficient incentive. So much anger against the lords had built up that it needed only a catalyst to explode.

Bazil digested all the information, along with a prodigiously good dinner, and tried to sort it out. At least the recce parties had filled their larder well. Scarcely a chicken could be left in the western hills. Norwul and Lumbee came to sit with him as they did every evening when they discussed the situation and tried to set strategy. They had evolved a triumvirate of command with many battle situations left to Bazil's decision. Bazil had been in enough fights to have assimilated the Legion knowledge of war.

Norwul was eager to plan for an assault on the main city gates, which were open at all times. The City of Slaves would be induced to riot and the slaves would come to the attackers' aid, storming the gates.

The Ardu looked to Bazil, who grunted dissent.

"Riots have happened before. The defense of the city gate is probably prepared for such things. Besides, neither slaves nor Ardu trained for assault on walls. This dragon know that without training, army not very good at assault on walls."

"If we surprise the guard, we might take the gate before they can close it."

"The guard will have been redoubled. They know we are here. They will have taken measures. Perhaps the gate itself is now shut more often."

Norwul was left nonplussed. The big brown eyes blinked in frustration. "But if we don't attack, what can we do? Mirchaz can raise an army to hunt us down. They kill us all eventually."

"In time, yes. We not give them time. We try a feint with the riot and a surprise attack. That will concentrate their attention on the gate and the south. It will make them a little nervous, perhaps."

"We must do more than make them nervous!" exclaimed Norwul, exasperated at the thought of not attacking the great enemy at once. He was impatient. He pounded a big fist into a palm.

"Norwul say we take the big club down there and we beat on Mirchaz. We make Mirchaz feel the pain he cause Ardu!"

Bazil shifted his tail, the dragon equivalent of a shrug. "While they got nervous, we send small group across the lake and attack the pyramid at night."

"They will see boat."

"No boat. We swim."

"Swim!" Lumbee and Norwul looked at Bazil with round eyes.

"Take best swimmers, then attack the pyramid. That where the Game is. That what they think is most important. We take control of their Game. Then we dictate terms of surrender."

"We kill them?"

"We cannot kill all of them. Too many. Perhaps not all of them deserve to die. We are too few to impose such things. We have to settle for less than complete revenge."

"What if Relkin is dead?"

"If they kill boy, then many will die, this I swear by the fiery breath of the ancestors."

As they thought about the idea, Lumbee and Norwul

began to see that it represented their best chance. Norwul was most impressed.

"Forest god make great magic. We have much power in this plan."

Norwul left to begin selecting swimmers. Lumbee stayed with Bazil to interview the slave representatives from the city.

Bazil and Lumbee had learned a few days before just what the Great Game did to the slaves put through the mind mass. All the Ardu fighters burned with redoubled anger. Bazil had heard that two-thirds of the released slaves from the mind mass were left completely witless—burned-out husks that had less mentality than an animal.

Now came three representatives of the city. Bazil was not sure what to expect. Lumbee introduced Jup, an older fellow with a bitter look. Heagle was a tall man with wide shoulders and impressive strength in his frame. He refused to sit and kept his hand on his sword the whole time, ready to cut his way to freedom if he had to. Redfenn was the only Ardu, but his tail had been cut off and sold to a gourmet club when he was young. You could only tell by the coloration of his hair and the slight slant to the eyes that he was Ardu at all.

Redfenn showed no dragon freeze. Jup and Heagle both froze when they looked Bazil in the eye the first time. Lumbee had long since learned the routine, though, and woke them both with snaps of her fingers beside their ears.

They shook their heads, blinked a few times, and avoided looking directly at Bazil, though they were clearly fascinated with him.

Redfenn spoke Ardu, which explained why he was there. He introduced the older men. Jup was a representative from the leading rebel group, the Outcasts. Heagle came from the guild, which represented all the mercenaries, thugs, soldiers, and freebooters of the city. Redfenn represented everyone else.

After initial introductions, Redfenn spoke to Norwul, assuming that he was in charge.

"I take it you are the one to talk to. I like the girl, but I do not talk with a female in this matter. Is she meant to be gift for me?"

"Certainly not!" said Norwul, taken aback. He had grown used to the triumvirate system that had worked out between himself, Lumbee, and the wyvern, and was shocked by the outsider's response.

Redfenn hardly seemed to notice his offense. "We have been waiting for your arrival. The kebbold is already a legend in the city. They all wait its arrival. And I have to say that it is an impressive kebbold. How do you keep it under such control?"

Bazil knew that "kebbold" was the Mirchaz word for pujish. His eyes popped and he swelled angrily.

"I am not kebbold," he said in loud, sibilant, but unmistakable Ardu. Redfenn's jaw dropped, Heagle's eyebrows climbed his forehead, and Jup goggled.

"It speaks!" gurgled Redfenn.

"I speak as well as you, in more languages. My name is Bazil. Yours is Redfenn. Do you understand? Can you?"

Redfenn swallowed hard. "I . . . yes, I think so, but it is hard. You look just like—"

"Good. Because we have a lot to do and we don't need to have you sitting around looking like an egg unhatched."

Heagle shook his head angrily. "I can't believe I'm hearing this. How can this animal talk?" he said to Redfenn in fractured Ardu.

Bazil understood enough. "I talk because I have a brain. All wyverns talk. We talk in our own tongue, which you do not talk. I also talk in Verio, the language of men in my homeland. And I talk the language of the tailed men."

Heagle and Jup followed this only remotely, since neither of them spoke Ardu fluently, but they understood that Redfenn and Bazil were having a conversation and they were stunned.

"It talks to you?" said Heagle.

"It speaks good Ardu."

"Is it a god?" said Jup.

"It is some kind of trick. A ventriloquist or something," snarled Heagle. "It's a damned kebbold, done up in some fancy trick. Either that or there's a man inside the upper part of it."

Heagle had lapsed into Mirchazese in his anger.

The word "kebbold" got through, though, and Bazil gave a grunt and surged up onto his feet.

With a sinuous move he unsheathed Ecator. In the flat rays of the dying sun the great blade glittered like glasss.

With a measured series of moves, Bazil put Ecator through its paces. The blade made the most terrifying hum when it swept over their heads and Jup cowered on the ground thereafter, not daring to resume standing until Bazil had finished.

Heagle drew his own sword, but some shred of self-preservation kept him from attacking the dragon. Instead he watched in awe as the huge creature went through its practiced routine with the blade.

Redfenn just stared, openmouthed, thinking he had never seen anything more dangerous in his life. It wasn't a kebbold. No kebbold could be trained to handle a weapon—and not just any weapon, but a battlesword that was longer than a man is tall.

Heagle was suffering a most peculiar sort of inner agony. He knew that the beast could not be a kebbold. Kebbold were uniformly vicious, stupid creatures. Nobody had ever kept one of the large types of kebbolds without it escaping and killing people. They were huge, active, and could not be tolerated where people lived. Kebbold could not exist that could fight with a sword, but Bazil existed, and so did Ecator.

Bazil stood there, looming over them while he rested his forearms on the handle of the sword.

"I am not kebbold."

"I agree," said Redfenn.

"To business, then. We have plans to make."

And while they schemed, the men barely able to contain their amazement, another piece of the prophecy of Bos was taking shape.

In the bottom tiers of the pyramid the fragmented, dying mind was swirling. And at the last, with annihilation approaching, there came something like a huge, soft

hand to catch it up and hold it from the finality of death.
Soft words played through the mind of the old one.

> *Hush,*
> *dusk purples to the night*
> *but dawn will come.*
> *First will come the knock,*
> *and then the coming of the old mind.*
> *Welcome.*

Chapter Forty-four

In a dark chamber, on a high floor in the Pyramid of the Game, the lords Zulbanides and Rasion met alone.

"The City of Slaves is upset. We think there are agitators, probably from these Ardu that are terrorizing the countryside." Rasion wore silver breastplate and greaves over light blue military silks.

"I've said it before," growled Zulbanides, still in his robes, "and I'll say it again. We should level that nest of vermin and send them out beyond the farms. Then they can steal and riot and do whatever else they wish to do and no one will care."

"Well, until we do that, we do have to care. The watch at the gates has been doubled again."

"Have the gates been shut?"

"No, it would wreak havoc on the merchants and farmers. The market has its busiest day tomorrow. The wagons will be coming in all night."

Zulbanides sighed. "But at the first sign of trouble the gates will be shut?"

"Of course."

"Well, thank Bos for that! The merchants would put us all at risk for the sake of a farthing. I've said that before, too."

"The city must eat. Tomorrow the market will be groaning as usual. Have you seen the new melons? Delicious!"

"Ah, yes, Rasion, but about the other matter?"

"The kebbold? Well, it is to be hunted down and exterminated. A force of five hundred guards, accompanied by three hundred volunteers from the slave-taking corps, will set out tomorrow to find and kill it."

"Eight hundred men to slay one kebbold?"

"There are hundreds of Ardu bulls accompanying it, Zulbanides."

"So they say, but they also say the most ridiculous things. This legend that it carries a sword . . . you've heard it?"

"Yes, of course. In fact, it may not be so ridiculous."

"What?"

"I have been investigating this phenomenon, and in the course of my researches I have discovered that there is said to be an army of such beasts. They are called dragons and they dwell in the far eastern lands of Ianta. There is a realm known as Argonath, part of an odd little empire, centered on the isles in the eastern sea. In the Celadon aeon it was the land of Gazzat. The mage lords ruled there from time immemorial."

Zulbanides' scowl intensified. That was where the boy had claimed to originate, too. Zulbanides had returned again and again to every nuance of memory of that meeting. Had he missed something? Was he losing his edge?

"You jest. A kebbold that wields a sword?"

"We have lost touch with the world beyond our realm, Zulbanides. Things have progressed. There have been developments undreamed of. As a result of a conflict with the Padmasan abbots, an army equipped with these unique kebbolds was sent to Eigo recently. This must be a straggler from that army."

"Incredible. Damn those upstarts in Padmasa. Their vile magic, all death-related, you know. Disgusting." Zulbanides stared into the dark. When he spoke again, his voice was husked with dangerous emotions.

"In all the aeons no one has dared to disturb us in our fastness. Now we have this savage intrusion by a kebbold with a sword. Someone mighty moves against us. It is in violation of the covenant at Gelderen."

"Lord, it fits the prophecy."

"The five things?"

"There is a 'forest god' mentioned there, is there not?"

"Yes."

"This kebbold is called the forest god by the Ardu. So I have been informed by our spies in the City of Slaves."

Zulbanides' response was cut off by a knock at the door.

"Who is it?"

"Captain Katun."

"Captain?"

"Well, he was before his disgrace. We recalled him to service with this emergency. He has considerable experience. Moreover, he was the one who captured our mystery youth upcountry and brought him in. Perhaps he can tell us something more about him."

"Ah, I see. I remember that he was disgraced, but clearly we must be flexible."

Zulbanides turned to the door. "Come in."

The door opened and admitted Katun, now wearing leather armor and helmet. He was weaponless, having been disarmed on entering the pyramid. No one like Katun would ever be allowed in the presence of such as Zulbanides and Rasion while he bore arms.

"Welcome, Captain Katun," said Lord Rasion.

Katun came to attention calmly and made a perfect salute. Rasion returned it rather less perfectly. Katun made a point of performing military punctilio with such precision that the elf lords always felt clumsy in their responses. It gave him a slight edge, which in dealing with the lords he found absolutely necessary to overcome their customary arrogance toward men. They were impossible otherwise.

Rasion drew himself up. Katun's massive physical presence was quite intimidating. He felt oppressed by Katun's proximity and took a step back.

"What have you to report, Captain?"

Katun waited half a second to respond. "There has been a disturbance in the City of Slaves. A foot patrol was attacked. A punitive force is being prepared."

"Is a punitive force a wise idea at this point?"

"The City of Slaves forgets itself once in a while, Lord. It needs to be taught a fresh lesson."

"Exactly," boomed Zulbanides. "A good point, Captain."

"I am only concerned because after tomorrow, we will have sent eight hundred of the guard off to pursue the kebbold and these Ardu bulls."

"Ah, that is a point, Rasion. We can't allow security standards to slip in the city. Life would become impossible."

"Still, we have to hunt this kebbold down, or they'll burn every farm around us. They have looted villas in the western hills."

"Ghastly, to imagine such a thing here, in our lovely refuge. We have our work, and what do we have to put up with? An interruption in the Game by this kebbold business. Villas looted, villages burned. We must put a stop to it."

"Exactly, Lord, which is why the expeditionary force must go out tomorrow."

Rasion turned to Katun. "So, Captain, have you obtained the new equipment?"

"We have equipped one hundred men with new pikes."

"Good. We want the beast's head on the spike over the gate as soon as possible. That will take the stuffing out of this rioting.

"Now, let us turn our thoughts to our mystery youth. Katun, you claim to have captured him originally."

"Yes, sir, up the Yellow River a ways. Where the kebbolds are thick on the ground. That's where these rebel Ardu were raising hell all season. I figured that's where the troublemaker would be. He was. We took him sneaking around our camp."

"Did he seem unusual in any way to you?"

"Unusual? I don't know how you mean, Lord."

"Anything magical, any sign of mystic powers?"

Katun cut off a bark of laughter. "No, sir. Just a little gutter rat. A soldier in some foreign army, I reckon. Straggler out in the forest. Of course, it was strange that he wasn't Ardu. Never seen a no-tailed man come out of that country."

"He spoke to you about this army?"

"Oh, yes, sir. Full of himself, he was, and very proud of the 'Legions,' as he called them. Claimed he had a pet kebbold, said it could talk. If you can believe that, you can believe anything, I reckon."

"A pet kebbold?"

"Yes."

"Like the kebbold that's supposed to be wreaking havoc out in the farms now?"

Katun compressed his lips, but made no response.

"Damnable damage's been done, Captain."

"So I have heard, Lord."

"The kebbold is fearsome, they say. It wields a sword."

"I'm not sure I believe that one, Lord. There are more rumors out there about all this than there are mosquitoes in the swamp."

Zulbanides spoke up. "Captain, the kebbold is fearsome, but I feel the need to question the scale of the force you propose to deploy. Do you really need eight hundred men?"

"Well, Lord, it's all guesswork at this stage."

"But surely you could do this with four hundred, couldn't you? And keep the guard on the city at full strength."

"Maybe, Lord. But maybe without the eight hundred, we lose the entire four hundred and don't capture this kebbold."

"Ah." Zulbanides' eyes widened and went blue. He had not thought of that.

Tactics again! Just like his problem with board play at the moment. Strategy was fine, but board play kept letting him down. Thankfully he had old Pitz to carry the boards. The line was fine, his pieces in firm competitive positions on all levels. Still, he needed more work on his own play. Something was lacking.

"Well, we will find out all about this kebbold when you return, won't we?"

"Even if we send eight hundred men, our force levels will be sufficient." Rasion took an active role in the military establishment. The guard was on its mettle here.

"I'm sure force levels will be sufficient to man the great gate. We will call up the second-line of reserves. That will bring in two hundred more."

Zulbanides bowed to Rasion's greater military knowledge. "Well, in that case I will turn my attention to other matters."

Rasion took control further. "And a punitive force might show them the error of their ways. That's worked many times before. Good thinking, Katun."

Katun saluted and left them.

"Let us question the youth," said Zulbanides.

"Can we get anything more from him? I thought we'd pretty well had it all."

"No. He hides and dissembles. He is more clever than that doltish exterior would lead you to think. He is not the Iudo Faex, of course, but he is something. He has some secret, and I shall have it out of him. Come, let us put him to the test. We shall each invade his mind. He cannot fight both of us at once."

Relkin was asleep when they opened the door to his cell. He awoke to a pair of guards unlocking his cuffs and hustling him out and down to another small, dark room, where he was forced into a heavy chair and cuffed to it at wrist and ankle. Instinctively he tried to shift the chair a little, just to see if he could move it. It was immobile.

He swallowed hard. No doubt about it, he was a mess. Both arms wrapped in bandages like a mummy, more bandages on his head. His face ached from his poor nose, which had been battered once again. Biroik had worked him over pretty thoroughly.

On top of that had come the questioning, the hours of interrogation by the elf lords. Zulbanides himself had been the driving force there. Relkin had kept some things back, but it had been hard. To lie endlessly and consistently was impossible. He was exhausted from trying.

And behind it all was a dull ache of horror from the death of Ferla, whatever she'd been, and possibly the death of the greatwitch, too. The horror burned on, endlessly. He didn't think he would ever recover. He laughed at himself. Recover? He wasn't even going to survive.

The dice had just rolled wrong for him. Old Caymo hadn't been up to the job. Maybe that was why folks had given up on the old gods: They were too capricious, they couldn't get the job done. They claimed a lot, but delivered little.

Dully, he wondered if he was in for more physical torture. The heavy chair bolted to the floor was an ominous indicator. If it was torture, he hoped he could hold out. He doubted that he could. Relkin had taken more than his fair share of cuts and bruises in life, but here he'd discovered the limits to his own fortitude. The hot iron pressed to the flesh was more than he could endure.

At the same time, he felt an odd sense of outrage. They were going to torture him when they had already heard everything he had to tell them. He hadn't held back very much.

And suddenly he noticed that they were back. They always came like this, silently, like wraiths out of the dark. Whether it was magic or simply an effect he could not tell.

He looked up into golden eyes.

Zulbanides he knew too well. Lord Rasion, too, had come to see him often during the interrogations. Now Rasion wore martial costume, with breastplate and greaves, while Zulbanides retained the more usual robes.

Zulbanides' face seemed to hover above him, as it had done for hours and hours already. The wicked sweet voice would begin in his mind again and he would have to lie and dissemble. And hide behind words. And try not to give away what he knew now.

He was the Iudo Faex.

It had come to him in that galvanizing flash. When the power had filled him for the first time and he had translated to the board. But he had refused to accept the knowledge. It was too mad, too dangerous. Now the knowledge had seeped back, little by little, and he knew in his bones that it was right.

But it might also be the end of the worlds. All worlds. Everything.

"I already told you what I remember. I don't know how I got to your precious board. I don't see why you always ask the same questions."

"Silence, child," said Zulbanides, not unkindly. "You

said that Mot Pulk was hurting you. And indeed, you have been sorely abused."

Like I told you, I was hurting bad. I kept going in and out of consciousness. And then I woke up on your board."

"You 'fainted' in Mot Pulk's pergola?"

"Something damn well like it."

"And you appeared next on the great board here in Mirchaz? With no magic involved, no spell from Mot Pulk, no use of an amulet of grade five or above? No, this is impossible. You lie, child. I can tell."

"What have I got to lie about?"

"That is exactly what puzzles me, child, and draws me on. What are you trying to keep from us? What exactly are you?"

"I've told you a hundred times, I'm a dragoneer, first class. Second Marneri Legion."

"What else are you, child? What else are you hiding from me?"

The two ancient mage lords bent their brows upon him and stared down. Their eyes seemed to glow as they summoned their power. Soon he felt them on the fringes of his mind, massing against him. Then he groaned and sagged as they began to press mental talons into his mind. It was the same horror as with Mot Pulk, except that they were stronger than the one-eyed lord. They were tricky, too. While one seemed to well up from below, flooding into his thoughts like water, the other came in a freezing wind that sought entry through any little crack.

He tried to resist, but this was beyond his strength. In comparison the great Heruta, lord of Padmasa, had been a crude brute on the psychic plane. These lords of the Game were past masters at this.

Relkin felt them overwhelm him. He was broken and flung on the rocks. They pegged down his mind and began to chew their way through his memory. He screamed with loathing at their mental touch and felt his legs kicking against the chair.

And then it happened again. Something inside him let go. Like an arrow released, it soared up, and then burst in a bolt of purple-white fury and the universe seemed to give way for a moment and he moved himself and left behind the chair in that cruel chamber.

He rode the magic power of the mind mass instead. He tapped into the raw power of the huge spell that bound them.

He stood on Ferla's hill looking down into the grotto. Alas, poor Ferla. Biroik was a statue again. Mot Pulk? The moons were high over Mot Pulk's world, but the one-eyed elf lord was not there.

There was nothing he could do here, except to kill Mot Pulk. He moved himself, and was somewhere else in the next moment, standing on a high cliff overlooking a valley. There were steep-walled mountains on the far side. A small blue-white sun hovered above the distant horizon.

A balloon, round and green, with its elaborate gondola beneath, swung across the sky, towed by a team of large birds flying in perfect formation. An elf lord guided the birds with reins and bells. The birds and the bells made constant music.

Relkin watched until the aviator balloonist was lost to view. There was haunting beauty in the worlds of the elf lords. He had to know more. If he was the Iudo Faex, there was much he had to learn.

He moved himself again and was gone.

Chapter Forty-five

The lake was surprisingly still and warm as they waded in at dusk. They were going to swim diagonally across, a much greater distance than just the width of the lake, which was rectangular and measured eight miles by one and a half miles. By swimming, their profile would remain very low, and in the murky conditions of night they would be invisible. The pyramid stood at the eastern end, still dimly visible in the gathering murk. There was only the faintest wind, from the south.

Because of the weight of their weapons and the distance involved, Bazil had decided from the beginning that he would tow the Ardu through the water. Four long ropes were attached around the wyvern's not inconsiderable waist and to these the Ardu would cling until they were close to their destination.

It took a while to get this to work—at first the ropes entangled themselves—but the Ardu learned to kick as teams and keep each ten-man rope separate.

Once they were all in the water and moving, Bazil hardly seemed to notice their weight as he surged on, powered by the big tail, with an occasional breast stroke added for direction or acceleration.

He had forty men with him, plus Lumbee, who had insisted on coming despite many entreaties from the Ardu men. Normally a female would not be allowed on such a mission, but Lumbee was not a normal female. Her place in the world had changed. She was, in a sense, a corrupted female because of her relations with Relkin, but those same links gave her power. In the crunch, when Norwul was tempted to use force to make her stay in the camp, the dragon backed her up and the Ardu gave way. If the forest god wanted her to come, then she would come.

She took a sword and strapped the scabbard over her shoulder in a crude imitation of the way the dragon carried the dragonsword. Miles slid past and the city on the shore grew larger in view. The ropes chafed somewhat on the leatherback's skin, but the discomfort was small compared to the satisfaction burning in his heart as he drew closer to their target. Bazil was eager for a chance to confront these enemies who had taken his dragonboy.

By the time they were halfway, they could see the red glare in the City of Slaves where caravans and warehouse buildings were on fire. The smell of smoke was strong. Soon they could hear the distant uproar, which grew steadily in volume. Everything was working perfectly. Right on schedule the slaves had risen and assaulted the gates to the Upper City.

The Ardu made jokes about the assault and renewed their determination to succeed. The dragon just kept swimming, with his big eyes fixed on the pyramid.

The moon was a huge yellow disk low in the sky behind the pyramid. Away to their right, the reddish glare silhouetted the crowded merchants' quarter. As they drew closer to the pyramid, so the glare was lost to view behind the houses of the Upper City. The noise still echoed off the high ridge to fill the whole vast bowl around the lake.

They passed out of the western lake when they rounded the Isle of the Dead. On their right was the glorious heart of Mirchaz, the walled Upper City, where the houses of the great were clustered on one side of a grassy median and the colleges of the mage lords on the other. Lamps burned on every corner and above every door. The white marble was lustrous and silken in the light of the moon. They could see people hurrying about urgent business, couriers, small groups of armed men moving at a trot. The Upper City was in ferment.

On they went, and though the dragon felt a degree of fatigue, he dismissed it and just riveted his attention on the target. It was quiet on the lake and there was nothing but the swish of water from their swimming and the distant uproar of the riot and the smell of smoke.

Later, a woman ran along the waterfront screaming at the top of her lungs. Victim of some great tragedy, she voiced a plangent lament. Meanwhile, the distant roar of the riot went on unabated, a steady growl.

The pyramid loomed much closer now. The torches set up at the main entrance showed figures in motion on the main staircase. Lumbee had never seen such an enormous structure. The whole city was so huge, so overwhelming, it shocked Lumbee to the depths of her Ardu soul.

At last they were within a quarter mile of the shore and the Ardu let go of the ropes and spread out and swam in an irregular line. Lumbee stayed close to the dragon. Bazil was relieved of the weight of forty Ardu, which had finally begun to wear him down, and now he surged forward ahead of them. Lumbee caught hold of Ecator's scabbard and rode behind his shoulders. As they came closer to the beach, they roused themselves to redouble their efforts.

The dragon touched bottom first and signaled to the Ardu with a wave. Their hearts rose and their weariness seemed to fade away. Ahead of them was a wide, muddy beach sloping up to a stone wall topped by a promenade with a railing and occasional steps set into the wall to allow access to the beach.

In a grim way Bazil had quite enjoyed the swim, a good long pull such as he hadn't had in too long. All the way across he had run through various possible plans of attack, just as Relkin had said Legion commanders would. Bazil was determined to not only rescue boy, but to impress him. They said dragons couldn't think much on their own. Dragons got set in their ways at an early age, couldn't learn so well. Well, this dragon would show them!

Unfortunately, all the plans came down to one consistent roadblock. The main entrance to the pyramid was a pair of metal-lined gates sixteen feet high that were normally kept propped open and guarded by six men of the caliber of Katun. As a result of the riot, there might well be more on duty. To reach the gates, one had to climb a broad staircase in full view of these guards. Indeed, to even get to the bottom of the stairs, one had to cross a wide-open plaza that was lit with a dozen huge oil lamps. There were people coming and going across these wide-open spaces, too, both singly and in small groups.

There was no way a dragon and forty-one Ardu were going to get to the gate unseen. The trick would be to postpone that moment of discovery until as late as possible. He slid on in closer, until the Ardu could touch bottom, then he settled into a four-footed gait to keep as low to the beach as possible. At this point they were still cloaked in the darkness over the lake and there was no light behind to silhouette them. But once they climbed onto the promenade level, they would be in plain view.

They crept up the beach until they were safely in the shadow at the base of the promenade. No cry of warning had resounded. So far, so good; they had made the first objective. Standing up, Bazil could look clear over the wall. Ardu swarmed up it to take a look for themselves and then dropped back while Bazil ducked down. The people hurrying to and fro on the far side of the plaza had not seen them.

In hurried whispers, they discussed their options. The best appeared to lie in making use of the gardens and shrubbery that surrounded the pyramid. The closest access to the gardens lay on their immediate right, perhaps one hundred feet across the promenade.

To their left, the promenade entered the wider plaza, lit with oil lamps hanging from posts. Across the plaza the staircase to the pyramid began, rising straight up to the entrance platform. The gates were open. In front were six guards.

They had not increased the guard. Bazil was most relieved on that score. Plus the fact that the gate was still open. Evidently the lords were not that concerned about the slave trouble. The slaves had rioted before, but had never succeeded in entering the city.

Bazil imagined that most of the reserves in the pyramid guard had been sent to the city gate anyway. They could hear the distant din. These things were in the attacking party's favor.

The task ahead was to get across the promenade and into the bushes of the park that skirted the pyramid's southern side. From there they could approach to within a hundred feet of the foot of the stairs, where the plaza was joined by an avenue. There were trees set along the edge of the park, and the foliage might cover them.

Bazil laid it out and then made the point that if they were discovered, they would revert to what he called the "crazy attack" plan, which was a simple mad dash for the stairs before the gates could be closed on them.

If they could do that, then success was in their grasp, and Bazil with Ecator in hand would see that it stayed that way. But getting to the gates before they were shut was imperative. The swiftest Ardu were Rekko and Ley Yey. They promised to make sure the gates were not shut.

Once inside, Bazil was confident he could take control of any large chambers inside and capture some prisoners. And then they could open the negotiations.

Bazil just hoped there was some food inside the building, because he would need to eat to rebuild his strength after that swim. To tell the truth, he already felt a definite hunger. But even if there wasn't food available, they could negotiate for that, too. If they controlled the building that was so important to these Lords Tetraan, then the lords would make a deal. They would have to. Their Game back in exchange for the boy and a lot of food, a hell of a lot of food. And beer.

They stepped off, Ardu first, skittering across the promenade and diving over the low wall into the bushes. Amazingly the people just a couple of hundred feet away on the stairs did not notice. Each Ardu was on the promenade for hardly a moment, flickering across in a few spiderish leaps. Finally it was Bazil's turn. With a prayer to the ancient gods of dragonhome, he squeezed his bulk up the rather narrow stairs to the promenade deck and ran four-legged for the bushes. The surface was hard; he could feel his talons skittering on it. The boy would have a fit when he saw those talons—they would be such a mess!

He was seen. A shout went up and then several screams.

"Crazy attack plan!" said Lumbee loudly in the bushes. Bazil skidded to a stop, almost fell over, and then

turned for the open plaza and the stairs. There were some
Ardu already sprinting across the open space. Bazil's
heart leaped at the sight. He'd been right about their
ability—they were running like champions. A moment
later the first pair turned onto the stairs. There were more
close behind them. And then came the rest of the Ardu all
bunched together. Bazil rumbled along in the rear, up on
his hind legs now, tail stiffly outstretched behind him like
a great pujish in attack mode. Thus did the wild wyvern
close in on seals napping on a beach. Thus did he run
down the walrus and the polar bear.

The screaming panic on the stairs had become general.
Elf lords and human servants ran for their lives. The
guards had set themselves with spear and shield to block
the way.

The first Ardu, Rekko and Ley Yey, crashed into the
guards, swinging huge war clubs with tremendous violence. For a moment the guards' formation almost broke.
One man was spun back by a blow on his shield. Another
saw his spear broken. Then the men on their flanks thrust
at the Ardu and drove them back.

More Ardu arrived a few moments later, but orders
were being screamed inside the gates and almost immediately they began to swing shut. They were massive gates
and they moved slowly. Once they were closed, though,
nothing would open them. They were sheathed in steel.

At the sight of the gates closing, Bazil let out a huge
roar. The Ardu went wild. They hurled themselves at the
spearmen. One fell, then another as spears found their
mark, but then the clubs hammered home and swords
thrust in and the guards were overwhelmed. Bounding
men with tails burst through the gates and into the interior
of the gatehouse. Another fierce fight broke out, but the
Ardu men were possessed of a rage that made them
almost superhuman. Nothing would stop them. Eight men
were slain in the tight little gatehouse in less than a
minute. But the gatekeeper broke off the long keys in
the door mechanism and froze the gates half open.

By then Bazil was on the scene. Ecator drawn, he
strode through the gates which had ceased to move. The
interior spaces of the pyramid were designed on a heroic

scale. The passageway was thirty feet across and twenty high, giving even a wyvern dragon room to move.

Within lay the atrium, a huge space which lost itself in gloomy darkness. Surrounding the open space were floor after floor of galleries, rising into the pyramid's upper mass. On the far side were a couple of wide openings, passages into the interior. Bazil made straight for the right-hand passage.

Both passages were clogged with a scrum of servants and elf lords, all trying to get away from the huge kebbold stalking toward them in the atrium. It was the ultimate nightmare of all in Mirchaz, to be devoured by kebbolds. As Bazil drew closer, they gave a collective shudder and pressed harder into the passage.

Then there came a squealing of metal on stone and a horrified screaming from many voices. Bazil drew close, Ecator held at the ready. The screaming went up a few notches and suddenly, like grouse bursting from cover, they poured out of the passage and ran for the farther reaches of the atrium.

Bazil peered into the passage and cursed. A portcullis had been dropped to block the way.

Then with an oath, he spun about and tried to sprint for the other passage. His big feet dug for traction on the marble floor and his claws left long scratches behind as he got himself into motion.

Even as he hauled himself around the corner and into the left-hand passage, he heard the rumbling and squealing and saw the spikes emerge from the ceiling and crash to the floor. A moment later the locking mechanism rang on the steel and a moment after that Bazil crashed into the portcullis and almost knocked himself senseless.

He rebounded, rubbing his nose and jaw. Through the portcullis he could see a group of nervous-looking elf lords who were staring back at him from inside it. They were safe from him, at least for now. The dragon had captured the pyramid, but not the Game board inside it.

Chapter Forty-six

When lords Rasion and Zulbanides met in the small map room of the Tendency, Rasion was still shaking from his experience lowering the portcullises.

"You cannot imagine the fear that possessed me. The mechanism was rusted shut! I pulled the lever and nothing happened! And the monster was heading straight for the left-hand passage. Mark my words, Zulbanides, this brute is not stupid. It lingered barely a moment at the right-hand passage when it saw the portcullis in place. Thank Bos that one worked properly, or I would never have had time."

"What did you do?"

"We oiled the mechanism and then hammered it open. I myself wielded a sledgehammer. Can you imagine?"

Zulbanides could not. In his experience, the golden elves did not lift hammers. Or anything else involving everyday work.

"It is incredible. You shall need to take a purifying bath. I recommend oils of enchilla."

"That monster almost got inside the Game hall!" Rasion's voice quivered with emotion.

"A kebbold striding around in the holy of holies. A disgusting thought!"

"Well, that kebbold is still in the atrium. We can't get out and it can't get in."

"Thanks be to Bos that it can't. And to you, Rasion, who were the instrument of Bos."

"Thank you, Zulbanides." Rasion was making a great effort to calm himself. "But now what are we to do?"

"We have a solution. It will be arduous, and even dangerous, but we can do it."

"What is that?"

"We will create our own warrior, a champion."

"An excellent idea, but who will it be, and how will he fare against a kebbold wielding a sword?"

"No, no, Rasion, it will not be one of us. We shall go into the *Book of Golgomba*. There are styles of magic that we have rarely made use of."

"Golgomba is proscribed by the treaty of Gelderen."

"Of course it is. And so is interference with the Game by outside forces that shall remain nameless."

"They are involved, aren't they? Our great enemies."

"Consider what has been happening here. What else could be responsible?"

"Golgomba, then. We will need sacrifice."

"We have sufficient servants in here. Probably too many, considering our food supply."

"Let it be done," said Rasion firmly. "Let us show them that we will not be trifled with."

They left the map room and passed through the suite to a gallery overlooking the atrium. A quick glance over the wall showed the atrium floor quite empty. The Ardu were down there, but they were out of sight. And no one had seen the kebbold for quite a while, not since a guard had grazed it with a spear thrown from the third floor. Still it was there, hiding in the shadows. And now the elf lords and their players were cut off from the outside world. The atrium was the only way in or out of the Game hall and the office suites above it.

After the initial panic had settled, Zulbanides had ordered a census taken of the lords who were present, and of their retainers. There were more than three hundred lords and a thousand servants. A third of the Thousand, in fact, drawn to the board that night by the dramatic play of Old Pitz, engaging Flannimi with Strengths and Leapers. They had a comforting sense of their own numbers. They were a strong group, but Zulbanides knew they were also a large group to feed on the available resources.

Unless, of course, they wished to eat the pap that was fed to the slaves of the mind mass. For beneath the board dwelled the mind mass and the access way lay through the hall of the Game. Of course the thought of eating pap never even occurred to Zulbanides or Rasion.

Zulbanides addressed the leading members of the Tendency first. There was a brief discussion and then agreement. It was a dark and dangerous path, but it would provide them with a force with which to tackle this kebbold.

They passed out the word, first in a meeting with the top six Cabal members present. The idea was accepted. Golgomba was the only answer. And they would act soon, because they had no food and the situation was intolerable.

Meanwhile, down below, in the passage between the gates and the atrium, the Ardu took turns to rest. A few even managed to snatch a few minutes of sleep. The dragon, furiously hungry now, hid out by the gates where he could see the city, the lake, and the open plaza below. Guards had appeared on the plaza in considerable numbers. Elf lords clad in blue and silver armor appeared and harangued the guards.

Bazil was glad of the breather, but he remained very hungry. Worse, things had not gone as planned. The attackers were trapped between two forces. By the fiery breath, he had never imagined that there might be portcullises. Just get to the gates had been his thought, and it'd been wrong. The only thing in their favor was that they had the Game lords trapped on the other side of the portcullises. There was only one way in or out of the Pyramid of the Game. Unfortunately, they could not shut the pyramid gates, since the operator had broken off the long keys inside the mechanism. The doors could not even be pushed shut, since they were controlled by immense gears, all governed by those keys. The whole thing would have to be taken apart to remove the key. Neither the Ardu nor the wyvern dragon had the skills or even the tools to begin such a task. Thus they were left with gates propped halfway open.

Bazil surmised that the elf lords down there in the plaza would realize there was some kind of problem. It would not take them too long, he imagined, to decide to try a frontal assault.

Bazil could not see it, but from the diminution of the sound coming from the southeastern end of the city he was sure the rioting had died down somewhat. The caravans had burned out in the commercial road, although there were still a number of buildings ablaze. The smoke was still rising into the night air. A lot of rioters had participated in breaking into the wine shops and were reeling around the gutters now, singing and shouting incoherently. At the city gates things had settled into a contest of rock throwing and archery. Guards held the city gates. The mob threw rocks at them, the guards occasionally sent an arrow down. Bazil imagined that reinforcements would soon be brought from the riot area to assault the pyramid gate.

His thoughts turned briefly to the captives they'd taken. They might prove worthwhile as hostages. They had five elf lords and twenty servants, some of them Ardu.

The servants were too terrified to raise their eyes from the ground. They could hardly even respond to the Ardu. The elf lords were haughty at first, until one or two had been knocked to the ground and kicked around a bit by vengeful Ardu. Disgusted with the cravenness of the servants, the Ardu herded all of them together into the gate control room.

There was a stir of movement down at the bottom of the stairs. A horn blew and a single man, wearing a helmet and leather armor, came up the stairs holding a white flag of truce. He reached the top of the stairs and came to a halt.

"I bring a message from the Lords Tetraan." He spoke Ardu with a harsh accent.

"Advance to the gate," said Bazil. "We will not slay you."

Captain Katun stepped forward warily. The gates were half closed. He could not see into the shadows until he stepped right into the center. Then he almost jumped out of his skin. A huge kebbold was standing there, hidden from view. Beside the kebbold stood an Ardu girl, and behind her were a number of Ardu men, some of them of impressive size. They would fetch good money in the slave market.

"Who is your leader?" said Katun.

"I am," said Bazil without a second's hesitation.

Katun's eyes popped and he went into a kind of dragon freeze. He sputtered, completely flabbergasted. After a half minute Bazil leaned over and poked the man with a talon.

Katun came alive, wide-eyed, face taut, spewing obscenities in Mirchazese.

"Speak Ardu," said Bazil.

Katun swallowed and took a couple of deep breaths. "I had not expected to be addressed by a kebbold."

"By the fiery breath of the ancestors, I am not a kebbold, any more than you are an ape!"

"How . . ." said Katun weakly. "Who . . ." He failed to finish.

"What do you want?" said Bazil.

Katun got a grip. "The lords wish to parlay with you. Do you have a list of demands?" Katun spoke to the Ardu; he still couldn't accept that a kebbold would speak.

"We have two demands," said Bazil firmly. "First we demand you free a captive. A boy taken in the Ardu country. He is dragonboy, my dragonboy."

Katun breathed an oath. That damned kid had told all these stories and Katun had never believed a word of it. Katun didn't know how they'd scared everybody out of their wits with a pujish, but he knew that pujish could not be tamed; they were simply too elemental—too stupid, perhaps. Pujish always ended up eating their handlers. But what was this thing that looked like a kebbold and yet spoke language?

"You did all this just to get back Relkin?"

"Relkin! You know my boy?"

Katun realized it was time to dissemble. "Yes, I met him."

"Relkin lives?"

"As far as I know. It is complex to tell. Are you capable of understanding?"

"I don't know . . . are you?"

"Yes."

"Then I think I will manage."

Katun swallowed again. Never had he dreamed that

things would come to this. He described the great, glorious universe of the magic of the elf lords. He spoke of
the whirling magical worlds, all created by the power of
the mind mass. Somewhere, one elf lord had made a
world and hidden it so cleverly that none could find it. It
was suspected that that was where Relkin was.

"If they have harmed boy, they will pay," growled the
dragon. Katun quailed. The dragon was leaning forward
on that scabbarded sword. The scale of the sword struck
Katun, who was highly familiar with swords of many
types. He blanched at the thought.

Bazil spoke again. "That is first demand. The second is
this: The slave raids in the Ardu land are over. If anyone
ever comes to the Ardu land again for slaves, they die.
And I will come back here and kill those responsible."

"I will tell them. They asked me to beg you to spare the
boards and the sweet lords of the Game. They have raised
great beauty in their worlds. Do not harm them!"

"None have been harmed. All are alive."

"Can we speak to them, to be assured that they are
alive?"

"No."

"Will you release them?"

"No. Go now, tell your masters what I say. Tell them
forest god has come to Mirchaz. Things will change."

Katun returned to the bottom of the stairs. Several lords
of the Tendency were waiting. He told them of Bazil's
demands.

"A talking kebbold. 'Tis extraordinary."

"We do not have the boy! This is the same damned boy
everyone was looking for because they thought he was the
Iudo Faex."

"No one knows where he is."

"Mot Pulk has him."

"Nobody knows where Mot Pulk is, either. Probably on
his hidden Game world."

"Then he can only be found by going through the Game
board."

"How can we do that when the kebbold holds the gate?"

"They hold the gate, but perhaps not the rest."

"The kebbold does not have control of the Game board."

"The portcullises, they dropped the portcullises. . . ."

"That is a comforting thought."

A few minutes later the guards were given the order to assault the gates.

Bazil saw the guards mass for an assault on a front ten wide and ten deep.

The elf lords had seen through the attackers' position. Perhaps there was a way for the elves inside to communicate with the elves outside. Or else something he had said had given it away. Damn! The dragon just was not wily enough to fool men.

Now they would have to fight. Unless the hostage option would work. He called for the captive elf lords to be brought out.

Quickly they were dragged out and displayed.

"Stop the attack and go back or we will kill these lords."

The guards came to a halt. Messengers ran up and down the stairs to the group of lords bunched at the bottom. Captain Katun was sent up to investigate. He reported back a few moments later. Five lords were being proferred as hostages. None were of higher rank than the eighth hundred, none had connections to the Tendency.

This confirmed the suspicions of the elf lords. The Ardu rebels had not secured the pyramid; they merely held the gate. The need to recapture the pyramid was paramount. A third of the Thousand was trapped in there. The lives of a handful of the eighth and ninth hundred were light in the balance in comparison.

Katun returned to the top and ordered the attack to begin.

Bazil realized his bluff was called. He ordered the elf lords shoved back into the gatehouse. He and the Ardu readied themselves for battle with a collective rasp of steel as they drew their swords and took up the slain guards' shields and spears.

As they did so, in the heart of the pyramid, in a chamber above that of the great board, the lords of the

Tendency were at work on the dread magic from the Old Red Aeon known as Golgomba.

A struggling servant, firmly gagged to prevent screams from breaking the general concentration, was bound over an altar. Words of power were recited by the group in unison. They reached out to the mind mass and established a connection by which to draw strength for their spell.

Zulbanides took up a sharpened knife and cut the servant, sending his blood running into a copper pan. The pan was then passed among the elf lords, who took sips of the blood to imbibe the slave's spirit.

Then Zulbanides cut out the slave's eyes, followed by his tongue, lips, and ears. Finally, Zulbanides cut the throat and the death energies gave power to the lords' dread spell. The room rocked, a sulfurous stench thickened the air, and the sense of imminence began to build.

Chapter Forty-seven

At the gate, battle began before dawn. The guards were seasoned mercenaries who had seen combat all over the southern part of the continent of Eigo, and many had experience dealing with kebbolds. But none had ever confronted a battledragon of Argonath. Thus, they were perhaps a little overconfident at first and made painful mistakes.

First they lit torches and set them at the edge of the platform, as archers took position along the top step. Spearsmen came in at a run, chanting a motto to inspire themselves as they chugged up the steps and started toward the gate. Bazil waited in the deeper shadows behind the gate until the last moment, so as not to expose himself to arrows and spears more than he had to. Then, as they began to bunch in front of the gate, he stepped out smartly and swung Ecator through the first rank at waist height.

Two tried to parry with their oblong shields. The shields were good ones, of steel on wood lapped with leather, but against Ecator at full power they parted and their owners were sent directly to hell in a spray of blood. Screams and cries of horror accompanied a mass drop to the ground by the rest of the first rank, all except for a fellow at the end who tried to jump and lost his legs just above the knees. The second rank jammed to a stop; some men fell down, and then rebounded and crashed into the third rank.

Ecator was just as quick on the backstroke and two more guards were cleft in twain, sending clouds of bloody viscera flying. The survivors of the front rank bolted back into the mass behind, which was bunching badly now and had slowed to a halt a good thirty feet from the gate. Bazil towered there in the mouth of the gate, that huge sword stained red. Lit by the savage fire of the torches, it was a terrifying sight. Then arrows flashed toward him and he stepped back into the shadows.

The guards were left shaking their heads, not looking at each other.

"Come on, you cowards," roared one of their leaders, a giant from Nuzt with a great battle-ax in his hands.

"Hasmone!"

"Hasmone will go up against the dragon!"

The guards took heart, sorted themselves out, and set off at a walk for the gate. Behind them the bowmen took aim. They pressed in on the gate, the long spears at the ready in front, with mighty Hasmone slightly ahead, waving his battle-ax. And then the darkness of the gate disgorged a line of robust Ardu, armed with swords as well the usual clubs. Some had taken up the shields of fallen guards.

The shock of impact rang out over the lake. Weapons of all sorts were instantly at work in a mad hacking, stabbing, ripping fight at close quarters. The Ardu had learned a few things about close-order combat with edged weapons. Both sides took casualties, but the Ardu were the clear winners. Hasmone struck down an Ardu, Lea of the Red Rock, before being gutted by a backhand strike from Norwul. A half dozen other guards were down by then, as were two Ardu stabbed through with spear and sword.

The floor of the pyramid gate was slippery with blood. The bodies of the slain covered the terrace. The Ardu fought with barely controlled fury. The guards could stand it no further and they broke back and withdrew. Again the archers struck and Usad of the Yellow Canyon went down and moved no more. The Ardu pulled back behind the gates, taking with them a valuable haul of spears and shields. But its value was not as much as that of Usad, or Lea or Usogon, who were now gone forever.

Guard officers were at work, forming up fresh troops in a phalanx with overlapping shields and long spears, ranked five deep. Pikeman would work along side, ready to drive home against the kebbold if it showed itself.

The Ardu met them with sword and club once more. But now it was the Ardu who took the heavier initial casualties, for the guards worked together well in the phalanx system, the first man wielding spear and shield, the second throwing a spear over his shoulder and then fighting with sword and ax.

Each Ardu fighter found himself engaged on two fronts at once. Edwal fell, speared in the groin. Then down went Yimt and Gadda. Then more fell; the spears were deadly. The Ardu could not stand against this well-organized attack.

Seeing their peril, Bazil roared his challenge and swung out to engage. Ecator flashed down and took a guard's head. Instantly arrows feathered his upper torso. A pike flashed in the torchlight as it drove in at him, but he parried with Ecator and spun the pikeman around before cutting him down. Another pike came from the other side, but too slowly. He dodged away while bringing the sword around in a backstroke that clove the point man of the phalanx and then continued on to slice through the pikeman, too. Bazil Broketail did not have to prove his skill with the great sword, but it was always manifest in battle.

The guards bolted back, but more arrows struck home before Bazil could get behind the gate.

He breathed a sigh of thanks for the toughness of leatherback dragonhide. That and the remains of the joboquin, which had stopped a few on its own. He had arrows sticking out of his shoulders and one was even embedded on the top of his head, but his eyes were all right and nothing had gone very deep.

It appeared that the attackers had gained a short respite. Bazil knew, however, that the guards would reform the phalanx and return.

Close to the equator, dawn came as swiftly as the night, and its first light fell across the land. Now the archers would have a plain target if he stepped out of the gate.

Lumbee came to him and began to remove the arrows, or at least to cut off the shafts if they were in too deep to be removed easily. Fortunately, none had struck through to an artery. Several were pretty painful, however. He leaned back against the wall and worked at overcoming the pain, using the technique Relkin had taught him. He took deep breaths, centered his mind on the battle situation, and ignored the physical sensations. Lumbee worked with knife and fingers. The light was not good, but she was deft.

He had not imagined this predicament. The lack of a shield was telling against him here. Occasionally a whistle escaped him as Lumbee cut and tugged. She wasn't clumsy, though, almost as good as a dragonboy, and she'd had no training.

He noticed that she had tears running down her face as she worked.

"Are you in pain, Lumbee?"

She looked up at him with eyes swimming. "No, I cry for the pain I must be causing you."

The wyvern put out a huge hand and let it rest for a moment on Lumbee's shoulder. "You do good job. Lumbee is dragonfriend, I know this."

Lumbee wiped away the tears with the back of her hand. "One of the men, Yord—he is of the Heather Hills, my kin—he is making the hand grip bigger on one of the captured shields. It might help a bit."

Bazil considered for a moment. "Any shield better than none in this kind of fight. And they don't have troll."

Lumbee did not understand the reference, or the word, for there was no Ardu equivalent, but before Bazil could begin to explain, Norwul came to speak with them.

He had a plan.

"Their archers are too dangerous. We have to pull back, make then fight us in here, inside the gate."

The wyvern clacked his jaws a moment. "Good idea," he said. "Pity we didn't bring Ium and Wol. They were getting pretty good with those crossbows."

"They could not swim that well. They went to aid the attack on the city gate."

"Now we fight inside the pyramid gate. But we need to draw them in, so Ardu must show themselves briefly, then retreat."

"Yord is adapting one of their shields for you."

"Lumbee told me. It is a very good idea."

"Yord is very skilled at such things."

And indeed, a few moments later a tall Ardu with a heavy beard came over with one of the captured shields. He had cut away the original hand grip and made a new grip from a doubled leather belt. It was nailed to the wooden backing with fasteners teased out of a wall panel in the gatehouse.

"Yord could have career in the Legion. Be dragonboy."

Yord bobbed his head nervously, overjoyed to have been of service to the forest god.

There were shouted commands coming from outside the gate.

"Here they come again," said someone.

The shield was small for a wyvern battledragon, but it was well made and the grip, though crude, was serviceable.

The guard phalanx stamped across the platform and bunched in the gate where the Ardu met them. The phalanx thrust on, the Ardu retreated, and the phalanx entered the gate. Now Bazil could engage and he swung, over the heads of the Ardu and down into the ranks of the phalanx behind them.

Ecator sundered several men from the world, but the phalanx did not break. Spearmen thrust up at his breast. Bazil shuddered away from the spears, felt something jab hard into the joboquin, and heaved himself back. A spear thrust into his tail as he turned, but it came loose a moment later and did no serious harm.

Norwul and the Ardu hurled themselves forward and grappled with the phalanx line just in front of the dragon. They used shields to sweep away the spear points and allow them to strike with sword or club. Such blows did they strike on the phalanx shields and helm that it fell back a step, giving the dragon time to get ready. Then the Ardu fell back, dodging low in terror of Ecator.

Bazil swung in and cut through the spears as if he were using a sickle on wheat. He lashed out with his foot to kick disarmed men out of the way. They fell back into the ranks behind them, and the whole phalanx was stalled and jammed up tight.

A guard hurled his spear at close quarters, but the borrowed shield deflected it into the wall. Another spear, however, sank into his leg and it went deep. Bazil knew at that instant that it was a bad wound.

Then Ecator was at work on the guards and since they were pressed together and unable to so much as duck, a swift, terrible carnage ensued. Within less than twenty seconds the phalanx of guards was a shambles, and the remainder had fled back through the gate and down the steps in complete panic.

A score of corpses lay mounded up in pieces around the blood-spattered figure of the dragon. Norwul's eyes were staring wide as he recalled what Relkin had told him, of how in Relkin's homeland they employed these giants in battle in groups of ten, hundreds at a time. It came home to him what it would mean to go up against such a force in battle.

The Ardu had regained control of the gates. But they had paid for it. A quarter of their number were gone, others were wounded. Arrows kept zipping in, occasionally finding a target. Still, they retrieved many more shields. Everyone had a spear, plus a sword now.

A study of the situation on the plaza revealed that the elf lords and the guard officers were arguing at the base of the staircase. The guards were massed behind them, except for the archers, who were lined up along the top stair shooting into the open gates. Arrows whipped in, ricocheted off the walls, and went on into the atrium.

For now they had a standoff. But for how long could they hold this place?

As long as the dragon could hold a sword and the Ardu could fight.

Just then there came a screech of metal on stone from inside the atrium. Heads turned.

One of the portcullises was rising.

Bazil gave a hiss. "They have a weapon," he said.

The portcullis jammed about halfway. For a moment nothing happened, then a shadowy shape appeared in the passage behind it. A huge hand reached into the portcullis and heaved it up with a fearsome screech of metal on stone. When it was high enough, a massive bulk slid through underneath.

The Ardu gasped. The gray thing was vaguely manlike in general proportions, except that it had no visible head and stood about eight feet high. It had enormous shoulders, massive arms and legs, and a torso ribboned with thick muscle. In one hand it bore a heavy double-edged sword, and in the other it carried a round buckler. Beyond that it appeared to have no armor, nor clothing, nor sex organs, nor tail.

It came straight toward them. Bazil took a deep breath. This attack on the pyramid seemed to have been a mistake. As the thing came closer, he saw that the barrel-shaped torso had a top like that of an onion. Around the top was a ring of round red eyes, with black pupils. It could see in any direction all the time. If it had ears, they were hidden. Perhaps the slits below the eyes were the ears. There was no mouth.

It stepped forward with a ponderousness that told Bazil that it was heavy, at least his weight, probably more. The question would be, how fast was it? And the other question would be, how fast was a wyvern dragon that had already been through a fight and was pretty cut up? The spear head jammed in his thigh hurt wickedly when he moved his right leg.

Bazil moved out into the atrium, Ecator swinging lightly in his hand. He could sense the unholy excitement that possessed the blade sometimes. The Golgomba thing stepped forward. It was not as tall as Bazil, but its limbs were longer. Warily the opponents circled, then the thing stepped forward, shield raised, and swung its sword.

Bazil parried, there was a flash of steel and he went on and tried a thrust for the monster's torso. It deflected him with the buckler. Its own counterstroke was a little slow and Bazil was able to get back on his hind foot and bring Ecator around to parry. Again the heavy impact. Ecator fairly sang with rage. Bazil felt his arm shake from the blow.

This was like exchanging sword blows with the Purple Green, a giant dragon.

He swung again. The thing defended with its buckler, but this piece of equipment was quickly beginning to disintegrate. Ecator had cut away a third of it already. Bazil felt a surge of confidence. He was the quicker of the two. And Ecator was by far the better blade.

It counterattacked with a waist-high sweep. Bazil parried and struck out with his good left leg. His talons raked down the thing's front. It took no notice. They swung together and he slipped the monster's clumsy sword and flicked Ecator on in a thrust straight for the center of that weird body. This time he was well ahead of the buckler. Ecator drove in but did not stab home, instead gouging along the thing's side. Bazil spun away and parried the enemy's counterthrust hurriedly.

What the hell was it made of? Ecator itself hummed with frustration. There was a long gouge, several inches deep running across its side, but it took absolutely no notice.

They engaged. Bazil checked it, feinted, and then swung down hard over the right shoulder. Ecator sank in halfway and then came free.

The thing staggered momentarily, then rocked back out of range for a moment and steadied itself. Then it came on. Its sword arm was unaffected. No fountain of gore appeared.

Again the question arose. What in all the hells was it made of? Bazil felt a distinct chill in his heart as he maneuvered, his right leg screaming all the time. Any normal living thing would have been incapacitated by that stroke. What was he dealing with here? What was this thing?

Chapter Forty-eight

The worlds of the Lords Tetraan were works of art on a high order. Most were jewels, designed like sensuous gardens but on the grandest of scales. Incredible artifice was commonplace in the construction of small alps, starkly beautiful canyons, and grottos with dramatic pools and ponds. Mountains and moons were set as decorations.

Homes and palaces for the elf lords were designed in a range of architectural styles. Some worlds had a single, perfectly placed structure, such as Zulbanides' beautiful Lone Tower, famous throughout the Game. It expressed the perfect proportion of pitch and harmony, looming over a subtly shaped grotto, with a single tree upon the opposite crag. When the huge moon rose at night, the tree was starkly illuminated. In its branches could be read a glyph that was Zulbanides' mark.

Many worlds had quite large populations of slave beings in villages and towns that supported the elf lords in their wondrous chateaux. In the hedonic rooms, the lords indulged a furious appetite for the sexual flesh of their slaves.

It was a rare castle that didn't have a combat room, with a pit where men fought each other to the death while the lords bet on the outcome. The lords were casually cruel to their slaves in many ways.

Still, they aspired to an artistic expression in the creation of their worlds. The pleasures these worlds returned to them were all but fractions of that expression. Like the combined flavors and colors of great wine, they sought a complex reward from the building of worldlets.

But then, here and there, among the beautiful, hedonistic worlds there were the other ones. The ones where a perverse cruelty had created an art from monstrousness.

As the Iudo Faex moved from world to world through the dimensions of the Great Game, he found more and more of these perverse horror worlds.

At one he found a flat land where people virtually carpeted the ground. He popped out perhaps a hundred feet above the surface, and he floated there in a bubble. A vast horde of stinking, filthy wretches stretched to the horizon in all directions. They could barely move, there were so many of them. As he watched, a cloud came over and rained down gray pellets and the people ate the pellets. And when the cloud made rain, the people stood there with their mouths open and were watered, like so much grass.

Then he found, to his horror, that was exactly how they were treated. Striding into view came an enormous four-legged creature, bearing on its back a small palace, complete with turrets and silken pennons flying from the tops. With each stride of its vast elephantine feet, the brute trampled a thousand pour souls to pulp.

The true horror was the speed with which the surrounding population ate the pulp and occupied the ground thus vacated.

The vast beast, like a short-necked shmunga, yet far greater than any shmunga that had ever lived, went past and bore the elf lord's castle away.

The Iudo Faex moved on.

Later he found his first war world, a horror of endless warfare between empires built and run by hundreds of millions of slaves. Guiding the warfare and directing the campaigns were the elf lords, for whom it was all part of the Game.

Vast, elegant battles were fought, and mounds of skulls were raised up to mark them. In time, the skulls would wither in the rain and sun and turn to dust, and still more mounds of skulls would rise in their place.

Here the elf lords could test military theories, run complex war games, and play at being generals. They were popular worlds, very draining on the mind mass, and so hey were usually the work of a power clique, such as he Tendency.

And then there were the more peculiar ones, such as the strange world inhabited by creatures with the heads of toothed birds, where great populations of people were kept as food animals. They were penned in tiny stalls, fattened on sludge, and then hung up, their throats slit, and left to bleed to death.

As raw meat they were fed to dog-headed things six feet tall that were kept as pets. Cooked, they were eaten by the rulers, the bird people.

The artistic point in this was not perceptible to him. Why had the golden elves of Gelderen descended to this degraded passion for the perversely cruel? What had driven them to this smallness of heart, this closed-in haughty disdain for all sense of decency?

He was sickened, standing on a hill watching two huge armies locked in combat on a muddy slope some five miles long. Shield walls clashed and men died by the hundreds, then the thousands as the attack was pressed on and on, past the endurance of the men until they simply collapsed. It was war by generals with no thought for the men involved. They were ciphers, things to be used and disposed of with no thought for consequence.

And here he felt the deepest contact with the wrongness of the entire, hideous enterprise of the Great Game, for he knew too well what was involved in such battle.

He moved on.

It was time to rest and collect himself. He would need all his strength for the next step. He knew the elves' trick for the use of the power of the mind mass now. He had learned it without knowing how he'd learned it; it had simply come to him. Then he had learned a deeper principle, directly from the mind mass. He could move through the worlds at will.

He sought solace on a pleasant world where purple clouds drifted through a yellow canyonland. The sun was square and dim. But the artificiality disturbed him and he moved again. He rediscovered Mot Pulk's hidden world. With his new powers he could pierce the skein of illusion that hid it from the other lords. He stood once more in the

pergola and recalled the happiness he had enjoyed there
with Ferla. He contemplated the grotto and his heart grew
heavy and tears came to his eyes.

The time was approaching. He had to prepare himself.
Flushed with emotion, feeling hate for Mot Pulk and all
the elf lords, he used a new power, one they had never
learned. He left the Game worlds instantly and made
direct transition to a spot well outside the Game board.
Where they would have spent hours slowly forging such a
transition, he accomplished it in an instant.

He stood alone on the promenade of the Overlook on
the Arkelauds as dawn broke over the mountains in the
east. The palace loomed behind him. A fountain played in
the ornamental pond. Tables and chairs were set along the
promenade and the city, laid out below, sparkled in the
first light. Across the lake the statue of Zizma Bos
gleamed. Smoke rose in the southwest, where the City of
Slaves was still burning. The smell was quite strong,
overwhelming the jasmine of the gardens. The lake was a
breathtakingly beautiful blue; the hills and mountains
formed a complete bowl around it. Relkin could appreciate why Zizma Bos had decided to build here. Such
natural beauty was rare.

For a moment his vision blurred and he felt faint. He
steadied himself on the rail, then sat on the nearest bench.
The burns still hurt horribly, but somehow he'd adjusted
to it. He needed to rest. Recuperate. He knew what he had
to do and knew it would take everything he had left.

The gestalt was there, but it was asleep. All that it did,
it did with dreaming minds, harnessed to the fell sorcery
of the elf lords. To wake it would be as if a pea wished
to awaken an elephant. All that was in his favor was that
he knew how to siphon off the energy of that selfsame
elephant.

Feeling desolate and cold, he looked out across the lake
to the ceremonial sites on the north bank. The loss of
Ferla, the torture . . . Relkin was about wrung out. The
world was on the other side of an invisible barrier and he
could see it, but he could no longer feel it. His dragon was
lost somewhere in the interior of the savage continent.
Lumbee was lost. Eilsa? She was on the far side of the

world and the way things were going, he would not survive to see her again.

If this was what it was that made you the Iudo Faex, he decided he didn't care for it much. He'd rather do something else. Dully, he wondered if he was going to lose his arms. They looked terrible. The burns had gone terribly deep.

Biroik had hurt his nose again, too. He found that blood had crusted inside the battered thing and was making it hard to breathe. There was blood in his mouth, which he spat out. He sighed softly. He was quite a mess. He'd never pass an inspection.

Incredibly, his head dropped and he dozed, exhaustion and shock combining at last to overwhelm the pain. When he awoke, he was no longer alone. An elf lady was sitting there watching him.

"Ah, there you are. Welcome," she said. The big eyes were completely blue.

He stared at her. It was Lady Tschinn, the one who'd started the madness when she'd named him the Iudo Faex.

"Come inside. We must tend to your wounds."

"You know what I am."

"Yes, child. I know."

"How can the Iudo Faex trust you?"

She went down on her knees and pressed her forehead to the ground at his feet. "I am your servant. I foretold your fate; now let me serve you."

She raised her head, sat back on her haunches. "You see, I understand that the Game must end. It has grown fell and evil. Our lords were not always as you see them now. Once they were the equals of great Althis."

"You know Althis?"

She gave him a strange glance. "Of course, we are the same people. Only we have descended. When we left Gelderen, when we were cast out of Gelderen, then began our fall from our true place in the world. Here we built our secret enclave, and here we have rotted."

The eyes were completely blue, milk and meek.

"It is a weirdness that has possessed our lords, something fell and foreign to their true nature. I think that it is the Game that has done this to them."

The lady sagged, as if by saying the words she had finally accepted the inevitable. Then she looked up at him.

"And yet not all of us have gone the way of the Game lords. Some of us still hold to the truth in our hearts. We earn nothing but scorn from them. And we do not play the Game. They offer us only the passions of spectators." She sighed.

"We remember Gelderen and the great life. We would keep our promise to the High. We will accept our fate. Thus we must serve you. You are the chosen instrument."

That sounded downright ominous.

"I need a drink," said Relkin.

"Come inside. I will bring you water or whatever you desire."

Still feeling dizzy, Relkin got to his feet and lurched across the promenade. The pain from the burns was fairly constant now. Moving didn't seem to make as much difference. She held the door for him and he shuffled inside to a large reception room set with plush furniture and thick rugs. The walls were a pale green.

He lay down on a golden divan. Three Ardu slave girls appeared at the tinkle of a little silver bell. They brought water and healing materials and set to work with Lady Tschinn to clean and dress his wounds. While the slave girls bandaged him, the lady performed healing magic. She burned bitter herbs on a small stone, sucked in the smoke, and then blew it over Relkin while she recited the words of the spell. Relkin accepted it as part of the healing. He had experienced too much magic in his short life to be surprised by such things.

The girls rebandaged his nose and cleaned the gouges and cuts on his back, where Biroik had ground him into the ground at one point. They dealt with the burns. Indeed, when they had finished, he was swathed in well-set bandages. He could scarcely move.

The girls left. Lady Tschinn sat beside him, singing softly while she did needlework. He tried not to think too much about what lay ahead. Eventually he spoke.

"They will kill me."

She paused, looked up, and nodded. "Yes. You are the Iudo Faex."

"It is hard when you feel so completely forsaken. Where are the gods now that I need their help?"

Old Caymo had thrown broken dice, bad dice, terrible dice. His last living worshiper was in desperate need of a change of luck. But Relkin felt certain that his gods did not rule in this dread place.

"Who knows what the gods do or don't do? I no longer believe in gods. Not since we were cast out of Gelderen."

And Relkin's fortunes were now entwined with the great gestalt entity that slept beneath the pyramid and that entity knew nothing of gods.

The slave girls brought him wine and bread and chicken broth. They soaked the bread in the broth until it was soft enough to swallow without chewing and fed him by hand as if he were some sort of precious animal. He had to force himself not to gulp the wine down and call for more.

He lay back and concentrated on breathing. Slowly he began to feel a little stronger. The food was a help. And there was something else, something deep within him that had turned around now. It was a distinct sensation that he had stopped retreating. Now he was moving the other way. Of course there was a long way to go.

He dozed off again.

Lady Tschinn cradled his head in her lap and sang elfin lullabies over him.

He was a brave young man, caught up in something far beyond his understanding. He had been sent, of that she was sure. Sent from the outside to bring an end to everything. He would destroy her, she knew, yet it had to be.

It all had to end. Her brothers, her father, her uncles, they had surrendered to the weird and the perverse. They had become cruel, disgusting caricatures of themselves. She knew that the moment was coming. The threads of the universe were approaching realignment.

She guessed that more was at stake here than even she could imagine. This youth had known of Althis. That could only mean that he was marked before he ever came to Mirchaz. What did this portend?

She knew. There was a ripeness in the moment. She sensed the fullness, the awesome fullness.

Chapter Forty-nine

In the pyramid, two giant gladiators circled, swords extended. Bazil's bad leg gave a twinge with every step. Sweat ran down his back, dripped from his chin, and soaked the remains of his joboquin. His sword arm was numb and the little jerry-built shield was disintegrating.

So were his hopes. Again and again he had beaten this eerie opponent and gone through to stab home, and still the thing kept fighting. Ecator had hacked deep into its shoulders, into the top of its tubular, headless torso, into legs and arms, and it took almost no notice. He had knocked it down, three times so far, and driven the blade deep into the region above the ring of eyes. Now it was coming back yet again, climbing off the floor for the third time. Its buckler was completely gone now, but its sword was still effective, though notched.

At least in that regard, the dragon could feel pride. Ecator was unmarked, still a ribbon of white steel imbued with a fell spirit that longed to feed on the lives of all enemies of the light.

The enemy thing had a limited repertoire of moves, and while it was not clumsy, it lacked grace. It never surprised him, but it always struck hard and accurately, so that to miss a parry was to risk a terrible wound.

Again they came together. He moved inside for a change, and used his bulk to stop it dead. Its arm flailed at him ineffectively since he was inside its reach and its sword was useless behind him. Now he reached up and stabbed down with Ecator, both hands on the handle, and drove the fell blade deep into the thing.

Ecator went in all the way, piercing it from headless shoulders to unsexed crotch. The thing thrashed for a moment, Bazil's heart leaped—at last a reaction! It quivered, shook itself, and moved away from him. He stepped forward in lockstep and tried to get Ecator out. The sword was stuck. He tugged. It stabbed at him with its own blade and he hugged it and felt the steel slice his hide along his ribs. Ecator still would not come free. Bazil hauled on it until the veins stood out all over the upper part of his body; still the blade was firmly held. He heaved and the beast came right off its feet for a moment, but Ecator remained trapped, skewering the brute.

It had shortened its arc of arm motion and was about to drive that ugly sword home into Bazil's belly. The wyvern was forced to step away and release his grip on Ecator. It was a desolate feeling, as if part of him had been lost.

There were shouts from above. He glanced upward and saw rows of elf lords gesticulating, on the galleries of the upper part of the atrium. They were applauding the creature they had made.

He stepped back, and back some more. The damned beast stood there, Ecator's hilt and handle sticking out of its topside, the blade rammed down into it like a new spine made of steel, and still it was coming at him. It moved deliberately, a step at a time. The useless buckler was proffered first to guard itself. Bazil snorted. By the fiery breath! It hadn't changed its battle plan at all; it still fought with the same stupid, ugly tactics. As if he were still armed.

It aggrieved Bazil to think he might die at the hands of such a clumsy opponent. Why, the Purple Green, bless his huge, cantankerous heart, was better with a sword than this insane, carrot-shaped thing. Still it swung its blade and he moved out of range smartly. He gave thanks to the gods that this place was big enough to give him a little room to maneuver. But in time his bad leg would make it impossible for him to keep that vital step ahead and then it would cut him down.

He had to get his sword free. Hope had dwindled to nothing without a sword. Fortunately, he was not completely alone. The Ardu were watching, and at that moment they were not being pressed at the gate. They called among each other and several edged out into the atrium to try to help. The thing ignored them and continued its pursuit of the limping leatherback.

Two Ardu ran in from behind and thrust their spears into its back. It cleared them away with a sweep of its arm, trailing fragments of the buckler, then continued the pursuit of the dragon. The sword hilt thrust crazily into the air above its head like some demonic sign.

A brave young man ran in and leaped up onto its back and jabbed at the eyes with his sword. This was a threat it took more seriously and it reached back to grab at him and forced him to slide down and tumble away. It turned and swung its sword at the Ardu, who dove to the floor as it hummed past.

This gave Bazil a last opportunity, and he knew he dared not waste it.

Stumbling on his bad leg, he threw himself forward, colliding with the thing and wrapping his arms around it as he bore it down. They fell to the marble floor with a crash and then wrestled there. Bazil stayed on top and pinned the thing with his knees, although it still retained its grip on its sword and kept trying to stab him in the back.

He grabbed hold of Ecator and began heaving back and forth, trying to work the blade loose. It gave a little, but it did not come free. Bazil needed more leverage. In desperation Bazil pushed himself to his feet, holding the thing down with his left foot while resting his weight on the bad leg. There was a lot of pain. He ignored it and pulled on the sword handle while pushing down with his foot.

The beast thrashed and tried to stab him, but missed. He pressed down and heaved on the sword, the muscles standing out all over his body, and there was a sudden give. Six inches of Ecator emerged.

At last.

Bazil gave a roar-scream and then a great groan of effort as he heaved again. The thing was still trying to stab him and he shifted around to dodge while still keeping his grip. Ecator came out a little more. Again the monster stabbed upward and he shifted and this time lost his grip, and the thing at once began to slide out from under him. Bazil desperately thrust out his right leg and pinned the thing facedown. Someone was screaming very loudly in pain; Bazil was not surprised to find out that it was him. He hauled on the sword's hilt and at last, with a sucking sound, Ecator came loose and pulled out and he staggered back and would have fallen except that he collided with the wall.

The thing was getting to its feet.

"No!" bellowed Bazil, and he pushed off from the wall, almost went down when he stepped on his right foot, but kept going and smashed into the beast and knocked it over again. He fell to his knees. There was blood all over the floor, and as he knew too well, only one of them seemed to have blood.

He had to get up, had to get up. Had to get back on his feet first.

And somehow, using the sword as a crutch, he did, beating the monster, which was still in the process of raising itself onto its knees. He planted his left foot on its back and pinioned it to the floor of the atrium once again.

With another roar-scream, he took Ecator in both hands and brought the sword up and over in a tremendous blow as if he were chopping through a log. There was a blur of steel and then Ecator sank deep into the thing, almost cutting right through its body. Bazil heaved the sword free before it could stick. Again he swung, with all his might, and again almost cut it in half. He moved into a frenzied state, swinging again and again. Pieces of the thing began to fly loose, cut off like chips of wood. There was a huge wound across its middle that didn't close up any longer. And yet it still tried to stab him and forced him to shift to his right foot again, which sent so much pain up that he almost blacked out. Once more he brought up the sword and swung it down with every ounce of strength he could muster, and this time Ecator cut through and sundered the thing into two halves.

To Bazil's horror, both parts still lived, thrashing and flailing on the marble floor. He kicked the upper part away, to ensure they couldn't somehow reattach and continue the fight.

The legged half kept trying to raise itself off the floor, but slipped on the dragon's blood and slewed around helplessly in circles. The upper half beat its arms on the floor, still clutching its sword.

Bazil felt sick. He leaned back against the wall, resting his arms on the hilt of the sword. He sobbed for breath, while sweat mingled with the blood running down his leg.

Norwul and Lumbee were there.

"How are you?" said Norwul.

"Not good right now. How is it at the gate?"

"We hold them, but many are hurt."

Bazil surveyed the scene. The pieces of the monster still wriggled and twitched in unkillable horror, but around the entrance to the atrium were piles of dead, both guards in leather armor and Ardu. Along the far wall, huddled for safety, were wounded men. Plainly they were in a desperate plight.

The leg hurt. It was pity about the leg; it curtailed his movement. Lumbee was tying a length of cord around his leg as a tourniquet. She tightened it and then had Norwul tighten it some more. As it took effect, it served to dull the pain a little. For the first time Bazil wondered if this wound was going to kill him. The spearhead was deep. In time it would infect and his entire leg would rot.

He glanced up and saw the elf lords still watching the proceedings with keen interest. When they saw that he was looking at them, they began applauding. Bazil damned them to hell in dragonspeech. He looked down and met Lumbee's gaze.

"We are trapped, Bazil," she said.

He nodded. His first attempt at mounting a rescue mission seemed to have come to a bad end.

"I am afraid I make mistake," he said.

Some of the elf lords had left the galleries. They had adjourned to the room above, where they began the process once more. They would conjure up another fighting beast, only this time it would be quicker.

"With our first effort in the Golgomba magic we erred too much on the durability of the creature," announced Zulbanides. "This time we will place less emphasis there and more on speed."

"Can we not improve its repertory of moves?" asked Lord Rasion.

"A good point, Rasion," agreed Lord Kyenn. "The dragon showed some superb fencing skill, did you not think so?"

"He did. A remarkable creature. I believe we should try and obtain a few. Properly armed and directed, they would make a formidable force."

Zulbanides nodded somberly. Indeed, he recalled that the little no-tail Ardu had claimed that in their homeland these dragon kebbolds fought in organized legions.

"It was a fascinating bout. Perhaps we should breed them and match them against each other. It could be enormously entertaining."

"Of course, of course."

A quivering servant was brought in and bound in place. They bent to the fell work, turning over the ancient screeds handed down from the long-dead Red Aeon. The words began to rise from their immortal throats; the magic to thicken in the air.

Chapter Fifty

The lull extended. The guards were busy reorganizing and readying some new tactic. Ardu watched at the gate. Bazil stayed back in the shadows and Lumbee worked on his wounds as much as she was able. The spearhead was deep in his leg, with the broken shaft projecting a few inches above the skin. She knew she didn't have the skill to cut it free, and she feared that if it was torn out, it would break major blood vessels and Bazil would bleed to death.

His other cuts and scrapes she could do something for, and so these she concentrated on. She removed arrowheads and cleaned the wounds. The supply of Old Sugustus was exhausted. All she had was a little water from a cistern in the gatehouse. For bandages there was nothing but strips torn from the shirts of dead guards. Still, it was something, and that was better than doing nothing.

Lumbee worked mechanically, trying not to think, but failing. She was aware that death was close for all of them. They had tried to free Relkin, but failed. They were trapped by the metal door that slid from the ceiling. There was no way back and no way out. The Mirchaz lords would be sure to make an example of any of them that fell alive into their hands. Lumbee would not let that happen, she swore. At her side she wore a sword and at the moment of utter defeat, she would stab herself in the heart with it.

There was a great sadness in the thought that she would never return to her people, never see her parents and friends again. She hoped the tribe would survive her disappearance and not break up into kin groups again. The troublesome Yellow Canyon grandmothers wouldn't give up easily. Further sorrow came from the thought that she would not see Relkin again. She had not said good-bye to him properly. Just to see him once before death, that would be enough. But such a choice was not to be hers, it seemed. The end of everything was growing closer.

The lord dragon was weakening. She watched him lying back against the wall, breathing slowly and deeply, the big intelligent eyes firmly shut. His terrible sword was in the huge scabbard and leaning beside him. His legs were stretched out, as was his curious tail with its twisted piece at the end.

Lumbee felt her heart rend at the thought of this magnificent creature dying in this way. She had never seen anything to match his fury in a fight. Whether it was troublesome pujish or a squad of Mirchaz men, the dragon and the sword were unstoppable.

And yet in other moments there was a gentleness and a kindness in the dragon that she had come to recognize in their months together. She realized that she loved the great beast as if he were one of her own kin. She had to wipe her eyes and look away for a moment. It was hard to breathe. She forced it and it came in a tortured sob.

One big dragon eye popped open and focused on Lumbee.

"Lumbee no cry. No cry. This be a good way to die. These damn lords not forget us for long time."

She laughed, despite herself. "Yes. We scared them, all right."

Bazil chuckled. "They won't come to the Ardu forest for a long time. Your people will grow strong."

"Yes." Her voice became small.

"Everything dies in the end. Some die in sickness, lying in the straw. Can take months for dragon to die. It better to die standing up, with the sword in hand. It better to die fighting."

Lumbee accepted this thought and came to see that there was truth to it, especially for a warrior such as Bazil Broketail. To die in battle was best, bringing a quick end to a life of war. Lumbee put her arms around the huge leathery neck and hugged as hard as she could.

They were interrupted by Norwul, who came and squatted beside them. Lumbee let go and wiped her eyes.

Norwul was feeling the effects of prolonged battle, and the emotions of impending death, too. It was hard to speak.

"They are preparing for another attack. It will come soon."

"I will be ready." Bazil started making motions to get up. Lumbee wanted to try to help, and gently he mocked her.

"What? You think this dragon is some kind of chicken that needs you to help him stand?"

He heaved up his bulk once again and winced. With a slow hiss he accepted the burden of pain from his leg. He reached for the sword. As his hand grasped the cat-headed handle, so he felt that mad exaltation that always came from the blade. He judged it good. If he had to die, then let him die with Ecator in his hands. Together they would take many heads before the end.

He was standing at last. He turned to the gate, where the remaining Ardu were preparing to receive yet another assault. They had armed themselves with spears and shields from the fallen guards and were forming a line across the inside of the gate.

The guards were coming up the steps, with drums beating to urge them on.

Bazil lurked back in the shadows to avoid arrows. The guards came on. They were a new lot, brought up from the city gates. The ones who had fought inside the pyramid would not obey the order to attack again. Their commanders were furious and ashamed, but there was nothing they could do. Men were sent for from the gate. The riot in the City of Slaves was burning down now anyway. There was no need for such a large force there. The slaves would never break the gates. The best they could do was hurl stones at them.

At the top the guards lowered their spears and jogged forward in a loose phalanx, with five feet between each rank. As they entered the gate itself, all the archers let fly a final volley and scores of arrows flicked through, some finding targets. Barely twenty Ardu men were waiting. Still they joined the fight with a counterthrust that gave them enough momentum to stop the guards in their tracks and back them up. The Ardu stabbed with their spears and then dropped them to use their swords. Their sword work was a little clumsy, perhaps, but very fierce. The guards took heavy casualties in that front line. Men from the second and third pushed forward and began to press the Ardu back.

Big Ohaga fell, a spear through the throat. Old Rufat went down, run through by sword and spear together. Ley Yey died while trying to pull Rufat's body away from danger. The Ardu were forced back, deeper into the gate passage, almost back to the atrium itself. Once they were forced into the atrium, they could be surrounded and slaughtered.

The guards, feeling the closeness of victory, pressed harder. They were good men, hardened mercenaries with a pride in their fighting skills. No bunch of wild-assed apemen from the forest was going to beat them!

Ohaga's brother Jumg was cut down and stabbed repeatedly. The Ardu fell back another step. The guards gave up a shout and threw themselves forward.

And the dragon stepped out of concealment again.

The guards saw him coming and hedged their spears in his direction.

"Lancemen to the fore!" came the shout. And from the rear rank came up men with ten-foot lances in hand, ready to flense the flesh of this unlikely kebbold that had frightened the other guards so badly.

Bazil slowed, keeping out of sight of the archers, letting the men with lances come forward. They thrust as a group as they came. He let them get within range and then struck with Ecator. Lanceheads flew as Ecator cut them away. A couple remained intact and were charged at him, their points aimed for his belly. He deflected them with the new shield that Yord had fashioned for him.

A thrown spear missed his throat by a fraction, and another grazed his shoulder, but Ecator on the backstroke cut into the men jammed up in the mouth of the gate and left six dead in a moment. At the explosion of blood and viscera, the others checked. Bazil swung again and smashed another line of guards. Then the Ardu sprang forward and rejoined the initiative and Bazil stepped back to avoid further spears.

The guards wobbled there, then Norwul crushed the man in the center with his war club and Yord cut down the one next to him and the phalanx lost all remaining cohesion in the center and began to collapse backward. The Ardu were emboldened and they swung their weapons with renewed fervor and two more guards were slain and the rest tumbled back out of the gate once more and retreated to the edge of the steps.

Arrows covered their retreat and forced the Ardu back into the darkness. Their cries of jubilation echoed around the pyramid. They had won again!

But now there were only fourteen Ardu standing, able to fight. They huddled back along the wall with eyes fierce and lungs laboring.

"The dragon says it is better to die fighting than lying sick in one's hut," said Lumbee, who had come to take her place with the men for the final battle.

"Forest god is right," seconded Norwul. "If we die, we die here!"

The others cheered hoarsely.

Their cheers were cut off by another sound, the unmistakable scrape of metal on stone. The portcullis gate was rising.

Bazil looked up with somber eyes. An all-too-familiar shape was visible behind the rising grid of steel.

"So," he hissed to himself. Another of the battle beasts had been hatched somewhere by these fell elves.

Wearily, he stepped forward to meet the deliverer of death.

Chapter Fifty-one

Relkin contemplated time with a hawk's-eye view above its flowing river. Time always flowed in a single direction, an inevitable processing of moments of now—each one following the last in its momentary stand on the stage before surrendering to the claim of oblivion that rendered it part of the past.

And yet, this was different. This particle of now was not the same.

Now! Something had changed, some line had been crossed. Time had ceased to be a series of anonymous moments, following one another into the infinity of the past. The fullness had swollen into the now. This moment had come, pregnant with awesome possibility, and from here on all would be different.

Relkin stirred. His eyes opened and he took in the lacquered walls, the shining floor of this room that spoke so well of the glory of the Overlook of the Arkelauds. Beside him knelt the elf lady, waving a fan over him and softly singing some ancient lay of her people. Her silver curls were hidden beneath a scarf of black silk

Now was come. He shifted on the divan and sat up. His face still ached from the beating his nose had taken, but the former agony of his arms had abated. He raised his arms to test it, and found the discomfort bearable.

"Thank you, Lady. Your healing magic has taken away the pain."

She looked up and he was startled to see that large golden stars had swollen in her eyes.

"Go," she hissed. "You must destroy our world."

He stood up, swayed a moment, and then recovered his balance. He could scarcely bend his arms, they were so heavily bandaged, but for what he had to do, his arms were unnecessary.

"I don't need a sword, anyway," he mumbled. His nose simultaneously itched and ached, an oddly unpleasant combination.

But he could walk and the moment, this weighted *now*, was calling him. He could not delay any longer, although something in him wanted to. He understood, of course. There was a part of him that didn't want to die.

He turned away from the accusing golden stars and walked to the door. He stepped out into a warm wind. The door banged behind hm.

Across the lake the statue of Zizma Bos beckoned. The pyramid's marble facings shone brilliantly away to his right at the eastern end. Below lay the glittering city of the golden elves. He stepped to the railing and raised his arms. The sun warmed his palms and he cried out in an ecstasy of love for the world even as he summoned the strength of the mind mass. In an instant he was gone and the wind blew alone on the terrace.

Lady Tschinn bowed her head and waited there for the end of the world.

In iambic nothingness he bounced in rhythm for a moment and then he was in the world once more, appearing a foot above the surface of the great board in the Game hall of the Pyramid. He landed clumsily and fell on the board, knocking over a set of Leapers that clattered as they rolled across the hallowed squares. Instantly heads came up and voices were raised in anger.

So much for any chance of surprise.

The shouting around him became general.

Then he heard other sounds, including one that was all too familiar to a dragonboy in the legions of Argonath, the mighty clang of huge swords wielded in combat.

What in all the names of hell? It came again, the huge sound of heavy steel in contact. Dragonsword? Did that mean that a certain wyvern dragon was in the vicinity?

He looked around himself. The board stretched away in all directions, dotted here and there with clumps of two- and three-foot-high pieces engaged in their own slow-motion, dumb panoply of war.

There were more shouts, men were running toward him across the board with drawn weapons. There was no doubt of their intentions.

It was time to be done with it. He dug into himself and called on the mind mass to hear him and awaken.

Nothing happened.

"Kill him!" screamed someone not too far distant.

He balled his hands into fists and called once more on the ten thousand who lay below powering the great gestalt.

"Awake!" he cried to the vast whale that turned slowly in ever-warm waters swimming up to the light. "Awake. Ye build and yet have no hearth. Ye make and yet have no bread. Awake!"

"Kill him!"

Still there was no response.

"Awake!" he screamed in sudden desperation, fearing for the first time that he might fail and the elf lords would slay him and prevent the Iudo Faex from completing the prophecy of Zizma Bos.

And then abruptly he realized that he had to "point" his call, to use his mind in a way he had never known before. He shaped and bent the thought and then drove his message into the vast entity like a rocket into a cloud and it burst within and touched something in the dark, something that stirred as enigma gave way to certainty.

There was an odd moment of complete stasis. Everything was still, as if the river of time itself had ceased to flow. Relkin was looking at a man with a drawn sword who was just a couple of yards away, preparing to hack him down. Relkin's death was written on that steel which seemed to float forward as slowly as the sun setting. A single second seemed to last a minute.

"Awake!" he sobbed.

And green lightning erupted from the board at his feet, soared up around him, and struck the ceiling, while a thunderclap detonated in the hall and deafened every ear. The scorched wretch with the sword was tossed twenty feet into the air. Those who were still ten yards away threw themselves flat or were knocked over.

The green flash vanished. Relkin was virtually blinded, but not scorched.

The swordsman was a smoking, charred heap among fallen Leapers.

The gestalt had awoken at last.

Screams of horror echoed all around the Game board. Too late. Too late. A line of termination had crossed from one aeon into another. They could never go back. The Iudo Faex had fulfilled the prophecy.

The gestalt awoke and looked about itself with a million eyes and saw the world in a million ways. And it looked beyond the one world and saw the other worlds and the worlds beyond those and beyond those and beyond those. And it looked close and saw the Game board of the elf lords and the scattered pieces and the faces turned up to it with horror writ large on their perfect features, and it understood. And then many things happened at once.

In thousands of magical worlds the light went out, the suns dimmed, the moons imploded, atmospheres blew away into nothingness, and fabulous foliage faded to black. Gaping elf lords were deposited back on the Game board with a sudden, brutal transition over which they had no control. The number on the board increased quite substantially. Others, perhaps less fortunate, vanished with their worlds.

In the atrium where the Golgomba beast was remorselessly pressing Bazil back to the wall, the green lightning roared. To Bazil's astonishment, the beast slumped, collapsed, and turned to a glittering gray dust that poured out upon the floor to form a mound barely knee high. The sword clanged to the ground, and the buckler made a tinny sound as it rolled away.

With a screech of metal on stone, the portcullis rose again. Nothing stood in the passage beyond this time. Bazil received the summons. He knew not from where, but the image it gave him was unmistakable.

"They kill my boy!"

He could not run, but he could stagger, and he passed under the portcullis and entered the Game hall with a curious gait, almost falling each time he put his weight on his right leg. But the fire in his eyes was beyond pain and the sword in his hand was a promise of death.

In the gatehouse, the long keys suddenly pulled themselves out of the mechanisms and flew across the room while the gates whirred shut on their own and closed with a clang.

The Ardu spun around and followed the dragon, their swords and spears in hand.

As he entered the hall, Bazil roared his challenge to the elf lords and they whirled, hands frozen, hearts stopped in terror. He looked past them with anxious eyes. Was he too late? As he had feared from the beginning?

There was a figure, swathed in bandages, swaying in the center of a ring of elf lords who had just gotten back on their feet. Many were singed. There was smoke coming from Red Elk's curls and he beat on his head with his hand to put it out.

The bandaged figure turned toward the dragon and raised an arm in greeting and Bazil felt his heart leap.

"Boy lives!" roared the dragon. He crashed across the board, smashing aside Strengths, Leapers, and all the rest. Ecator hummed through the air and an elf lord who had dared to plant himself in the way with drawn sword was sent to eternity.

The others either ran for their lives or also readied themselves with swords in hand. Ecator scythed through the air with a howling viciousness that Bazil could feel through the handle. The sword was exercised as it had only ever been when they cut off Heruta's arm and sent his soul to hell. A half dozen elven princes were annihilated.

The rest of the elf lords fled, their resolve collapsing in the face of the fate of their fellows.

Then boy and dragon were reunited. Huge arms enfolded the bandaged figure and hugged it.

"Careful," said Relkin.

"Yes, be very careful with fool boy. How you come to be taken here?"

"If we live through this, I'll be glad to tell you the whole story." Bazil set him down with exaggerated care. The wyvern had to agree that their chances of getting out of this were slim. They were still surrounded, cut off inside the pyramid, with a large force of guards outside.

"I knew this dragon would find you." Bazil sounded absurdly happy with himself.

"You know something? That joboquin is just totally ruined!"

"Ha! That is very good. Boy is nothing but a big bandage."

"Wonderful timing, Baz. Got here just in the nick."

"I not have much choice."

But then Relkin waved a hand, suddenly consumed with a new thought.

"No, I'm serious. Really! I just realized what I can do. It's going to be all right, Baz. I haven't finished. There's still work to do. I'm going to leave now and finish the job I began here. Don't worry about me. You'll see some magic—at least I think so. I'll see you in a while."

Bazil was too happy to have found his boy to think much about these words. He waved at the elf lords. "Should I kill them all?"

"No. That isn't for us to do. If they are to die, let it be by the hand of those they have oppressed so long."

They fell silent. Relkin gathered himself and then raised his arms again and called on the mind mass.

It was still there, but now it had eyes that looked into his soul. Great burning eyes that it turned this way and that, seeing all. He made no attempt to hide from it. To this being, so new, like a newborn baby in some ways, he had no need to hide a thing.

In a moment he felt the response. It understood what was needed. And Relkin "moved" once more, vanishing from the Game board and reappearing in front of the city's main gate. Behind him stood the mob, drawn by the call they had all heard in their heads. The time had come. Mirchaz would fall.

Relkin reached up to the gates, pressing his palms to them, and the gates broke asunder in coruscations of green lightning, and the way to the city was open.

The slaves lifted their voices in a great shout and advanced past him where he stood, shaking a little, feeling emptied by that green flash of violence that had coursed through his body. For a moment he had been the conduit of the mind mass. That sensation would never leave him.

Chapter Fifty-two

Like fragments falling away from an explosion, the effects of the awakening of the gestalt being struck near and far, right across the world, and beyond.

In the city of Andiquant, thousands of miles to the east, an unconscious body, lovingly cared for by old Gert, shook in sudden spasm and then awoke with a strange, keening cry.

Gert ran in from the kitchen, her eyes widening. The lady's body was thrashing on the sheets. She sat down on the bed and reached to try and comfort her mistress, but at her touch the lady suddenly sat up and grasped her shoulders in hands that felt like steel claws.

"Gert!" cried the witch, eyes glowing as if she had seen the goddess in the face. "The giant sleeps no more. And I who was dead am still alive."

Ribela's eyes brimmed with tears. Gert swallowed, astonished.

"It is sweet to be alive. I have just rediscovered this fact. Very sweet."

"So glad, my lady, so—"

"It sheltered me. It was as if it knew I was coming. There is much I do not understand yet, but I have glimpsed a new mystery. And I never felt a thing! Not since . . ." and in her mind's eye she saw the grotto below as she fell into it, in Ferla's body. It was all a magical illusion, but Ferla's impact on the rocks below had felt real enough.

She hugged the astonished Gert and let the tears flow.

"Oh, Gert, sweet gentle Gert. I think I have learned a little about contrition. I must talk to Lessis someday."

On higher planes of existence beyond Andiquant,

beyond Ryetelth itself, the tremors from Mirchaz were felt clearly. Something unique had come into existence on the Sphereboard of Destiny. Others took note of this event with mingled awe and concern.

Closer to the city, in the western hills, the people came out in wonder as they saw the volume of smoke that now arose. The burning of the City of Slaves had produced a fair-sized cloud already, but now the whole sky was alight, the great city itself was burning.

In the palaces and grand houses, the former slaves avenged themselves most horribly upon their oppressors. Many an ancient name was extinguished, often with horrifying cruelty. Lord and Lady Filguince were roasted alive over a bonfire in the avenue outside their mansion. Others suffered similar fates.

There were survivors, and many houses were left untouched during the killing spree, the simple cast of the dice of chance determining who died and who did not.

Lord Pessoba escaped by hiding in the foul gutter beneath the barrels in his wine cellar. The tall, elegant house was sacked by the mob, but Pessoba survived. And so did Master Lum, who pretended to be one of the rioters.

When the gates went down, Katun and the guards saw their peril clearly. They moved to seize control of the buildings of the Astrologers' College. The elf lords sought shelter there, too, since it was the most easily defended building in the Upper City. It even had a high surrounding wall. The guards were in a nasty trap. They began to think differently of their contract with the elf lords.

The elf lords tried to hold the guards in line with sorcery. The guards learned of this before it became effective and turned on the elf lords, thrusting them out to the waiting mob. The men nominated Katun to speak for them in negotiating a way out of the trap. They wanted safe passage south.

The elf lords received no mercy. Some were torn to pieces on the spot. Then the slaves built fires and when they were blazing high they threw the elf lords onto them alive.

Later the killing subsided. The fires burned themselves out. Whole sections of the graceful city of the elves had been reduced to rubble.

The plaza in front of the pyramid became a focus of new organizational energy, with Norwul and Lumbee taking charge.

The Ardu recruited as many able-bodied as were willing from the rioters and armed them from the equipment abandoned or lost by the guards. Their task now was to impose a new kind of order on the city. Killing had to stop. Looting, on the other hand, was justified and could continue, at least for now. Fires were to be put out.

A handful of surviving elf lords were brought to the plaza. The atrium of the pyramid was being used as a temporary prison to hold the former rulers.

Near the city gate, Ium and Wol found Relkin leaning against a warehouse wall on the commercial road. He was dazed and incoherent and barely able to stand.

They brought him to shelter and then sent for help. Soon Relkin was borne to safety by a crowd chanting "Iudo" over and over.

While chaos raged in the city, he was cared for in a house in the City of Slaves. The destruction here had been limited to the commercial road and the warehouse zone around the city gates. The tenements and mean houses of the City of Slaves had survived. He rested there in the house of a horse trader. He slept, briefly.

When the orgy of destruction and murder had subsided a bit, the Ardu bore him into the city and along the shore promenade to the pyramid. Here they found Baz, lying back against the staircase to the pyramid with his leg propped up on a stack of shields. They had stretched a sheet of cotten over him to shade him, and they had promised him food and beer.

Bazil lay back, propped up with piles of shields and armor stripped from the guards. Relkin hugged the great beast, and was hugged in return so hard the breath went out of him.

"You came to find me, right?"

"Found boy."

"Well, it has to be said, you showed up at just the right moment."

The dragon chuckled indulgently. "Elf lords lucky they not kill boy."

Relkin looked over to the group of survivors. They all looked so similar, with the identical stiff faces and the silver curls, it was hard to be sure, but he thought he saw Pessoba. They seemed such a sad, dislocated group. In the flash of a moment, their gaudy worlds had been undone and they themselves dispossessed.

Lucky?

Relkin was examining the wound in Bazil's thigh. There was no getting around it, it was really bad, probably mortal. The spear had gone a foot deep and had moved around as the dragon continued fighting. To remove it would risk cutting major arteries, and that could be fatal. To leave it was to ensure gangrene. The leg would have to come off at the minimum.

It was a sickening thought, but Relkin could see no other way. The elf lords had skilled surgeons among their servants, they had already been sent for and they concurred with Relkin's first impression.

He sat there stumped. He wondered how to explain it to Bazil. If ever Caymo and the Old Gods were going to help him, now was the time.

"Baz—" he started.

The dragon waved a huge hand. The eyes fixed on Relkin's. "This dragon know end is coming. Spear in too deep. Leg already infected. You want to cut off leg. It better to be dead."

"Baz . . ."

"Besides, you look like your end is coming, too." The dragon clacked his long jaws in amusement.

Relkin had to agree he looked like he was already embalmed, wrapped in bandages. And yet his wounds had continued to heal rapidly since the elf lady's healing magic. Even his battered nose, though still swollen, was no longer an active source of pain.

"Baz, we have to take off the leg. It's the only way."

"This dragon not live one-legged."

"You could retire. Live by the sea. I'm sure the Legion would give you dispensation."

"This dragon not live without one leg."

Relkin confronted the realization that the dragon would be immovable on the subject.

"Then we still have to try and take it out, or else you will die."

"Die anyway, why bother?"

"No! I think we can do it. There has to be a way to get it out."

Bazil groaned. "Dragons feel pain, just like you."

"I know, Baz. But we'll get the elf lords to use their healing magic. I have felt it. The lady, she healed my arms. I thought I was going to lose them, they were burned so bad."

"Magic not work on dragons. Not easy."

"We can't just let you die. I won't give up without trying."

There was a long moment. Both of them thought about the agonies involved. Relkin set his jaw. He would not let the dragon die. Somehow.

"All right, you torture me before the long sleep." Bazil stared at him again with something like fury. "But first we eat."

Bazil's sensitive, top-predator nose had informed him that there was food in the offing. From the surviving houses in the city came the makings a fine dinner rolled out by Master Lum and a squad of cooks for the houses of the elf lords. Bazil devoured a side of beef, spit-roasted over hot coals, plus a couple of sides of bacon, along with two dozen loaves of bread. He washed this down with a barrel of dark beer rolled up from the cellar of the pyramid.

While Bazil ate, Relkin turned away. His thoughts were a whirl of confusion and fears. How would he live without the dragon? Could he? It seemed unimaginable. He pushed himself to investigate the pyramid. Anything that might take his mind off the problem at hand. What had become of the entity he had felt arise here? It was something entirely new in the world, he could not guess at its powers, especially considering the load it had carried in operating the Game worlds of the fallen Lords Tetraan. Yet he imagined that the ten thousand would still need to be fed and cared for. Their physical bodies were the essential basis for the grand gestalt they had fused into. They would have to be kept alive for the gestalt to survive.

Relkin walked through the catacombs, past row upon row of stone cribs in which lay the silent slaves. He wondered how many thousands had been used up in these cold cells, consumed and tossed aside like so many sheep or swine. The place fairly reeked from the horror of what had been done here.

The cells and corridors were oppressive. He soon decided to leave the ten thousand to their quiet darkness and returned to the dragon's spot beside the great staircase. There was still a little left of the keg of beer Bazil had been working on. Relkin took a cup in a silver mug. It was heavy, and sweetish, but it was still recognizably beer. It went down very easily. He had another cup.

He called for Lord Pessoba to be brought out, if he still lived. He did, and he was.

"As you are aware," Relkin told Pessoba, "circumstances have changed. Your Great Game is gone forever. Something new has replaced it."

"The world is shattered. Such wanton slaughter! Did we deserve such?"

Relkin shrugged. "I have seen Game worlds with ten thousand times as much slaughter. You destroyed the lives of millions for your pleasure. I can understand why the slaves did what they did."

"And now you are the master?" said Pessoba.

"No. The Ardu are the masters now. But they might spare you if I ask them."

"Oh, please do, please do. Really! I have no desire to be thrown to the flames."

"There is work for you to do."

"What is that?"

"The ten thousand in there, they must be cared for. You will organize it. They have to be fed and cleaned. Until we know what else they want. Something very great and very mysterious has happened. We will have to wait and see how it manifests itself."

"What has happened? I am not at all sure that I understand the progress of recent events. You came to me from Katun. I thought you charming, of course. We visited the Arkelauds. That damned woman claimed you were the Iudo Faex. Nobody believed her, but they still wanted to kill you. Then you vanished. Just up and vanished. Finally Mot Pulk was sought for the crime. Mot Pulk, he has a great deal to pay for."

"Mot Pulk is dead. He was caught when the worlds went down. He did not return to the Game board."

"Then he escaped full punishment."

"None of you will escape punishment. The folk you oppressed shall rule the city now. You shall serve them."

"Of course, I understand this. I will see that the ten thousand are tended to. They shall be fed and watered just as they always have. The pap they are fed is nutritious. The system is stable. We shall change nothing unless they so order it."

"Good."

Pessoba was dismissed. Relkin lay back against the wall. The dragon was picking through the remains of the feast. He turned big eyes on Relkin.

"You listen to me, boy. This dragon not live one-legged."

"I know, you told me."

"I not be one of the cripples. That is no life for a wyvern dragon."

Relkin thought his heart would break. That damned spear would kill Bazil unless it was removed, and pulling it out would probably prove lethal, too, and would only cause the dragon much pain before he died. Taking off the leg was the only option open to them.

"It has been a good life. This dragon has seen much, done more. We have made our enemies fear us, eh?"

"Yes, Baz, we did."

"They sing of us for a long time to come."

Bazil set down the empty barrel and cradled his big arms across his belly and went to sleep as if quite unconcerned for the future.

Relkin lay beside the dragon and felt tears course down his cheeks. The wound was seeping blood at a steady rate. Relkin wondered if Bazil would last until morning. Perhaps it would be better if he didn't, if he went in his sleep. He knew he would not try to pull the spearhead out; it would only cause agony. He would have to let go, let Bazil go peacefully, but it was hard, very hard indeed.

Somehow, perhaps because of the underlying exhaustion, he slipped into sleep, curled up next to the dragon for the last time.

Late in the night Bazil stirred, drifting in light sleep. The leg throbbed evilly, but it was not the pain that had awoken him. He sensed a presence close by. He opened one eye. There was nobody there, and yet he felt the weight of someone, something. It waited there patiently.

"Who are you?" he said softly in dragonspeech. "Are you death come to take me to the dragonstar?"

There was no answer, just a breeze stirring off the lake.

Bazil's hand strayed to Ecator's hilt. There was a familiar faint tingle, which meant the spirit blade sensed troll or some other manifestation of foul magic.

If it was death, then it could not be fought with the sword this time. There was no point in preparing for battle. Still the presence hovered there. The dragon grew sleepy again and after a while dropped off once more into a troubled sleep.

Bazil awoke as the first fragile light of dawn tinged the sky. He came awake suddenly, feeling a great rushing in the air, but not from the wind, and a sensation of unbearable pressure began to build.

Relkin woke up with a sudden yelp.

And there came a blinding flash of green light that seemed to pass through the dragon's leg. It was gone in an instant, leaving only a smell of ozone and a medley of screams and cries from the plaza. It took a half minute or so for vision to return.

"My leg itches!" said Bazil. "Oh, whooo! It really itch."

He reached to scratch his wound and discovered that the broken stub of the spear shaft was no longer projecting from his leg. The itch came from inside the leg, and there was no way to scratch it.

Relkin discovered that the spear shaft was gone a moment later.

"Gone!" he cried. New hope burgeoned, incredible hope.

The surgeons came forward and examined the wound. They backed away, astonished. "The spearhead is gone. The wound is deep, but it is empty."

"Use honey to dry it up," said Relkin.

"It is healing very rapidly on its own."

"It itches. Oh, it itches."

"Maybe, but it looks like we won't have to cut it off."

"Better to die. But something came. I think it was your friend. It was there for a long time. It not speak, but I knew it was there. Then this."

"I think it's going to be a force for good in the world. I wonder what it will be."

Later, Relkin went back into the pyramid and down into the catacombs where the ten thousand were stacked.

"I don't know if you can hear me, or if you'd care to listen. You may have more important things to do, but I want to thank you for saving my dragon. I woke you up, you saved my dragon. Good luck to you, whatever you are."

There was no response from the silent figures lying in their stone cots. But then, as Relkin was leaving, he felt a chill run through him and he sensed the presence he had felt before standing on the Game board. It was there now watching him somehow. It made no communication that he could understand, so he thanked it again and left.

Chapter Fifty-three

The smoke cleared; the rubble lay where it fell. Days in the ruined city drifted into weeks. Bazil's leg healed swiftly, as did Relkin's arms, though his nose would never be quite the same again.

Slowly the chaos in the great city subsided and a new order obtained. A new population, formerly the outcast and excluded, had taken up residence in the surviving grand houses, the colleges, and the palaces. Working for them were the former slavers and elf lords. A few lords and ladies, including Lady Tschinn and Lord Rasion, had found posts as healers and administrators.

Of the former slaves and freebooters who made up this new ruling caste there were no Ardu. The Ardu folk all voted to return to their homeland and they began to leave at once in large parties, heading up the river to the Lands of Terror and the Plain of Three-Horns.

The former mercantile class, which had occupied the lower-status western end of the city, had survived more or less intact. They paid indemnities and gave bribes and soon regained their position as the city's link with the outside world. Caravans began again, although for a while insurance rates were going to be sky high.

Relkin acquired a stonemason's wagon and a team of six powerful horses. When the day came for the parting of ways, he and Bazil were set to join a caravan heading south for the coast. That same day Lumbee and another party of the Ardu were setting out to return to their homeland.

Lumbee and Relkin were able to go for one last walk together along the dusty south road just beyond the city gate. In the midst of the caravan, out of sight of the other Ardu, they enjoyed one last kiss.

"I am sorry to see you go, Lumbee."

"Relkin, we had our love together. It was a true love, but it was as if we lived alone, with no one to worry about. We are from different worlds. I could not live in your world. I would be the only tailed person. You must go back to your own land. You have people waiting for you there."

Relkin knew she was right, but his memories of the sweet time they had had on the river would always haunt him. It was hard to let go.

"I will never forget you, Lumbee."

"And I will not forget you, Relkin."

After a while they rejoined the rest of the Ardu and Relkin bade farewell to Ium and Wol, and big Norwul.

"We will keep the tribe strong," said Norwul. Relkin could sense that Norwul would be the first tribal chief of the Ardu. Norwul had learned an enormous amount about the world and had adjusted his thinking. At the same time he was physically one of the most imposing Ardu, six feet tall and solid muscle, a great warrior, and smart, too. Relkin thought it was a good combination for the job he could envisage a chief having to do.

Ium and Wol and Relkin all embraced. They had been hunting brothers, and Relkin knew that Ium and Wol would carry the ideas of the tribe with them for all their lives. If Norwul was chief, they would be among his top captains.

Lumbee and the others all made their final farewells with the dragon. The forest god was leaving, going to the outside world where he belonged. The Ardu had all come to respect the forest god's decisions, although they would miss his presence in their camps upon the Plain of Three-Horns.

"Farewell, Lumbee dragonfriend."

Lumbee could barely speak all of a sudden. "Lumbee try to be dragonboy. Not succeed."

The dragon shook his head. "Lumbee succeed. Dragon always remember Lumbee."

The time had come. Relkin climbed onto the driver's

seat of the massive wagon. He lifted the reins and cracked the whip to get the team in motion. They were beautiful animals, well trained and used to hauling heavy weight. Bazil would get a thoroughly deserved free ride on this trip.

They left the Ardu singing one of their ancient songs as the caravan got under way and, with wagon wheels rolling, set off down the long south road.

Relkin had bought the wagon and team with some of the gold he'd found in the ruins of Mot Pulk's house. Twenty gold tabis, hidden in hollow bricks cemented into the wall. Fire had damaged the wall and cracked open one of the bricks. A golden gleam had caught Relkin's eye and he broke away some of the scorched brick, and out tumbled a golden tabi, a fat, sleek square of pure gold.

Now there were nineteen gold tabis sewn into the lining of Bazil's new vest, which went under the remains of the joboquin. Reduced to scraps of leather and a few intact belts, the joboquin would would have to be replaced entirely.

The south road was a torturous affair, winding back and forth in long loops as they climbed the pass through the mountain ranges that led to the narrow coastal plain. Throughout this part of the trip it rained, a constant cold drizzle that sorely tried Relkin's patience. Bazil was wrapped in a big cloak and stayed more or less dry as the wagon bounced along the rutted road.

The first mountain range was the Mindor Ath, a line of medium-sized peaks with trees growing up their flanks and just a little snow on their tips. The way here was hard, but not that bad. Then came the more serious task of crossing the high pass through the Ath Gahut, which were mighty mountains with long rocky ribs rising to snowfields and glacier-clad shoulders. This part of the journey was very arduous and Bazil was forced to get out and walk on the worst stretches since the horses simply couldn't manage his weight and the wagon. The air grew thin and it was hard to draw a decent breath, while the cold seemed to bite through clothing to the bone. At last, though, they came over the top of the pass and looked out on a green plain and the distant ocean.

The descent was also hard going, with more slogging through slushy snow and stiff winds that drove ice into their pores, but after a week of hell they left the snow line and entered warmer air.

On the south side of the mountains they rolled through the pleasant south coastal lands: farmland in the dells and woods on the hills, with a well-maintained road and occasional coaching inns to stay at. Bazil was used to the gawping stares and stiff dragon freeze faces wherever he went. He would put up with a lot in exchange for good beer and a roof over his head when it rained all night.

Eventually they came down into the coastal town of Zund.

Relkin sold the team and the wagon, for not quite what he'd paid for it, and they sat in the Shore Inn stables for the next two weeks until a ship came in that was big enough to carry a two-ton dragon in reasonable comfort. Throughout this period it rained almost continually, which, they learned, was the usual pattern for this time of year.

The first reasonable vessel was a dull cog, *Helida*, a squat two-master, crewed by Samander Islanders who were fond of wearing bones pierced through their noses and ears. Relkin paid for the use of the entire vessel, to carry them around the southern capes and up to Sogosh. That was about as far into the western ocean as the Samanders would venture.

Relkin paid with a gold tabi, which sent unworthy thoughts through the minds of the Samander Islanders. Within an hour, though, he and Bazil went aboard and stowed themselves in the hold. Bazil would sleep at one end on a mound of straw and Relkin oversaw the construction of a bunk close by. The crew was disconcerted to a degree by this promptness, and some protested, but Relkin had already paid for the vessel and he had had extra supplies of food delivered, tons of noodles, plus ten casks of beer. *Helida*, indeed, was weighed down in the water with it all.

The islanders grumbled and plotted together as the cog caught the west wind and moved out onto the ocean. Then Bazil came up from the hold and sat in the waist with

Ecator in one hand and a whetstone in the other. The dragon no longer limped; his wounds had completely healed. The sword was as cruel and hungry as ever. As the whetstone worked over the long, deadly slab of steel, the crewmen took note.

After Bazil had finished sharpening Ecator, he worked the blade briefly through a few exercises, constrained, of course, by the limits of the small ship. Still, it was enough. The crewmen buried their unworthy thoughts and the voyage was uneventful. On one occasion pirates had approached, but the Samanders had been unconcerned. The pirates had come up close so that a row of evil-looking faces could be seen grinning over the rail. Then Bazil stood up and drew Ecator and made a few more moves with the blade.

The pirates drew away. Their sail was soon well down on the horizon.

The Samanders were pleased with this outcome and their captain offered Bazil a lifetime job if he would sail with them.

Bazil was tempted. Any wyvern was tempted by the very smell of the sea, but in the end he was not tempted enough. He was heading back to the life he'd always known, with his friends and regular meals. He preferred it that way.

For his part, Relkin kept a sharp eye on the Samanders and kept them from ever discovering where the rest of the gold tabis were hidden.

The *Helida* caught the southwest trades after rounding the Cape of Winds and made a quick and uneventful voyage to Sogosh.

At Sogosh Bazil and Relkin were feted by the local governor. A message was received that ordered them to stay in Sogosh until the king himself, great Choulaput, could come down from the capital at Koubha to greet them. Once, Bazil and Relkin had saved the great king from assassins and he had never forgotten.

Another great festival was held when the king appeared. Choulaput gave them gold rings and gold chestplates that hung around their necks on golden chains. Relkin had a special chest made to hold their newfound vealth. It was very stoutly constructed, with the best lock e could find in Sogosh. It was not very large, but it was lready filling up. And when the local elite of Sogosh organized a subscription for the health of all the fighting dragons, Relkin took charge of that, too, two hundred pieces of gold coin, full doubloons. With these on top of he tabis and the rings and chestplates, the chest was full.

The Legion post in Sogosh had been reduced to just a couple of men, who worked out of the embassy of the Empire of the Rose, a modest two-story house on the edge of the commercial sector of the city.

Relkin and Bazil found a warm enough welcome there and a safe harbor for the chest of gold. Relkin had become just a little concerned now, since they were carrying with them a moderately huge fortune in gold. And apart from their own future, there was gold for all the dragons that had served in the Eigo campaign. Relkin felt the responsibility and was intensely concerned.

Choulaput stayed three days, and they dined with him every night. Even Bazil was feeling pretty stuffed after the final night of banqueting in the Bogoni mode.

The only problem was that the next ocean trader scheduled to visit was the *Oat*, which would be on her way back to the Argonath after visiting the Bakan coastal ports. *Oat* was expected in a month. On the other hand, the life in Sogosh was spectacularly comfortable. They had no duties, no war, no troubles at all. Every big family wanted to feed them and the local dark beer was really excellent. Both of them had quickly come to enjoy this wastrel life. Bazil was putting on weight. Even Relkin was filling out a little.

And then a week later a frigate, the *Lyre*, put in unexpectedly to Sogosh harbor. *Lyre* was on the return leg of a voyage to Kadein after mapping the far western shores of Eigo.

Captain Keperson sought them out at the embassy and offered them immediate passage to the Argonath city of Kadein. *Lyre*'s carpenters set up a section of her hold for the dragon's stall and Relkin bunked there as well. The crew were honored to ferry the famous Broketail dragon

back to the Argonath. Bazil and the dragonboy were quite
sorry to see old Sogosh dwindle behind them.

Captain Keperson was out in time to catch the rest of
the southwest trades and make a quick passage to the doldrums. There they were unlucky for a week or two, but
then were caught in the fringes of a tropical storm, and
that drove them north and right out of the doldrums in
less than a week. From there they reached the Ourdhi Gulf
on the last bits and pieces of the monsoon and they
rounded the cape and beat up the Bright Sea and three
weeks later were in the port of Kadein. Winter was
coming in, but in Kadein the trees still had their leaves
and the grapes were being harvested and pressed.

Once again there was a wild welcome for the famous
Broketail dragon. Relkin took the opportunity to bank
some of the gold. He took half the tabis and the gold coin
subscription and placed them in an account at the Royal
Landbank. The other tabis he kept sewn into a belt around
Bazil's waist.

There was another great banquet and then they tran-
shipped to an older, cargo vessel, the *Durable*, and sailed
for Marneri at last. This voyage was marked by a nasty
winter squall that made all the passengers seasick, except
for the dragon, of course.

In a thin, cold wind they stepped ashore on the strand at
the white city six months after leaving Mirchaz and more
than two years after setting out on the expedition to Eigo.
There was a huge, tumultuous welcome waiting for them.
The city toasted its most famous dragon, returned miracu-
lously from the dead, with a huge party that lasted right
up to Fundament Day.

Chapter Fifty-four

It was deep winter in Dashwood, where the Marneri Legions worked the immense woodlots in order to feed the boilers both in the city and in the Dashwood barracks. The 109th Marneri Dragons were back at Dashwood that winter, paired with the 167th, a new unit that was now commanded by the 109th's old dragon leader, Turrent.

It had been a very mild winter with little snow. The ground was a faded green, the stark trees the only obvious sign of winter. The ponds were scarcely frozen and while working in the woodlots the men wore no more than shirts.

Dragons wielding immense axes—captured troll axes, in fact—cut down trees. Wood was felled, split, sawn, carried, and stacked in a continuous process, replacing the seasoned wood that was now feeding into the lines of wagons that came up from the city.

It was an especially happy season in the Dashwood dragonhouse, a sprawling great place with the best steam room of any dragonhouse in the Legions. The dragons always enjoyed time at the woodlots. They liked the hard physical work and the huge meals that accompanied it.

In this season, though, they had an extra reason for joy, since they had been reunited with their old comrade Bazil Broketail, presumed lost for about a year after the battle of the volcano. With his return the 109th had finally come together as a social unit once again. The new dragons, Churn and Gryf, were fitting in much better all of a sudden. Morale had soared.

It had been a tumultuous few weeks since Bazil and Relkin stepped ashore at Marneri. But even before they returned from the dead, their saga had preoccupied the

109th for months, ever since the first miraculous word that Bazil and Relkin were alive but lost in the dark, ancient heart of the southern continent. After that there had been nothing, no word until the dragon and the dragonboy returned to Kadein aboard *Lyre*. The dragons had lived for every rumor, every scrap of news.

Until that moment when they'd finally stepped ashore in the Argonath, there'd been mounting concern, fear for the pair, alone in that fabled city, hidden in the depths of the southern continent. It was said to be a nest of magic where deadly elves devoured human flesh.

And then out of the blue, just like the first bulletin, came the word. The famous pair had stepped off a ship at Kadein completely unannounced. They walked in on the dragonhouse and caught everyone napping. The surprise had been total. Gigoth, the huge brass that ruled the Kadein dragonhouse, thought that Bazil was a ghost!

Then a few days later they came ashore at Marneri and into a parade up Tower Street to the Tower of Guard and the dragonhouse. There they found the 109th waiting to greet them. They formed up in drill fours, and Bazil took his place with Alsebra, the Purple Green, and old Chektor, as he always had. The new dragonleader, Cuzo, read the official welcome and then dismissed the parade. The scene dissolved into a chaotic roaring and stomping that was positively dangerous for humans, who took shelter in the nearby accessway as huge forms jumped and shook and bellowed together.

Since then, the squad had come together once more. Morale was high. Even the Purple Green bent to the work, which was good and hard and active. In the evenings they had an extra barrel and sang until sleep claimed them. The rest of Dashwood camp became accustomed to falling asleep while the 109th were still in song. Animals for miles around fled the scene; game would be scarce for months.

Among the dragonboys there were new faces, as it was among the dragons. Gryf was a green dragon from the Blue Hills town of Mud Lake. His dragonboy was Rakama, a bluff, solidly built youth of sixteen. Rakama was a fighter. Already he and Swane had bumped heads and Swane had only just prevailed. Big Swane was used to being the top boy in the squad. Rakama was going to test him.

Relkin fit back in as he had been before, one of them and also something else, someone who had gone to another level. They took it that he had wisdom—or more than they, did at least—and he became the one that people went to, to talk about problems. He had been there from the beginning of the unit. Only Mono, Chektor's dragonboy, came from the same draft. The 109th had seen more than its share of battle and might well have been dissolved on a couple of occasions, casualties had been so high. The battle standard of the squadron had more decoration than any other in the Second Marneri Legion. And Relkin had the Legion Star, which was the senior decoration in the Legion—and at an age when no one had ever received such an honor before! The younger boys naturally looked up to Relkin, and when they found that he was usually approachable, they came to him when trouble called.

There was something slightly different about him now, a subtle thing that all the older hands were aware of. His eyes had an emptiness sometimes and he spoke with a weary earnestness that was new.

Swane was aware of the changes, too. Swane's old antagonism came back sometimes, but in the main he was awed by Relkin's ability to survive.

"I don't know how he does it," he told the younger boys, "but he survives. You got to copy Relkin. He's the one who knows how to get through the worst stuff. No one's seen harder action than Relkin."

The younger boys all knew they were entering a hallowed unit, one of those that had stood at Sprian's Ridge and stopped the great invasion of Arneis. The competition for the places had been intense. The names of the other dragonboys were known throughout the Legions and the society surrounding them.

To them, Relkin was a mysterious fellow, older than they and with a different order of experience. He accepted their deference quietly. In truth, Relkin was looking for the quiet life until he could retire from the Legions.

For the most part he thought he might get it, except for Rakama. Relkin knew that eventually he would have to butt heads with Rakama. He would pick his time. He wasn't going to rush it. But he could see that Rakama was starting to pick on some of the others.

Among the dragons, Gryf was also a bit of a handful and had already had one brush with the Purple Green, who was far too big for Gryf and none too gentle. Alsebra had broken a table over the Purple Green's head to get him to release Gryf. Since then, things had shaken down in the squadron. Along with Gryf there was a big new brass, named Churn. His dragonboy was a mild fellow named Howt and they were from a village in Seant.

There was also a trainee dragonboy, named Curf, unattached to any dragon, but kept as a spare. This was a new policy. Curf was given plenty to do, since he was supposed to help anyone with just about anything.

And then there was the fly in the ointment, Dragonleader Cuzo. Cuzo had taken command when their former dragonleader, Delwild Wiliger, resigned his commission and left the Legions. Wiliger had never recovered from the battle at the volcano. A dark, wiry man, Cuzo had transferred out of the administration department, determined to get back into a fighting unit before he was forever condemned to a desk. So far, however, he had had little success in getting on good terms with the dragons. He resolved to try to build a good relationship with Relkin and perhaps thereby get some help in dealing with the wyverns.

One day, while the dragons cavorted in the plunge pool, the dragonboys worked on equipment problems, repairing joboquins and scabbards and the like. There wasn't much to do, in fact. Dragonleader Cuzo was fierce about equipment and the polish thereof. So most things already glowed. Soon card games were going while a group began plotting how to acquire a double ration of beer to cover this beer feast.

Swane was losing money as usual when there came the word that a party of five riders had appeared at the main gate. They wore plaid garments, and one among them was a girl with long golden hair.

The boys in the 109th knew at once, and went out en masse to welcome Eilsa Ranardaughter, who had fought at their side at Sprian's Ridge.

She was accompanied by her uncle Traim and her aunt Bream, plus two burly Wattel clansmen.

She was welcomed by Major Beenks, to whom she showed a military scroll, signed by General Klendon of the Tower of Guard in Marneri. The orders were for Dragoneer Relkin and Dragon Bazil and they allowed for a four-month special leave, to be taken at any time within the next half year.

Major Beenks sent an orderly to give the news to Dragonleader Cuzo, but Cuzo was not to be found at that moment.

Relkin had already heard, of course, and came racing up from the bread locker dusted with flour and found Eilsa standing with a small group of folk in the plaid of Clan Wattel. He ran in with a shout and swept her up in his arms.

She laughed and kissed him and then made him set her down before her uncle's scowls turned into anything worse.

"We must behave, Relkin. This is my uncle Traim. He is here to keep us to our vows before marriage."

She had flour all over the dark plaid shawl around her. She knocked it loose with her fingers while she smothered a giggle.

Traim bowed. Relkin saluted. Traim favored him with a hard stare. Relkin did not return it.

"And this is Aunt Bream."

She was an older woman with penetrating eyes peering out from under the fold of her plaid scarf. Relkin felt the keen inspection he was getting from both of these chaperones as their eyes raked him for the slightest fault. And, of course, he had flour dusted all over his shirt and trousers, and probably on his face, too. They must be thinking he was a wild fool by this time.

The introductions over with, Eilsa handed him the scroll from General Klendon. Relkin read it carefully and then leaped in the air with a happy shout.

When he came down, he found Dragonleader Cuzo

glaring at him, having returned from his mission to the staff office.

"What is going on? Why are these civilians in the dragonhouse? This is great regulations." Cuzo seemed quite upset. Relkin bit his lip. He could understand Cuzo's instinctive response to the presence of a beautiful young girl in the dragonhouse.

Relkin saluted and proffered the scroll from General Klendon.

"Sir! This is Eilsa Ranardaughter of Clan Wattel. She's brought this order from General Klendon."

Cuzo read it with a deepening scowl.

"You've already been absent from the unit for two years, and now you take a four-month leave! This is most irregular."

"Yes, sir," said Relkin, who had learned long before that the only way to deal with dragonleaders in such situations was to agree with them.

Cuzo balanced the scroll in his hand. In theory he could protest and ask for a reappraisal, but then what would that gain? He shifted his ground.

"When did you last have official leave, Dragoneer Relkin?"

"Ah, three years ago, sir."

"Well, I'm sure you deserve this, then." He gave Eilsa a smooth smile, nodded to Uncle Taim. "Delighted to meet you, Lady Ranardaughter. I will see to it that space is prepared for you and your horses." Cuzo departed.

The watching dragonboys were amazed. The terrible Cuzo had become a kitten in the hands of Relkin, or so it seemed. Relkin's stock soared among them. If anything could ameliorate the harsh rule of Cuzo, they were for it.

Relkin looked around. This was not exactly how he would have liked to meet Eilsa, but it was going to have to do.

"At last," said Relkin, his heart too full to say anything more.

"Yes, my love, you are alive, despite everything, and I am here, and we shall be wed if you still wish it."

"I do, I do very much."

They went into the dragonhouse and took stools and sat

in Bazil's stall. The wyverns were still in the plunge pool, so for a moment they had the place to themselves. Relkin let the curtain fall.

Uncle Taim and Aunt Bream sat outside the stall while the clansmen toted their belongings up to a suite of rooms that had been opened up for them.

Relkin and Eilsa were shy and a little hesitant at first. There was a great deal to say and neither was feeling very articulate.

"So long, I sometimes thought you would never return," she said.

"Eilsa, I . . ." Relkin realized that there were some things you just shouldn't tell your beloved and he fell silent.

"What, Relkin?"

"I'm so grateful that you waited for me. Not much to wait for, I know, a dragonboy coming out of a war. But things have taken a surprising turn. Bazil and I have come away with a small fortune from this last thing. Found some gold—quite a lot of gold. So, what I wanted to say was that our prospects won't be just forty acres and Bazil."

"Relkin, I would wait for you even if you had no land at all. And besides, I have title to land in Wattel Bek. No, I waited for you and our life together. Believe me, they tried to change my mind. They've tried everything. I can't tell you how many handsome young Wattel men they have made me meet."

She laughed at the memories. "But I said no to all of them, because I knew somehow that you would survive. I don't know why, but something told me you weren't dead."

"Well, they came close this time."

"Yes, I can see that." And Eilsa looked into his eyes and saw the ocean of hurt and the wild realizations produced by Relkin's work on the Game board of the Lords Tetraan. He had changed, perhaps grown more cynical. She resolved to try to change that.

"You have been tested, and not for the first time."

Surreptitiously they stole a kiss or two, but kept the conversation going so that Uncle Taim would not be moved to investigate. Relkin told her about their journeys in the interior, leaving out a few salient points.

When the dragons came out of the plunge pool, a herd of giants splashing water with every movement, Bazil found Eilsa and Relkin in the stall.

"Ho-ho!" he bellowed in greeting.

First they had to get Uncle Taim and Aunt Bream out of dragon freeze, which wasn't easy in her case. Then Bazil hugged Eilsa and almost crushed the breath out of her.

Then he swung to Relkin with big eyes filled with happy thoughts.

"Ah-hah, boy gets another opportunity for the fertilizing of the eggs!"

Eilsa laughed. "And what does that mean?"

Relkin gulped. "Oh, it's just a figure of speech. Dragons always say that. They're not very well versed in courting, if you see what I mean."

Relkin glared at Baz. "You promised!" he hissed in dragonspeech.

The wyvern chuckled. "I keep your secret."

"What are you two hissing at each other about?"

Relkin turned back to her. "Oh, nothing, just some missing equipment."

Eilsa looked at him with just a trace of suspicion. "Nothing too important, I hope."

"Oh, no, just a missing dragon brain," muttered Relkin to himself.

They were crowded together now that Bazil was in the stall. A two-ton leatherback dragon could do that. Uncle Taim was getting hot-eyed again.

"You must get something to eat," said Relkin. "You've been on the road a long time. I will just finish up with the dragon and join you in the refectory, main hall. Curf will show you to your rooms."

Eilsa left with her chaperones and Curf.

Relkin turned back to the dragon. "You nearly sank me, there. You've got to be more careful, Baz."

"Heh, heh, this dragon agree entirely with that."

**Don't miss Bazil and Relkin's next adventure,
Dragon of Argonath. In this action-packed
preview, new members are settling into the
109th unit and causing tension among the older
fighters until tempers—and steel—fly.**

Unfortunately dragons have minds of their own and they
are all individuals, all different. Most different of all, by
common consent, were hard greens. These were wyverns
with a slim body build, unusual height in a two-footed
stance and deep, dark-green skin. They had a reputation
for being difficult to work with, of carrying grudges, and
sometimes killing a dragonboy in anger. Still, they were
often very skilled with dragonsword, providing the most
fluid movements, balletic spins and turns imaginable, for
beast weighing two tons.

Rakama's dragon was Gryf, a young green, very hard,
from Mud Lake. When Gryf heard the story of the fight,
he was upset by Relkin's interference. Rakama would
probably have won, in Gryf's view, and so Relkin had
taken victory from Gryf's dragonboy. Gryf found this a
bad thing in principle and he complained loudly in the
dragon house on his return from sword practice.

"Dragonboys fight. That is natural. Why not let
Rakama finish the job?"

The others ignored him. Bazil was in the plunge pool
and out of earshot, but the Purple Green's eyes took on a
dangerous tinge. The Purple Green had had several run-
ins with Gryf already, and the smaller wyvern dragon had
been saved again and again by the intervention of the
others.

"Vlok! Where is Vlok?" called Gryf.

"This dragon is Vlok," said the leatherback from his
stall. He emerged a moment later with a question of his
own. Vlok might appear stupid, but in his own way he
often hit on certain truths.

"Dragonboys are hurt," he said. "This fight go too far.
Why waste dragonboys?"

"Listen to Vlok," sneered Gryf. "My boy beat your boy. that is the truth of it."

"By the fiery breath," roared Vlok instantly enraged.

"My boy will beat yours, you know it, he knows it. I know it," Gryf said loudly.

"Enough!" hissed Purple Green. "We all tired of you and your boy."

"Who was talking to you? Not me, that's certain."

"Well, I am talking to you, and that too is certain." The Purple Green rose up to his full massiveness. Gryf's shoulders came up and a snarl escaped him.

"You stupid thing, wings cut, useless, can hardly wield sword!"

There was a brief moment of shock as this insult hung in the air and then the Purple Green charged. Gryf tried to dodge but was caught up in giant arms and swept back against the wall of the dragonhouse, which shook under the impact. The Purple Green had returned to his atavistic nature. His huge jaws snapped down on Gryf's shoulder, which fortunately was still encased in leather armor from his work on the sword butts. Nevertheless, Gryf roared in pain.

The building shook. Shouts of alarm rang out as men ran for the stairs throughout the central block. Two-ton wyvern and four-ton wild dragon grappled briefly on the wall, and then Gryf escaped the wild one's grip and broke away. The Purple Green came after him, but stumbled over a dragonboy stool that disintegrated to matchwood in the process. With a second to spare, Gryf now drew his sword from his shoulder scabbard.

Suddenly, the incident had moved into truly dangerous territory. A dragon with sword in hand became the most lethal thing in the world. The Purple Green was still enraged, but Gryf was in an insane place, beyond any reason, black eyes flared in mad battle rage. The Purple Green seemed doomed. Dragon murder hung in the air.

Then Vlok interposed his sword, Katsbalger, and in a moment there was a fearsome flash of steel on steel as Gryf and Vlok were engaged in sword battle, right in the middle of the dragon house.

Dragons tumbled out. Eventually Vlok lurched out,

defending himself desperately from a Gryf gone completely berserk. Vlok barely deflected the blows that were coming, any one of which would have slain him instantly. He was forced back across the yard, Gryf swinging with a speed and skill far beyond that of poor, old Vlok, who had never been much more than a middling hand with sword and shield.

Bazil Broketail, a leatherback of a little more than two tons, was out of the plunge pool now and standing by. He could see that Vlok was in a perilous state, outmatched and only just fending off Gryf's assault. But there was no sword to hand, and Bazil watched helplessly for a moment as dragon blades rang off each other just a few yards away. Then his eye caught the nearest wooden butt. Huge pieces of the wooden sword butts were constantly being cut away when dragons exercised upon them. Bazil grabbed up a hefty slab some six feet long and ran at Gryf from the side.

The young green never noticed him, too intent on finally getting through Vlok's guard. Bazil swung, but not too hard, and brought the balk of wood down on the back of Gryf's head and neck. The green was bowled over in a heap.

Unfortunately, this didn't quite do the job. Gryf was a hardheaded wyvern. He rolled over, sat up, and let out a shriek of rage and started to get back on his feet. Bazil instantly regretting holding back. He should've swatted Gryf with everything he had.

Vlok was standing nearby, panting, struggling to get a breath after his defensive struggle across the yard. Gryf was getting up. Bazil reached over and grabbed Vlok's arm and pulled him close.

"What you want?"

"Sword," said Bazil, twisting Katsbalger out of the other leatherback's astonished grasp.

Gryf was back on his feet and his sword, Swate, was coming up in front of him. Bazil shoved Vlok away and moved to engage.

Gryf swung, Bazil parried. Gryf swung again and again and was parried with a neat efficiency vastly unlike Vlok's hurried strokes. Once more Gryf came on, but

Bazil parried and then turned Swate with a deft move, forcing it to the ground. Bazil struck on the rebound and Gryf was forced to stumble back. The situation had changed radically. He wasn't fighting Vlok anymore. Bazil hefted Katsbalger in his hand. It wasn't Ecator by any means, but it was a well-made sword and light for its size. He came on at Gryf with speed and precision, and the hard green was forced back, helplessly on the defensive.

Gryf roused himself twice, coming close to regaining the initiative, but each time Bazil responded with a trick or two that absorbed Gryf's energy and kept the situation as it was. Finally, Bazil came overhead, their blades rang together and the leatherback and green came belly to belly. They struck at each other, but Bazil was the quicker and his forearm scored a solid smash that sent Gryf wobbling. For a second or two, the green was virtually defenseless. Katzbalger came around in a flash and struck Gryf's forearm with the flat of the blade and knocked Swate loose.

The green gave a shriek and tumbled backward, clutching his arm. The other dragons, lead by Roquil and big Churn, seized Gryf and subdued him by brute strength. They dragged him over to the pool and dunked him head-first to cool him off. Then they escorted him to the infirmary. Along the way, everyone let him know that if he wanted to survive in the 109th fighting Marneri he would never draw steel on a dragon again like that. Next time he would die.

Gryf was silent, his head hung low. The enormity of his folly was coming home to him.

Later, the old core group of the unit gathered by the pump house to talk it over.

"This can't go on," said Bazil. "Trouble every day. That green is just the worst of it. We're all getting crouchy."

"I know, I have occasionally wanted to draw steel on the Purple Green, myself these past few days," said Alsebra, the green freemartin renowned for her skill with dragonsword.

The Purple Green just glowered at her, but bit back his retort.

Bazil noted the wild one's restraint.

"You are quiet, this is unusual."

The Purple Green exhaled slowly and ominiously. Sometimes Bazil could easily imagine the wild dragon venting the fiery breath of the great ancestors.

"I am insulted, but I understand. She is right. We are all upset."

"Does the Red Star ride high?"

"Not yet."

"Is Gryf unstable?"

They shrugged. Greens were all a little odd. The Purple Green hunkered down.

"This dragon tire of Gryf and sharp tongue."

"We've noticed," said Alsebra, who had broken a few things over the Purple Green's head to stop him attacking Gryf.

"We have to make Gryf part of the squadron," said Bazil. "He not fitting in, yet."

"The other new dragons are fine. Churn is a good brass, very strong," said Alsebra.

"Ah, this dragon see," gurgled the Purple Green. "You have the eggs to fertilize. You wish to go to the mountain-top with young Churn."

Alsebra flushed somewhat purplish herself, then swung to Bazil with wide, staring eyes. The most sensitive thing to any infertile female dragon, known as freemartins in the legion, was her lack of eggs.

"You see?" she said. "He provokes me."

Bazil shrugged in sympathy and turned harsh eyes on the wild dragon. "Alsebra has no eggs, she freemartin, you know that. Why upset her? She take sword and kill you right quick. She very good with a sword, as you know."

The Purple Green withdrew into himself. His big mouth had done it again. His sword work, though improved over the years was still crude. Time and again, the others had saved him in battle. But his vast strength and utter ferocity had compensated. He had burst clean through the lines of trolls with his mighty shield alone. Yet in a sword fight with Alsebra he could only lose. It was time for him to be silent. Along the way he had learned to be quiet sometimes, too. This had not been easy for the former Lord of Hook Mountain, but this he recognized was one of those times when he was better off not saying anything.

Bazil sighed, glad to see his wild friend withdraw into silence. "Gryf remains a problem. Good with a sword and bad with his temper. Perhaps this time he learn a lesson."

"He knows now that he isn't the best dragon sword in this squadron," said Alsebra.

They all nodded agreement to that.

"Good thing that Cuzo wasn't around."

"Very good thing," agreed Alsebra.

"So much trouble and why? We have nice quiet life here. No marching, no fighting, very quiet. Food is adequate."

"Maybe that's the problem," said the freemartin.

"I think she right," said Purple Green aroused once more by the thought of food. "We bored."

"Good legion food. Good beer."

"Bah, legion food is bland. Noodles day after day. Not enough akh."

"Always plenty of it."

"I want to eat horse again."

"Oh, no, not that again. We ate horse."

"It was good. I had never had it roasted before. This roasting of meat is best thing men ever invent."

"That's why the ancestors had fiery breath. They roasted their own meat on the spot."

The Purple Green looked at Alsebra with astonished eyes.

"I think you are right."

The bell was ringing to announce the first boil of the evening. They set off for the refectory in a group, making the ground shake under heavy feet.

"Never enough akh!"

ABOUT THE AUTHOR

Christopher Rowley has written over a dozen science fiction and fantasy novels, including the Bazil Broketail series and *The Wizard and the Floating City*, a novel set in the Bazil Broketail universe. He is currently working on further adventures of Bazil and Relkin.

THE FORGING
OF THE SHADOWS

Book One of The Lightbringer Trilogy

OLIVER JOHNSON

Seven terrible years ago, Lord Faran Gaton, High Priest of the Go
of Darkness, immersed the mighty Thrull, city of the God of Ligh
into an era of shadow. His army of vampires swept down upon a
unsuspecting people and few escaped the savagery of these undea
hordes. Now Thrull is a nightmarish place, where the living lock the
doors against the risen dead. And the sun's power wanes with eve
tortured day. Desperate to thwart the coming of the Eternal Nigh
three champions of the God of Light join together within the ghast
shadows of Thrull. Against all odds, they search for legendary artifac
with powers to keep the awesome forces of shadow from plunging th
world into endless darkness prowled by the living dead. . . .

from **R⊙C**

*Prices slightly higher in Canada.   (455657—$14.95